PRAISE FOR RANDY SINGER

"As a lawyer, Randy Singer has lived the drama of the gun issue as it plays out in the courtroom. In *The Justice Game,* he brings that drama to life in a riveting story that captures the passions of both sides of the American gun debate."

DENNIS HENIGAN
VICE PRESIDENT FOR LAW AND POLICY AT THE BRADY CENTER TO PREVENT GUN VIOLENCE AND AUTHOR OF *LETHAL LOGIC: EXPLODING THE MYTHS THAT PARALYZE AMERICAN GUN POLICY*

"A great read! In *The Justice Game,* Randy Singer has crafted a fast-paced, suspenseful ride through our legal system. This entertaining story will draw you in from the opening scene. And, as a good book should, it will make you question and consider your own views of gun control."

ALAN GURA
ATTORNEY, CONSTITUTIONAL LAW, WHO SUCCESSFULLY ARGUED LANDMARK SUPREME COURT GUN RIGHTS CASE *DISTRICT OF COLUMBIA V. HELLER* (2008)

"Encore! Randy Singer does it again with another intense, thought-provoking novel that leaves his reader wanting more. *The Justice Game* invokes readers to question long-held opinions and consider the difficult aspects concerning weapon control."

MISTY BERNALL
MOTHER OF SLAIN COLUMBINE STUDENT CASSIE BERNALL AND AUTHOR OF *SHE SAID YES*

"What a page turner! In *The Justice Game,* Singer captured me from page one with brilliant storytelling and a gutsy message about gun rights in our country. Just when I thought his stories couldn't get any better, this book is even better than his last. Do not miss this read!"

AARON NORRIS
TELEVISION AND FILM PRODUCER/DIRECTOR

"Singer hooks readers from the opening courtroom scene of this tasty thriller, then spurs them through a fast trot across a storyline that just keeps delivering."

PUBLISHERS WEEKLY
ON *BY REASON OF INSANITY*

"At the center of the heart-pounding action are the moral dilemmas that have become Singer's stock-in-trade. . . .an exciting thriller."

BOOKLIST

ON *BY REASON OF INSANITY*

"In this gripping, obsessively readable legal thriller, Singer proves himself to be the Christian John Grisham. . . ."

PUBLISHERS WEEKLY

ON *FALSE WITNESS*

"[Singer] delivers a fresh approach to the legal thriller, with subtle characterizations and nuanced presentations of ethical issues."

BOOKLIST

STARRED REVIEW, ON *DYING DECLARATION*

"Singer . . . hits pay dirt again with this taut, intelligent thriller. . . . [*Dying Declaration*] is a groundbreaking book for the Christian market. . . . Singer is clearly an up-and-coming novelist to watch."

PUBLISHERS WEEKLY

"Singer delivers Grisham-like plotting buttressed by a worldview that clarifies the dilemmas that bombard us daily. Don't miss this book."

HUGH HEWITT

AUTHOR, COLUMNIST AND RADIO HOST OF THE NATIONALLY SYNDICATED *HUGH HEWITT SHOW* ON *DYING DECLARATION*

"Realistic and riveting, *Directed Verdict* is a compelling story about the persecuted church and those who fight for global religious freedom."

JAY SEKULOW

CHIEF COUNSEL, AMERICAN CENTER FOR LAW AND JUSTICE

THE JUSTICE GAME

TYNDALE HOUSE PUBLISHERS, INC., CAROL STREAM, ILLINOIS

RANDY SINGER

Visit Tyndale's exciting Web site at www.tyndale.com

Visit Randy Singer's Web site at www.randysinger.net

TYNDALE and Tyndale's quill logo are registered trademarks of Tyndale House Publishers, Inc.

The Justice Game

Copyright © 2009 by Randy Singer. All rights reserved.

Cover photograph copyright © by Matthew Antrobus/Getty Images. All rights reserved.

Author photo copyright © 2008 by Don Monteaux. All rights reserved.

Designed by Dean H. Renninger

Published in association with the literary agency of Alive Communications, Inc., 7680 Goddard St., Suite 200, Colorado Springs, CO 80920, www.alivecommunications.com.

Some Scripture quotations are taken from the HOLY BIBLE, NEW INTERNATIONAL VERSION®. NIV®. Copyright © 1973, 1978, 1984 by International Bible Society. Used by permission of Zondervan. All rights reserved.

Some Scripture quotations are taken from the *Holy Bible*, New Living Translation, copyright © 1996, 2004, 2007 by Tyndale House Foundation. Used by permission of Tyndale House Publishers, Inc., Carol Stream, Illinois 60188. All rights reserved.

Some Scripture quotations are taken from *The Holy Bible*, English Standard Version®, copyright 2001 by Crossway Bibles, a publishing ministry of Good News Publishers. Used by permission. All rights reserved.

This novel is a work of fiction. Names, characters, places, and incidents either are the product of the author's imagination or are used fictitiously. Any resemblance to actual events, locales, organizations, or persons living or dead is entirely coincidental and beyond the intent of either the author or the publisher.

Library of Congress Cataloging-in-Publication Data

Singer, Randy (Randy D.)
The justice game / Randy Singer.
p. cm.
ISBN 978-1-4143-1634-5 (pbk.)
1. Trials (Murder)—Fiction. 2. Extortion—Fiction. 3. Assault weapons—Fiction. 4. Firearms industry and trade—Fiction. I. Title.
PS3619.I5725J87 2009
813′.6—dc22 2009009854

Printed in the United States of America

15 14 13 12 11 10
7 6 5 4 3 2

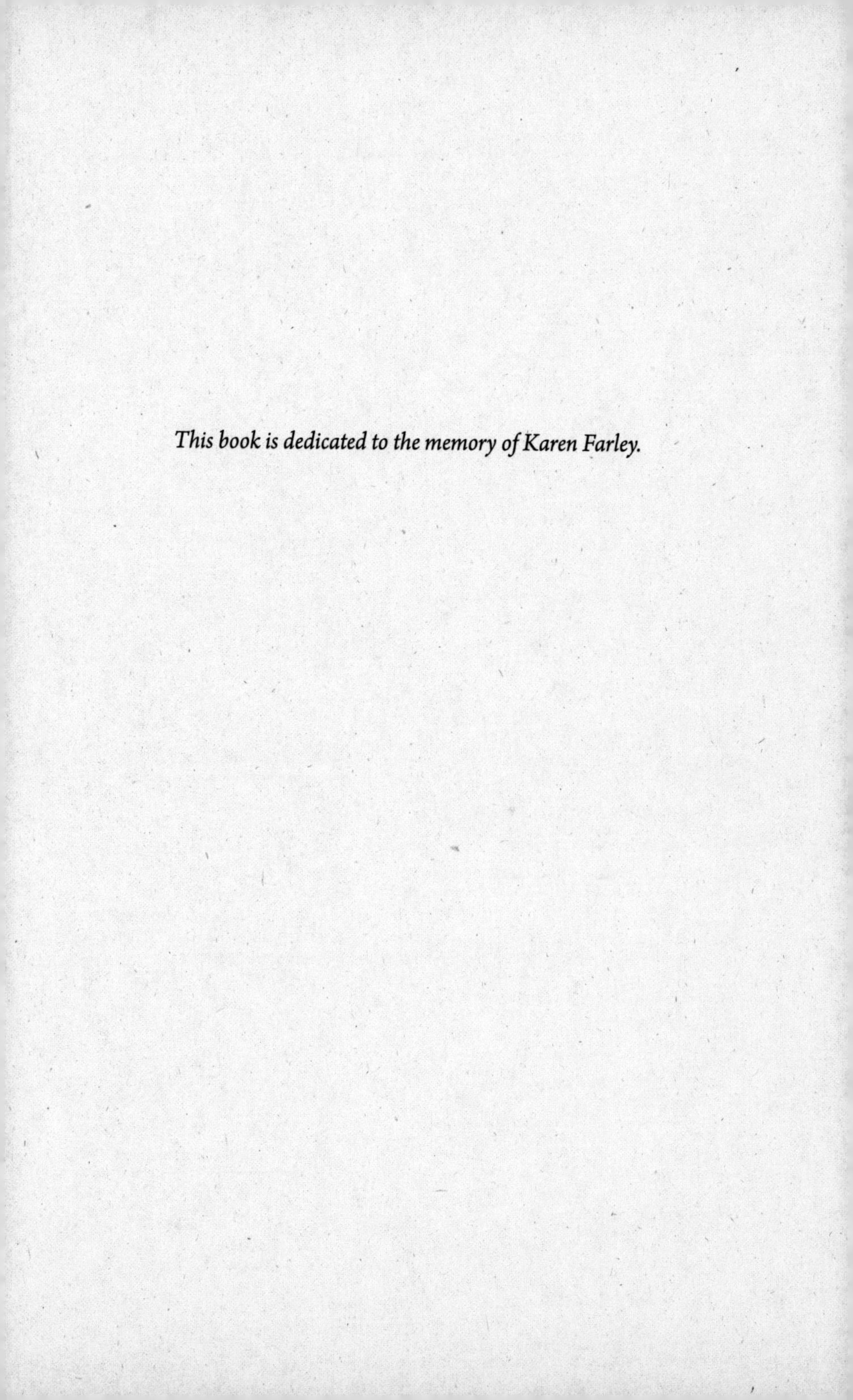

This book is dedicated to the memory of Karen Farley.

AUTHOR'S NOTE

This one is personal.

On December 16, 1988, a sixteen-year-old student named Nicholas Elliot took a semi-automatic handgun to Atlantic Shores Christian School and opened fire. He shot and killed a teacher named Karen Farley and wounded an assistant principal, then burst into a trailer where a Bible class was meeting. When he attempted to open fire on the students huddled in the back corner of the trailer, the gun jammed. The Bible teacher, Hutch Matteson, tackled Elliot and prevented the kind of tragedy that hit Columbine High School in Colorado several years later.

Atlantic Shores was the school where my wife taught. It was the school my kids attended (though they were not there that day).

And when I learned that Elliot had purchased the gun illegally from a gun store in Isle of Wight County through a transaction referred to as a "straw purchase," I represented the family of Karen Farley in an unprecedented lawsuit against the gun store.

The verdict shocked everyone.

That trial was seventeen years ago—my baptism by fire into the national gun debate.

With this book, seventeen years later, I willingly wade back in . . . wiser (I hope), more cautious, and with a better understanding of both sides. My goal is not to make converts (at least, not in the Second Amendment sense) but to fairly present both perspectives and let the reader decide.

I tried to create compelling characters on both sides of the debate. In fact, I was so determined to be balanced that I did something I've never done before and, as far as I know, no other novelist has ever done either.

I asked my readers to determine the verdict for this book.

We put together an online video showing a news report about the fictional case at the heart of this book and portions of the closing arguments for both lawyers. We asked readers to watch the video and render a verdict. The verdict in this story reflects the verdict of a majority of my readers.

Thanks for taking this journey with me. In a very real sense, you are always the jury. And just like in my real trials, I've got a few butterflies as I submit my case to you.

For *The Justice Game*, the jury is out. . . .

PART I

WRONGFUL DEATH

1

RACHEL CRAWFORD CLOSED HER EYES while the show's makeup artist, a spunky woman named Carmen, did a quick touch-up.

"The sun looks good on you," Carmen said. "The Diva's fake 'n bake turns her orange."

"The Diva" was WDXR prime-time anchor Lisa Roberts. Lisa treated the staff like dirt and was easy to hate. Five foot ten with long, skinny legs, Lisa always complained about how much weight the camera added to her figure. Her chair had to be adjusted higher than everyone else's, the camera always had to be positioned to capture her left side (exposing a mole on her left cheek that she considered sexy), and her water had to be cold with just the right amount of ice.

"Maybe my next report will be on tanning beds," Rachel said. Carmen removed the makeup cape, and Rachel checked herself out in the mirror.

She was no Lisa. A little shorter, heavier, with more of a girl-next-door look. But Rachel had one thing Lisa didn't—it was the reason for her glow.

"I hear tanning beds cause cancer," Carmen said, perking up with the thought. "Not just skin cancer, either—liver, thyroid, all kinds of nasty stuff."

Rachel did a subtle sideways twist, so casual that Carmen didn't notice. The blouse Rachel wore fit loosely—not so much as to be obvious, but just loose enough. She would have a few more weeks before her secret was out.

As a new reporter for the WDXR I-team, Rachel had been working on a piece about the effect of cell phones on pregnant women. In two weeks, she would break her own exciting news on air as part of that piece. For at least one night, Lisa wouldn't be the center of attention. Tonight, however, she had a very different story to cover.

"Thanks, Carmen," Rachel said. She scooped up her pad and water bottle and headed toward the door. "This water's way too warm," she said, mocking Lisa's perfect diction. Carmen cackled.

"Plus, it goes straight to my hips," Carmen shot back, cocking her chin in the air as she gave Rachel a dismissive little shake of the head.

Rachel smiled and left the makeup room, settling into investigative reporter mode. Most of tonight's report was already on tape. Things had gone well during the 5 p.m. newscast. What could possibly go wrong at six?

She loved her job. Yet she loved the thought of being a mother even more. She wanted to do both—part-time I-team reporter and full-time mom. But that was a conversation for another day.

◁▷

Rachel fiddled with her earpiece, listening to the show's producer give Lisa Roberts and Manuel Sanchez, Lisa's co-anchor, instructions about the next few segments. Rachel sat up as straight as possible, though she would still be a few inches shorter than Lisa, and smiled at the camera. The show's producer started the countdown. Lisa didn't change her scowl until the man said zero, triggering a magical transformation from spoiled Diva to devoted and caring newswoman.

"Over three thousand international college students come to Virginia Beach each summer to work in the resort city," Lisa said, reading the prompter. "An unlucky few end up being victims of the sinister human trafficking industry. I-team reporter Rachel Crawford has the details."

Lisa held her pose as they transitioned to the I-team tape. She might be hard to stomach, but she was a pro. Lisa's cover-girl looks and unshakable poise would soon carry her beyond the Norfolk market, away from the place Lisa scornfully referred to as a "dead-end Navy town," the place Rachel loved and called home.

Rachel watched the report for about the fortieth time and allowed herself a brief moment of pride. The segment started with a few shots of The Surf, a popular Virginia Beach hangout, with a voice-over from Rachel about the way international student workers helped keep the place afloat. They had video of two Eastern European women tending bar, waiting tables, even taking out the trash. The camera angles had been carefully selected so the viewers could never quite get a good look at the students' faces. The tape cut to Rachel, standing in front of the bar, a serious tilt to her head.

"But a few of these girls, who talked to WDXR under condition of anonymity, said there was a dark side to their summer at the Beach."

The next shot featured Rachel interviewing one of the workers. The editors had blocked out the student's face and digitally altered her voice. She talked about the owner of The Surf—Larry Jamison—the man who had promised the girls jobs and paid for them to come to America.

"If you didn't become one of 'Larry's girls,' you could never get out of debt, no matter how hard you worked. Plus, there were threats."

As Rachel explained the scam, a Web site appeared on-screen. The girl's images were distorted but it was obviously a porn site, one that Rachel had traced back to Larry Jamison.

"We asked Mr. Jamison about these charges," Rachel said on the tape. "He refused to be interviewed for this report."

In a few seconds, they would be live again. Rachel checked her earpiece and turned toward Lisa. She heard a pop that startled her—it might have been a few pops—something like firecrackers, coming from the other side of the studio's soundproof door. She glanced at the doors but nobody else seemed bothered by it.

"Five seconds," said a voice in her ear. "Four, three, two, one . . ."

A cameraman pointed to Lisa, and she turned toward Rachel. "Those girls you interviewed seemed so vulnerable," Lisa said. "Did they understand they could press charges against this guy?"

Out of the corner of her eye, Rachel noticed a flash of commotion at the back of the studio. Like a pro, she stayed focused on Lisa, explaining why the girls were not willing to come forward.

"Hey!" someone yelled. "He's got a gun!"

Shots rang out as Rachel swiveled toward the voices, blinded by the bright lights bearing down on her. She heard more shots, screams of panic and pain—pandemonium in the studio. "Get down!" someone shouted.

There was cursing and a third barrage of shots as Rachel dove to the floor, crawling quickly behind the anchor desk—a fancy acrylic fixture that certainly wouldn't stop a bullet. Overhead, the suspended "on-air" monitor blinked off. In the chaos, Rachel looked over to see Lisa, wide-eyed with fear, her fist to her mouth, shaking with a silent sob.

For a moment, everything was still.

2

RACHEL HUDDLED BEHIND THE DESK, paralyzed by fear. Her breath came in short, staccato bursts, miniature explosions into the deafening silence. She pressed both hands against her face, half praying, half listening—shaking with terror.

She heard footsteps and heavy breathing.

She gasped when she caught the gunman in her peripheral vision, towering over her—Larry Jamison, the target of her I-team report. The man was wild-eyed, his gray hair disheveled, his face red and stubbled. He pointed a flat black pistol at her that looked like a chopped-off version of a weapon from a Rambo movie. He hit the magazine release and jammed a second magazine into the gun as the first one hit the floor.

"You're the one," Jamison hissed, grabbing her by the hair and yanking her to her feet. He pressed the barrel into the small of her back. From behind, he wrapped his left arm around her neck and wrenched her close. Rachel could smell sweat and alcohol, his putrid breath moist on her ear.

"Everybody at your posts!" he demanded. "I want this show live in two minutes or this sweet thing dies."

Trembling, Rachel scanned the studio. One of the cameramen, a gentle giant Rachel had spoken with on many occasions, lay next to his camera, blood pooling from his chest. She noticed a young female camera operator hunched in a corner. The control booth had been deserted. She couldn't see Lisa and Manuel—they must have crawled to the other side of the anchor desk.

"Get back to your camera!" Jamison shouted at the woman in the corner. He fired several rounds into the wall above her head. Sparks flew and she screamed, scrambling to her station. "Two minutes," Jamison repeated. "I'm talking to one of my partners on my Bluetooth right now. He's waiting for the television signal."

Rachel fought for breath as Jamison squeezed his left arm tighter around her neck, dragging her toward the end of the anchor desk where Lisa and Manuel sat huddled together on the floor. Jamison pointed his gun at Lisa. "Looky here."

He laughed as she stared at him in horror. "Get back behind your desk. We've got a show to put on."

Trembling and sobbing, Lisa stood. She backed slowly away from Jamison, climbing into her anchor seat.

"Good girl," he said. He pointed his gun at Manuel and squeezed Rachel's windpipe tighter with his left arm. The room was beginning to spin.

"We're not on the air yet," he hissed, his frustration showing. "Somebody get in that control room."

Manuel glanced quickly at the booth. "They're gone."

"I can see they're gone!" Jamison shouted. He turned and unloaded another stream of bullets toward the control booth, the gunshots echoing in Rachel's ear. The bullets shattered the glass of the booth into tiny shards that dropped onto the sound and edit board.

He again pointed the gun toward Manuel. "Get us on the air."

Manuel shook his head, beads of sweat popping on his forehead even in the clammy cool air of the studio. "I c-can't . . . don't know how."

"Then you're useless."

Manuel opened his mouth—a silent plea, too scared to talk.

Rachel was losing consciousness fast, the edges of her vision going dark. *How many shots has Jamison fired? How many are left?* She said a quick prayer and threw her elbow backward into his gut, heard him grunt, and tried to squirm free. She had nearly twisted out of his arm, but he drove the corner of the gun's rectangular magazine against her skull. The blow knocked her to the ground. Dizzy, she could feel blood oozing down her forehead.

She looked up at Jamison with blurred vision. She blinked and crawled a few feet backward.

"You think I'm playing games?" Jamison asked.

Terrified, Rachel shook her head. He smiled at her and popped a second magazine out, quickly jamming a third into place.

Jamison tilted his head back and shouted. "We're not on the air! Every minute we're not on the air, somebody dies!"

He took a step closer and looked down at Rachel. "Maybe I'll start with you." His eyes flashed with excitement. "Put your hands behind your back and lie facedown."

Rachel did as she was told, fighting panic. To her left, she saw a flicker of movement, a crouching figure. She forced herself not to look. She hoped it was Bob Thomas, the show's director, a tall and lanky man who had disappeared once the gunshots started. Bob would not let her die.

Jamison walked over to Rachel. He stepped over top of her, straddling her. His breath came in short, hard bursts.

"Beg."

For a split second contempt battled her fear. She wouldn't beg for this man—he'd fire anyway. But she knew she needed time. She closed her eyes. "Please don't hurt me," she said. "I can help you get out of this."

Jamison laughed—a fake, contemptuous chortle. "Look at me," he said softly.

She opened her eyes and looked over her shoulder, her neck craned as she stared at her tormentor. He bent closer, his face twisted with the pleasure of revenge. The black barrel of the gun dominated her field of vision, his maniacal grin forming the backdrop. "You need to learn a little humility," he said. "You don't know what it means to beg, do you?"

He grabbed her hair and pulled her head back farther. "*Please,*" she said, tears stinging her eyes. Pain throbbed on her cheek and radiated from her neck. She closed her eyes, but the image of the black barrel and Jamison's face wouldn't go away. "*Please* don't shoot."

"That's not begging," Jamison said. He let go of her hair and her head dropped toward the floor. She braced herself, feeling helpless, waiting for the impact of the bullet. She thought about Blake, her husband. About the tiny life sheltered in her womb. It was supposed to be a safe place.

"Open your eyes!"

She did. Just in time to see Jamison turn the gun on Manuel Sanchez. "Say good-bye to your buddy."

"No!" she shouted.

Before Manuel could move, Jamison fired. Rachel gasped as a small hole opened in the middle of Manuel's forehead. He grunted—the air fleeing his body—and slouched to the floor.

Rachel saw Manuel's eyes go glassy as blood poured from his head. She turned away, vomit rising in her throat.

"You need to learn how to beg," Jamison said, his voice flat. "Now get in your seat."

Rachel got to one knee, and the room started spinning. She hesitated, wiping blood away from her eyes and mouth. She watched Jamison kick Manuel's lifeless body, rolling the co-anchor onto his back.

"Hurry up!" he said.

She stood slowly, thinking about Manuel. Watching him die had changed things. Instead of making Rachel more afraid, it somehow steeled her. She felt responsible for Manuel's death—this whole thing was *her* fault. Jamison was here because of Rachel. Now it was up to her to think clearly. Somebody had to make sure there was no more bloodshed until help arrived.

She staggered to her seat, keeping a wary eye on Jamison. He had moved behind Lisa.

"Get us on the air," he said to Lisa.

"I'm trying," Lisa said, her voice shaking, lips trembling. "But *please* . . ." she choked out, "stop pointing that gun at me."

"You've got thirty seconds," Jamison said.

Lisa caught her breath. She pointed to a spot on the right side of the studio. "Behind there," she said, "is our director. He can run the control booth."

"Nice," Jamison said.

He walked over to the camera and forced Bob Thomas out of his hiding spot, ordering him into the control booth. A minute or two later, the large television on the floor in front of the anchor desk and the other television suspended from the ceiling changed from a technical difficulties message to a live shot of the desk. Rachel was shocked by her own appearance, blood streaking down her face and staining her blouse. She pushed back her hair and waited.

How long before a SWAT team storms this place?

Jamison was just one man. Surely if the four of them acted together . . .

Jamison settled in next to the sole camerawoman operating the huge boom camera. She had it on a wide-angle shot that showed both Lisa and Rachel. Jamison kept the gun on Rachel, periodically glancing over his shoulder to check the studio door.

"This is Larry Jamison!" he yelled, his voice loud enough to be picked up by the wireless mikes that Lisa and Rachel wore. "You've just seen vicious lies broadcast by this television station. Now you're about to hear the truth.

"Introduce yourself!" Jamison shouted. He pointed the gun at Lisa.

"I'm Lisa Roberts," she said, her voice unsteady, an octave higher than normal. Out of habit, she looked straight at the camera.

Jamison swung the gun toward Rachel. For a moment, just long enough to show the slightest flicker of resistance, Rachel didn't speak.

"And I'm Rachel Crawford," she eventually said, "a member of the WDXR I-team."

"Ten minutes ago, this woman lied to you!" Jamison shouted. "And now she's going to stand trial for it."

He checked over his shoulder one more time and then moved forward, circling around behind the anchor desk so that he stood between Lisa and Rachel. Rachel watched as Jamison checked himself out on the TV monitors, then pointed the gun at the side of her head.

God help me.

3

JAMISON KEPT THE GUN POINTED AT RACHEL, his eyes darting from her to Lisa to the large boom television camera capturing everything. "I'm Larry Jamison," he said, stealing a glance at the camera. "The report you've seen about me is a total crock. And that's because this station, WDXR, cares more about ratings than truth."

He took a half step toward Rachel. Not close enough for her to reach him but close enough so she could smell the body odor from the half-moons of sweat under his armpits and the lines of moisture just under his chest that plastered his shirt to his body.

"Who are your anonymous sources?" he asked Rachel.

She hesitated—a journalist's instinct to protect her sources.

"Tell me!" Jamison yelled, raising the gun over his head as if he might step forward and pistol-whip her again.

"Nysa Polides and Tereza Yankov."

"Nysa. Tereza." Jamison spit the words toward Rachel. "Did you know *they* asked *me* if they could be part of my Web site? Did you know they planned to blackmail me all along?"

Rachel quickly processed the allegations. The women had seemed so reliable. Innocent. Naive.

Jamison's face darkened, the veins on his neck rising to the surface. "They wanted a thousand bucks a week or they would go to the media with their lies. A thousand a week! Where am I supposed to get that kind of money?"

He spun toward Lisa. "Your network let them conceal their identities? You're responsible for this too! Nobody checked them out!"

Lisa shook her head quickly, her eyes wide with fright. Jamison took a few steps in her direction until he was close enough to touch her. He was breathing hard, nearly hyperventilating, his eyes wild with hate. Lisa trembled, looked up at him, then at the studio door, then back to Jamison.

Rachel glanced at the back door too. *Where's the SWAT team? How much time can they possibly need?*

Jamison pressed the barrel of his gun against Lisa's temple. She closed her eyes, sobbing. He looked over his shoulder at Rachel. "You'd better apologize to your viewers. This time, make it good."

Oh, God, don't let him shoot. "I'm so sorry," Rachel said quickly. "Don't shoot her. Please. This report is mine, not hers. She had nothing to do with it."

Jamison smiled thinly and leaned over so he was in Lisa's face. "Is she guilty?" he asked. "Do you agree that it's *her* fault?"

Lisa shuddered. Her words were hard to decipher, punctuated by sobs: "She . . . made . . . a . . . mistake."

"I say she's guilty," Jamison replied, standing to his full height, the gun still pressed against Lisa's temple. "What do you say?"

"Ask her. Not . . . me."

He pivoted just as the studio door blew open and everything happened at once. Smoke bombs exploding, Jamison squeezing off as many shots as possible in Rachel's direction, his own body convulsing from SWAT team bullets, Rachel diving for the floor, trying to roll as she fell, turning her back to protect the innocent life in her womb.

She felt something slice her shoulder, a blow to her back, and another bullet rip into the base of her skull.

A millisecond of images followed—her husband, the new life growing inside her. For the tiniest fraction of a second she reached out for them, but then they exploded into a blinding flash of light.

She was gone before she could even say good-bye.

PART II

THE COMPANY

4

A CONTINENT AWAY from the chaos in the WDXR studios, Jason Noble approached the jury for the most important closing argument of his young career.

"Let's talk about the hair," he said, surveying the inquisitive expressions on the faces of the jurors. Some were literally gaping; others suppressed a smirk. Jason pretended not to notice.

"Mr. Lockhart argues that the hair evidence creates reasonable doubt. 'Forget about the defendant's rage when she learned that her husband and her best friend had an affair,' he says. 'Forget the fact that her best friend also happened to be a very talented backup singer whom the defendant's husband could turn into a star the same way he made the defendant a star. Forget all that. If the hair testing shows that Carissa Lawson had been taking drugs for several months, then the cause of death must be a self-administered drug overdose, not poisoning.'"

The jury was only half-listening, but that was okay with Jason. They were too busy staring.

The night before, on a whim, Jason had dyed his hair platinum blond and spiked it—the hairstyle of the victim. And the change was more than symbolic.

Months earlier, when Carissa Lawson's autopsy showed fatal amounts of oxycodone and cocaine in her blood, the medical examiner had declared the death an accidental overdose. But then the rumors started surfacing. The backup singer had been involved with the husband of rock star Kendra Van Wyck. When Van Wyck found out about the affair, she became consumed with jealousy and rage. She owed her fame to the efforts of her husband, a wealthy recording executive who had "discovered" her. His love for someone else, especially someone as talented as Carissa Lawson, ate at Kendra Van Wyck like a cancer.

Van Wyck was eventually indicted for murder. But the prosecution's case was largely circumstantial, and Van Wyck had the best legal help money could buy. The defense lawyer opposing Jason, a pit bull named Austin Lockhart, had built his case on the popularity of Kendra Van Wyck and the lab tests of Carissa Lawson's hair.

Van Wyck had not taken the stand in her own defense. Instead, her lawyers had relied on a distinguished toxicologist named Dr. Richard Kramer, a man who lectured the jury about the wonders of testing hair for drugs. According to Kramer, as hair grew, its roots were fed by blood. In a chronic drug user, the blood would contain trace amounts of the drugs in question, which would become entrapped in the hair's cortex. Since hair grew at the rate of about a half inch per month, you could test different segments of a person's hair and tell how long that person had been using drugs.

Kramer testified that hair testing for Carissa Lawson showed high levels of oxycodone and codeine in all segments of her three-inch hair. The obvious conclusion? Carissa Lawson had been abusing cocaine and painkillers like OxyContin for months and had died from a self-inflicted overdose.

As he approached his closing argument, Jason knew that the jury was looking for a reason to spring the popular defendant, consistently ranked by *People* as one of the hottest female performers. Her husband's divorce petition and the murder trial had only garnered more attention, fueling album sales. Plus, the rock star cried on cue during the trial.

"Murder by poisoning? Or accidental overdose?" Jason asked. He paced back and forth in front of the jury. No notes, just a spontaneous little chat. He had memorized every word.

"Carissa Lawson had stopped seeing the defendant's husband. But that didn't mean he loved her any less. And that didn't mean he wasn't planning on dumping the defendant and making Carissa the next big thing.

"Did Kendra Van Wyck have motive? 'Hell hath no fury like a woman scorned.' By killing Carissa Lawson, the defendant could punish both Carissa and her husband at the same time.

"No doubt—the defendant had plenty of motive.

"The defendant was seen with Carissa Lawson early in the evening on the night Carissa died. When the defendant found out about her husband's affair, she never confronted him. She never confronted Carissa either, choosing instead to remain friends so that Carissa wouldn't be leery about spending time together. The defendant had access to OxyContin pills for pain relief and to cocaine from any number of close associates, two of whom have pled guilty for possession with intent to distribute.

"In other words, the defendant had opportunity.

"But Mr. Lockhart argues that the affair between Caleb Van Wyck and Carissa Lawson occurred just two months prior to her death. Why would the defendant begin poisoning Carissa Lawson six months earlier? According to Mr. Lockhart, the hair evidence proves that Carissa Lawson is a drug addict who died from an overdose rather than as the victim of a one-time poisoning."

Jason paused. He now had their attention. "And so . . . it all comes down to the hair. Other than the toxicologists, not one witness has linked Carissa Lawson to drug use. Does the hair really show six months of drug use, or should we throw out the hair testing results as unreliable?

"You will recall my cross-examination of Dr. Kramer. He admitted that hair can be contaminated by drugs from external sources, things like sweat or running your hands through your hair. This can make the results suspect." Jason paused for effect. One of the things he had learned by studying courtroom advocacy was the impact of silence. An advocate who wasn't afraid of silence showed confidence. Silence helped refocus the jury.

It also helped Jason remember his script.

"You heard the coroner describe the type of slow and painful death Carissa Lawson suffered. In large quantities, cocaine and oxycodone shut down the lungs, causing the victim to suffocate as fluid collects and breathing becomes impossible. Eventually, Carissa drowned in her own lung fluid, probably while her best friend watched, pretending to call 911 as Carissa gasped for breath."

Jason shook his head and ran his hands through his hair. "Was Carissa Lawson sweating as she died this slow death, fighting to get air?" He paused again, looking from juror to juror. "You decide. One thing that's not open for question—if she was poisoned, her sweat would have contained high quantities of these drugs and contaminated her hair.

"But Dr. Kramer says we shouldn't worry about that. Before testing the hair, he washed the samples twice with methylene chloride, a solvent guaranteed to remove any contamination. But you also heard our toxicologist, Dr. Chow, say he believes that drugs contained in sweat cannot be removed from the hair through mere washing because they form ionic bonds with the hair follicles. As a result, hair testing can't tell us whether the drugs present in the hair are due to contamination from sweat after a one-time poisoning event or from long-term use.

"And so, last night, I came up with a harebrained idea, if you'll pardon the expression. I dyed my hair platinum blond—the dye representing external contamination that bonds to the hair particles." He walked over to his counsel table, speaking over his shoulder as he went. "You'll recall that Dr. Chow testified that the same chemical reaction that explains the incorporation of hair coloring into hair follicles also takes place with drugs like cocaine and oxycodone."

Jason pulled a towel out of his briefcase and picked up two plastic bottles from the floor. He walked back toward the jury and smiled briefly at two young female jurors—Jurors 5 and 7—who had been nodding as he made his points.

Jason could usually count on the younger women. He didn't have the stone-carved jaw of a movie actor, but he was in good shape and had received more than a few comments about his eyes. "Sleepy." "Intriguing." Or on courtroom days like today, when he had his green contacts inserted, "piercing."

Jason did fine with women at a distance—like the ten feet that separated him from the jury panel. The ones he let in close always gave him trouble.

"I asked my expert to provide some methylene chloride," he explained. "And I'm going to wash my hair right here in front of you, using the same chemical and the same procedures that Dr. Kramer used before he tested the victim's hair."

"Objection!" Austin Lockhart could apparently stand it no longer. Most lawyers avoided making objections during closing arguments, since they tended only to underscore the opponent's points. But Lockhart had made a career out of arguing even minor matters until he was red-faced and furious. Which he was right now.

"This is outrageous," he said. "The chemical makeup of hair dye and cocaine is hardly the same. And how do we know that's even methylene chloride in that bottle? This is nothing but showmanship, and it's highly improper."

Jason acted stunned that anybody would object to this. Instead of responding immediately, he looked up at the judge, as if the objection wasn't worthy of wasting his breath.

"Mr. Noble?" asked Judge Waters.

"For starters, Judge, I didn't have any cocaine or oxycodone handy last night, or I would have used them instead. But if I were a juror, I'd like to at least know whether this vaunted solvent that Dr. Kramer used could remove a little hair dye."

"That's . . . that's just . . . ridiculous," Lockhart stuttered. "It's not *relevant* and it's highly prejudicial, and if he wanted to do a demonstration, he should have done it with his expert so I could cross-examine Dr. Chow about it."

"I'm sorry, Your Honor," Jason responded quickly. "I must have been absent from evidence class the day they said showmanship was inadmissible."

When he heard a few jurors snicker, Jason knew he was on the right track.

"Plus," Jason continued, "Dr. Chow would look even more ridiculous in platinum blond hair than I do."

"There may be some differences of opinion on that," said the judge, drawing her own set of chuckles. "Objection sustained."

Jason turned back to the jury and noticed that Juror 5 still had a thin smile on her face. He would reinforce the feedback with a generous portion of eye contact. "Now that we've established how much confidence the defense puts in its hair washing procedures, let's talk about the affair. . . ."

◁ ▷

In a luxury suite at the Westin hotel, Robert Sherwood, the CEO of Justice Inc., watched the courtroom drama unfold on closed-circuit TV. He studied the images on the split screen—one camera following Jason around the courtroom, the other catching the expressions on the jurors' faces. Sherwood was willing to bet $75 million of his firm's money on the outcome of this case.

Like most larger-than-life rock stars, Kendra Van Wyck supported a labyrinth of companies. Her husband's record label, a designer line, her own reality TV show and production company. All were highly profitable ventures, but all would be worthless if the diva was sentenced to life in jail. If she won, on the other hand, the companies would skyrocket in value. Until today, until this ingenious stunt in the closing argument, Sherwood thought that Van Wyck would be the biggest celebrity acquittal since O. J. Now . . . he wasn't so sure.

"The kid might be too smart for his own good," Sherwood said, shaking his head. "Skewing the results."

He rubbed his forehead, the pain of another migraine setting in. His firm had spent hundreds of thousands of dollars diligently researching this case, selecting the perfect jurors, scrutinizing each piece of evidence. Now Jason Noble was blowing the whole thing apart with a piece of choreographed drama in his closing argument.

"We can't let this happen again," Sherwood said. "Let's make this trial his last."

5

JASON NOBLE WATCHED coverage of the shootings at the WDXR studios on the television in his hotel room—an oceanfront suite at the Malibu Beach Inn on the California coastline.

Until the footage grabbed his attention, he had been focused solely on waiting for the phone call signaling that the jury had reached its verdict. He was oblivious to the luxury surrounding him—the beautiful white sands of Carbon Beach, the ever-observant hotel staff ready to meet his every need, the Hollywood A-listers who occasionally frequented the lobby bar. None of that mattered as he speculated about the jurors' progress, tried and retried the Van Wyck case in his mind, and steeled himself for the worst. The same young lawyer who demonstrated poise and a devil-may-care attitude in the courtroom was a world-class worrier when the jury was out.

But in the last several minutes, he had forgotten all about his own case.

According to Fox News, the whole sordid affair at WDXR had been broadcast live to the Virginia Beach and Norfolk markets. Now, two hours later, he was watching a replay of the shootings for the third or fourth time. Each time they ran the tape, a newswoman told viewers with weak stomachs to turn their heads, and a scroll across the bottom of the screen warned of graphic violence. Jason probably qualified for the weak stomach category but he couldn't turn away, staring in morbid disbelief as Jamison fired at Rachel Crawford while the SWAT team's bullets slammed into Jamison's body, the final shots tearing off portions of his head.

Jason clicked to other channels, all of which were breathlessly replaying the tape (though some excised the last few grisly frames) and analyzing the siege from different angles. CNN had a civil rights lawyer criticizing the SWAT team. They should have moved in quicker. They should have used tear gas earlier. The usual armchair quarterbacking. NBC featured a forensic psychiatrist who tried making sense of Jamison's twisted mind. CBS focused on the gun.

A woman from the Handgun Violence Coalition argued passionately for a renewal of the assault weapon ban. "This gun has no legitimate purpose. You can't hunt with it. It's no good for target practice. It's used for only one thing: mowing down innocent human beings." Her righteous indignation was palpable. "What we've seen today is the reason this gun is sold."

CBS anchor Jessica Walsh—young, photogenic, and expressive—nodded. "According to police, the gun in question is an MD-9 semiautomatic assault weapon, manufactured by a Georgia gun company named MD Firearms. We have that company's CEO, Melissa Davids, joining us live from Atlanta."

A shot of a smug-looking brunette filled half the screen. Jason guessed she was about forty-five or fifty years old. The woman had a long face with striking brown eyes, a protruding chin, and sharp cheekbones; a few pounds less and she would have looked anorexic.

"Good evening, Ms. Davids," Walsh said.

"Good evening."

"What about the argument that the MD-9 is used primarily by criminals and has no law-abiding purpose? Without rehashing the whole debate about whether guns kill or people kill, can you tell us why you manufacture a weapon like this?"

"Because people buy it."

Walsh waited for a more detailed explanation but Davids just stared at the camera. Unblinking. Unapologetic.

"But that's the point," Walsh said, her brow furrowed. "Criminals are buying the gun in disproportionate numbers, often illegally or through straw purchases. Why would legitimate buyers who use guns for self-defense and hunting ever need a weapon like this?"

"Why do they make cars that can go faster than the speed limit?" Davids asked, her words clipped and uncompromising. "Your questions miss the point. Why isn't anybody asking about laws that keep honest citizens from having guns at work? If somebody in that studio had a gun, Rachel Crawford and the other victims might be alive today."

Walsh made a skeptical face, twisting the corners of her mouth. "Then you feel no responsibility for these deaths?"

"No, I don't. The first tragedy in this case is that the *only* person who had a gun in that studio was a deranged killer. The second tragedy is that networks like yours keep showing the footage over and over to increase ratings." Davids narrowed her eyes, her contempt for the media slithering through. "And *you* feel no responsibility for *that*?"

From Jason's vantage point, it seemed like the question caught Jessica Walsh off guard. *She* was supposed to be asking the tough questions. Her eyes darted away from the camera for a moment, but she made a nice recovery. "We always warn viewers about graphic footage," Walsh explained. "But still, it's our commitment to show newsworthy events even if they might sometimes be disturbing."

"You let the viewers choose; we let the buyers choose," Davids said. "It's a free country."

Walsh responded with a sarcastic little grunt—the sound of disbelief escaping before she could catch herself. "Melissa Davids," Walsh said, "CEO of MD Firearms. Thanks for joining us."

"My pleasure. And Jessica?"

"Yes."

"I want to express my sympathy to the victims' families."

It was, Jason thought, a performance his dad would admire. A city detective in Atlanta, Jason's dad had seen more than a few senseless homicides. Yet he would probably be the first to defend the rights of gun manufacturers like MD Firearms and gun advocates like Melissa Davids.

Jason flipped through a few more channels and watched lawyers speculate about who should be blamed. The victims couldn't sue their own employer, WDXR, because the workers' comp laws prevented such a suit. A suit against the SWAT team would be nearly impossible because cops had sovereign immunity for judgment calls like this. And it was generally assumed that the killer himself had no assets squirreled away. For lawyers, it was the greatest of all tragedies—a death without someone to sue.

A ringing phone brought Jason back to more immediate concerns.

"We need you here in fifteen minutes," the caller said. "All three panels have a verdict."

Jason glanced at his watch; the jurors had taken every minute of their allotted time. "Does juror number five look happy?" Jason asked. He was pretty sure the young lady was on his side.

"I can't tell," the caller said. "They all look mad to me."

Jason put on a new layer of deodorant—clinical strength—a fresh white T-shirt, and the same white shirt he had worn earlier in the day. He buttoned the shirt and pulled his tie snugly into place. He slid into his loafers and quickly combed and gelled his hair. He could feel his stomach roiling, the coiled nerves of a big verdict winding tighter with each minute of anticipation. He had barely eaten all day—a bowl of soup and a few crackers for lunch, an energy bar and a smoothie after court. He often lost three or four pounds a week during an intense trial, weight he couldn't afford to shed.

Jason gave himself a pep talk and focused on getting into character. In a few minutes, he would saunter into the courtroom and listen to the bailiff announce the verdicts. If he lost, Jason would stare at the jurors as if they were idiots and then would walk over and shake Austin Lockhart's hand. If he won, he would shrug it off as if he expected nothing less. Twenty minutes from now, when the verdicts were announced, you wouldn't be able to tell the result by the look on Jason's face.

He would be stoic. A first-class actor. A devil-may-care trial lawyer.

He brushed his teeth and gave himself the once-over in the bathroom's full-length mirror. He flashed a bright smile, accentuated by a gleam in the intense green eyes. There was nothing he could do about the small crook in the bridge of the nose, an old soccer injury, but it didn't seem to deter the female jurors.

"We would like to have the jury polled," Jason said, turning serious, envisioning the worst-case scenario. "And we move for a new trial based on defense counsel's discriminatory strikes during the jury selection process and our previously filed *Daubert* motion."

He narrowed the eyes, an intense stare for the imagined jurors who had turned on him. The look wouldn't melt steel, especially with the platinum blond hair mocking his seriousness, but it would certainly let them know that, in Jason's opinion, they had just sprung an unrepentant murderer. Right after the stare, the jurors would have one more chance to get it right while the judge polled them individually and asked if they agreed to the verdict.

Okay, he was ready for the worst-case scenario. He would take the blow, congratulate his opponent, and spend a few days analyzing what went wrong. Afterward, he would move on to the next case. That's what lawyers did. But he also knew a loss would stick with him for months, maybe years. Obsession? Most definitely.

He shrugged. *It is what it is.* Underneath the laid-back exterior, a 24/7

Oscar performance designed to lure others into underestimating him, Jason was a warrior. He lived to compete.

Knowing he could survive the worst case, he banished any further thoughts of losing. Today, he would play the role of the gracious victor, and he allowed himself to imagine the scene in his mind. He would barely react to the verdict, as if it were just a formality, as if he'd known all along.

Van Wyck would be sentenced to life in prison. And Jason would start getting ready for the next case.

6

JASON PULLED into the student parking lot at Pepperdine Law School. He parked and quickly found his way to the second-floor courtroom, where a private security guard stood with his arms crossed, a listening device in his right ear.

Jason nodded at the man, entered the courtroom, and spent the next few minutes giving the broadcast crew and court clerk a hard time. He had liked trying the Van Wyck case here. The school had recently renovated the courtroom, installing state-of-the-art technology, including three wall-mounted cameras and two ceiling-mounted ones, all controlled remotely from a soundproof booth. The inconspicuous technology had been less distracting than in other trials, where Jason felt like he was trying a case and acting in a movie all at the same time.

Jason clipped his battery pack to his belt, threaded the wire between the buttons on his shirt, and clipped the miniature mic to his tie. He did a quick sound check, poured himself a glass of water, and took a seat at counsel table, leaning back and crossing his legs—left ankle on right knee. It was the pose of indifference. *What—me worry?* Austin Lockhart paced in small circles near his own counsel table, exchanging small talk with his client.

A few minutes later, the bailiff entered the room and called the court to order. Judge Waters followed close on his heels, took her seat, and had the bailiff bring in the jury. She glanced quickly at both lawyers, and Jason gave her a faint smile, which she chose to ignore.

Jason wiped his hands on his pant legs and folded them on the table. His moist fists made a little water stain on the polished glass and he discreetly pulled them back, his right arm on the armrest and left hand under his chin. He had won every case in the last two years, but his nerves still frayed at the sight of a jury shuffling into their seats, heads down, somber-looking.

Juror 5 was definitely not smiling. Juror 7, a single mom who shopped at Costco and read Janet Evanovich novels and Ann Coulter books, was not smiling either.

Despite his earlier bravado, Jason did not have a good feeling about this one.

He reached for his glass and took a sip of water.

"Do you have a verdict?" Judge Waters asked.

"We do." The foreperson was Juror 4, a nicely dressed middle-aged woman in the back row. She worked in PR for one of the Hollywood studios. Drank Diet Mountain Dew. Subscribed to *Entertainment Weekly*. Voted Democrat. Contributed to green causes and PETA. Definitely not Jason's choice for forewoman.

She handed the slip containing the verdict to the bailiff, who in turn handed it to the judge.

Judge Waters studied it for a minute, seemingly enjoying her chance to torture the lawyers. *How long does it take to read the word* guilty*?*

She handed it back to the bailiff and nodded. The bailiff walked to the center of the courtroom, and Judge Waters asked the defendant and her lawyer to stand. The bailiff held the paper in front of him, as if preparing to read from an ancient scroll of Scripture in the middle of the Temple. He waited, soaking in the moment.

"We the jury, on the count of murder in the first degree, find the defendant . . ." The bailiff hesitated.

Time stood still. Jason wanted to puke.

" . . . guilty." The bailiff looked straight at the defendant and Austin Lockhart. Jason barely reacted, other than a quick glance at his two favorite jurors accompanied by a slight nod. They both acknowledged the look with a discreet smile, proud of their role in the deliberation process.

Austin had the jury polled while Jason leaned back in his seat, watching each juror affirm the verdict as their own. After a series of mistrial motions, all of which were denied by Judge Waters, the jury was dismissed and the bailiff led them out.

One jury down, two juries to go.

◁ ▷

This first jury, the one that got to watch the case unfold live, was the most important. But there were two other similar juries, seated in two other moot courtrooms, each watching the proceedings on closed-circuit TV. All three of these shadow juries were made up of Los Angeles–area residents and were designed to mimic the exact characteristics of the real jury, who had been impaneled a few days earlier to hear the actual case in a downtown L.A. courtroom.

Jason's company, Justice Inc., was a sophisticated jury consulting and research firm. For major trials, they impaneled three shadow juries as soon as the actual jury was seated. The company rushed through a confidential mock trial in a few days of intense proceedings, arriving at a verdict well before the real trial concluded. A prediction for the real case would then be communicated to privileged investors and would result in millions of dollars of stock purchases or option sales surrounding the affected companies.

The shadow jurors were paid handsomely and sworn to confidentiality. In addition, they would only know the verdict for their own panel, so even if they broke the confidentiality agreement, they would not be able to leak complete results.

The first shadow jury, the one privileged to view Jason and the other lawyer in person, was the jury that most closely mirrored the actual jury. But the president of Justice Inc., Robert Sherwood, never liked putting millions of dollars on the line unless all three shadow juries reached the same result. Even then, the votes of individual jurors were fed into the company's complex profiling software so unexpected results could be flagged and studied. The company's high-priced analysts would also study the shadow juries' deliberations for hours to make sure the outcomes weren't a fluke, perhaps driven by one juror's strong personality or a quirk in the mock trial proceedings that might not occur in the real case.

Jason settled into the second courtroom and watched the jurors assemble in the jury box after Judge Waters gave the word. For the first time in three days, the large screen on which the jurors had been viewing the proceedings had been replaced by live participants. Jason had not seen these jurors before and always found it interesting to compare the back-up mock jurors to the first-stringers. Even though the micromarketing profile of each juror had been carefully screened to reflect the micromarketing profile of the corresponding member of the real jury, each shadow panel looked significantly different from the others. For example, this panel's Juror 5, one of Jason's main allies according to her profile, was thinner and had a skeptical scowl that had never crossed the face of Juror 5 in the main moot courtroom.

But looks weren't the key. As Robert Sherwood phrased it, "Man looks on the outside, but Justice Inc. looks at the heart." It was classic Sherwood—part satire, part arrogance, and dead-on accurate. He was a man to be feared and respected, if not entirely admired.

Each shadow juror had been selected based on how closely they tracked the micromarketing profile of an actual juror. Political parties, medications taken, shopping habits, magazines read, religious backgrounds, favorite Internet sites and TV shows, sports teams, ages of children, even the type of car each juror drove—all of these factors and a hundred more had been carefully researched and analyzed by Justice Inc.'s massive investigative team. Complex software programs weighted each factor according to the type of case involved, then filtered the prospective jurors using an algorithm based on the weighted factors, identifying virtual clones of the actual jurors.

The system worked. During Jason's year and a half at the company, the shadow juries had only been wrong once, and that was a split decision where two of the shadow juries came down on one side and the third went the other way.

Today, the second jury fell in line with the first and declared Van Wyck guilty. Jason nodded at the jurors and kicked back in his chair while Austin had them polled and gave them his best scowl. Once again, the jurors held their ground, and the lawyers, judge, and court personnel moved on to the third courtroom.

By now, Jason was barely sweating. He had already won the case. The only question left was whether it would be unanimous.

It may have been his closing. Or his clinical dismantling of the defendant's lead expert. Or perhaps the fact that Van Wyck had decided not to take the stand in her own defense. Something was swaying these jurors. Later, Jason would study the tapes and find out exactly what it was.

"Does the jury have a verdict?" Judge Waters asked.

"We do," the forewoman said. It was Juror 7, a single young mom, a sure sign that Jason was about to go three for three. She handed the form to the bailiff, stealing a quick glance at the defendant. Normally, the eye contact would have worried Jason, but this time he blew it off. This was Juror 7, whose profile screamed law-and-order, a sure bet to love Jason's side of the case. Plus, women in general tended to like Jason and hate the arrogant defendant. It was the men who fell under the rock star's spell.

Maybe Juror 7 just wanted the chance to see a look of hope in the defendant's eyes, just before the verdict shattered it.

Judge Waters studied the verdict and handed it to the bailiff, instructing the woman who had been filling in for Kendra Van Wyck to stand alongside Austin Lockhart.

Again the bailiff took his spot in the middle of the courtroom. "On the count of murder in the first degree, we the jury find the defendant . . ."

As always, he hesitated.

". . . not guilty."

"Yes," Austin Lockhart responded, under his breath but loud enough for Jason to hear.

Jason looked at the bailiff in disbelief, as if he had misread the result. Then he reminded himself—*play the part.* The stoic lawyer. Unflappable. All in a day's work.

"Do you want to poll the jury?" Judge Waters asked.

Jason eyeballed them. They looked tired. Most avoided eye contact. They seemed sure of what they had done.

"Nah," Jason said with a shrug, as if the judge had just inquired about a lunch recess. "I think they probably meant it."

7

TWO HOURS LATER, Jason knocked on the door of room 301, a large corner suite in the Malibu Beach Inn occupied by Andrew Lassiter, the brains behind Justice Inc.

As was his custom, Jason came bearing a large pizza—half meat-lover's and half cheese—an order of spicy chicken wings, blue cheese, a six-pack of beer, and a bottle of Diet Coke. The beer, wings, and meat-lover's side of the pizza were all for Lassiter, a string bean of a man whose metabolism was off the charts. Jason had never seen Lassiter exercise, but his brain cells alone probably burned more calories than most people's entire bodies.

Tonight, Lassiter answered the door in pleated brown dress pants, a tucked-in T-shirt, and socks with a small hole on top of the right big toe. His shaggy brown hair hung down over his forehead, kept out of his eyes by a funky pair of black-rimmed glasses. He had a touch of gray around the temples, the only thing that hinted at the fact that he had graduated from MIT nearly twenty years and two bankruptcies ago. At age nineteen.

He took the pizza from Jason and locked the door behind them while Jason unloaded his other goodies on the round table in the middle of the room.

"State's Exhibit 12," Jason said. It was a game Jason played with the man who possessed a photographic memory that never ceased to amaze him.

Lassiter stared at Jason for a minute as if reading an imaginary teleprompter. He blinked a few times, a distracting nervous habit.

"Lab results," he said. "Toxicology tests for hair evidence. You want the numbers?"

"I trust you. Let's try Juror 6—religious affiliation."

Lassiter blinked again and put a few wings on a plastic plate, opening the small container of blue cheese. Jury information was his specialty. "Former Catholic. Attends Mass twice a year. Married a backslidden Baptist."

Jason shook his head. "Sometime, you'll have to show me how to do that."

Lassiter popped open his first beer and opened a video file on his computer screen. "Let's go straight to the third panel."

"Might as well," Jason said. Following each case, the two men would get together to watch the deliberations of the main jury panel, learning a little more about what made jurors tick. Tonight, Lassiter apparently had the same idea as Jason—better to watch the panel that Jason lost and try to figure out what went wrong.

Jason moved his chair around for a better view. Lassiter started in on the wings.

"It was probably Juror 7," Lassiter said between bites.

"Seven?" Jason asked. He walked over to the couch, where receipts, case information, and folded clothes were stacked in neat piles. He moved one of the piles aside and found the large black spiral notebook for the third shadow jury, containing detailed profiles for every juror. Each data point in the book was also lodged someplace in Lassiter's brain. "Why Juror 7?"

Lassiter finished devouring a wing and leaned back in his chair as the jury deliberations came up on the screen. "Her husband had an affair," he said. "Ended up in a painful divorce messier than Juror 7 on either of the other panels. She probably didn't like your little nod to William Congreve—'Hell hath no fury like a woman scorned'—or the fact that the jilted wife is always the state's number one suspect."

Jason absorbed the news in silence. He stood behind Lassiter and kept one eye on the computer monitor as he glanced through the profile of Juror 7 in the black notebook.

On the screen, the jury was busy selecting a foreperson. Juror 4, a middle manager at a software company, was the first to put his name in play. But Juror 7 suggested that, since the defendant was a woman, maybe they should consider a woman for chairperson.

Before Jason could blink, somebody had suggested that Juror 7 take the role. She put up a token protest and was promptly voted in anyway.

Jason sat down next to Lassiter. He pulled a slice of pizza free and placed it on his plate, though he was already starting to lose his appetite.

"They'd already cut the deal," Lassiter said. "I watched them huddle together earlier in the case. Juror 10 agreed to nominate Seven for chairperson. They probably had two or three others with committed votes."

"Just like *Survivor*," Jason said. Sometimes it was discouraging to watch jurors operate.

"The point," Lassiter responded, "is that Juror 7 was dead set against you from the start and looking for a way to control the deliberations."

Jason hunkered down with his pizza, soda, and black notebook. Technically, he wasn't supposed to have access to this tape of the deliberations. But after a few months at Justice Inc., he had befriended Andrew Lassiter, the man who shouldered the ultimate responsibility for making the prediction about the real case based on the shadow jury results.

Each time Justice Inc. targeted a major case, Lassiter watched the entire deliberation process for every shadow jury. He often stayed up most of the night after the juries returned their verdicts, analyzing and reanalyzing. He was the mastermind behind the entire system—the inventor of the micromarketing software at the core of the company's process. His mind was a rare blend of scientific genius and psychological insight.

A year ago, Jason had pleaded for the chance to join Lassiter while he analyzed one of the panels, arguing that it could enhance Jason's own trial skills and give Lassiter some company. Lassiter eventually broke down, though he swore Jason to secrecy. The two men hit it off instantly—Lassiter as the laser-focused professor, Jason as the studious trial lawyer—brought together by their insatiable desire to scrutinize the dynamics of jury deliberations.

After a few trials, the review process had developed its own quirky routine—like a private premiere party. They discussed the things that worked for Jason and the things he could have done differently. They talked about the idiosyncrasies of each juror and whether anything peculiar had happened in the mock case that might skew the results. After a night of reviewing the video, Lassiter would have a final meeting with a team of other analysts and then call Robert Sherwood with a consensus prediction for the real case.

"Why didn't you tell *us* about Juror 7's husband?" Jason asked.

"You know the rules. You only get access to the same data that the real lawyers have."

"They don't know about the affair?"

"I don't think so. Juror 7 and her husband agreed on a property distribution without going to trial. Cited irreconcilable differences. Neither likes to talk about the real reason."

"I would have argued the case differently."

"I should hope so." Lassiter popped open his second can of beer, blinked at the screen a few times, and took a long swallow. By now he had a nervous bounce going with his left leg—the carbs burning up as soon as they entered his system.

"How did *you* find out about the affair?" Jason asked. He knew Justice Inc. maintained a slew of investigators who looked under every rock when compiling the micromarketing profiles for the citizens who had been selected for jury duty during the term of the case in question. The investigators checked each juror's trash—technically not a crime since it was abandoned property. Often they gained access to a juror's computer files through some genius hacker who reported directly to Andrew Lassiter. A handful of jurors would agree to a telephone survey Justice Inc. conducted under the guise of a time-share company promising a free round-trip airline ticket just for participating. There were rumors of more nefarious methods as well, though they were never discussed in Jason's presence.

"We know lots of things," Lassiter said, picking up another wing.

"You have guys following the jurors?"

Lassiter gave Jason a look, out of the top of his eyes, with just a hint of annoyance. They had been over this before—there were some things Jason could never know.

"Okay," Jason said. "I'm just saying, it's hard to believe that Juror 7's husband had an affair, and the actual lawyers trying the case, with their own high-priced jury consultants, don't even know about it."

"Please," Lassiter said. "You might as well hire a palm reader and just skip the so-called jury consultants. They don't hire real investigators. They just hazard wild guesses based on the same information everybody has. What they do is roulette. What we do is science."

For the next hour and a half, Jason watched the tape with Lassiter, occasionally checking a juror's profile information. As usual, Lassiter provided insightful commentary, tying the remarks of the jurors to the data in their profiles. He stopped at three beers and left his plate of half-eaten chicken wings on the table, his leg bouncing, eyes blinking, working on a spreadsheet the entire time the jurors argued—his screen split between a window showing the deliberations and the spreadsheets that predicted their outcome.

Eventually Jason cleaned off the table and put the leftovers in Lassiter's refrigerator. His friend stayed hunched over his computer, massaging the data even as he talked to Jason and listened to the jurors prattle on.

After two hours of deliberations, Juror 7 decided it was time to take another vote. This would be the fourth or fifth vote—Jason had lost count—and each time the number of jurors in favor of acquittal had increased by one or two.

"Eight to four in favor of acquittal," Juror 7 announced after a quick show of hands. There were a few groans from the ones who had been in favor of acquittal from the start. They had obviously been hoping for a few more converts.

During the last hour of the video, Jason watched helplessly as Juror 7 and her comrades tore apart his case and bullied the other jurors. He had an answer for every question, but he would never get to voice them.

In two years, he had never lost a case at Justice Inc. Not a single shadow jury had turned against him. But now it was happening right in front of his eyes, and he couldn't think of a single thing he could have done differently to prevent it.

"The prosecution's going to lose, aren't they?" Jason asked, referring to the real case.

"Why do you say that?" Lassiter stood for the first time in two hours and stretched. "You won two of the three panels."

"But Austin Lockhart's not much of a trial lawyer. And Juror 7 is on a mission from God. Nobody had better accuse a jilted wife of murder . . . not on her watch."

"She's a little out of control," Lassiter admitted. He blinked and cleared his throat. "But you won the other two panels, so it obviously wasn't as much of a factor there. Personally, I'm more concerned about the Jason Noble factor."

Jason knew it was intended as a compliment—a reference to his superior advocacy skills and whether they had skewed the results. Jason didn't put much stock in it himself. He was certainly better than Lockhart, but not enough to completely alter the outcome.

"I glanced at the beginnings of the other deliberations before you got here," Lassiter said. "The other juries were nearly unanimous for a conviction right from the start. Sure, you out-lawyered Lockhart, but you had more to work with. Nine times out of ten, Kendra Van Wyck is going to jail."

"I don't know," Jason said. "I've got a bad feeling about this one."

"That's the point. You operate on feelings. I operate on facts."

8

ROBERT SHERWOOD and his guests grilled steaks and drank wine for nearly two hours aboard his sixty-eight-foot yacht, *Veritas*, being careful not to discuss any business until they were beyond the territorial jurisdiction of the United States. Sherwood constantly reminded his guests that they were doing nothing illegal, but you never knew when some headline-grabbing prosecutor would think of a creative new way to twist the law and go after you, based on the theory that nobody should make this much money without a little hassle from the feds.

Sherwood's guests each represented a major hedge fund. They were part of an exclusive club of Wall Street boy geniuses, a few of the lucky survivors who had bet on a bear market even before the collapse. But it was still Sherwood who dominated the conversation, holding forth on politics, baseball, Manhattan real estate, golf, and yachting—just about anything the great man wanted to talk about. Except business—that could wait until later.

Sherwood was fifteen years older than the oldest guest and outweighed most of them by at least twenty pounds. The man wore his years well, and people routinely expressed surprise when they learned he was pushing sixty. He dyed his hair, bleached his teeth, and worked out every day. He stood six-two and weighed a solid 210 pounds, the same weight he had carried in law school nearly thirty-five years earlier. Sherwood was loud and confident and generally found a way of mentioning his black belt within a half hour of meeting someone new.

He knew that two of his guests would never cross him, never dare to argue with a Robert Sherwood recommendation. But then there was Felix McDermont. McDermont was the most unimposing man in the room—slender and soft-spoken with feminine features and wire-rimmed glasses, protruding cheekbones that made him look like a POW, and teeth too large for his mouth. He always aggravated Sherwood with a persistent list of innocent-sounding questions, but Sherwood kept inviting him back because McDermont routinely made the biggest investment of any of Sherwood's clients. And once McDermont made his play, a dozen other hedge funds would follow suit within twenty-four hours.

Plus, he had one other endearing trait. Every time he made a hundred million or so for his fund, McDermont donated generously to Sherwood's current philanthropic cause, which at this moment happened to be the AIDS epidemic in Kenya. Sherwood could put up with a lot of nonsense for someone as generous as McDermont.

At 2:30, Sherwood led his guests into the ornate main cabin area, pulled out his laptop, and hit a switch that caused a large television screen to rise out of a cabinet. The hedge fund operators poured themselves stiff drinks from the bar—they knew their way around—and settled into the plush leather furniture. All but McDermont, who quietly drank water and sat on a barstool, his laptop open on the bar in front of him.

Sherwood turned on the cabin lights and lowered the power blinds on the windows. He lit a fat stogie—not an expensive imported brand but a blue-collar Phillies cigar manufactured in the City of Brotherly Love—and pulled up a PowerPoint presentation that had been prepared by Andrew Lassiter. Sherwood roamed the cabin as he talked, blowing smoke and stopping occasionally for a nice long pull on the cigar, pointing with the lit end to emphasize his arguments.

Sherwood had done this drill forty-one times before. He had correctly predicted the winner in thirty-four cases, and five other cases had settled during trial. He had been wrong only twice. One of those times, in the early days of Justice Inc., had nearly bankrupted the startup operation.

As of today, Sherwood was on a nineteen-case win streak. Each win further emboldened his clients, causing them to raise their bets on subsequent cases. Sherwood would never know exactly how much each hedge fund gambled, but on a big case like the Van Wyck trial, with the ripple effects that might impact a number of different companies, a savvy hedge fund operator could easily put a hundred million dollars at play without raising suspicions. With the right jury verdict, Sherwood's investors would double their money.

For thirty minutes, Sherwood bored the men with background

information they already knew—the charges against Van Wyck, the perceived strengths and weaknesses of the lawyers, general information about the jurors. The real trial had started four days earlier, and the lawyers had estimated it would take three weeks to finish. Public opinion was split on who was winning—a perfect scenario for Justice Inc.'s advanced research techniques.

The hedge fund operators listened patiently. Felix McDermont typed as fast as Sherwood spoke, recording every detail, presumably so he could scrutinize it later. The other guests didn't need details—they just wanted the bottom line.

Sherwood walked over to a glass bowl containing mixed nuts, picked out a few cashews, and munched on them before calling up a new slide. This one featured information about Juror 7, including complete details about her husband's affair.

"How good are your sources?" McDermont asked without looking up.

"We used Rafael Johansen's company, same as every other case."

McDermont made a note. Johansen's information could be trusted.

The next slide was the clincher, the reason each firm in the room paid Justice Inc. nearly $150,000 apiece, enough to recoup every dime of the company's cost for the mock trials.

"Two out of three shadow juries returned a guilty verdict," Sherwood said. He paused, allowing this information to sink in. Justice Inc. typically made recommendations only when all three shadow juries reached the same result. He watched the disappointment register on his guests' faces. "But we think the third jury is an aberration, driven by Juror 7's emotional connection with the defendant. In hindsight, we think Juror 7 on the third shadow panel has a much stronger personality than Juror 7 on the actual jury. We're prepared to predict a guilty verdict despite the outcome of the third shadow panel."

"Doesn't the scientific evidence favor the defense?" McDermont asked. "Jurors hate to ignore CSI evidence these days."

Sherwood agreed but took the next several minutes to talk about the holes in the hair testing evidence, weaknesses that had been exposed by Jason Noble. He showed a video of Jason's cross-examination of a toxicologist who was playing the role of Dr. Kramer. By the time Jason finished, it was clear to everyone except Felix McDermont where the case was headed.

"I watched the prosecutor's opening statement and examination of the first few witnesses," McDermont said. "Frankly, I wasn't that impressed.

From what I've just seen of your man's cross-examination, he may be better than the actual prosecutors, invalidating the results."

It was a good point—and one that troubled Sherwood as well. The previous night, he had argued with Andrew Lassiter for nearly two hours. *Maybe we just need to be patient. Juror 7 worries me. Jason Noble is better than the actual prosecutors. And maybe Austin Lockhart isn't as good as the actual defense lawyers. Seventy-five million is a lot to put on the line when we have split results from our juries.*

But Lassiter had been insistent. He had verified this sixteen different ways, he said. The third shadow jury was an aberration. There were no guarantees, but this one was close to 90 percent.

He had eventually sold Sherwood, who that morning had authorized the investment of seventy-five million dollars in short sales and put options on various companies that would be hurt if Van Wyck was found guilty. Seventy-five million of Justice Inc.'s own money! It was too late to turn back now.

Sherwood calmly took another drag on his cigar.

McDermont spoke into the silence. "I don't like the prosecution's theory of the case. They don't understand the scientific evidence. I've looked at their credentials. They aren't used to trying circumstantial cases like this."

This was what Sherwood hated about McDermont. Sherwood had been a successful trial lawyer. He had an instinct for juries. McDermont had probably never seen the inside of a courtroom. "Do you want me to send one of our trial lawyers over to your company so they can give you advice on natural gas futures?" Sherwood asked.

McDermont stopped typing, crossed his arms and leaned back on his bar stool.

"We've tried dozens of these cases," Sherwood said, meeting his stare. "This is our area of expertise. If we're not sure, we don't come to you with a recommendation."

"Give me a percentage," McDermont said.

"Ninety," Sherwood said.

McDermont thought it over.

The silence was broken when two of the hedge fund managers pronounced themselves in. Even in the midst of the Wall Street turmoil, Justice Inc.'s predictions had generated enviable returns and earned their trust.

"What about you?" Sherwood asked McDermont.

"I'll think about it. Your track record is strong. But this one has some hair on it."

Sherwood knew McDermont was a stubborn man. Sometimes, the harder Sherwood pushed, the more McDermont resisted. "You pay us to give our best recommendation," Sherwood said. "We've done that. The rest is up to you."

"Thanks," McDermont said. Sherwood took it as a cue to move on.

"These next few slides deal with our foundation's efforts in Kenya," Sherwood said.

Images of Kenyans with hollow eyes and skin hanging from their bones flashed on the screen. Moms. Children. Men whose look said they had lost all reason to live.

"In Kenya, millions of people have been diagnosed with the HIV virus but can't afford a cab ride to the hospital so they can get a treatment that could send the disease into remission. Even if they get there, they usually can't afford the costs of the medication."

Sherwood paused and snuffed out his cigar in an ash tray. "A child with the HIV virus can live her entire life within the shadow of a clinic that has a life-sustaining vaccine and still die because she can't afford it. In Kenya, the poverty level is one dollar per day."

A slide popped up showing the faces of young kids rummaging through garbage, gazing up at the camera. "This is why Justice Inc. exists," Sherwood said. "America has men like us who are obscenely rich. We can save millions of lives if we're willing to part with just 10 percent."

The hedge fund managers looked somber. They would donate 10 percent; they knew it was the price of admission. All but McDermont. If he got on board, he would give 20 percent.

"Our goal as a company is to donate $50 million to our Kenya foundation this year. We would be honored if you chose to join us."

Sherwood looked from one face to the next. He exited the slide show, knowing he had pushed his cause as hard as possible. His screen saver replaced the PowerPoint slides, showing a beautiful young lady in the mountains of Pakistan—Marissa Sherwood, his only child. Dead at the age of twenty-five. She had gone to the war-torn country on a humanitarian mission, helping to provide clean drinking water to areas of the country devastated by conflict and poverty. She was killed in the cross fire between two warring tribes.

Sherwood didn't say a word about her. These men had already heard the story many times. Today, he let Marissa's clear blue eyes say it for him.

There are some things in life more important than making more money.

◁▷

The next day, Felix McDermont invested nearly a hundred million hedge fund dollars in various short sales and put options that would pay off if Kendra Van Wyck was convicted—and fail miserably if she walked.

When the phone call came, Robert Sherwood breathed a huge sigh of relief. When smart money managers saw hedge fund money bet big against Van Wyck, they would assume the funds had inside information about the trial. In response, the money managers would start dumping stock in Van Wyck's companies, causing the stock prices to plummet even before the verdict.

Justice Inc. would no longer need a conviction to double its money. By the time the jury decided the case, Justice Inc. would have already cashed out.

The pattern held on the Van Wyck case, and within three days of the meeting on the yacht, Justice Inc. had doubled its investment and started pulling its money out.

By the time the jury began its deliberations, Justice Inc. had banked its eighty million in profits. Others might lose their shirts, but Justice Inc. no longer had its own money at risk. Sherwood's reputation would take a huge hit if the rock star was acquitted, but his profit and loss statement would remain unblemished.

And it was a good thing. Three weeks after the meeting on the yacht, the jury emerged from two days of intense deliberations and announced its verdict.

Kendra Van Wyck was acquitted on all counts.

9

THE JUSTICE INC. WORLD HEADQUARTERS was spread over two floors in a high-rise office building at 125 Broad Street in the heart of New York's financial district. Because "associates" like Jason Noble traveled so much, they did not have offices at Broad Street. Instead, Justice Inc. provided BlackBerries, laptops, and a generous rent allowance. When he was in New York, Jason used the corner of his studio apartment, located two blocks from Central Park, as his office. He paid through the nose for his proximity to one of the few green areas in the city, sacrificing apartment size for convenient access to the park.

The morning after the Van Wyck verdict, Jason was savoring his last day in New York before flying to Houston for a long and complex mock trial involving price fixing at one of America's largest oil companies. Getting this verdict right would serve up enormous investment opportunities for Justice Inc. and its clients. It was rumored that Justice Inc. alone might invest nearly two hundred million. It would be the most scrutinized case Jason had tried during his time at the company.

It was nearly 8:30 in the morning on a gloomy mid-September day with an overcast sky that threatened steady rain. Jason laced up his running shoes, determined to get a quick run in before the showers started. He listened to the legal commentators try to make sense of yesterday's verdict in the Van Wyck case.

Though he knew Justice Inc. had backed the wrong horse, he personally took satisfaction in the result. Jason had done what the real prosecutors could not. At the same time, he had told Andrew Lassiter that he had a bad feeling about the prosecution's case—a hunch that had been proven right.

I operate on facts, Lassiter had said. *You operate on feelings.*

Chalk one up for feelings.

Heading out the door, Jason heard the double vibration of his BlackBerry, signaling a new e-mail. He knew he should let it go, but that was impossible. The devices were called "CrackBerries" for a reason.

The e-mail was from Robert Sherwood, requesting a meeting with Jason at 10 a.m. in Sherwood's office.

Jason stared at the e-mail for a moment, his mind racing with the implications. Unlike Andrew Lassiter, Mr. Sherwood was not inclined to hang out with young associates. In fact, Jason had been in Sherwood's office on only three prior occasions, and one of those preceded his hiring.

It probably had to do with the upcoming case in Houston or maybe the Van Wyck verdict. Whatever it was, Jason had an uneasy feeling about the meeting.

He pulled off his running shoes and headed for the shower. There were stories about young lawyers who kept Mr. Sherwood waiting. None of them had happy endings.

◁ ▷

Jason exited the cab at 9:50, tipped the driver, and ran through the drizzle into a lobby that had given him goose bumps just eighteen months earlier. A white marble floor with tastefully placed brown marble squares, a granite rectangle that housed an oasis of green plants and flowers in the middle of the lobby, mirrored brass trim all around, and a security guard/receptionist smiling behind a mahogany wood desk all symbolized New York power, prestige, and status. This was the heart of New York, New York. Serious money was made here.

Jason rode the elevator to the twentieth floor, studying his own reflection during the rapid rise. He was the only associate who would think of attending a meeting like this without a suit. Instead, he wore plain black pants and a button-down, long-sleeved shirt with the sleeves rolled up. Jason was from Atlanta, where business casual was an art form. But more important, he worked hard to project a kind of casual attitude, a veneer to hide the ultracompetitive overachieving personality that lurked just beneath the surface. For close observers, there were hints of the real Jason Noble, like the fingernails chewed down to a nub during a stressful trial. But he had become a pro at hiding most of them.

"Good morning, Mr. Noble." A pretty receptionist flashed a blinding smile.

The firm ought to issue sunglasses.

Jason checked in, and a few minutes later an equally stunning woman showed up to escort Jason down the hall to Robert Sherwood's office. Jason thought about the snide comments made by young female associates who belittled the obvious importance of looks as part of Justice Inc.'s hiring criteria for staff. Funny how the male associates never complained.

The woman ushered Jason into the inner sanctum of Sherwood's large corner suite. "Mr. Sherwood will be right back," she said. "My name is Olivia. Please let me know if you need anything."

Olivia stepped out, and Jason took the opportunity to glance around. His other visits to this office had been part of quick meetings with Mr. Sherwood and other attorneys—never alone like this. Though he worked hard not to be impressed by the trappings of success, the view out the bank of windows on the west wall was breathtaking even on a rainy day. The Statue of Liberty, the green trees on Ellis Island, a few boats navigating the choppy water of the Hudson River—it was all a little overwhelming for a cop's kid from Alpharetta, Georgia.

But the view was not the most talked about aspect of Sherwood's corner office. That honor fell to a mundane navy blue leather chair positioned just in front of Sherwood's desk. The faded leather was cracked, and the wooden armrests were stained dark on the ends—the result, Jason suspected, of years of accumulated palm sweat. The old chair looked almost comically out of place amid the other expensive office furniture; the navy blue color didn't even match the rich brown decor of the other furnishings.

But the blue chair had been known to strike terror into the hearts of even the most intrepid young associates. The Justice Inc. rumor mill said that the blue chair was only used for tongue-lashings and firings and similarly unpleasant events. When Mr. Sherwood asked you to have a seat in the blue chair, you'd better have your résumé updated.

When Sherwood entered the room, Jason was rubbing the small brass knobs on the top of the backrest, wondering how many lives had been changed in that chair.

"Thanks for coming," Sherwood boomed, causing Jason to start. Sherwood walked over and shook Jason's hand with a grip you might expect from a football coach. The man was old school—white shirt, red tie, black wing-tip loafers. He patted Jason on the shoulder. "Have a seat."

Jason took a breath and slid reluctantly into the blue chair. Without speaking, Sherwood walked around his desk and sat in his own desk chair. Jason slouched down just a little and crossed his legs by resting his left ankle on his right knee. He wasn't intimidated . . . much.

Before Sherwood started speaking, Olivia poked her head back in the office. "I'm sorry," she said, "but it's Mr. McDermont, and he's insisting on speaking with you."

Sherwood looked annoyed. "I've already talked with him twice. Tell him I'll call back later."

Olivia's face fell, as if she knew McDermont would take it out on her. "I'll let him know," she said.

As soon as Olivia disappeared and closed the door, Sherwood pushed his chair back and stood, grabbing a sealed envelope as he did so. "They say you should never have a desk between yourself and someone you're talking with. Creates a barrier or some such nonsense." He walked out from behind his desk and motioned to a small round table. "Let's move over here."

Jason smiled to himself—a student of head games, he was watching a master. He joined Sherwood at the conference table that overlooked the river, suddenly feeling a little more confident after being liberated from the blue chair.

"Did Olivia offer you something to drink?"

"I'm fine, thanks."

"You tried a heckuva case in Los Angeles," Sherwood said.

"Thanks." Jason felt a small burst of pride—after all, this was the head honcho. But he also noticed that the envelope Sherwood absentmindedly tapped on the table had Jason's name on it.

"Too bad the real prosecutors didn't use your playbook."

Jason thought about his "playbook," including the hair dye stunt. He had used another product after the trial to regain his natural brown hue. "They played it safe. Prosecutors always play it safe."

Sherwood frowned at the thought and nodded. "You know what makes our system work?"

"Sir?"

"Do you know what makes our criminal justice system work? What allows juries to get it right most of the time?"

Jason could think of a thousand things—the presumption of innocence, the right to confront one's accusers, a jury of one's peers—but he wasn't sure where Sherwood was headed. "I haven't really thought about it in those terms," Jason admitted.

"The adversarial nature of it," Sherwood responded, as if the answer was obvious to any idiot. "When two equally matched and well-prepared advocates zealously represent their clients in front of an unbiased decision maker, the truth generally wins out."

He rotated the envelope in his hands, zeroing in on Jason. "Now, what screws the system up? When does it *not* work?"

"When lazy or incompetent lawyers get involved. When the juries or judges are biased."

"Right," Sherwood said. "There's an old adage about the definition of a jury. It's twelve men and women from the local community who come together to decide which client hired the better lawyer. When exceptional lawyers with enormous resources outwork and outsmart their adversaries, they win. But in the process, justice loses."

Three years of law school and two years of practicing law, and Jason had never heard it expressed quite that way. Sherwood had a reputation for cutting to the core issues.

"That's what happened in the Van Wyck mock trial," Sherwood continued. "You out-lawyered Austin Lockhart. You pulled out a conviction when the evidence demanded an acquittal. You cost a few hedge fund managers millions of dollars."

Jason didn't quite know what to say. It felt like he was being accused and congratulated at the same time.

"I think you're giving me too much credit," he managed.

"That's what Andrew Lassiter said. And I listened. It cost me a lot of credibility, Jason. It cost my clients a lot of money."

Jason squelched the desire to apologize. What had he done wrong?

"It's not your fault," Sherwood said, as if reading Jason's mind. "We told you on day one that we wanted your best efforts in every case. The only way this works is when both lawyers go all out." Sherwood flashed a quick smile, almost a wink. "Unfortunately, your best efforts are too good.

"I've never fired anyone for being too good at their job, Jason. But there's always a first time."

Sherwood twisted his neck back and forth, casually stretching his neck muscles as if he fired someone every day.

Am I hearing this right?

The CEO put down the envelope and stood, his bulky frame hovering over the table. He walked to his credenza and pulled out a box of cigars. He held them toward Jason, a surreal gesture that made Jason realize this moment would become part of Justice Inc. folklore. His friends wouldn't believe this! He was getting fired for doing his job too well—and then offered a celebratory cigar as if he and Sherwood had just won the NBA championship.

"No, thanks," Jason said.

Sherwood set the box on the table and unwrapped one for himself. He bit off the end and spit it into a trash can. He placed the cigar in his mouth without lighting it and chewed on it as he talked.

"I'll pay you for the remainder of your two-year contract," he said, sliding the envelope toward Jason. "I would probably pay you a bonus for exceptional performance if you hadn't set the company back a year or two by winning a case you should have lost."

Jason bit his tongue and eyed the big man curiously. It was hard to know whether Sherwood was being sarcastic or serious.

Sherwood shrugged and gave Jason a knowing smile. "I know this sounds stupid. But it's like a college football player declaring early for the draft. You're better prepared to try a big case than 90 percent of the litigation partners at the largest law firms in this city." He chewed a little more on his cigar. "You've got a knack, Jason. And I want to help you land at the right place."

Sherwood paused, as if he was spontaneously thinking this up. But Jason knew better. "You're licensed in Virginia, right?"

"Yes, sir."

"And don't call me 'sir.' We went over this before."

"Right."

"I've got some friends at a few of the larger D.C. firms. Starting salaries are about one-fifty." Sherwood went to his desk and grabbed two manila folders and plunked them on the table in front of Jason. "I've already made a few calls if you're interested."

Jason looked at the names on the folders—two prestigious K Street firms. Not bad for a guy who graduated from the University of Georgia Law School.

"I appreciate it," Jason said. He pulled the folders toward him and stacked them neatly together. "But I've actually thought about starting my own practice. Criminal defense. Plaintiff's contingency fee work. I'm not sure I'd be happy working at a big firm where I'd spend my first five years in the library."

Sherwood chewed on his cigar, studying Jason as if he were some kind of lab experiment.

"I'm a courtroom lawyer, Mr. Sherwood, not a desk jockey."

"It's Robert. And I knew that." He grinned. He walked to his phone and hit the speaker button, summoning Olivia into his office. "Can you get Jason the contact information for Dr. Rivers?" he asked. "And bring me the Jacobsen and Bakke files."

He turned back to Jason after Olivia left. "Dr. Rivers just retired as the chief toxicologist for the Commonwealth of Virginia. She's setting up a consulting firm in Richmond, Virginia, to work the defense side of the aisle. She knows all the skeletons in the closets, Jason, all the places the bodies are buried, so to speak. But she's just an expert. She needs to team up with a really good trial lawyer."

Richmond, Jason thought. Far enough from Atlanta to escape the past. Big enough to make a name for himself.

"I've already talked to Rivers about you," Sherwood said. "She's working two major criminal cases right now that will hinge on hair testing evidence. Maybe you move to Richmond. Maybe you and Rivers become the go-to team for cases involving hair evidence."

It sounded good to Jason, almost too good. But things were moving pretty fast. From New York to Richmond. From mock trials at Justice Inc. to real cases with lives on the line. Was he really ready to try a major criminal case just two years out of law school?

Of course you are, he said to himself. He had watched a lot of mediocre lawyers on the actual cases that Justice Inc. had been tracking. They were afraid to take risks. How could he do any worse? After all, he'd just been fired for being too good.

Sherwood gave Jason that look that said he knew exactly what Jason was thinking. "Make sure you get sizable retainers up front," Sherwood advised. "That's the first and most important rule for criminal defense attorneys."

His own practice. Two new clients. A top expert witness as a partner.

Jason cast a disdainful look at the blue chair. "Maybe I *will* have a cigar," he said.

10

JASON SPENT NEARLY AN HOUR in Sherwood's office, by far the longest amount of time he had ever spent with the CEO of Justice Inc. He learned that Sherwood had served nearly ten years as managing partner of a large New York law firm, and Jason soaked in law management tips, at one point even asking to borrow a legal pad and pen so he could get it all down. The conference ended only after Olivia interrupted again, reminding Sherwood of his next appointment.

"Okay," Sherwood said, "we're wrapping it up."

When Olivia left, he turned back to Jason. "You've heard me say it a hundred times before, but I want it to be the last thing you hear from me. You're going to make an obscene amount of money in your life. But there will always be someone making more, and it will never feel like quite enough."

Sherwood's dark eyes burned with an intensity he reserved for this issue alone. "We've given you better training than most elite lawyers will ever receive. Like other Justice Inc. alums, I'll stay in touch and help you however I can. I only ask for one thing in return. Do your part to alleviate suffering in a third world country. We give 10 percent of our gross profits to such causes. I'd ask you to think about doing the same."

Jason nodded and took the unlit cigar out of his mouth. It suddenly seemed a little pretentious.

"I'm going to turn you over to our HR department now," Sherwood said. He stood and Jason followed suit. "We've got some severance documents for you to consider and some draconian security processes in place, but don't take it personally. There are millions of dollars at risk on every case, and we've got to be careful."

"I understand," Jason said. He shook Sherwood's hand, threw his cigar in the trash can, and gathered up the envelope that contained his severance check along with the legal pad on which he had jotted three full pages of notes. He thanked Sherwood for the amazing experience of working with Justice Inc. and then followed Olivia to the office of Michael Ortberg, Justice Inc.'s director of Human Resources.

There, Jason filled out a small mountain of paperwork—a severance agreement, health insurance elections, a non-compete and confidentiality agreement, and other similar documents. He reluctantly surrendered his firm-issued BlackBerry, thinking about how many personal e-mails and voice mails the device contained. The blow was lessened somewhat when Ortberg explained that Mr. Sherwood had authorized Justice Inc. to provide a replacement BlackBerry with the first year's service agreement paid in full. As a convenience, Ortberg said the company would transfer Jason's contact list to the new device, though they couldn't do the same with the e-mail.

"I'm sorry," Ortberg said. "Company policy. That e-mail address belongs to Justice Inc., and we have to maintain complete control over it."

Ortberg explained that Jason could transfer his e-mails from his firm computer to a flash drive before he turned in his computer. "We'll also erase all your personal data on the hard drive before we reissue it," Ortberg said.

"Do you want me to bring the computer in tomorrow?" Jason asked.

"Actually, we have a policy about that too. We'll have one of our folks follow you home and bring everything back to the office. It's not that we don't trust *you*. But some of our attorneys and employees are released on less than favorable terms and we have to apply the policy the same way for everyone who leaves."

"I understand," said Jason, though he actually didn't. What happened to all the trust the CEO of the company had expressed just an hour or so earlier? "I'll need to delete some passwords for my bank accounts and other personal things before you take the computer back."

"Rafael can handle that."

Rafael Johansen showed up a few minutes later. Jason decided the man must have arrived fresh from the studio lot of Hollywood's latest action flick. Dark-skinned and buff, Johansen was wearing a short-sleeved, button-down shirt and white slacks. The shirt was loose, hiding the man's biceps, but his forearms had the bulging veins and rock-hard look of a steroid abuser. Rafael had thin hair and a trim beard that followed a granite jawline, and he wore a Bluetooth earpiece and dark sunglasses even though the forecast called for more rain.

Jason tried to begin a conversation during the taxi ride to his apartment, but Rafael apparently specialized in one-word grunts. They rode most of the way in silence.

Once inside Jason's apartment, Rafael produced a checklist of items he needed according to the contract Jason had signed when he first started work for Justice Inc. They started with Jason's laptop. Jason downloaded his personal items to a flash drive and deleted those same files from the hard drive. Rafael watched over Jason's shoulder the entire time.

Next, Jason gave up all the flash drives, CDs, and paper files he had produced while at Justice Inc. His contract called everything a "work for hire" and specified in no uncertain terms that it all reverted back to the company. Rafael called somebody on the phone and spoke to them in Spanish. Twenty minutes later, two men appeared at Jason's apartment and started loading everything into boxes.

They reached a point of impasse when Rafael insisted on personally inspecting Jason's desk drawers and the drawers of his filing cabinet for additional Justice Inc. materials. Jason refused, challenging Rafael to point out contractual language that entitled him to invade Jason's privacy.

"I am just ensuring that you've complied with your contract," Rafael insisted. "This is for your own protection. If proprietary information gets leaked, I'll be able to certify that it didn't come from you."

"I'll take my chances," Jason said.

Rafael stared at Jason for a moment. He had slipped his sunglasses on top of his head an hour earlier, revealing emotionless dark eyes that he now used to try to bully Jason.

Instead of intimidating Jason, it only made him mad.

"I'll have to make a phone call," Rafael said.

He called Michael Ortberg, who asked to talk with Jason and played the role of good cop on the phone. It was nothing personal, Ortberg said. He acknowledged that Rafael had no contractual right to look in the drawers but he urged Jason to let Rafael look anyway. "I know you've got nothing to hide," Ortberg said. "So if you could just humor him on this, it would make things a lot easier."

"What's next, my sock and underwear drawer?"

When Jason's sarcastic comment was met with momentary silence, he became even more agitated. "You're kidding," he said.

"Yes, I'm kidding," Ortberg said. "Let me talk to Rafael."

Rafael took the phone and walked into another room. When he returned, he told his men to make sure they had everything boxed up and labeled. He removed a form from a folder and asked Jason to sign it.

While the men taped and labeled the boxes, Jason studied the form. It was a certification that he had returned everything—every piece of data and information he had ever generated or collected while at Justice Inc., whether stored electronically or contained on paper or in any other manner. Jason read the form, opened his desk drawer, and handed another flash drive to Rafael, then signed the form.

Rafael took the form, then handed Jason a plain white envelope with Jason's name on it. "Mr. Sherwood wanted you to have this," Rafael said.

After Rafael and his men left, Jason sat down at his desk and opened the envelope. Any warm fuzzies he'd had about his time at Justice Inc. had largely disappeared. Rafael had made Jason feel like a convicted felon trying to steal the company's proprietary secrets.

The envelope contained a letter from Robert Sherwood, expressing his gratitude for a job well done. *I've never terminated anyone for being too good,* the letter said. *Seems like that might merit a small bonus.*

Enclosed was another check for $75,000—half a year's salary. It made his total severance $150,000.

Though it still seemed like a strange way to leave a company, Jason no longer felt underappreciated.

He sat for a few minutes in silence, contemplating how quickly his life had changed. It was times like this when he most longed to pick up the phone and call his mom—a remarkable woman who had lost a six-month struggle with cancer when Jason was in junior high. Until she died, Jason had always been his mother's son, soaking up the attention and unconditional love that came as natural to her as breathing. She died after the cancer metastasized from her colon to her liver. Fourteen years later, Jason still teared up just thinking about her.

At the time, people simply shook their heads. "She was so young," they'd said.

His mother's death left Jason with his father—a strict disciplinarian who never remarried. Jason now felt obligated to call his father and let him know about these recent developments. His father had grudgingly accepted Jason's going to work for Justice Inc. but had always dreamed of Jason becoming a prosecutor. Instead, Jason would have to tell his dad about his plans to become a criminal defense lawyer, joining the "dark side."

His father would curse and let Jason know he was disappointed. He would remind Jason, as he had many times before, that Jason would be serving time behind bars if not for the fraternity of the men in blue—the way they looked out for each other's families. He would do everything within his power to send Jason on another guilt trip.

But it would only backfire, reminding Jason of the reason he had chosen this path in the first place. If other cops were as willing to work outside the law as the ones Jason knew, all kinds of innocent people would need good defense lawyers.

His father would never understand that. He would accuse Jason of being a sellout.

But Jason knew the truth.

It was his father who had sold out. The system had already purchased his father's soul.

◁▷

Robert Sherwood looked up at a knock on his office door.

"Come in."

The door swung open, and Rafael Johansen stepped in. "We're all set," he said.

"Do you think he's got copies of the software?" Sherwood asked.

"Maybe. He wouldn't give us access to his desk drawers and filing cabinets."

Sherwood thought about this for a moment. Given the enormous sums at risk, Justice Inc. had always been obsessed with protecting its proprietary information.

"I think he's a straight shooter," Sherwood said. "But let's put surveillance on him for a year or so just to play it safe."

11

IT TOOK JASON three days to call.

The first two days, he pulled up his father's contact information a half-dozen times and scrolled the BlackBerry wheel until it shaded his father's phone number. But he couldn't bring himself to place the call.

The third day, in the solitude of his apartment, Jason found the courage to push the wheel and initiate the call. The phone rang three times with no answer, raising Jason's hopes that he might be able to just leave a message.

But then his father answered. "Jason, I'm in the middle of something. Can I call you back?"

"Sure."

An hour later, when Jason was walking down the Avenue of the Americas, he felt his BlackBerry vibrate twice. His father's name and number appeared on the screen.

"Hey, Dad," Jason said.

"Hey, Jason. Sorry I had to go earlier. I was in the middle of a department meeting. What's up?"

Justice Inc. placed a premium on confidentiality, so Jason needed to be somewhat vague, even with his father. In the past, he had described his job as "legal research for investment firms."

His father had scoffed at the "desk job" but tolerated it because he knew Jason was making $150,000 a year, enough to take a healthy chunk out of his student debt. The unspoken assumption—at least his father's unspoken assumption—was that Jason would take a job as a prosecutor once he finished his two-year commitment.

"Um, I'm leaving New York early, Dad. As in next week." Jason paused—it was never easy to talk with his dad. "I finished my projects ahead of schedule, and they're paying me the rest of my salary."

This brought an extended silence. Jason imagined the scowl on his dad's face—the block jaw tensing as the forehead wrinkled in displeasure. It was, in Jason's opinion, a face that bore little resemblance to his own. "You're not telling me something," his dad said. "You had a two-year contract. Something must have happened."

"Nothing happened," Jason said. He started getting a little perturbed. Why couldn't his father just accept that Jason had actually done something right? "I finished my research projects . . . ahead of schedule. They loved my work, made a ton of money off me, and now they're going to help me get my own practice started."

Jason held his breath, ready for the explosion. He was standing at a street crossing, waiting for the light to change, elbow-to-elbow with a couple dozen New Yorkers. It felt like everyone was listening.

"Your own practice?"

"The president of the company has some connections. He's setting me up with a few clients and an expert witness who recently retired from her post as Virginia's chief forensic toxicologist. I'll have my own law office in Richmond."

The light changed, and taxis immediately blew their horns. A large tour bus revved its engine as it went through the lower gears. Jason started walking again, moving with the masses.

His father said something but Jason had to ask him to repeat it.

"What type of clients?"

"All kinds. Trial stuff. Civil as well as criminal."

This brought another pause. His father didn't need it spelled out—private lawyers who handle criminal cases represent criminals. In his father's view, only the prosecutors wore the white hats.

"Heckuva way to make a living," his father said. "Plea bargains for rapists. Attacking cops and victims for what—a couple hundred an hour?"

Jason didn't want to have this conversation right now. His father was stubborn, a trait Jason *had* inherited. "There are good lawyers on both sides, Dad. You know that." *And crooked ones too,* though Jason left that part off.

"Interesting way to show your gratitude," Jason's father said. Jason knew the comment was coming, but it still stuck in his craw. It was a reference to *the incident,* the point in Jason's life when he learned that cops could be bought and sold, with loyalty if not with money. The same event that, in his father's eyes, indebted Jason to his dad forever.

The incident had haunted Jason for the past ten years, beginning with nightmares and bouts of depression that eventually gave way to a lingering cynicism. It was, though his father would never understand this, the reason Jason had decided to be a defense attorney.

"Matt Corey put his career on the line—his entire life's work—so you could have a chance," his father reminded him. "You would have never made it to law school if Matt hadn't valued our friendship enough to do that. Why do you want to spend your life attacking men like that?"

"That's not what I'll be doing, Dad." It was a small lie, but Jason just wanted off the phone.

"Are you calling to ask me about this or tell me about it?"

Jason took a breath and stepped to the edge of the sidewalk, out of the traffic flow. "I'm going to do this, Dad. And I'm going to do it the right way. I've made up my mind."

Jason's father didn't respond immediately, perhaps hoping that the uncomfortable silence would cause Jason to change his mind. If so, he was wasting his time.

"There is no right way," Jason's dad eventually said. And with that parting comment, he hung up the phone.

PART III
ADVERSARIES

12

Eight weeks later

KELLY STARLING SNUCK a discreet glance at her watch, taking care to ensure the recruit sitting across her desk didn't notice. She liked this young man—Geoff, a second-year from Georgetown with good grades and a track record of serious community service. Kelly's firm, one of the largest and most prestigious on K Street in downtown Washington, surely could have used another idealist like Kelly. But she knew it wasn't going to happen.

"I read the article about your work with victims of human trafficking," Geoff said, admiration flashing in his eyes. "It's one of the things that attracted me to the firm."

He was talking about a two-year-old *Washington Post* story detailing the way young women were lured to America with the promise of jobs and then forced into prostitution or pornography to pay off insurmountable debts. As a second-year associate at Burgess and Wicker, Kelly had started taking a few of those cases *pro bono*—filing suits to wipe out the women's debts and pushing prosecutors to indict the men who brought them here. The article made great press, and now B&W included it in all their marketing and recruiting materials, as if the firm had a serious commitment to *pro bono* work.

Kelly had retold the story in dozens of interviews, mesmerizing law students with a side of D.C. most of them never knew existed. At the same time, she was careful not to imply that they might have a shot at being another Kelly Starling. B&W was interested in billable hours, not crusades.

Kelly was one of a kind—a fortunate beneficiary of publicity that had helped the firm's image and eased the conscience of its senior partners as they hauled down more than a million a year. One Kelly Starling was good for a firm like B&W, softening its image. The firm "cover girl," the other associates had labeled her. But a bunch of Kelly Starlings would destroy the financial model of the firm, butchering the cash cow that funded Bentleys for the partners and college educations for their kids and plastic surgery for their spouses.

Stifling a yawn, Kelly told Geoff her sex-trafficking story, leaving out the gory details in a PG-13 version of the events. Most recruits expressed horror that such things could go on right under their government's nose in the nation's capital. A few of the more confident male recruits—usually former jocks—would try to flirt a little or let Kelly know that they might have taken matters into their own hands and busted a few heads when nobody was looking.

Kelly was used to this—men trying to impress. She had been a swimmer in high school, fast enough to earn a few college scholarships, which she had promptly declined. She still tried to stay in shape, but her sedentary job was taking its toll. Plus, there were some things you couldn't fix at the gym.

To her own critical eye, her shoulders were a bit too broad, and she lacked the curves of most women her age, compensating instead with toned arms and flat abs. She still remembered the article they ran in her hometown paper in high school. It was probably supposed to be a compliment, but it didn't seem that way to a sixteen-year-old girl who had grown to an awkward five-ten: *She has the perfect swimmer's body. Her posture is gangly, loose and cocky, like a teenage boy's. Her body resembles an inverted triangle—broad shoulders, long torso, thin hips—and provides a significant advantage in leverage over the other more muscular female swimmers she regularly beats.*

An inverted triangle—not exactly an endorsement for Hollywood's next leading lady. But it worked for Kelly. Some said she had "natural" beauty, probably a backhanded comment on the fact that Kelly wore little makeup and kept her dirty-blonde hair short and layered, requiring minimal fuss between her morning swim and hitting the office. More honest assessors used the word *handsome* to describe her slender face, an adjective perhaps engendered by the firm jaw or high forehead. She squinted when she smiled, flashing dimples and perfectly aligned white teeth, thanks to the wonder of orthodontics.

The *Washington Post* article had called her a cross between Dara Torres and Greta Van Susteren—quite a stretch in Kelly's opinion. The same article had described her as somewhat obsessive, an "A+++ personality," in the words of the reporter. The fact that Kelly could still remember the exact quotes nearly two years later probably proved them right.

In any event, the recruiting director at B&W was no dummy—she sent Kelly nearly twice as many male law students as females.

But Geoff didn't try to play it cool or demonstrate his machismo. "That's amazing," he said after Kelly finished. "I would have never had the guts to do half that stuff."

Geoff was big and a little goofy, his blond hair moussed into spikes, but his transcript was littered with As. If B&W hired him, he would be stuck in the library, researching complicated tax shelter schemes or leveraged buyouts. He wouldn't have a minute to spare for the homeless or elderly.

Kelly wrapped up the interview as efficiently as possible and ushered Geoff to the next attorney's office five minutes early. She walked quickly back to her office so she could fill out the interview form before her next appointment. She gave Geoff a few scores below five on a scale of one to ten, low enough to guarantee he wouldn't make the cut. Kelly really liked the kid, so much so that she wasn't willing to subject him to the pressure cooker at B&W. Only the strong survived at Kelly's firm. Her partners would chew Geoff up and spit him out.

13

LATER IN THE DAY, Kelly waited in her office for the receptionist to call. She tried to busy herself with other files, but it was useless. Finally, at a few minutes after one, the call she had been waiting for came through.

"Mr. Crawford is here."

"Can you set him up in 12A? I'll be down in a couple minutes."

Mr. Crawford. Blake Crawford. Grieving widower of Rachel Crawford, the reporter gunned down in the WDXR studio two months earlier. A week ago he had called Kelly out of the blue, claiming he had been referred to her by the Handgun Violence Coalition. He wanted to talk about suing the manufacturer of the MD-9—the gun Larry Jamison had used to execute Rachel.

At first, she thought it was a prank, but she kept herself from saying anything stupid. Once she realized it really *was* Blake Crawford on the phone, she started running through the legal analysis in her mind. Though the case sounded like a stretch, Kelly didn't want to say no until she had at least researched it. She didn't get calls from potential clients with national name recognition every day.

It was complicated, Kelly had said, explaining that he had caught her between meetings. Could they schedule an appointment? Would first thing next week be soon enough?

Kelly's next call had been to the director of the Handgun Violence Coalition, who said he had indeed referred Blake Crawford to her. The director explained that he had received a call from a big donor who suggested Kelly might be the perfect lawyer to represent Blake Crawford against the gun manufacturer. The donor had faxed a copy of the *Washington Post* article to the director, noting that both Kelly and Rachel Crawford had been active on the issue of human trafficking. "Maybe you should call Blake Crawford," the donor had suggested, "and explain the basis for a suit against MD Firearms, referring him to Kelly Starling."

Kelly had asked for the name of the donor.

"He wants to remain anonymous," the director said.

After a few days of additional research, Kelly had some solid answers. The case had potential. And she would pull out all the stops to get it.

Letting Blake Crawford sit for a few minutes in conference room 12A, the crown jewel of B&W's Washington office, would be a good start.

Nearly half of B&W's 450 lawyers set up shop in this smoked-glass office building with the prestigious K Street address. Others worked out of equally plush addresses in Atlanta, Singapore, Paris, Bangkok, and London. Conference room 12A had seen its share of Fortune 500 CEOs and United States senators. Billion-dollar deals had closed on its forty-foot mahogany table. Bill Gates had been deposed here. Press conferences had been held here. National political campaigns announced. Even a few office affairs had been consummated here in the wee hours, the participants evidently unaware of the hidden cameras.

From 12A you could gaze out over Farragut Square, contemplate your problems while staring at the U.S. Chamber of Commerce building, or catch a glimpse of the Capitol on the horizon. Kelly met with her sex-trafficking clients on park benches and in greasy restaurants, but Blake Crawford would get the full treatment, including an extra five-minute wait so he could admire the authentic paintings and realize that Kelly was a very important and busy associate in a very successful firm.

"Sorry I'm late," Kelly said, bursting into the conference room and shaking Blake's hand with just the right touch of assertiveness. "Something to drink?"

"I'm fine," he said. Blake was dressed in khaki pants, a light blue shirt, and a black suit coat. He had dark circles under his eyes and a quiet voice, the strain of the last few months showing on his face.

Kelly had admired his restraint when he appeared on TV. He had steadfastly refused to cast blame on anyone except Larry Jamison—not WDXR for having lax security; not the SWAT team for failing to intervene early enough; not the gun dealer for selling the gun illegally; not the manufacturer of the weapon. "I don't know why this happened," Blake Crawford had said. "But I just have to trust God that He's got His reasons. Pointing fingers won't make the pain go away."

Kelly trusted God, too. But sometimes, in Kelly's view, God needed a good lawyer.

Kelly sat across the table from Blake, suddenly feeling silly for meeting in such a large and imposing room. "Thanks for coming in," she said. "I'm sorry for your loss."

"Thanks." Blake looked at Kelly for a moment and then down at the table. "I almost cancelled," he admitted. "I still don't know if this is the right thing to do."

"I understand that," Kelly said. "Let's just take it one step at a time."

She asked Blake some introductory questions and jotted a few notes on a legal pad so she could fill out the new client intake form. "I haven't completed my investigation yet, but I've got some preliminary opinions," Kelly said. She noticed the blank look in her potential client's eyes—the pain of the tragedy had apparently morphed into a certain kind of numbness. She had seen the same look from her human trafficking clients when they gave up hope.

"Let's start with the gun dealer." Kelly opened a file she had compiled on Peninsula Arms, the shop that had sold the gun Larry Jamison used to murder Blake's wife.

"Jamison had a felony record and was ineligible to purchase a firearm under federal law," Kelly explained. "The gun was actually sold to a twenty-three-year-old man named Jarrod Beeson. As you know, Beeson originally said that somebody had stolen his gun and that he just didn't bother reporting it. But the next thing you know, some guy serving time for illegal firearms possession tells the authorities that Beeson was one of the men used as an intermediary in other straw purchase transactions from this same store. The ATF agents pressure Beeson and he cracks, admitting his role as a straw purchaser."

Blake Crawford nodded absentmindedly.

All this information had already been broadcast to the entire nation, Kelly knew. Beeson had signed a confession acknowledging his role in multiple straw purchases from Peninsula Arms. He even admitted that sometimes the clerks at Peninsula Arms would give his cell number to potential customers who couldn't clear the background check on their own. Three weeks ago, the feds indicted the owner and a store clerk at Peninsula Arms. Last week, the store and its owner filed bankruptcy.

"This is not an isolated case." Kelly slid a nineteen-page Excel spreadsheet across the table. It contained a long list of guns sold by Peninsula Arms that had been traced to crimes in New York City, Washington, Baltimore, and Philadelphia.

"A few years ago, several municipalities filed suit against rogue gun dealers who demonstrated a pattern of engaging in illegal transactions—selling guns to eligible purchasers acting as stand-ins for ineligible purchasers. New York City even sent undercover agents as phony shoppers to the gun stores.

"The first agent would select a gun but balk at the paperwork when it came to questions about whether he was a felon or had been involuntarily committed to a mental facility. A few hours later, that same person would come back with somebody else, point out the gun right in front of the same store clerk, and give the new agent the money to buy the gun. The clerk would have the new undercover agent fill out the paperwork and would sell the gun, then watch as that person handed the gun to the illegal purchaser. The dealers never even reported this to the ATF."

Kelly waited a moment as Blake glanced over the chart. With the help of the Handgun Violence Coalition's attorneys, she had distilled the statistics from each of the East Coast cities that had filed a lawsuit. "In 2006 alone, the last year for which we have stats, Peninsula Arms sold 251 firearms linked to murders or aggravated woundings in these four cities. Only one other dealer had a greater number of guns traced to crimes. Between the two of them—Brachman's Gun Shop and Peninsula Arms—they had accounted for more than 30 percent of the guns that turned up in these cities linked to violent crime.

Kelly stopped, waiting for Blake to make eye contact. He seemed to have a little more spark in his eyes this time.

"Not one of the guns linked to Peninsula Arms was used in the crime by its original purchaser," Kelly continued. "We're talking about a massive number of straw purchases, Blake. Three separate citations by the ATF. And guess what the gun of choice was for one out of every four crimes?"

"The MD-9," Blake said, his voice more sad than irate.

"The MD-9," Kelly repeated. She said it with more feeling, as if she could somehow stiffen Blake's backbone with an injection of her own determination.

Next, Kelly opened a folder on MD Firearms and started building her case against them. According to Kelly, the company's CEO, a woman named Melissa Davids, knew that the MD-9 was designed for one thing—killing people. That's how they marketed the gun. And it was working. The dull black semi-automatic was preferred by street thugs everywhere, as demonstrated by the factual evidence distilled from the cities' lawsuits.

"The company makes nearly two hundred bucks each time it sells one," Kelly explained. "And they sell hundreds through Peninsula Arms, even knowing that many of the guns are being peddled to convicted felons through illegal straw transactions."

Blake nodded, the sad eyes finally showing some flint. "I've seen Melissa Davids on a few TV shows," he said. "That's one of the reasons I'm here." He paused, and Kelly noticed his lip tremble a little. "She says she's not worried. She says there's a federal law protecting manufacturers from lawsuits like this one. There's no remorse about her gun being used in this crime. It's almost like she's proud of it."

The short speech made Kelly realize again how much she wanted to file this case. A crusader needed a crusade. And here was a decent man whose life had been torn apart through no fault of his own. Her heart ached for him.

"There *is* a federal law," Kelly said. "It's called the Protection of Lawful Commerce in Arms Act. It protects dealers and manufacturers from getting sued if a firearm operates the way it was intended and causes injury through criminal activity. But a few courts have declared it unconstitutional. Plus, there is one very important exception."

Kelly turned to the statute and read the exact language—every word mattered. "This act does not include 'an action in which a manufacturer or seller of a qualified product knowingly violated a State or Federal statute applicable to the sale or marketing of the product.'"

She looked up at Blake and thought maybe she detected a thin ray of hope. Family members of victims often tried to find a larger meaning in the death of a loved one. A cause. A greater good.

"I know a lawsuit won't bring her back," Blake said. "But maybe it will prevent someone else from going through the hell I'm going through. Maybe it will make Melissa Davids think twice about selling guns to places like Peninsula Arms or this other dealer you mentioned. I just need to know we're not tilting at windmills."

Kelly resisted the urge to tell him that tilting at windmills was her specialty. This case wasn't hopeless. Other crusaders had prevailed on similar facts.

"Remember the D.C. area snipers?"

"Yeah."

"They got their gun through a straw purchase as well. Bull's Eye Shooter Supply ran such a shoddy operation that it couldn't even find the paperwork for 238 guns it sold, including the Bushmaster assault rifle used by John Allen Mohammad and Lee Malvo. The victims filed suit against both Bull's Eye and the gun manufacturer. They settled for $2.5 million."

Blake considered this for a moment, studying his hands. When he looked up at Kelly, she saw big tears pooling in his eyes.

"I know you hear this all the time," he said. "But it's not about the money. If we file suit—and I still haven't decided to do it—but if we do . . . we're not going to settle."

Kelly had been litigating at B&W for five years. Every client swore it was a matter of principle. For most, the principle that mattered most was the amount of money the other side offered in settlement. She sensed that Blake might be an exception.

"A case like this won't be easy," she said. "It could take years. You and I will be ruthlessly attacked by the NRA and their affiliates." She paused to emphasize the seriousness of her warning. "Are you ready for that?"

In response, Blake reached into his back pocket and pulled out his wallet. He opened it up and retrieved a small piece of folded paper with a grainy brown and white image on it. He gently unfolded the paper and slid it across the table.

"Here." He rotated the paper, and the image became clear. It was a 3-D ultrasound. The small baby inside Rachel's womb was in the traditional upside-down fetal position, looking cozy and content.

The image rocked Kelly. "How far along?"

"Twenty-two weeks."

Kelly hesitated, trying to divorce her personal life from her professional one. She needed to focus on Blake and Rachel. "Did you know if it was a girl or a boy?"

"A little girl."

"Had you picked out a name?"

"Rebecca."

Rachel and Rebecca. Biblical names.

"I'm sorry," Kelly said. She folded the paper carefully, as if handling a priceless artifact, and handed it back to Blake.

The news media had reported that Rachel was pregnant, so that part was no surprise. But actually seeing the ultrasound and hearing the name somehow made it real. A person. A tiny baby in the safest place imaginable, violently slaughtered.

These were the kinds of thoughts Kelly had been carefully avoiding the past seven years. This case, if the screening committee let her pursue it, could be tougher and more personal than any Kelly had tried yet.

14

FOUR DAYS LATER, on a cold Friday morning in November, Kelly presented her proposal to the stone-faced B&W screening committee.

Despite all of its marketing and recruiting pitches to the contrary, B&W was still firmly entrenched in the "good-old-boy culture." The five unsmiling faces on the screening committee belonged to old, male, white, Ivy League–credentialed lawyers. They were also five of the most conservative and pessimistic partners in the firm, strategically placed on this committee because the firm believed that the best time to fire troublesome clients was five minutes before signing an agreement to represent them.

Kelly made it about halfway through her presentation before the questions started.

"What about the theory of independent superseding cause? Don't the actions of this guy . . . what's his name?"

"Jamison."

"Right. Don't his criminal actions cut off the right to pursue MD Firearms?"

Before Kelly could answer, another member of the committee piped in. "She's not proposing a negligence theory. She's saying this company creates a public nuisance by selling to rogue dealers. Causation is analyzed differently under a nuisance theory."

"Actually," Kelly said, "I'm proposing both."

"Even if we take this on a contingency fee, who's going to pay the out-of-pocket costs?"

"I'm proposing that our firm would advance them."

"Could be a hundred thousand or more," somebody murmured.

"Have you seen the polls on gun control?" one of the members asked. "A majority of Americans *support* the Second Amendment."

"What's that got to do with anything?" countered another committee member. "We're not attacking the Second Amendment."

"That's semantics," the first member shot back. "You know as well as I do this is just a backdoor way to take guns out of the hands of American citizens."

And so it went. The pro-gun members arguing with the anti-gun members and Kelly hardly getting a word in edgewise. The men staked out their positions early, and nobody changed anyone else's mind. At the end of the meeting, the committee authorized Kelly to take the case by a 3–2 vote.

There *was* an unexpected twist, however. John Lloyd, the chairman of the committee and a vote in favor of the case, proposed that B&W take the case *pro bono* instead of on a contingency fee basis.

At first, Kelly hated the idea. If the firm handled the case on a contingency fee basis and obtained a large verdict, the money collected would count toward her billable hour requirement. But *pro bono* cases were extra—community service work done above and beyond the normal oppressive billable hour quota.

"If we take the case on a contingency fee," Lloyd said, "the media will portray us as a bunch of ambulance-chasers trying to profit from gun violence. If we take it *pro bono*, they'll applaud us as principled advocates for reform."

"And we might leave a million dollars on the table," somebody protested.

Lloyd motioned toward Kelly. "We're gonna have our firm's prettiest face all over *The Today Show* and *Nightline* and *20/20*—no offense, Kelly. How much do you think it would cost us to buy that kind of publicity?"

Kelly blushed a little. She wasn't afraid of the publicity, but it would be nice to be more than just the firm cover girl. "I think that's a mistake," she said. "This case could lead to other cases just like it. This could develop into a very lucrative practice area."

That thought generated looks of grave concern on the faces of the two partners who had voted against the case. "B&W is a business litigation firm," one said. "Not a plaintiff's personal injury firm. I for one don't want to be known as the law firm that declares war on the Second Amendment."

John Lloyd took off his glasses and spoke with the gravitas of a peacemaker. "Those are valid concerns, and I'm not proposing that we declare war on the Second Amendment. We're taking one case, milking all the publicity we can out of it, then going back to our bread and butter."

It wasn't exactly a ringing endorsement, but Kelly just wanted out of the room with her case intact. Even though she couldn't possibly handle her billable hours requirement *and* this case, in a way it wouldn't matter. If she won, her reputation would soar, and her lack of billable hours wouldn't matter. If she lost, all the billable hours in the world wouldn't save her.

The more she thought about it, the more she liked the idea of taking the case *pro bono*. Lloyd was right. The liberal media would portray Kelly as the white knight, riding in to save the day against gun violence. Her firm could take the next case on a contingency fee.

"You really want me to do this *pro bono*?" she asked. Her tone made it clear that it would be a major sacrifice, one she would reluctantly make for the good of the firm.

"I'm afraid so," John Lloyd said.

"All right," Kelly said, resisting the urge to smile.

15

TWO WEEKS LATER, a B&W runner filed a thick lawsuit in Virginia Beach circuit court. A press release quickly followed. In the lawsuit, Kelly was required to provide only general allegations, but she had gone much further. She beefed up the pleadings with lots of specific facts about the MD-9 and the way Peninsula Arms supplied much of the black market in New York, Philadelphia, Baltimore, and D.C.

Fortunately for Kelly, all four of those cities happened to be major media markets.

A week earlier, B&W had hired an outside PR firm to arrange interviews on the most prestigious morning shows for the day after the filing. Accordingly, while the lawsuit was being file-stamped by the Virginia Beach court clerk, Kelly was on a flight from D.C. to New York. She was nervous, but she had learned from the rainmakers at B&W that building a law practice consisted of one part skill and two parts marketing. Besides, this would be a great opportunity to influence the public's perception of her case, including potential jurors in Virginia Beach. She would look into the cameras and pretend she was talking to a few friends over a nice dinner. How hard could it be?

On Tuesday evening, Kelly was greeted at LaGuardia Airport by PR consultant Jeff Chapman and a limo driver holding a sign with Kelly's name on it. On the way to the hotel, Jeff briefed Kelly on each interview scheduled for the following day and the types of questions she might expect. Jeff was a big man, gregarious and confident, and his briefing helped Kelly calm down. He seemed to be on a first-name basis with all the hosts and assured Kelly that most of the interviews would be very sympathetic.

"They'll have to ask hard questions because that's what they do. But remember, secretly they'll be cheering you on. If you stumble, they'll ask a softball question so you can end strong."

"And then there's *Fox and Friends,*" Kelly said.

"Even there, they'll have to be careful how hard they push. There's a lot of sympathy for your client."

◁▷

At each studio, Jeff Chapman introduced her to the producers and makeup crews, chitchatting with them like old friends. Kelly breezed through the first few interviews, her only disappointment being that Matt Lauer was taking the day off. Her third interview, ABC's *Good Morning America,* was smooth sailing until Diane Sawyer popped the experience question: "If you don't mind my asking, how long have you been practicing law?"

"Five years," Kelly replied. She had flashed her smile often that morning, on the advice of Jeff Chapman. But she didn't smile now. "I'm the same age Rachel Crawford was when she was gunned down."

"Great answer!" Jeff said after the interview. All morning long, he had been telling her that she was a natural.

I could get used to this, Kelly thought.

◁▷

CNN was probably her best interview. They had assembled a whole package of graphics based on the statistics Kelly had highlighted in her lawsuit. As an extra bonus, they had uncovered some details about several other crimes involving guns sold by Peninsula Arms, particularly the MD-9. Toward the end of the interview, they actually produced an MD-9 on the set, assuring Kelly it was not loaded.

It looked evil, lying on the anchor desk—flat and boxy, dull black with a blunt barrel. "Do you think guns like this should be legal?" the anchor asked.

In response, Kelly launched into her speech about why criminals prefer guns like the MD-9. Law-abiding citizens have no use for them, she argued. And the NRA can no longer use the slippery slope argument, saying if we outlaw guns like this we will eventually come after hunting rifles and pistols. The Supreme Court took that possibility away in the *Heller* case.

Fifteen minutes later, Kelly was being whisked into the less friendly environs of the Fox News studios. Jeff made his usual round of introductions and Kelly was ushered into makeup. As she climbed into the chair, Jeff explained that he had some other pressing appointments and had to run. This was her last interview. Kelly should just call a cab to take her back to the hotel. Jeff would meet her there for lunch.

Kelly thanked him and settled into the chair while a perky young woman touched up the makeup that had been layered on at the other shows. "You don't need much help from me," the woman said.

"Thanks."

"You've got about five minutes before they start your segment," the woman said when she had finished. "The greenroom is right down the hall."

Kelly thanked her and headed to the greenroom. Things had been happening so fast all morning, she needed a few minutes to clear her head. So far, she had survived her media baptism relatively unscathed. One more interview and she could return to the safety of her office in D.C.

The Fox News greenroom was a clone of the other greenrooms Kelly had seen that morning. A sofa, a few leather chairs, a coffee table, and a large mirror on a side wall. Plaques hung around the room along with signed photos from celebrities expressing best wishes to the hosts. Munchies and drinks lined a table along one wall, while a flat-screen LCD television broadcast Fox News on the other. A middle-aged man with a full head of gray hair was talking to a razor-thin and diminutive woman in the middle of the room. They stopped talking when Kelly entered.

The man extended a meaty hand. "I'm Congressman Parker," he said.

He looked older in real life, his skin wrinkled and beginning to spot. He was a conservative icon, sixty-five or seventy years old, certainly no fan of gun litigation.

"Kelly Starling."

They shook hands, Parker squeezing hard enough to send a message. "I know who you are."

Kelly ignored the comment and extended her hand to the woman standing in front of her. She estimated the woman to be about five-two or -three and could tell she was wound tight.

Maybe it was because Kelly had just sued her company.

Melissa Davids ignored Kelly's outstretched hand. Kelly smiled and withdrew it.

"I didn't know we were appearing together," Kelly said.

"Now you do," Davids responded.

16

KELLY SAW NO REASON to get into a big argument in the greenroom. "It's nothing personal," she said. "I'm just representing my client."

She started to walk away and take a seat, but Davids had other ideas. "Have you ever been raped?" she asked.

Kelly stared at her for a second, sure she'd misunderstood the question. "Excuse me?"

"I was. At age sixteen. I spent two years learning jujitsu and was assaulted again at age eighteen. That's when I bought my first gun." Davids took a half step closer and lowered her voice. "Nobody's touched me since."

This woman is hard-core.

"Look, I know you mean well," Davids continued. "You're no doubt one of those big-hearted liberals all fired up about women's issues. You want to empower women?"

Kelly crossed her arms, choosing not to respond.

"Teach them to shoot. A gun is a woman's best friend."

If Kelly hadn't heard it with her own ears, she probably wouldn't have believed it. Davids was like a character from a comic book.

"Thanks for the advice," Kelly said.

◁ ▷

The fireworks started again as soon as Kelly and Davids were situated next to each other on the set. For most of the segment, Kelly felt like she was being cross-examined by the show's host with Davids looking for fun places to pile on. On a few occasions, Davids interrupted Kelly's answer, raising her voice until Kelly let her talk.

"We've been sued thirteen times when some psycho uses one of our guns in a crime," Davids said, her eyes narrowing. "We've been sued in New York,

San Francisco, Boston, Philadelphia, and Detroit." She paused for emphasis. "We've yet to pay a dime. The only people making money in these cases are the lawyers, not the victims."

"Those were different legal theories," Kelly countered. "Based on your design and marketing of the gun. This case is different. It's about supplying the black market—"

"That's no difference," Davids interrupted. "That's just lawyer talk."

Both women argued at once but this time Kelly spoke louder. "I'm not finished!" she said emphatically. "I let you finish; I'd appreciate the same courtesy."

The host smiled and held up his hands. "One at a time," he said. "Ms. Starling first and then Ms. Davids can respond."

"Our firm is taking the case *pro bono*," Kelly said. "Every dollar recovered goes to the client. In addition—"

"And I suppose you aren't in it for the publicity, either," Davids sarcastically interjected. "Which is why you've sprinted from one morning show to the next all day long."

"You're not very good at letting people finish," Kelly countered. She knew this tit-for-tat made them both look stupid; she needed to get back to her talking points.

"She's right," the host said, grinning at the fireworks.

"Are you honestly saying you didn't know that Peninsula Arms was a rogue dealer?" Kelly asked. "You never watched the videotapes of New York City undercover agents conducting straw purchases at Peninsula Arms? You didn't know about the 251 guns used in crimes traced to Peninsula Arms in 2006? The media was all over this stuff—how could you not know?"

Davids leaned forward and stared back at Kelly. "You want to hear what I know? I know you didn't sue the estate of the man who actually shot your client's wife. I know you didn't sue the gun store that you say illegally sold the gun. Instead, you sue my company, and we didn't even know about the sale. And then, as soon as the suit is filed, you make the rounds of every talk show in America. That's what I know."

Their host started to wrap up the segment but Kelly cut him off.

"May I respond?" Kelly asked.

"We've only got fifteen seconds," the host said. "I'll give you the last word."

Fifteen seconds? The competitive instincts kicked in. Kelly was tired of being pushed around.

"I told you in the greenroom it was nothing personal," Kelly said to Davids, her teeth gritted. "I lied. It *is* personal. Your cavalier attitude cost Rachel Crawford her life. I take that very personally."

Davids scoffed and started to respond.

"I'm sorry," the host insisted, talking over Melissa Davids. "We really are out of time." He read a few sentences on the teleprompter as the producer counted down to the next break.

As soon as the red light flashed off, Davids stood and took off her lapel mike. She ignored Kelly, thanked the Fox News host, and headed to the greenroom.

Kelly tried to be gracious, mustering a fake smile as she also thanked the host and then moved off the set. She stood behind the cameras for a few minutes, watching the start of the next segment. Congressman Parker, a regular guest on the show, pontificated about the purpose of the Protection of Lawful Commerce in Arms Act. It was, according to the congressman, legislation specifically designed to stop this sort of unmerited lawsuit.

"Let me read what the legislation says about these kinds of civil actions," the congressman said. "They are an abuse of the legal system, they erode the public confidence in our nation's laws, they threaten the diminution of a basic constitutional right and civil liberty, and they constitute an unreasonable burden on interstate and foreign commerce."

Kelly had heard enough. She left the set and returned to the greenroom to pick up her folder. Fortunately for her, or maybe fortunately for her adversary, Melissa Davids was already gone.

17

ON HER WAY BACK TO THE HILTON, Kelly checked her BlackBerry. Lots of enthusiastic e-mails awaited her—friends and family gushing about seeing her on television, other attorneys at B&W telling her she did a good job. She checked her missed phone calls—thirteen in just the last few hours—and immediately dialed the one number she cared about most.

"My friends said you were great on the morning shows," Blake Crawford told her. "I didn't have the heart to watch them myself."

"Did any of your friends catch *Fox and Friends*?"

"A couple. They said Melissa Davids was a jerk."

Kelly was relieved to hear that assessment, even if it was from a totally biased perspective.

"I think it's safe to say she's not going to roll over on this one."

"You told me that in your office."

"It's a little different when you meet her in the flesh. You know those folks who run around with the bumper stickers saying, 'You can have my gun when you pry it out of my cold, dead hands'?"

"Yeah."

"I think Davids probably views them as sellouts."

This brought a small courtesy chuckle from Blake. In her limited contact with the man, Kelly sensed that it had probably been a long time since he had truly laughed. And who could blame him?

"My friends say you were not exactly a pushover, either," Blake said.

It was the one comment Kelly needed to hear. She felt like she had been played on the Fox interview and caught off guard. But the client felt good about it. Funny thing with clients, they didn't always care how smooth or eloquent you were; they just wanted to know you were fighting for them.

"Thanks," Kelly said. "I think we're off to a good start."

◁▷

It took two discreet calls from conservative pro-gun senators, both friends of Robert Sherwood and major beneficiaries of Sherwood's political donations, before Melissa Davids would agree to the meeting. Ultimately, she acquiesced, provided that they could squeeze it in first thing in the afternoon, before her return flight to Atlanta. Sherwood had a driver pick Davids up at the Fox News studio and drive her to his waterfront estate in Greenwich, Connecticut. Privacy was of utmost importance.

Sherwood met her at the door himself and was struck by how much smaller she looked in person than she did on television. When they shook hands, her grip had the tensile strength of iron; when she spoke, she talked in clipped sentences with a military staccato and no trace of a Southern accent. She looked at Sherwood with the same kind of suspicious intensity one prizefighter uses to intimidate the other just before the bout.

Robert Sherwood liked her immediately.

"Something to drink?"

"No, thanks."

"How was your trip out here?"

"Fine."

Visitors normally couldn't resist gawking at the cavernous entranceway to Sherwood's manor or staring through the house to the bank of windows overlooking the water. The view from the front entrance was breathtaking. One could see past the plush marbles and rich woods and antique furniture of the interior, through the floor-to-ceiling windows that lined the back wall, straight to the layered terrace and exquisite landscaping leading down to Long Island Sound. On a clear day, you could stand at Sherwood's front door and see sailboats, pleasure yachts, and other vessels dotting the sound for more than a mile in each direction.

Sherwood's neighbors were some of the wealthiest men and women in America—not the flashy *nouveau riche,* television stars and athletes with limited earning capacity, but the old-time money with real fortunes—hedge fund operators and brokerage firm executives savvy enough to have survived the stock market meltdown of 2008. These were the men and women who made more each year than the combined payroll of the New York Knicks.

Yet Melissa Davids, to her credit, was apparently impressed by none of this.

"I don't have long," she said, hardly even glancing around. "I suggest we get down to business."

"All right," Sherwood said. "But first I want to show you something."

He led her through the massive family room that stretched across the back of the house, past a wet bar, and through a door that opened into another large room spanning the house's east side. It had few windows and no view of the harbor. Its design was more rustic, with a stone fireplace and a number of trophy kills hanging on the walls—African lions, Alaskan bears, Canadian elk.

Sherwood took his guns seriously. His collection contained more than forty firearms, including four rifles and two pistols manufactured by MD Firearms.

Melissa Davids's lips curled into a little smile. "Your friends told me you were a collector."

They spent nearly a half hour in the trophy room, with Davids critiquing her competitors' firearms and even pointing out a few flaws in her own. A dry wit came to the surface, and she allowed Sherwood to talk her into a drink.

"Scotch? Brandy?" Sherwood asked.

"I'm from the South," Davids replied. "We drink whiskey and beer."

Over Bud Lights, they swapped hunting stories. For lunch, Sherwood served sandwiches and chips on paper plates.

Halfway through the meal, Davids checked her watch. "Okay," she said, "you pass the bona fide gun nut test. Now, let's get down to business. Senator Michaels said you might be able to help with the Crawford case."

"I run the best jury consulting firm in the world," Sherwood said. He put his sandwich down and launched into an explanation of the micromarketing techniques that Justice Inc. employed to predict jury verdicts.

Davids looked skeptical. "I spend a few million bucks on lawyers every year. If you're so good, why haven't I heard of you?"

Sherwood lowered his voice. This was the critical part. "We've spent millions perfecting the system. But to be frank, companies like yours can't afford our services."

Davids didn't flinch, but he could tell he had her attention.

"We impanel mock juries who very closely mirror the actual juries. Other consulting firms know how to use shadow juries. But our jurors so closely track the real jurors that they're more like clones. We hold mock trials with these jurors, working around the clock to predict the actual verdict days or even weeks before the real trial concludes. We sell our research to hedge fund operators and investment firms."

Davids had stopped eating and Sherwood could see the look in her eyes, the dawning realization that this might be an asset she hadn't considered before. A different league. What could be more valuable than the ability to predict exactly which jurors might be most sympathetic to her case?

But she was a tough negotiator who knew better than to act impressed. "And because you're such a big fan of guns, you're going to make an exception in this case," Davids said, with a twinge of sarcasm. "For the meager sum of a half million or so, you're going to tell us exactly which jurors to strike and which ones to keep."

Sherwood smiled. "I already told you—you can't afford us."

"Then what's your angle? Why this elaborate show?"

Sherwood got up and grabbed another beer from the refrigerator. "I want you to win," he said. "I like your side of the debate. Plus, if I intend to make a lot of money on the case, I can't afford to be surprised by the verdict."

"Then let me put your mind at ease," Davids said. She took another bite of her sandwich. Sherwood waited while she chewed. "We haven't paid any plaintiffs yet. We don't intend to start with Blake Crawford. We'll win, Mr. Sherwood. You can put your money down right now."

Robert Sherwood shook his head. "We ran three mock juries on that Indiana case that was headed to trial until Congress bailed you out with the Protection of Lawful Commerce in Arms Act. You would have lost nearly ten million. You haven't paid anything yet, but only because you've never actually gone to trial in a case like this one."

Sherwood watched the lines on Davids's face tighten, the eyes narrow. She didn't like hearing this, but he kept his voice steady, matter-of-fact. "Your high-priced lawyers and in-house counsel have lost almost every critical hearing this past year in the cases currently pending against you. So far, courts in New York, Indiana, and the state of Washington have either held the Protection of Lawful Commerce in Arms Act unconstitutional or found other ways around it. It's just a matter of time before you have to start facing real juries on these cases where you're allegedly indirectly supplying the black market, and our research is not encouraging."

Davids finished her beer and wiped her mouth. "I've got enough people telling me how bad things are going," she said, her words terse. "I'm fully aware that inner-city juries are just dying to tag a gun manufacturer like us with a huge verdict. It's the American way, Mr. Sherwood. Everybody's a victim. Sue the big, bad corporation. I didn't really need to come all the way up here for the civics lesson."

"I've got a solution," Sherwood said. She gave him a don't-we-all? look. "Wait," he said, "hear me out."

"My plane leaves in two and a half hours. It will take thirty minutes to get to the airport."

"All right, let me get right to it." Sherwood said. "Virginia Beach is a good town for a test case—it's pretty conservative and mostly Republican. But there's not much of a gun culture there. You need a different type of lawyer to handle this case. Somebody young. Somebody who doesn't fit the stereotype. Somebody who can relate to a Virginia Beach jury."

"And I suppose you have just the person?"

"He's the best young trial lawyer I've ever seen. I had to release him from our program because he was too good—skewing the results. He would win cases that most of us thought were unwinnable."

Sherwood could tell from the look on her face that Davids was not buying it. "I've already got plenty of lawyers," she said. "And I need true believers, not somebody who, as you say, 'goes against stereotype.'"

"Humor me," Sherwood said. "Just spend fifteen minutes watching this kid on tape."

Davids put up some initial resistance but ultimately agreed. They went to a flat-screen television hanging on the wall, where Sherwood had the highlight film ready to go—portions of an opening statement, Jason on cross-examination, a slice of Jason's best closing argument. Sherwood provided running commentary, explaining that Davids could use her in-house lawyer to drive the overall strategy and Jason to try the case.

"This kid is magic with a jury," Sherwood reiterated. "You can teach him how to use guns, why they're important. Someone like Jason who is less immersed in the gun culture will be better at explaining those concepts to the jury in a way they can understand."

Davids looked like she was thinking about it, so Sherwood pressed his point. "He's licensed in Virginia, and you need someone young. Kelly Starling is young and fresh and easy on the eyes. You think that's a coincidence? The handgun-control folks know that men typically go our way.

"On the other hand, our preliminary research shows that young women would typically be sympathetic to a victim like Blake Crawford. Jason could help win over that demographic."

Davids nodded a little and seemed to relax. "I'll think about it." She was silent for a moment, then asked, "Why would you own a Russian SKS?" She motioned toward to one of the guns in Sherwood's collection. "It's a piece of junk."

"It was a gift," Sherwood explained. "I haven't fired it more than twice since I got it."

Davids seemed to accept this and turned the conversation to hunting. She didn't leave until two hours later, flying south on Sherwood's private plane. On the return trip, Sherwood's pilot called and shared some good news.

"She contacted her company lawyer and asked him to do a background check on Jason Noble," the pilot said.

When Robert Sherwood hung up the phone, he poured himself a glass of scotch and water. Before he went to bed, he stepped back into his gun room and looked around at his trophy kills hanging from the walls, the pictures of Sherwood and his hunting buddies, the guns that had brought him so much pleasure.

Until the day his daughter died.

Just prior to his meeting with Davids, he had thought about putting away the hunting pictures but decided against it. They added so much authenticity to the room. Besides, he hadn't changed that much in five years. Davids apparently hadn't noticed that there were no recent pictures.

He turned off the light and locked the door. The details he had learned about his daughter's violent death flashed through his mind. He would pour himself another drink before he called it a night.

18

HE WAS ONLY SIX WEEKS into private practice, and Jason Noble was already tired of the grind. He loved the practice of law; he just didn't have time for it. He had become Jason Noble, office manager, rather than Jason Noble, trial lawyer. He kept telling himself things would be different once he put all the systems in place.

At least he had a sweet office space. Sherwood had strongly suggested that Jason secure a Class A space on Main Street. "Nobody wants a lawyer who can't afford a Main Street address." Jason initially protested, calculating the cash flow he would need until serious fees started rolling in.

Sherwood wiped out that objection with one phone call.

"You've got a hundred-thousand-dollar line of credit with Bank of America," he said when he called back. "You can probably double that after six months if you make your payments on time."

At first, $100,000 seemed like a lot of money. Six weeks later, Jason had already burned through half of it. An interior designer (another of Sherwood's suggestions) cost $5,000; office and conference room furniture was $15,000; computers and software another $5,000; a lawyer to incorporate, insurance, an independent bookkeeper, a cleaning crew, etc., etc. For the first two weeks, it seemed that the only legal work Jason did was negotiating contracts with vendors. During his third week, he started interviewing assistants and opened his first legal file.

Jason spent the next few weeks trying to learn the procedures in the criminal courts in and around Richmond. As promised, Sherwood delivered a few major cases to Jason's door, all dealing with hair-testing evidence. Three more cases came as referrals from Dr. Patricia Rivers, the commonwealth's former chief forensic toxicologist. By week six, Jason had seven cases in his filing cabinet.

The call from Robert Sherwood, promising case number eight, was totally unexpected.

"You ready to take that job with the big firm in D.C.?" Sherwood asked.

"Just about."

Sherwood laughed. "Hang in there. It'll get much worse before it gets better. Trust me—I've been there."

"Thanks for the encouragement."

"How many cases you got?" Sherwood asked.

"Not many," Jason admitted. He felt a little embarrassed about the exact number. He had never been much of a marketing guru. "Ten or so."

"That's not bad for the first few months," Sherwood said. "Any civil cases yet?"

"Not yet."

"You ready for your first one?"

Jason felt a surge of adrenaline. He had already figured out that landing the cases was half the battle.

"I think I can squeeze it in."

"You may not want it," Sherwood said, his tone playful. "It'll take lots of time. Probably bill about two fifty, maybe even three hundred an hour. The client will have no trouble paying. Plus, it's high profile."

"Maybe I'd better stick to criminal work," Jason said, playing along. "I'd rather work for less money and keep worrying about getting paid."

"Okay," Sherwood said. "Have a good day."

"No . . . wait! Are you serious?"

"It's a good case." This time Sherwood sounded more somber. "But there's a catch."

Jason waited. There was always a catch.

"The case was filed in Virginia Beach. The plaintiff's lawyer is not the kind to settle. It seems to me that any lawyer taking this case would have to spend a lot of time in Virginia Beach, maybe even move there. It's the kind of case where you've got to get inside the heads of the jurors. From your time with us, you know how important that is."

"I've spent time in Newark. I think I could survive a few months in Virginia Beach."

"Good. The client will be calling you any day. Her name is Melissa Davids. She's the CEO of MD Firearms. She wants you to defend the Rachel Crawford case."

Jason didn't respond immediately; he was not at all sure that he had heard the man correctly. "The *Crawford* case?"

"She wants a fresh face to represent the gun industry," Sherwood said. It sounded like he was having fun breaking the news. "Someone who might also happen to be a pretty decent trial lawyer."

Jason was at a loss for words. Most lawyers waited an entire career for a case like this. "Am I going to serve as local counsel?"

"Not just local counsel. As far as I know, they're looking for you to help try the case. Maybe serve as co-counsel with their in-house lawyer."

"That's unbelievable. . . ." For a split second, the euphoria lifted Jason. The next second, reality set in. "What makes them think I'm qualified?"

"They're going on my say-so. And trust me, Jason, you're more than ready."

19

MELISSA DAVIDS did not waste any time. She called Jason the day after his phone conversation with Robert Sherwood and summoned him to Atlanta for an urgent meeting with herself and Case McAllister, general counsel for MD Firearms.

Jason scheduled his flight for 6:30 a.m. on December 12, two days after the initial phone call. He woke at 4 a.m. and rummaged around his closet for a few extra minutes before deciding on the perfect attire for meeting with a gun-manufacturing client—jeans, a white shirt, and a sports jacket. The windchill was supposed to be near freezing, but Jason hated traveling while carting around a heavy winter coat and briefcase. Since 95 percent of his time would be spent indoors or on planes, he decided to leave the overcoat at home.

His commuter flight got bounced around a little by the wind gusts. When it finally landed, they had to sit on the runway for thirty minutes waiting for their gate to clear. Jason fought his way through the crowded terminal to the underground transit and up the long escalator to the baggage claim area.

A driver holding a poster-board sign with Jason's name printed neatly in black Magic Marker waited for him. For the first time in his life, Jason felt like a big-time lawyer.

"Welcome to Atlanta," the man said. "You must be Jason Noble."

They shook hands and Jason mumbled, "Thanks for coming for me."

"Let me get that," the man said, grabbing Jason's briefcase.

"Thanks," Jason said, though he felt a little silly letting an old guy carry his briefcase. The driver was about seventy or so, with stooped shoulders, a thin, pointed nose, and gray hair slicked back so that it curled around his ears. He was wearing a suit, a red bow tie, and cowboy boots.

Jason followed his driver to short-term parking, buttoning his sports coat along the way as the wind knifed through him. His driver seemed to be limping a little.

"Where's your overcoat?" the driver asked.

"I hate lugging them around," Jason said. The cold air in the parking garage bit into Jason's face, and he felt a little stupid.

The driver led him to a Ford Taurus and beeped it unlocked. "This baby's got a good heater," he said. "You can ride in the backseat. But most folks prefer to ride up front with me."

Reluctantly, Jason took the hint and climbed in the front. He had actually been looking forward to daydreaming while he rode through Atlanta, spurring a few positive memories and repressing negative ones as he recognized familiar landmarks. The drive to Buford would take close to an hour in the morning traffic.

The man carefully placed Jason's briefcase in the backseat and popped open the trunk. He retrieved a black pistol in a shoulder holster and strapped it on under his suit coat.

"We've been in a big fight with Hartsfield-Jackson," he explained, climbing into the car. "They don't want guns anywhere on airport property—parking lots, nothin'—but we've taken 'em to court a couple of times. The Second Amendment is the Second Amendment. The feds get to take your guns at the metal detectors, not before. I've got a concealed-carry permit and bring my gun every time I come to the airport, just out of spite."

Jason resisted the urge to tell him that he agreed with the feds on this one. The thought of thousands of passengers running around the airport premises—even outside the metal detectors—with guns hidden under their suit coats was not a comforting one.

Over the next hour, Jason had no time to stroll down memory lane. The driver engaged in conversation virtually nonstop, even after Jason tried to make it clear at the outset, by giving only one- or two-word answers, that he wasn't interested in talking. The driver chatted about the Second Amendment, hunting, frivolous lawsuits, his ostrich skin cowboy boots, Jason's choice of vehicles, the Georgia Bulldogs, illegal immigrants, and lenient judges. The driver even pried information out of Jason about his father, a homicide detective in Atlanta.

"Cop's kid, huh. I'm surprised you're not a prosecutor."

"So's my father."

They eventually pulled up to a nondescript one-story redbrick building on a small industrial road off Lawrenceville-Suwanee, basically in the middle of nowhere. There was a large cinder block manufacturing facility behind the office building and a parking lot on the side, full of hundreds of cars. There were a few 18-wheelers parked near the loading docks.

Out front, there was one small sign with the address of the facility and the name MD Firearms. A few neatly trimmed shrubs lined the sidewalks. The Georgia crabgrass that passed as a lawn in these parts had gone brown for the winter.

Jason had envisioned a far different facility. The infamous MD Firearms, in the fulcrum of so much national media attention, looked like any other law-abiding small American manufacturing facility, piecing together a product and struggling to make a buck.

"That's our manufacturing plant out back," the driver said. "There's a shooting range on the other side of it—can't really see it from here. And this one-story building in front that looks like a renovated elementary school—that's the worldwide headquarters of MD Firearms."

Jason thanked the driver, who dropped him off at the front door and handed Jason his briefcase. "The receptionist knows you're coming," the driver said.

Jason peeled off a five-dollar bill from the other money in his pocket and tried to hand it to the driver.

"No, thanks," the man said. "I work for the company. We're not allowed to take tips."

"Okay. Well, thanks again." Jason drew a deep breath and headed into the facility.

20

THE INAUSPICIOUS SIZE of the building was only the first of many surprises. Melissa Davids met Jason in the lobby and gave him a personal tour of the manufacturing facility.

She was nothing like the fierce advocate he had seen on television. She knew most of the line workers by name and asked questions about their families' Christmas plans. Even though Davids was a small and nondescript woman, her personality dominated everyone in her presence. She had this thing for calling people by their last name and somehow made that feel more informal and intimate than if she had used their first name or a nickname. The place was neat and businesslike, the kind of atmosphere you might expect to find at any top-notch manufacturing plant.

After the tour, Davids took Jason back to her office, located at the front corner of the building. It was about half the square footage of Jason's office. Pictures of Melissa's husband—an accountant, according to Jason's research—and children adorned the walls. She picked up the phone and asked Case McAllister to join them.

A few minutes later, Jason's driver came into the office, a sly smile on his face. It took a second for Jason to piece it together. Stunned, he casually shook the man's hand.

"We've met," Case said. "Had a good ride from the airport together."

Jason felt like an idiot for failing to get the man's name. It was probably some kind of litmus test, seeing how a lawyer would treat a lowly driver for the company. Quickly, Jason scrolled through his conversation with Case, trying to remember if he'd said anything stupid.

"Has Melissa told you the meeting rules yet?" Case asked.

Meeting rules? "No."

"She hates meetings," Case said. "Believes that committees and meetings are the places good ideas go to die. Any meeting at MD Firearms involving Melissa is a stand-up meeting. If we can't finish it in a half hour, we do it off-line."

"Good rules," Jason said.

"How'd he do on the ride?" Davids asked.

Case checked a notepad he was holding. "A little more liberal than most of our outside lawyers. Not much of a hunter or gun aficionado. Doesn't detest frivolous lawsuits with quite the same passion you and I might."

Jason felt himself going a little red and started wondering how he might explain this to Robert Sherwood. *I lost the client before I even got to their facility.*

"Any good points?" Davids asked.

"A couple. He drives a Ford F-150 truck, and his dad's a cop." This elicited an approving nod from Davids. "He's also a Georgia Bulldog fan. Graduated from UGA Law."

"Salvageable," Davids said.

"Barely," Case said.

The whole exchange felt surreal, like being a draft pick and watching the front office evaluate you. They were talking past Jason, as if he didn't exist.

But then Case McAllister addressed him. "We've interviewed two other prospective lawyers who both assured us we could get summary judgment based on the Protection of Lawful Commerce in Arms Act. Said they could make the case go away in less than six months. Have you looked at that issue?"

The question threw Jason even more off stride, not because he hadn't looked at the Act but because he hadn't known he was in a beauty contest with other law firms. He really wanted this case, and Robert Sherwood had made it sound like it was Jason's just for the asking. But he couldn't fudge his legal advice just to land a client.

"The way I read the complaint, it falls within an exception to the Act," Jason said. "And if we decide to leave the case in state court, which I recommend based on the conservative nature of Virginia Beach juries, it will be almost impossible to get summary judgment. Virginia is the only state that doesn't allow the use of depositions for a summary judgment motion. If we don't get a judgment on the initial pleadings, which is unlikely based on my review of the complaint, then we're going to trial."

Jason paused for a second, trying to read how this blunt honesty was impacting his potential clients. "With respect, Mr. McAllister, you need a good trial lawyer, not somebody who's going to waste his time filing unwinnable paper motions."

That assessment was followed by a brief silence, and Jason still couldn't read the faces of his hosts. Case McAllister made a check mark on his legal pad.

"I like him," Davids said. "It's the first honest piece of advice we've received on this case. Plus, Robert Sherwood assures me he's an excellent trial lawyer."

McAllister nodded his assent, and Jason felt his neck muscles relax. He took note of how Davids had made a point to insert Sherwood's name into the conversation.

Melissa Davids took a half step forward and looked Jason dead in the eye, as if she was somehow measuring the strength of his character.

"They're going to demonize us," she said. "Make you feel like you're literally the devil's advocate. You're going to have to look at that jury and tell them a poor grieving widower doesn't deserve a dime. You're going to have to learn about guns and the gun culture. You're going to have to defend the Second Amendment like it's your firstborn child. Can you do all that?"

She said it with the seriousness of wedding vows. *Man, these folks are intense.*

"Yes," Jason said, setting his own jaw to show that two could play this game. "But you're going to have to let me call the shots at trial. And let me coach you as a witness. And go along with some wild gambles I might cook up along the way. And let me—and only me—select the jury. And one more thing—you're going to have to pay my bills on time and send in a seventy-five-thousand-dollar retainer." He hesitated, trying to make sure he hadn't forgotten anything. "Can *you* do all that?"

"I *really* like this guy," Davids said to Case McAllister.

21

A FEW MINUTES after Melissa Davids made her pronouncement, Case McAllister escorted Jason down the hall to Case's office, bigger than Melissa's but every bit as austere. The two men talked litigation strategy for nearly an hour. They agreed not to remove the case to federal court and decided to immediately file a Motion to Dismiss, though neither of the men thought the motion would be successful.

As they were wrapping up, Davids stuck her head in the door. "Grab your overcoat, Noble," she said. "I'll meet you at the shooting range in five minutes."

Before Jason could respond, she was gone.

Case rose slowly, the limp more noticeable this time. "Bum knee," he said. "Need a total replacement but I keep putting it off. It's worse after I've been sitting for a while."

Case pulled a long overcoat from a hanger on the back of his office door. "Here," he said, handing it to Jason.

"I'm fine. Really."

"Don't be a hero," Case said. "You'll freeze your butt off out there. Melissa loses track of time."

Jason took the coat and tried it on. It was black and came down to his knees, like something Doc Holliday might have worn to the O.K. Corral. The sleeves were short, and the coat was tight. "Maybe if I take my sports coat off." He removed his jacket and tried the overcoat again. The sleeves still crawled up Jason's forearms.

Case sized him up. "Close enough," he said.

◁▷

The MD Firearms outdoor firing range was located behind the factory on a large slice of land that backed up to woods full of pine trees. Jason had seen an indoor firing range on the tour provided by Davids. But according to Case, Melissa Davids much preferred to do her target practice outside.

A few minutes after Jason arrived, the company's CEO showed up carrying two gray attaché cases.

"He's all yours," Case said. "Just bring him back to the office when you're done." The lawyer retreated toward the building as Davids set down the attaché cases and handed Jason earmuffs and safety glasses.

"Have you ever fired a gun before?" Davids asked.

"No."

She looked at him in disbelief. "And you're a cop's kid?"

"It's a long story."

Davids shook her head. "We'll psychoanalyze that later. For now, let's start with some basics."

After a brief safety lesson, Davids opened the first case. It contained an MD-9, the same gun used by Larry Jamison to mow down Rachel Crawford. Even to Jason, who was now being paid $275 an hour to represent the manufacturer, the gun looked evil.

According to Jason's research, the MD-9 had become popular with gangs after it made the lyrics of a few ubiquitous rap songs. The gun had a dull black finish and a boxy design—none of the smooth, glossy, machine-finished surfaces of pricier weapons. It featured a stubby barrel and a square pistol grip that jutted down from the center of the gun, not the rear. Davids began loading the slender gray magazine with thirty-two brass 9 mm cartridges.

"What do you know about gun terminology?" she asked.

"Not much. What I've read."

"Gun control folks like describing guns as 'automatics' and 'semi-automatics,' to make it sound as if a gun like this is a machine gun. A fully automatic keeps firing as long as you hold down the trigger. A semi-automatic, like this gun, fires one round each time you pull the trigger."

Jason had read some information about how easily the MD-9 could be converted to a fully automatic before it was redesigned in the early 90s. But he decided to save that topic for later.

"You'll also hear people use the term *automatic* when referring to a pistol like the MD-45. In that context, what they mean is that the pistol automatically reloads, using the explosive force of the cartridge to load and cock itself after each shot. These pistols are actually auto-loading or semi-automatics."

She looked up at Jason. "Does that make sense?"

"Sure," he said. In truth, it was a little confusing. But he'd figure it out.

Melissa Davids demonstrated the proper handling and shooting techniques for the MD-9, instructing Jason in the best stance as she downed several man-shaped targets about fifty feet away. Jason noticed that even in Davids's expert hands, a few of the shots missed their mark.

She took off the earmuffs and turned to him. "Attorney-client privilege?"

"Of course."

She looked at the gun, weighing it in her hands. "This thing's a piece of junk. It's awkward and bulky and kicks like a mule. It's good up to about twenty-five feet, and that's it."

Jason resisted the obvious question: *Then why do you sell it?* For one thing, he didn't want to alienate the company CEO on their first meeting. For another, he already knew the answer: *People buy it.*

She handed the gun to Jason and pushed a button that made the targets pop back up. Another button moved them to twenty-five feet away.

The gun felt heavy and awkward in Jason's hand, like it needed a second handle at the back of the gun so his left hand could provide some stability. He tried to mimic Davids's stance but didn't quite get it right.

"Bring that one leg back just a little," she said, tapping his right foot until he slid it back. "Competitive shooters use a squared-off stance, but in a true self-defense encounter, you're more concerned about balance and the ability to move laterally.

"Now, keep your strong arm straight and stiff, with your support arm slightly bent." Davids demonstrated as she talked. "Bring the gun straight up into your line of vision until the sights are lined up and on-target."

Jason did as he was told. His hands trembled a little, partly from the cold, partly from nerves, partly from the unexpected weight of the gun.

"Fire away," Davids said, her voice loud enough to penetrate the earmuffs. "Empty the magazine."

The trigger action was quick and required little pressure. But the gun bucked, and Jason's first few shots were slow and off-target. He gained a feel for the gun and started squeezing faster, adjusting on the fly after each errant shot. Even after all the targets had dropped, Jason kept squeezing and firing, aiming at a piece of wood farther down the range, peppering the ground with 9 mm bullets. Shell casings flew past him, one hitting the rim of his safety glasses. He emptied the magazine in a matter of seconds.

Davids was smiling. They both hung their earmuffs around their necks.

"Whoa," he said. "That was a rush. No piece of dirt is safe when I'm firing an MD-9."

Davids eyed him with a look that seemed to indicate a slight reappraisal. "Most first-time shooters start a little more cautiously," she said.

The second attaché contained a shiny pistol that Davids handled with the pride of a first-time parent. "It's a prototype," she explained. "An MD-45. Five-inch barrel. Blue carbon steel and aluminum alloy frame. Rosewood grip. Two ten-round magazines."

She loaded the gun and handed it to Jason. It felt a ton lighter than the MD-9, with a comfortable wooden grip that fit nicely into the contour of Jason's hand. Davids popped the targets up and moved them back down the range to fifty feet.

Jason sighted in the gun, and Davids corrected his stance. "Relax a little more. Bring the gun straight up. Don't lock your elbow."

Unlike its evil cousin, the MD-45 felt smooth and comfortable in Jason's sweaty hands. The trigger had a crisp let-off and very quick reset. He fired efficiently and with much greater accuracy. The gun had a larger-caliber bullet but only about half the kick. The longer barrel and precision machining made it easier to hit the targets even at this greater distance—not exactly in the heart but at least a shoulder wound or maybe one that strayed down to the thigh. He only missed the entire target once.

After he finished, Jason and Davids removed the earmuffs and safety goggles.

"You like it?" Davids asked.

"Yeah."

"We're going to order you one, Noble. I'll ship it to a dealer in Virginia Beach. It's a prototype that will have all of our latest safety features including—are you ready for this?"

"Sure."

"A built-in GPS system for tracking the gun. That way if it ever gets stolen, you'll be able to trace it. It'll also have a fingerprint-activated safety lock that will allow the gun to be fired only by you."

Jason knew those types of guns were in the works—some of the lawsuits he had researched even suggested it was negligence not to use safety locks like that in the design of every gun. But Jason didn't know that MD Firearms was working on this prototype.

"I thought owning this type of gun might come in handy for media interviews or maybe even your closing argument," Davids said. "You'll hear a lot of talk about how we push semi-automatic assault weapons and how we're the great merchant of death. Might be helpful for you to say that you own an MD Firearms gun, one equipped with a GPS system and fingerprint safety lock. Also, the publicity wouldn't hurt our marketing."

Jason wasn't so sure. He still thought it might be more powerful to say he'd never owned a gun in his life. That way, nobody could accuse him of being part of the industry. But Davids wasn't exactly asking his permission. He had the sense that nothing would alienate his client quicker than disrespecting her product.

"Let's shoot a few more rounds and then get you fingerprinted," Davids said, reloading the prototype. "Our market studies have shown just one glitch with the MD-45 so far."

Jason waited, still wrestling with the thought of being a gun owner.

"With all those safety features, nobody wants to buy it."

◁▷

Jason left town without stopping by to see his father. He hadn't spoken to his dad in at least a week, and his dad would have no way of knowing that Jason had flown into Atlanta.

Christmas would be here soon enough, and it would be mandatory for Jason to visit. He would keep it short—Christmas Eve and Christmas Day—making sure that some crisis in his law practice required him back in Richmond the day after Christmas. Jason's older sister had married and moved to California. She only showed up every third year, and this would not be one of them.

Jason hated Christmas.

22

One week later

ROBERT SHERWOOD wanted to wring Andrew Lassiter's scrawny little chicken neck but instead gave himself twenty-four hours to calm down. The drug patent verdict was the second time in three months that Justice Inc. had called it wrong. Sherwood's clients were lighting up the phone lines. His efforts to calm them met with limited success. Felix McDermont, Sherwood's largest and most unpredictable client, was beside himself.

"Take me off your list," he told Sherwood. "I can flip a coin and get the same results."

"Don't do anything precipitous. We're still batting over 90 percent."

"Being forty million short based on your recommendation was precipitous," McDermont replied. "Ending our relationship is not."

After the phone call, Sherwood had begun polling his board members. When he had garnered the votes, he'd arranged a meeting with Andrew Lassiter for this morning.

The timing was lousy, but what options did he have? His entire life, Sherwood had made it a habit to deal with problems as soon as they reared their ugly heads. Problems only got worse with time, never better. Besides, if he waited until January, Lassiter might catch wind of the plan. He would lobby the board members, and they might soften once the heat from the patent verdict dissipated.

Sherwood had the votes now. There was no guarantee he would have them in January. He couldn't change the fact that Christmas was only one week away. No doubt he would become legendary for this, the comparisons to Scrooge almost too easy.

But he had no choice. Lassiter could no longer be trusted.

⊲⊳

"He's here," Olivia said.

Sherwood blew out a huge breath. If he listened carefully, he could hear the songs of the season echoing up from the street. The lobby of Justice Inc. was decorated with a large tree and the politically correct amount of white Christmas lights. The two failed predictions had cost the firm's clients a lot of money, but the firm itself had been immensely profitable this year. Sherwood had just signed some hefty bonus checks.

Now this.

Olivia showed Lassiter into the office and closed the door. The two men shook hands. Lassiter was hunch-shouldered and red-eyed, wearing a ratty navy blue sweater and jeans, his laptop tucked under his arm. Sherwood had seldom seen Lassiter without the laptop. Lassiter's hair looked like he had just rolled out of bed, and he blinked a couple of times behind his thick glasses. *Why are the brilliant ones always so socially inept?*

The two men had initially made a formidable team. Lassiter had developed the software and micromarketing formulas to predict jury verdicts, while Sherwood had worked the venture capitalists for financing and developed the hedge fund clients who paid so handsomely for Justice Inc.'s service.

As the company grew, Sherwood became the face man for interacting with board members, investors, and clients. Lassiter obsessively focused on the study of the human mind, constantly refining the formulas and models for predicting jury behavior.

But now he had lost his touch. And Sherwood was the one who got stuck cleaning up the mess when Lassiter was wrong.

"Have a seat," Sherwood said. He motioned to the navy blue chair. He knew the rumors about the chair and had never done anything to discourage them. It was a useful way to signal bad news without actually saying anything. People could brace themselves.

Lassiter's eyes reflected confusion and hurt, like a loyal dog tossed out of the house when a new baby comes home.

He twitched once and stepped to the side. He took a seat in the other chair facing Sherwood's desk, the brown leather chair.

Interesting.

Sherwood took a seat behind his desk.

Without prompting, Lassiter started in, the blinking on overdrive. "I watched the mock trial deliberations again last night and tweaked the program. Part of it was the limited *voir dire* that Judge Davis allowed in the real case. Plus, the defense lawyers alienated the jurors when they attacked every witness who took the stand. We can't factor in for bad lawyering, especially when the reputation of that firm was so strong."

Sherwood kept his tone businesslike. "But Andrew, all three shadow juries came back with a defense verdict. The real jury found patent infringement and $325 million in damages. Our clients don't want excuses; they want results."

"We *have* given them results, Robert. It's science, not a guessing game. Let me show you a couple of things."

Lassiter moved his glasses to the top of his head and opened his computer. Sherwood knew what was coming—detailed explanations of formulas and micromarketing techniques, a mishmash of algorithms and spending preferences and consumer psychology. There were others in Sherwood's organization who could apply the models but didn't have half the baggage.

"Put the computer away, Andrew. We're beyond that point."

Lassiter looked up at Sherwood with alarm bordering on panic. "What do you mean?"

Sherwood leaned forward. He hated doing this, but Lassiter's reaction was confirming his decision. "The company needs to move on without you, Andrew. Our clients are losing confidence in us. These last few months have been tough. The board agrees that it's time for change."

Sherwood paused so the words could sink in. It was clear he had stunned Lassiter. The man stared into space for a moment and then gingerly placed his computer on the floor, as if continuing to hold its weight was more than he could bear.

"I'm sorry," Sherwood said. "I know this is terrible timing, but I've gone to bat for a good severance package."

Lassiter started to speak but couldn't. He looked like he might break down at any second. "You had a board meeting already?" he finally managed.

"I've spoken to every member."

For the next several minutes, Sherwood explained the details of the proposed severance deal. The payout was $2.5 million. In addition, Lassiter would keep his 15-percent stake in the company and could cash in if the company went public. In return, Justice Inc. needed a signed release and confidentiality agreement.

By the time Sherwood finished, Andrew Lassiter had regained some of his composure. The glazed-over look had faded. He put on his glasses, picked up his computer, and stood. He cleared his throat. Once. Twice. "You can't do this," he said. "I designed virtually every program we use."

"Those are all works for hire." Sherwood's voice was more emphatic now. He stood as well. "You know that, Andrew. This is the best way."

Lassiter was trembling but had his jaw set. "I'm not your employee, Robert. We're partners. We started this company together."

"You don't want this fight, Andrew."

"I'm going to see a lawyer."

Sherwood sighed and moved out from behind his desk. He put a hand on the outside of Lassiter's arm. Lassiter stared at him, through him. "We've had a good run, Andrew. And I hope we can still be friends. But I've got a fiduciary duty to our shareholders and the board, not to mention the clients." He gave Lassiter a squeeze on the arm. "I could have had our HR department do this, but I felt like I owed it to you to do this myself. I really am sorry."

Lassiter stared for an awkward few seconds, saying nothing. He blinked, took a sideways step, and headed toward the door.

"Wait a second," Sherwood said. "I need the computer."

Lassiter looked down at his laptop and back at Sherwood, his mouth open in disbelief. Sherwood held out his hand. "I need it now."

Lassiter cradled it like a football. His eyes took on a wild look, as if he might explode at any second.

"There are folks in your office packing all your personal stuff as we speak," Sherwood said. He kept his voice steady, like he was talking a person down from a ledge. "Rafael is waiting right outside to escort you out of the building. I need your computer and keys. Don't make it any harder than it already is, Andrew. You know our policies."

Lassiter hesitated for another few seconds, his face twisted in pain, before he handed the computer to Sherwood. He reached in his pocket and retrieved a key ring. With trembling hands, he removed his office keys.

He looked so pathetic. Tears welled in his eyes. It was as if Sherwood had just ordered him to the electric chair rather than offering him a multi-million-dollar severance package.

"Are you going to be all right?" Sherwood asked.

Lassiter stared at him for a moment, as if he couldn't believe that Sherwood had the audacity to ask such a question.

"This isn't right," Lassiter said. There was no throat-clearing this time. "It's just not right." He turned, as if in a trance, and opened the office door.

Rafael Johansen was waiting outside.

After Lassiter left, Robert Sherwood sat down at his desk and lit up a cigar. He knew that Lassiter would review the offer with a lawyer and see the light. Sherwood probably should have handled this the way other CEOs would have—let the HR guys do it. But that had never been Robert Sherwood's style.

He took a long draw on the cigar, calming his frazzled nerves. Andrew Lassiter was a good man. Off-the-charts brilliant. Justice Inc. would never have made it without him. But Sherwood had his fiduciary duties, and he couldn't let friendships interfere.

Sometimes he hated his job.

23

THE PHONE MESSAGE took Jason by surprise. He hadn't heard from Andrew Lassiter since leaving Justice Inc. three months ago.

Call me as soon as possible. It's important.

Jason returned the call from an office phone. Lassiter answered on the first ring.

"Are you alone?" Lassiter asked.

"Yes."

"I got fired from Justice Inc. Sherwood squeezed me out. I need your help."

Through the phone lines, Jason could hear Lassiter's desperation. The man was breathless, spitting his words out quickly.

"They've got all my software, my programs, everything. Sherwood lined up the votes from the other directors and called me in yesterday. One week before Christmas. Can you believe this? He had his goons escort me out of the building."

Jason was having a hard time processing all this. Andrew Lassiter wasn't just an employee; he was a cofounder, the brains behind the micromarketing formulas.

"You're a shareholder. How can the board just vote you out?"

Lassiter cleared his throat, his nervous habits on full throttle. "Technically, they can't take away my stock. But if they don't take the company public, my shares will be worthless. They'll increase Sherwood's salary, send more money to Kenya, do everything they can to eliminate year-end profits. They can manipulate the books to pay stockholders whatever they want."

Jason knew Lassiter was overreacting a little. Minority shareholders could audit the books to ensure that profits weren't being hidden. Still, the urgency in Lassiter's voice was unmistakable. This wasn't really about the money.

"What reason did they give?" Jason asked.

Lassiter spent several minutes describing his meeting with Sherwood. He got sidetracked for a few minutes explaining why the miscalculation in the drug patent case wasn't his fault. The formulas worked fine, and his prediction would have been right if the real-life lawyers had done their job. Unfortunately, the defense lawyers had been pitiful.

Back on track, Lassiter detailed the terms of the proposed severance agreement. Two point five million might sound like a lot, but it was a pittance compared to the real worth of the company.

Jason listened patiently, asking appropriate questions as he tried to figure out what he should do. He felt a special bond with Andrew Lassiter. Others at Justice Inc. had a strictly business mind-set. They sweated over P&L statements, the intricacies of stock deals, budgets for the mock trials.

Lassiter, on the other hand, was more like Jason. Their obsession was figuring out what made juries tick. For Lassiter, being wrong on a jury verdict was like being unfaithful to your wife. It was a character flaw, not just a bad business prediction.

In a way, that compulsive behavior made Andrew Lassiter a kindred spirit. Normally, Jason, who had his own obsession with winning, would go out of his way to help.

But not when it meant taking on Robert Sherwood. The man had his faults, but he wasn't the personification of evil that Lassiter was making him out to be. He was a tough business executive, and the squeeze play on Lassiter did not entirely surprise Jason. But Robert Sherwood also had a heart. He genuinely cared about social justice. And he had certainly helped Jason in the three months he had been on his own.

"What do you want *me* to do?" Jason asked.

"Represent me," Lassiter said, his voice tense, a half octave higher than normal. "I need somebody to file suit—somebody who won't be intimidated."

"You don't need me," Jason protested. "You need somebody with experience in business law. Somebody who hasn't worked for the company."

This brought silence on the phone line, followed by the trademark throat-clearing to which Lassiter resorted under pressure. When Lassiter finally spoke, his voice was cracking, the raw emotion coming to the surface. "You're wrong, Jason. You care about the same things I care about. This case will be tough. Other lawyers could be bought off or intimidated. I need somebody I can trust."

Jason swallowed hard. He hadn't asked for this—the plea of a desperate man. He felt like a kid in the middle of a nasty divorce.

"I'm not asking for a favor, Jason. I'll pay whatever your rate is."

Jason tried to imagine himself suing Robert Sherwood. The only way to get Andrew Lassiter reinstated would be to threaten the entire business plan of Justice Inc. Perhaps Jason could challenge the non-compete that Lassiter had signed, freeing him up to start a similar business. If other companies could use the same micromarketing formulas to predict these seminal cases, Justice Inc.'s business would take a major hit.

But Justice Inc. had treated Jason fairly. If not for Robert Sherwood, Jason wouldn't be where he was now. His biggest clients had all been referrals from Sherwood. And what had Andrew Lassiter done for him?

"Andrew, I'm sorry. I just can't take the case. I've got too many conflicting loyalties."

Jason waited. The silence became awkward.

"You're better off with another lawyer," Jason insisted. "Somebody without the conflicts."

"Thanks for your time," Lassiter said, his voice cold. Before Jason could respond, his friend hung up the phone.

Jason walked over to the window and stared at the street below. He rubbed the back of his neck and watched the small flakes of snow dot the afternoon sky, a novelty in Richmond, particularly in December.

Was he intimidated by Robert Sherwood? A little. Was that the reason he had turned Lassiter down? Not really. It was a business decision. Jason had acted in spite of fear many times in the past. If he had to take on men like Robert Sherwood, he would do it.

At least that's what he told himself.

This wasn't the case of a little guy like Lassiter being taken advantage of by a powerful man with all the resources. If it were, Jason would feel compelled to intervene. Wasn't that one of the things he had learned at Justice Inc.—the Robin Hood philosophy of justice?

No, this was just a business dispute, and Jason didn't need to get in the middle of it. Besides, Andrew Lassiter would land on his feet. The guy was a certifiable genius.

But the questions wouldn't go away—that gnawing in the pit of his stomach. Was he just scared? Was he betraying a friend?

It was just a business dispute, he reminded himself. Between two grown men.

24

THE DAY BEFORE CHRISTMAS, Jason boarded a plane in Richmond for his second flight to Atlanta in less than two weeks. He ended up sitting next to a mom and her elementary-age son, who was excited to see his grandparents. When Jason deplaned in Atlanta, Hartsfield-Jackson was jammed with people, thousands of smiling and excited faces dragging kids and luggage through the terminals. Jason always felt an extra stab of loneliness and envy this time of year.

What would it be like to go home to a normal family—a mother who showered unconditional love on her kids, a father who didn't try to control and manipulate, a sister who was there more than once every three years?

He would never know. For Jason, this Christmas would once again consist of arguments with his dad, followed by long periods of uncomfortable silence. The traditions and expectations of Christmas had a way of magnifying family shortcomings, like watching an episode of *Father Knows Best* followed by *The Osbournes*.

On his way to the baggage claim, Jason checked his messages. His father had called. He would be working the three-to-eleven shift, covering for an officer whose wife had been recently diagnosed with cancer. Detective Corey would pick Jason up at the airport. His dad left Corey's cell number and said he was looking forward to seeing Jason later that night.

From the tone of his father's voice, Jason doubted it.

◁▷

Detective Matthew Corey was one of the youngest-looking forty-five-year-old men Jason knew. For starters, Corey spent about ninety minutes a day in the gym, tossing around the big plates, sculpting his muscles and toning his already impressively flat abs. He had thick dark hair, bushy black eyebrows, and skin that looked like it belonged on a shaving commercial. The only concessions to his age—particularly to his twenty-two years on the Atlanta police force—were the wrinkles starting to spiderweb away from the corners of his eyes.

"Thanks for coming," Jason said.

"You're family," Corey said. He put on his turn signal and pulled away from the curb. "You're lookin' great," he added, without conviction. It was a perfunctory greeting from a man whose favorite hobby was checking himself out in the mirror. He was probably fishing for a return compliment.

"You look like you're getting a little flabby," Jason responded.

Corey smiled. "Always the smart aleck. Glad to see law school hasn't changed you."

Years ago, as a rookie, Matt Corey had drawn Jason's dad as his patrol partner. At least two times and maybe more, depending on who was telling the stories and how many beers they had polished off first, Jason's dad had saved Corey's life. Even after both men were reassigned—Jason's dad as a homicide detective, Corey to the narcotics unit—they had remained tight.

"There's nothing I wouldn't do for your dad," Corey had told Jason. "*Nothing.* I mean that."

On the way to the house, they filled the ride with idle talk—Jason's job, the investigations Corey was handling, Corey's family. Corey had a need to impress even someone as insignificant as Jason, so he spent a fair amount of time bragging about this case or that drug bust, especially the arrests where the suspects put up a fight . . . and lived to regret it later.

When they were about five minutes from the house, the conversation turned to Jason's dad.

"He's drinking more," Corey said. "Alone. And he's been missing work."

The news didn't surprise Jason, but he was at a loss about what to do. His father had been drinking for years. The alcohol made him brood and loosened his tongue. He lashed out at those who tried to talk with him about it. Jason's solution was to stay away.

"He's proud of you, Jason," Corey said, keeping his eyes on the road. "He probably never says anything to you, but he's always bragging *about* you—his son, the big-shot lawyer."

If Corey had just said he'd married the queen of England, Jason wouldn't have been more surprised. Jason's dad never said such things around Jason. He only criticized, always nitpicked. Words of praise were not in his vocabulary.

"That surprises me," Jason said.

"He would rather have you wearing the white hat, of course. But he's still proud of you."

He hides it well, thought Jason. Nevertheless, he appreciated Detective Corey's telling him this. It might make the next twenty-four hours a little more bearable. All Jason had ever gotten from his dad was a deep sense of disappointment. He wanted Jason to play football, but Jason chose soccer. He wanted Jason to become a Navy SEAL, and Jason wanted to act. When Jason entered law school, his father talked about the prosecutors he respected. Now Jason was a defense attorney.

They reached the house, and Corey pulled into the driveway. "It's great to see you doing so well," he said. He turned and looked straight at Jason. "I'm glad you took advantage of your second chance. I knew at the time you were a good kid."

Jason had been half expecting Corey to bring up that night from ten years ago, the night that had changed Jason's life forever. It was the night he learned that cops sometimes write their own laws. But still, the words made his stomach clench.

Once every few years, Corey mentioned it. Jason sensed the detective was trying to make sure his secret was still safe, that Jason still acknowledged a debt he could never fully repay.

"I'm not so sure about that," Jason said. He stared out the front window, the guilt pressing in on him. This was the reason he didn't like being around Corey; it was a constant reminder of the worst night of Jason's life. "Good kids don't betray their friends."

"Everybody makes mistakes," Corey said emphatically. "And one stupid mistake shouldn't haunt you for life."

Jason nodded. He knew there was no sense arguing the point. He ought to be grateful to Detective Corey, not resentful.

"I know," he said.

He swallowed the words he really wanted to say. *It's haunting me for life anyway.*

25

JASON ONLY MADE IT HOME once or twice a year. The last few times, he had been struck by how much the place had changed. It was a small, one-story brick house in one of the few older Alpharetta neighborhoods. Jason's father had bought the place to escape the home that held so many memories of Jason's mom.

It made Jason sad to see the gradual deterioration of this house—the weeds overtaking the yard, the stained carpeting that needed to be replaced, the faded tile on the bathroom and kitchen floors.

The house smelled like stale beer.

In a halfhearted nod to the season, his dad had moved a chair in the living room and erected a fake Christmas tree. He had not bothered to decorate at all on the outside, making the house an oddity in a neighborhood that sparkled with all manner of gaudy outdoor lighting.

Jason threw his stuff in his old bedroom, a room that now doubled for storage, and stepped around the extra furniture, the old StairMaster, and the boxes that cluttered the floor. He thought about calling a few high school friends but remembered that they usually had family activities planned. Instead, he alternated between TV and surfing the Internet on his dad's desktop computer.

Next year, he would think of a good excuse to skip Christmas in Alpharetta altogether.

At 11:30, Jason's dad came home and apologized for being late. He had traded shifts with a young detective who had a sick wife, and Jason resisted the urge to make a snide comment. He could smell the alcohol when they shook hands, his father placing his left hand on the outside of Jason's shoulder—a Noble family "hug."

After his father changed clothes, he immediately poured himself a beer... almost certainly *another* beer. "Want one?" he asked.

"No, thanks."

"Loosen up, Son. It's Christmas."

Jason had sworn off drinking ten years earlier. He wasn't about to start up now, especially seeing what it had done to his dad. "I'll just take some soda."

His father shook his head and mumbled something that Jason didn't catch. He handed Jason a two-liter bottle of Coke from the refrigerator, and Jason poured himself a glass. The Coke was flat.

They took seats at opposite ends of the kitchen table like two gunslingers squaring off for a fight.

Jason studied his father—the old man's deterioration seemed to match the house. Jason had his mother's build, her average height, high metabolism, thin bone structure. His father was broad and stocky, about three inches shorter than his son, powerful as a bull. He had put on a little more weight in the last year, and his skin had the red, splotchy complexion of an alcoholic, matched by a large nose and perpetually bloodshot eyes. He looked older than fifty-two.

"Tell me about your practice," his father said.

His tone said he might actually be interested, despite the disappointment he had expressed when Jason opted for a career as a private lawyer. Jason remembered Detective Corey's comments and decided to start by describing the gun case he had just landed. His dad worshiped at the altar of the Second Amendment. There had been guns in the Noble house for as long as Jason could remember, though Jason himself had never fired one. This case might help break his dad's perception that Jason was just defending a bunch of crooks and cop killers.

"You remember the shooting that occurred in that television station in Virginia Beach—the one everybody played live on the air?"

"Yeah." His dad was wasting no time downing the beer.

"That reporter's husband filed suit against the gun manufacturer for allegedly knowing about the illegal sale of their firearms and doing nothing to stop them."

"MD Firearms," his dad murmured as he took another drink.

"Right. They asked me to represent them. Some say this could be the biggest Second Amendment case in years." Jason took a sip of his Coke as his dad made a face and digested the news.

"What do you know about them?"

"What I've read online and in the papers." Jason decided to omit the fact that he had toured their plant, just a short drive from his father's house.

"Maybe you ought to investigate a little more before you take that case."

The tone deflated Jason. He hadn't taken the case in order to gain his father's approval, but he hadn't thought it would hurt. "Meaning?"

His father played with his beer glass for a few seconds, apparently deciding whether to proceed. "Have you heard about what they did with silencers?"

Jason shrugged. He didn't even know they made silencers.

"Buncha years ago, your potential client decides to make a few extra bucks by diversifying into silencers. The only problem is that, according to ATF guidelines at the time, anybody who orders a complete silencer has to register it. So MD Firearms—which was back then called Buford Arms Corp., or something like that—went into partnership with some other Georgia companies to sell parts for a silencer. I think your client sold the tubes and the others sold the internal parts."

Jason's father paused to take another drink. "Finally the ATF got a warrant and raided the facilities of all these companies. They seized records showing something like six thousand sales of silencer parts, but only four buyers had registered their silencers, and about fifty of 'em were sold to folks with prior felony convictions."

Jason listened intently, knowing that this information would be paraded around by the plaintiff's lawyers. This kind of rule bending seemed out of character for the Melissa Davids he had met at MD Firearms.

"So the ATF gets all this evidence and takes these companies to court to revoke their licenses, but the judge throws it out—says nobody can prove they intended to violate the registration laws. Might have just been legitimately trying to sell silencer parts." Jason's dad snorted. "What a crock."

"Was Melissa Davids there at the time?" Jason asked.

"She was working there." Jason's father went to the refrigerator for his second beer, on top of who knew how many earlier that night. "A few years later, her husband's family helped her buy the company from the original owners and she promised to clean it up. But all she did was change the name of the company and the guns. Right up until the assault weapons ban, they pumped out their MD-9 by the truckload, knowing that people were converting it to a fully automatic. The ATF traced hundreds of converted guns to crimes, including one here in Forsyth County where a cop got mowed down by a drug gang. When the ban expired five years ago, they brought the MD-9 back in all its glory, more popular than ever."

Now Jason understood why his father recalled all these facts. Forsyth County was right next door. A police officer had been killed. A line had been crossed.

Jason's father sat down with a thud and twisted the cap off his drink. This time, he didn't bother with the glass.

"Do me a favor, Son. Don't take that case."

He stared at Jason, waiting for a reply.

"Son?"

Jason looked down. He didn't want to trigger his dad's temper. Not tonight. It was Christmas Eve. They hadn't seen each other in months. One cross word and the Noble men would be at each other's throats with dizzying speed.

But he wasn't going to lie. And he wasn't about to let his father start dictating what cases he should take. Did he tell his dad what crimes he should investigate?

Jason took a deep breath and faced into his father's bloodshot eyes. "I already have, Dad. Everybody's entitled to a defense."

His father cursed, his face reddening. "Why do you insist on embarrassing this family?"

"My client didn't shoot that woman." Jason argued. He thought maybe he could play his dad like a jury member, appeal to the man's bias. "You hold that company liable in a case like this and it's only a matter of time before they go after Glock or Smith & Wesson. This is a Second Amendment case, Dad."

"That's bull," his father said in an angry whisper. "And you know it. You want this case because you want to make a big name for yourself. Jason Noble. Big-time defense lawyer."

Jason took the bait. He couldn't help himself. Somehow his dad always managed to get under his skin. "That's right, Dad. You know all about me. You've got me all figured out." Jason felt his anger quickly spiraling out of control, the thing he had pledged would not happen on this trip. "Everything I do is wrong. I can never be good enough for the vaunted Noble name. The hard-working detective." Jason scoffed. "If only they knew."

"I don't need your attitude." Jason's father stood, staring at Jason with disgust. "You've been here five minutes and you're already starting in with this crap."

Jason lowered his gaze to the table, seething. He had physically squared off with his dad just once, a few months prior to leaving for college. His father had thrown Jason to the ground and scrambled on top, pounding Jason until he begged for his dad to stop.

His dad had stood towering over Jason for a few seconds afterward. "You think you can beat the old man?" he taunted. Jason had lain there on the ground, gingerly touching his lip, blood streaming onto the carpet. He shook his head meekly.

"Clean up the carpet," his father had said. Then he walked away.

His father was quicker and stronger than he looked. Every time they argued, that fight came cascading back, relodging itself so strongly in Jason's memory that he could almost taste the blood. But then there were times, like right now, that Jason was so angry he didn't care. Plus, Jason was older now. Stronger. His old man had undoubtedly lost a few steps.

In the heat of the moment, Jason wanted to jump up and start something, either beat the old man once and for all or force him to beat Jason so severely that it would end their relationship forever.

"You want to try the old man?" The words were taunting, echoing from eight years ago. They knew each other's hot buttons.

Jason looked up, tears stinging his eyes. "What do you want to do, Dad? You want to hit me again? Go ahead and hit me." Jason stood, holding his hands out to his sides, palms open. "Will that make you feel like a real man—beating up your kid? Maybe you can do some permanent damage this time."

His father stood there, rage coloring every feature. Jason half expected the fists to fly at any moment. This time, he wouldn't even defend himself. He would let his father do whatever damage he wanted. He would make him pay by never speaking to him again.

The face-off only lasted a few seconds, and then his father nodded his head a little, as if he couldn't believe what a jerk he had raised for a son. He sat down in his chair, scoffed at Jason, and took another drink of beer.

Jason walked away, heading down the hall toward his bedroom.

"Where are you going?"

"To bed, Dad. Merry Christmas. . . . Thanks for making it so special."

26

FOR KELLY, there was comfort in going to church. She sat in the second row with her family—her mom, two older brothers, and two younger sisters. Of the Starling family, only Kelly remained unmarried, though the church members had been doing their best to set Kelly up since she arrived home a few days earlier. Who needed dating services when you had a whole church full of scouts and matchmaking geniuses?

Four grandchildren would enliven the Starling household tomorrow, reminding the adults of the simple joys of Christmas. Four was plenty, in Kelly's opinion. She loved her nephews and nieces. But she also loved leaving the little rascals behind when she left her family's chaotic home in Charlottesville and headed back to D.C.

Tonight, on Christmas Eve, there was a kind of somber peace inside the ornate church where Kelly's dad served as pastor. Traditions, especially religious ones, had a way of soothing the spirit and bringing eternal perspective. The carols, the liturgy, the candles, and her dad's short homily on hope all had a way of distancing Kelly from the turmoil of her legal practice. She hated the fact that Christmas snuck up on her at the law firm—her once-favorite season lost in a blur of billable hours and *pro bono* projects. Year-end reviews and bonus checks competed for attention with the baby in the manger.

Kelly felt a little guilty, sitting in church as part of the pastor's perfect little family, knowing that she had probably cost her dad goodwill with some of his more conservative parishioners. Being one of the pastor's daughters had always put her in the spotlight here, but it was compounded this year by publicity about the Crawford case. Unlike the *Washington Post* article chronicling her work with victims of human trafficking, this case had the potential to split the church—liberal social activists versus hunters and gun enthusiasts.

But out of respect for her dad, even the church members who secretly hoped Kelly would lose the case had not said a negative word to her.

The service ended this Christmas Eve, like every Christmas Eve before it, with her dad leading in Communion. At the appropriate time, the attendees would file to the front of the church, be handed a small wafer, and take a sip from one of several chalices.

Kelly could still remember her first Communion, after she understood the true nature of repentance and the role of Jesus Christ in her salvation. Her dad had explained how Christ had commanded His church to take Communion as a remembrance of His sacrifice. The Communion elements, he explained, were powerful symbols of the body and blood of Christ.

Her eyes had filled with tears the first time she walked forward with her mom. "The body of Christ, the bread of heaven," her father said as he handed her the wafer. She walked a few more steps and dipped it in the cup. "The blood of Christ, the cup of salvation," one of the church leaders said. Kelly nodded solemnly and ate the wafer. She had returned to her seat and watched the rest of the church file forward, many seeming like they were only going through the motions. She had promised herself then, as a thirteen-year-old girl, that she would never take Communion lightly.

Her father's words punctured the memories, bringing her back to the present. "We welcome anyone who has accepted Christ's salvation to participate in this symbolic ceremony we call Communion. Remember that the baby who came to give the world hope is also the Savior who died to give the world life.

"But we also urge you to remember the words of the apostle Paul. Nobody should participate in Communion unworthily. If your heart is not right, or if for some other reason you don't wish to participate, just come forward and fold your arms across your chest. Instead of Communion, one of the other leaders or I will pray a blessing over you."

They began the liturgy, her father reading, the congregation responding. The first part of the liturgy contained a prayer of repentance.

"Let us confess our sins against God and our neighbor," her father said.

The congregation responded in unison, "Most merciful God, we confess that we have sinned against You in thought, word, and deed, by what we have done, and by what we have left undone."

The prayer continued, but those first few words lodged in Kelly's heart.

By what she had done. By what she had left undone.

For five years, Kelly had carried the burden of what she had done and the knowledge of what she had left undone. She hadn't confessed it to anyone, not even her dad. She hadn't tried to make it right with the authorities. God had become distant, prayers infrequent, church attendance all but nonexistent.

She was busy. She was tired.

And honestly, she was running from God.

As her row stood and marched forward, Kelly found herself sandwiched between her two brothers. As always, they lined up in front of her dad. Last year, she had taken Communion, compounding her guilt. She had brushed off the warning of the apostle Paul for a few days so she could enjoy Christmas, but later the guilt had come charging back. Along with regret. And hypocrisy.

By what we have done. And by what we have left undone.

She stood in front of her father. He had a wafer in his hand, waiting for Kelly to cup her hands and receive the symbol of Christ's broken body.

Instead, she crossed her arms.

Her dad didn't flinch. He reached out and placed a hand on her shoulder, closed his eyes, and asked the Lord to bless her.

◁▷

On the way home, Kelly's dad arranged it so she rode with him. She welcomed the chance to be alone with him for a few minutes before they hit the pandemonium of the house on Christmas Eve. It reminded Kelly of high school, how her dad would get up early every morning and drive her to swimming practice, even though she had her own license.

"Did you like the homily?" he asked.

"Fifteen minutes. What's not to like?"

"People don't want a long sermon on Christmas Eve. They just need a reminder. They need a chance to take a breath and remember."

"It was great, Dad. They always are."

Her dad kept his eyes on the road. "I'm really proud of you, Kelly. You're an exceptional young lady." He paused. She could sense a *but* coming, and he didn't disappoint. "But you've always been so hard on yourself."

This from a man who knows how to pile on the guilt. Her dad had a gentle, soft-spoken way, but he knew how to trip-wire every emotion. Especially remorse.

"I've had a good teacher."

He gave her a knowing smile. Her dad was too honest to argue the point. Nobody was harder on himself than Kelly's dad. "Is there something you need to talk about, Kelly?"

She let the question hang in the air for just a second. It was tempting to tell her dad everything. Somehow, after the initial shock, she knew he would understand. But something more powerful held her back—maybe the pain it would cause him; maybe her own shame at what she had done; maybe the fact that time had started to dim the memory and she didn't want to fully open the painful wound.

"I'm fine, Dad. I'm just not in a place where I can take Communion right now."

This brought a prolonged period of silence. It was an old trick that Kelly had wised up to in college. Her dad would just wait her out. Sooner or later, she would confess, driven by her overactive conscience and the deafening sound of silence. But she was older now. Wiser. A lawyer.

"I'll work through it, Dad. It's one of those things I've got to do on my own."

27

ON CHRISTMAS MORNING, Jason's father woke at ten, had two cups of coffee, and downed a few ibuprofens for his headache. Then he apologized.

"I didn't mean what I said last night," he managed, speaking quietly with a thick tongue. "That was the booze talking."

"Don't worry about it."

"You've got a job to do. Give 'em hell."

"I intend to."

Jason fixed pancakes, though his father didn't have much of an appetite. They went for long periods without saying anything, emphasizing the fact that they no longer had much in common. By noon, it was time to open gifts.

First, they both unwrapped presents mailed by Jason's sister. Afterward, Jason pulled a small package out of his briefcase.

"Thanks," his father said, unwrapping it gingerly. The man had big hands, and Jason noticed they shook a little, making the gift opening more of a chore. His dad eventually got down to the single piece of paper at the center of a small box.

"Based on what you said last night, you might want to trade it for another model," Jason offered.

His dad pulled out a picture of an MD-45, the gun Jason had fired at the shooting range. Underneath the picture was a gift certificate to the Bulls Eye Marksman store in Cumming, Georgia.

"I called the store and found out how much the MD-45 would cost. That gift certificate is for the exact amount. But seriously, Dad, I won't be disappointed if you get a different gun. You can use that certificate for any gun in the store."

"I never said they didn't know how to make a good gun," his father said. He looked at Jason, a spark of pride in the bloodshot eyes. "I never thought I'd see the day that I got something like this from you."

Jason opened his father's presents next. A new briefcase—soft leather. A gift certificate to Office Depot and another to S&K Menswear. Jason had to admit—his dad had tried.

"What kind of guns do you own?" Jason asked his father.

His dad perked up at the question and rattled off a list of the weapons in the Noble family armory. Then he had a brilliant idea.

"If you're going to be the Great Defender of the Second Amendment, it might help if you knew how to shoot a gun. Your mother never let me take you when you were little, and by the time middle school rolled around . . ." Jason's dad looked a little melancholy. "Well, we didn't spend much time together. You want me to see if I can get us into the Fulton County shooting range this afternoon?"

Jason thought about it for a minute. They could sit in the house and risk another argument. Or they could spend a few hours at the shooting range. Maybe he would learn something that would prove useful in the case. Plus, it would serve his dad right—loud noises to exacerbate the hangover.

"Sounds good. I just need to be at the airport no later than eight."

28

One month later

JUDGE ROBERT A. GARRISON JR. had been presiding over Virginia Beach Circuit Court, Courtroom 8, for the past seven years. Short, pudgy, pale-skinned, and bald, he looked more like an accountant who had just survived a hectic tax season than a judge. But with the power of the gavel, the man transformed into a monarch. He ran a tight ship, routinely starting court one or two minutes early. He liked to lecture criminal defendants and their lawyers, favoring prosecutors blatantly enough that nobody could accuse him of being soft on crime.

Garrison had a knack for finding the spotlight and ran into controversy a time or two over his unique ideas about proportional punishment. Two eighteen-year-olds accused of vandalizing public schools were told to return to his courtroom when they each had a half gallon of gum they had scraped off the bottom of public school desks. To make sure they didn't cheat, Garrison appointed a deputy sheriff to supervise. Another defendant, accused of violating the noise ordinance with his car stereo, had been sentenced to twelve straight hours of Barry Manilow, again supervised by a poor deputy sheriff who hadn't done a single thing wrong.

Garrison's main qualification for the bench was not his intellect, demeanor, or trial experience. Instead, it was his daddy. Old Man Garrison was one of the most successful developers to ever bulldoze trees and destroy wildlife in Hampton Roads. Fortunately for his son, he used his largesse to patronize local Republicans now serving in Richmond. They returned the favor by appointing Robert Jr., a nondescript real-estate lawyer, to an open slot on the Virginia Beach Circuit Court bench.

The partisan nature of the appointment created a small uproar among the local bar, but soon the Virginia Beach lawyers discovered more pressing matters to complain about and left Garrison alone.

Garrison played the part of the proper Southern gentleman, donning seersucker suits starting on Memorial Day and wearing them under his robe at least twice a week until Labor Day. Other accessories included wire-rimmed glasses, membership in the Princess Anne Golf Club, a home on Sixtieth Street just two blocks from the ocean, a beautiful wife, two kids, and a membership in a large church in the Little Neck area of Virginia Beach. He seldom attended.

Garrison knew the other judges found him useful because he didn't shy away from media attention and loved the high-profile cases. When the Rachel Crawford case hit the desk of the chief judge of the Virginia Beach Circuit Court, Garrison knew immediately that she would assign it to him. Nobody else would want to mess with all the cameras in the courtroom, the public scrutiny, the lawyers hotdogging for the TV audience. Nonetheless, the chief made Garrison wait until just one week before the first hearing on the case—a Motion to Dismiss based on the Protection of Lawful Commerce in Arms Act—before she let him know.

Garrison, however, was one step ahead. He had already discussed the case with his Republican cronies at the Christmas cocktail parties, being careful not to express a legal opinion about the merits. He had never owned a gun himself, preferring sailboats and golf clubs, but his friends all did. In their considered opinions, this was just a money grab based on a tragedy over which MD Firearms had no control. What was next? Suing beer and wine companies when a drunk driver caused an accident? Why not sue Boeing for manufacturing the planes that the terrorists flew into the World Trade Center?

Garrison couldn't argue with them. He, too, thought the lawsuit was an abuse of the legal system. After all, hadn't Congress already legislated these types of lawsuits out of existence?

A pro-business judge like him, especially one who believed in the Second Amendment, would dismiss this case so fast the lawyers (both of whom lived out of the area) wouldn't even have time to figure out where the bathrooms were in the courthouse.

But when the file hit his office early on Friday afternoon, he ran into an unexpected snag. It seemed that the federal statute contained an exception for lawsuits based on aiding or abetting illegal activities. Crawford's attorney was claiming that the manufacturer knew about the illegal straw purchases and did nothing to stop them.

Dismissing the lawsuit would not be as easy as Garrison had thought.

He decided to have a law clerk do some additional research over the weekend. Even in the absence of a federal statute, he could probably dismiss the case on the theory that a manufacturer couldn't be held accountable for the criminal acts of a third party who was not acting as its agent.

On Monday, Garrison rushed through his morning docket, ate a quick lunch, and spent the afternoon digging into the case law the clerk had provided. Unfortunately, the law was murky. His gut told him to dismiss the case, but his head cautioned that he might get reversed. A seat on the Virginia Supreme Court was a long shot for any judge; getting reversed on this case would end all hope.

The rules didn't allow cases to be dismissed at the pleadings stage unless there was no possible way the plaintiff could win even if everything he claimed in the lawsuit was true. Maybe Garrison should wait until further down the road, after the plaintiff produced his evidence at trial, and dismiss the case then. But if he did that, he would have to endure a wave of criticism in the meantime from the very party that had placed him in office.

By Monday evening, the news was out that the case had been assigned to him. Tuesday morning's paper carried a feature story on Garrison, complete with quotes from local lions of the bar who called the judge "fair" and "evenhanded" and "exacting."

A highly regarded big-firm lawyer named Mack Strobel summed it up best: "He's no Lance Ito."

Garrison shut his office door and read the article several times. There were a few sentences he might have written differently, but for the most part, the reporter got it right. Garrison came across as a no-nonsense judge in control of his courtroom.

He folded the paper and placed it carefully in his briefcase. He couldn't use the office copier to make copies—someone might notice. He would stop at a Kinkos on the way home. The newspaper would yellow over time but the copies would maintain their color.

This wasn't just another news story. He sensed that years down the road, in the scrapbook of his life, this story would take on pivotal importance. If he played his cards right, it could be his ticket to the Virginia Supreme Court.

And who deserved it more?

PART IV
PRETRIAL

29

ON FRIDAY, JANUARY 30, Jason picked up Case McAllister at the airport and headed to Virginia Beach Circuit Court for an 11:00 a.m. hearing. They had agreed that Jason would introduce Case, move for his admission to the Virginia Bar *pro hac vice*—for this case only—and Case would argue the motion. If the case ended up going to trial, Jason and Case would be co-counsel, with Jason taking the lead. But Case wanted to argue this first motion, and Case was paying the bills. Enough said.

On the way to the courthouse, Jason expected to talk strategy, but Case was more interested in talking football. He asked about Jason's dad as well, and Jason gave him the CliffsNotes version of Christmas. His father took him out shooting, Jason said. A few days later, he'd picked up the MD-45 Jason had ordered. The father-son fights, of course, were none of Case McAllister's business. Jason quickly changed the subject.

"When do you think I'll be able to pick up my special order?" Jason asked, referring to his customized MD-45.

"Not long," Case replied. "We were backed up for Christmas and haven't caught up yet. Prototypes can take a while to produce."

◁▷

The Virginia Beach courthouse was a mammoth fortress attached to the city jail by an underground tunnel and located on the edge of a sprawling municipal complex composed of matching colonial-style redbrick buildings. Years ago, when the city complex had sprung to life in the southern, agrarian part of the city, it had been surrounded by cornfields. Now it was surrounded by housing developments, office buildings, and commercial establishments. Trees had been turned into asphalt parking lots, wildlife replaced by convenience stores and fast-food restaurants.

As they approached the building, Jason was surprised to see a small band of protestors wandering around, carrying signs, allowing themselves to be videotaped by the half-dozen television cameras. Jason knew this was a high-profile case, but all this attention at a Motion to Dismiss hearing seemed a little unusual.

At least the hardy band of protestors, who were braving temperatures in the thirties and a biting wind, appeared to be on his side. Two signs in particular caught his attention. *We were meant to be armed—the Lord gave us a trigger finger.* And another, neatly printed in large black letters for the TV cameras: *God created men; MD Firearms made them equal.*

Jason and Case walked past the protestors and cameras, their eyes straight ahead. As they were climbing the steps, Case taking his time because of the bum knee, Jason could have sworn he heard a protestor mumble something meant only for Case McAllister's ears. It sounded like "Get 'em, Case," though Case didn't even acknowledge the man.

Case checked his sidearm at the courthouse metal detector like a real cowboy and exchanged small talk with the deputies. The two lawyers rode the escalators to the third floor and followed the signs toward Courtroom 8. When they reached the hallway outside the courtroom, Jason encountered his second surprise of the morning.

The place was crawling with people. They were pressing forward, trying to get a look inside past three beefy deputies who stood in the open doorway and formed a human blockade. Jason and Case elbowed their way through the crowd, and this time there was no mistaking it. Several folks said hello to Case, shook his hand, or wished him luck.

"You know these folks?" Jason asked.

"Kindred spirits."

Case and Jason showed their bar cards to the deputies and were allowed into the courtroom. There were only a dozen or so wooden benches in the spectator section, but every seat was filled. A television camera—the "pool" camera that would relay the feed to local affiliates—was set up along one wall. The other walls were lined with people standing, surely a violation of some fire code.

The crowd was overwhelmingly white, overwhelming male, and overwhelming middle-aged. It didn't take a genius to figure out that Case or some other person at MD Firearms had called the local gun enthusiasts and told them to rally the troops. Maybe he was trying to send a message to the judge. Maybe he was trying to influence the jury pool.

Whatever the reason, this was a far cry from the secluded trials Jason had cut his teeth on at Justice Inc.

◁▷

Muscling her way through the crowd, Kelly Starling thought about what an obvious and stupid ploy this was. A few hundred gun nuts, stripped of their weapons at the metal detector, were not going to intimidate her. Even Judge Garrison, a hard-core conservative and a bad draw for Kelly's case, would probably be offended by this stunt—as if he might be swayed by pressure from the crowd.

Blake Crawford and a few friends and family members were already inside the courtroom and seemed a little shaken by all the attention. Nobody had treated them rudely, Blake said, but Kelly could see concern in his eyes. He probably hadn't anticipated a crowd that would be so overwhelmingly against a grieving widower.

There was something else in Blake's expression that fed Kelly's fervor. It was the dazed look of a client who was trying to make sense out of tragedy, a threadbare hope that the justice system could bring good out of a horrendous evil. At times like this, clients would irrationally pin their hopes for recovery on the outcome of a civil case: *"Maybe I can keep others from suffering like this. Maybe my wife's death won't be in vain."*

To balance her client's tentativeness, Kelly put her own confidence on overdrive, asking the deputies to clear out a few seats in the front row behind Kelly's counsel table so Blake's relatives and friends could have a place to sit. That maneuver earned her the barely muted hostility of the crowd, especially since she did it over her client's objection.

"We can stand next to the wall," one of Blake's brothers offered.

"Don't be ridiculous," Kelly said, loud enough for the first few rows to hear. "They've packed the entire courtroom. We're entitled to one lousy row."

When Jason Noble and Case McAllister came walking down the aisle, Kelly sized them up, positioning herself so it looked like she was talking to her client. McAllister looked old, weathered, and confident, walking with a slight limp. His thin, rounded shoulders revealed his age, but his eyes were sharp, and he had a sly half smile on his face, as if surveying a masterpiece he had just painted. Jason Noble was young and decent looking, in a carefree surfer sort of way. He had penetrating green eyes and dark shaggy hair. He looked like maybe he had just left a frat party at the University of Georgia, the yin to Case McAllister's yang.

Kelly made a note—Jason would probably do okay with young female jurors. But other than a kind of roguish charm, she couldn't figure out why MD Firearms might have chosen him to help on the case. He was only two years out of law school—nearly five years younger than she. And Kelly herself was relatively young and inexperienced to be trying a case of such magnitude. Jason, she concluded, was probably just there to carry Case McAllister's briefcase.

She approached the defendant's counsel table and extended her hand.

"Kelly Starling," she said.

Jason's grip was firm, but his hand was cold and moist. Nerves.

"Jason Noble," he said.

He turned and motioned toward Case McAllister, who had just settled into his seat. "This is my co-counsel, Case McAllister."

Kelly took a step toward the man, expecting him to rise and shake her hand. Instead, he looked up at her disdainfully, gave her a curt nod, and turned back to his papers.

"Nice to meet you, too," Kelly said.

She returned to her own counsel table, blood pounding in her temples. The man was rude, but she wouldn't let it throw her off focus.

They could bring a big crowd and they could play mind games, but Kelly wasn't about to back down. McAllister might have experience, a sympathetic judge, and a federal law on his side, but Kelly had a grieving widower, a horrific shooting, and the mainstream media in her corner.

And she also had one other thing. Her own little secret weapon. The reason she was supremely confident about today's hearing.

Kelly had a lawyer's holy writ—legal precedent. A case from this very same court. Not a ruling from Judge Garrison but from one of his respected colleagues from more than a decade ago. It was, to use a bad analogy, her silver bullet.

Farley v. Guns Unlimited. *Let's see how the great Case McAllister deals with that.*

30

AFTER BEING GRANTED *pro hac vice* status, Case McAllister rambled on for nearly half an hour about why Judge Garrison should dismiss the case. Kelly could hear the murmurs of agreement coming from the cheap seats.

McAllister's primary argument was that manufacturers should not, as a matter of law and policy, be held liable for misuse of their products. He went through an illustrative list of products. Knives, of course. And what about cars? If somebody drives a car into a busy shopping center, should the manufacturer be liable? Then there was fertilizer. Nobody had sued fertilizer companies after Timothy McVeigh used a fertilizer bomb in Oklahoma City.

What about cigarettes? Kelly wanted to ask. But it wasn't her turn yet.

McAllister then turned to the Protection of Lawful Commerce in Arms Act—a law he claimed was designed to prevent exactly these types of frivolous lawsuits. He explained the rationale, quoting extensively from the legislation itself. He spoke at a deliberate pace, with just a twinge of a Southern drawl: "Civil liability actions against gun manufacturers are based on theories without foundation in hundreds of years of the common law and jurisprudence of the United States and do not represent a bona fide expansion of the common law."

He paused and glanced up at the judge, then continued reading. "The possible sustaining of these actions by a maverick judicial officer would expand civil liability in a manner never contemplated by the framers of the Constitution, by Congress, or by the legislatures of the several States."

Judge Garrison's face seemed to redden a little at the reference to a maverick judicial officer. "Isn't there an exception for illegal acts by a dealer or manufacturer?" Garrison asked. "Including the types of straw purchase transactions alleged to have occurred in this case?"

It was a good question, Kelly thought, the first indication that maybe Garrison wasn't totally drinking the Kool-Aid.

But Case McAllister just shrugged it off. "The exact language of the act says that a manufacturer or seller must aid or abet or conspire with another person to sell a gun to somebody who does not qualify. Here, my client didn't sell the gun—the dealer did. And my client certainly didn't aid or abet that sale. We didn't even know about it until after the shooting."

"Why isn't that a jury question?" Garrison countered. "Questions of fact, like whether your client's conduct was aiding or abetting, should be decided by a jury, not a judge."

McAllister didn't hesitate. "Because for hundreds of years criminal acts of third parties have cut off the liability for a seller or manufacturer. The only reason we're here, with all due respect to Mr. Crawford, is because my client is the only entity associated with this gun that isn't bankrupt."

McAllister paused and swallowed, as if he didn't like making this next part of his argument. "Larry Jamison shot Rachel Crawford. Jarrod Beeson bought the gun illegally. Peninsula Arms sold the gun illegally. My client violated no laws, yet we're the only one who gets sued.

"We're here because Mr. Crawford believes MD Firearms has deep pockets. Mr. Crawford wants somebody to pay for what happened to his wife, even if that person or entity acted entirely properly, selling guns legally to a federally licensed firearm dealer. Unfortunately for Mr. Crawford, my client is a gun manufacturer, not an insurance company. No reasonable judge would let this case go to the jury."

McAllister packed up his papers and limped away from the podium. Garrison scribbled a few things on his legal pad, his red ears reflecting his displeasure at the tone McAllister had adopted.

"Ms. Starling," Garrison eventually said. "Your response?"

Kelly stood and walked confidently to the podium. "On December 16, 1988, Nicholas Elliot, a sixteen-year-old kid, walked into his Virginia Beach high school with a semi-automatic assault weapon. He executed one teacher and wounded another. He had an entire class of students huddled into the back corner of a trailer, praying for safety, as he prepared to fire on them as well. The gun jammed, the teacher tackled Elliot, and the lives of all those students were saved."

Kelly found her stride and picked up confidence with every word. She was right about the law. She had justice on her side as well. She just needed to make sure Garrison understood that.

"It was later discovered that a notorious gun store in Isle of Wight County named Guns Unlimited had allowed Nicholas Elliot to buy the gun through an illegal straw purchase, using his uncle as the paper purchaser of the gun, even though store employees should have known that Elliot was the real purchaser. The family of the slain teacher sued the gun store, and Judge John Moore faced a Motion to Dismiss very much like this one."

Kelly had done her homework. Judge Moore had retired, but his opinions still held weight. The opinion itself was never recorded in the law books—at that time, only appellate court decisions were recorded. But the Handgun Violence Coalition had monitored the case and provided Kelly with the opinion.

Kelly handed a copy to Case McAllister and another copy to the judge.

"Judge Moore allowed that case to go to the jury against the gun dealer. His reasoning was based on common sense. Congress prohibits certain persons, like kids and felons, from purchasing firearms. When a dealer engages in an illegal straw sale to one of these prohibited persons, and then the purchaser commits a criminal act, the dealer can't try to hide behind the doctrine of intervening cause as if they couldn't anticipate those criminal actions. I mean, why does Congress prohibit sales of pistols to kids and guns to felons in the first place? Because the danger is obvious, not something unanticipated."

Kelly paused for a moment, allowing Garrison to read a few lines of the opinion.

He looked up. "Continue," he said.

"Mr. McAllister says that no reasonable judge would make such a ruling. I didn't have the privilege of appearing in front of Judge Moore. But from everything I've heard, he was the epitome of reasonableness."

Judge Garrison took off his reading glasses and studied the back wall for a moment.

He turned back to Kelly. "Anything else, Counsel?"

The question was judge-speak. It meant shut up and sit down while you're still ahead.

"Not at this time, Your Honor."

"Then this court stands adjourned for a brief recess."

"All rise," called the bailiff. The silence held until Judge Garrison disappeared out the door behind the bench. His exit was followed by a buzz of excitement and frustrated murmuring, as if the home team had just thrown an interception.

At Kelly's table, Blake worked hard to contain his elation. "That was brilliant," he said, his voice an excited whisper.

"We'll see," Kelly said, because that's what sophisticated trial lawyers were supposed to say. But in her heart, she was agreeing with Blake.

That *was* brilliant.

31

DURING THE BREAK, Case McAllister handed his copy of *Farley v. Guns Unlimited* to Jason. "Did you know about this?"

Jason shook his head.

It was only a question, asked in a civil tone without any inflections, but Jason knew what Case was really saying. *You're local counsel. We're paying you a lot of money to know about cases just like this one—cases that are part of the local folklore but don't show up in the law books or in electronic databases like Westlaw.*

Jason quickly glanced through the opinion. In the *Farley* case, the manufacturer had actually been dismissed, and the case had proceeded only against the dealer. But it would be useless to argue that distinction. The manufacturer in the *Farley* case had not known about the troubled history of its dealer, and therefore the plaintiff had proceeded against the manufacturer on other grounds. But here, Kelly Starling had been clever enough to use the exact language of the exception in the Protection of Lawful Commerce in Arms Act, alleging that MD Firearms had "aided, abetted, and conspired" with Peninsula Arms to sell firearms illegally. The statute got Kelly in the front door. The *Farley* case prevented MD Firearms from walking out the back door based on an unforeseeable intervening cause.

In short, they were toast.

"We knew this hearing was a long shot," McAllister said. "I just don't like surprises."

"Yes, sir," Jason said.

◁▷

Garrison took the bench scowling. He gaveled the court to order, and a hush engulfed the courtroom. Jason knew that a best-case scenario would be the court taking the case under advisement. Worst case would be an immediate ruling against MD Firearms, allowing the case to proceed.

Garrison turned his attention first to Blake Crawford. "What I'm about to say is meant as no disrespect, Mr. Crawford," he said. Jason's heart began to beat a little faster. Could it be?

"I know you've suffered a terrible loss and undoubtedly feel like someone needs to be held accountable for that loss."

Jason glanced at Crawford, who looked stricken. Jason didn't want to get his hopes up . . . but it sounded like Judge Garrison was winding up to dismiss the case.

"While I understand those emotions and want to personally express my condolences at what happened, in my view the person responsible for your wife's death is Larry Jamison. At most, you might also be able to lay some blame at the feet of the store that illegally sold him the weapon—Peninsula Arms."

Jason couldn't believe he was hearing this. Not in a million years had he thought a judge would dismiss the case this early. It was almost too good to be true.

"Nevertheless . . . ," Garrison said, pausing.

The word was like a sledgehammer to Jason's midsection.

"My personal view is not what matters. When I took the bench, I took an oath to follow the law."

The judge sighed and looked out over the courtroom. "The law in this case leaves me no choice. There is an exception in the federal statute protecting manufacturers, and that exception leaves room for suits against manufacturers who aid or abet illegal sales.

"In addition, I'm duty-bound to follow the precedents of this court, especially a case by someone as respected as Judge Moore."

Garrison turned his attention to Jason and Case. "The motion is overruled. I'm not saying this case will necessarily go to the jury. But for now, the plaintiff has alleged enough to state a cause of action."

Jason could hear some murmuring behind him, and the judge banged his gavel. Garrison was trying to play the role of ally to the gun groups even as he ruled against them. Nobody in the courtroom was buying it.

"Ms. Starling," the judge said, "please draft an order reflecting the ruling. Anything else?"

"No, Your Honor," Kelly Starling said, half-standing as she addressed the court.

Garrison looked at Jason and Case. Case just sat there, waiting long enough that Jason considered standing and responding himself.

When Case finally spoke, it seemed like he was talking to himself. "There are going to be a lot of dealers out of business."

"What's that?" Garrison said, clearly perturbed.

Case stood. "If we can be accused of aiding and abetting illegal sales on facts like these, we'll have to stop selling guns to a lot of dealers."

Tension lined every wrinkle on Garrison's face. He wasn't used to lawyers talking back.

"Speak to Congress about that," he said. "You're wasting your breath in here."

"That last statement is something we can agree on," Case said.

Judge Garrison seemed stunned by the comment. Livid. But he apparently thought twice before jumping down Case's throat. His Republican friends would already be upset that Garrison had denied the Motion to Dismiss. No sense making things worse.

"Court adjourned," Garrison said.

◁ ▷

Before she left court, Kelly had one more job to do. She pulled a deposition notice out of her briefcase and checked it one last time. Normally, lawyers called the other side and mutually agreed on dates to take sworn pretrial testimony of key witnesses. But sometimes, when Kelly wanted to make a statement, she sent out deposition notices without even checking. This typically ignited the other side's fuse, resulting in a big argument.

Eventually a date for the deposition would be established by mutual consent.

But the message would be sent.

This particular notice was for Melissa Davids. Ten o'clock. Kelly's office in Washington, D.C. She had scheduled it for February 9, just a week and a half away. The defense lawyers would undoubtedly object to the time and place, and Kelly would agree to reschedule—so long as Davids was the first witness to be deposed.

She walked to the table where Case McAllister and Jason Noble were packing their briefcases. She placed the deposition notice in front of Case.

"It's a notice for Melissa Davids's deposition," Kelly said. "I'm willing to be flexible on time and place as long as she goes first."

"That's very considerate of you," McAllister said. He didn't look at Kelly. Nor did he pick up the document.

She stood there for a second, then returned to her client. "Let's go," she said, packing her stuff. "Look straight ahead. Don't respond to anybody."

Blake nodded and put on his game face.

As they turned to leave, Kelly noticed that Case McAllister and Jason Noble had already departed. Her deposition notice was still sitting there on the defense counsel table, untouched.

"Jerks," she said under her breath.

32

KELLY STARLING AND BLAKE CRAWFORD emerged from the courthouse side by side, family members and friends trailing in their wake. The protestors gave the entourage room to pass and refrained from yelling slogans in their face. They were on their best behavior.

The media was not.

Cameramen walked backward with their cameras just a couple of feet from Kelly's face. Reporters fired questions at will.

"Ms. Starling, how do you feel about the court's ruling?"

"I feel great."

"What evidence do you have that MD Firearms knew about the sales?"

Kelly smiled. "Lots."

"Is it true that the investigative report about Larry Jamison was flawed?"

"What's that got to do with anything?" Kelly shot back, before she could remind herself to keep her mouth shut.

"Could the defense raise that as contributory negligence?"

Kelly picked up the pace. "Of course not. That's ridiculous."

Kelly fielded a few more questions on the fly, until she and Blake outdistanced the reporters. When she parted company with Blake at her car, about a half mile from the courthouse, there were tears in his eyes.

"I'm glad I found you," he said.

Kelly gave him a quick hug and imagined what a wonderful husband he must have been to Rachel. The man was sensitive and not afraid to show it. And though she hated herself for being so obsessively analytical about it, he would make a strong witness.

"We've got a long way to go," she warned.

She spent most of the ride to D.C. thinking about Blake and Rachel, even pulling a picture of Rachel from her briefcase to remind herself of the woman's innocent charm. The rest of the time, she was on the phone with the firm's public-relations director. There would be four local television stations waiting for her in a firm conference room when she returned. The partners were proud of her. They thought a press conference would be a good way to capitalize on the free publicity.

Kelly sighed, but what choice did she have? She would prefer to try her case in the courtroom, but Melissa Davids would probably be all over television that night, spouting off about this money grab by Rachel Crawford's family.

It couldn't hurt to even the playing field a little.

◁▷

On the way to the airport, Case McAllister didn't seem to be at all bothered by the hearing. He had tossed his suit coat in the back and slouched down in the passenger seat, relaxed and talkative. "We knew going in that we were going to lose," he reminded Jason. "I've got some friends in the Virginia legislature. They've got ways of getting the word to Judge Garrison. We may still win this thing on a Motion to Strike at trial."

Jason wasn't so sure. He would prepare for the case as if it were going to the jury. Judge Garrison's ruling had not left a lot of wiggle room for a Motion to Strike.

For most of the trip, Case talked about everything except the lawsuit. When they pulled up to the curb at the airport, he reminded Jason not to talk with the press. "Melissa likes to handle the publicity aspects herself," Case said.

No kidding, Jason thought.

"You just focus on trial prep," Case said.

After he dropped Case off, Jason spent a few minutes analyzing the day's events. Case seemed supremely confident, almost as if he had an inside line on Judge Garrison. But if he did, why would Garrison have ruled against MD Firearms today? Could it be that Davids and McAllister actually wanted to lose this hearing, realizing that the free publicity for their company would be worth millions?

The thought that his own client might be pushing this case toward trial troubled Jason. Maybe it was just the product of his cynical and imaginative mind. Or maybe Case had been through so much controversy in his day that this was just a blip on the radar screen. Either way, Jason still felt it odd that the same ruling that had sent his own stomach into a relentless churn had not seemed to impact Case at all.

But then he thought about the moment that Kelly had first pulled out the *Farley* ruling. Case had seemed understandably frustrated. And surprised. So maybe he just got over things quickly.

When Jason reached the interstate, instead of heading north toward Richmond, he took the second entrance ramp, heading south and eventually east to Virginia Beach. There were certain things he couldn't control. The judge, for example. Maybe his client as well.

But Jason had a job to do, and he needed to focus on that. He had to assume this case would ultimately go to trial.

Today had given him a chance to analyze Kelly Starling, and he had been impressed. She was businesslike and well prepared, but she also had a quick smile, lively brown eyes, and a short, layered haircut that gave her an all-American image. She could do Wonder Bread commercials. Plus, she seemed to be a true extrovert, not a private person like Jason who just played the part of a trial lawyer.

But he could count on at least one weakness. She was from Burgess and Wicker, a traditional big firm that taught traditional big-firm trial prep. She would focus on pretrial depositions, file truckloads of legal motions, and try to bury Jason in a mountain of paperwork. She would view the trial as a battle of evidence, hers versus his, a procedural competition with the verdict as the prize.

But Jason had been trained differently. At Justice Inc., under Andrew Lassiter's watchful eye, Jason had discovered that the courtroom was not about *debate*; it was about *drama*. The trial was a play, the jury the audience, the lawyers the actors. What mattered most to Jason was not this piece of evidence or that piece of evidence. What mattered to him was the audience. What did they value? What motivated them? How could he touch on the issues they cared about most? It was Cicero, not big-firm training, that formed the basis for Jason's playbook: *Touch the heart, move the mind.*

That was the key to advocacy.

But there were practical concerns as well. He had overlooked a critical case in his prep for today's hearing because he wasn't part of the local legal culture. That was why smart companies usually hired local legends for their trials as opposed to nationally known out-of-town lawyers. Every courthouse had its own culture. Every city and county had its unique jury pool with a unique set of values, fears, and hot buttons to push.

Let Kelly Starling focus on evidence and legal motions, Jason decided. He would work hard on those aspects of the case too, but his real focus would be elsewhere. He would become part of the Virginia Beach culture. Tonight he would spend time hanging out in Virginia Beach. Tomorrow he would look for a temporary place to stay for the next few months, just like Robert Sherwood had suggested.

In six months or so, unless Case McAllister took care of things behind the scenes, Jason would play a starring role in the case of *Crawford v. MD Firearms*.

It was time to start getting into character.

33

JASON SECURED A ROOM at an oceanfront hotel, then drove up Laskin Road, looking for a place to eat. He had been on edge at lunch and hadn't had much appetite. Now he was famished.

About half a mile from the oceanfront, next to an abandoned movie theater, Jason found just the place. He pulled into a burger joint with a purple roof and a sign that promised thick shakes. The Purple Cow. If he wanted to find an authentic slice of Virginia Beach life, this looked like a promising place.

The interior featured purple booths, an old jukebox playing "Help Me, Rhonda," a soda bar, a giant gum ball machine, children's crayon drawings of purple cows pasted to one wall, and a colorful assortment of life-size figures covering the others, including a picture of Bill Clinton dressed up like Elvis and singing next to an image of Marilyn Monroe. The place was about half full, not a bad crowd for a weeknight in the winter, and the hostess said Jason could sit anywhere he wanted. Jason picked a booth in the back corner and studied the menu.

Jason guessed his waitress was a local high school or college student. Her name badge said *Kim,* and she tried to talk Jason into ordering a purple milk shake, pointing out a family at the next table where the kids sported purple teeth and tongues.

"You can't come to the Purple Cow and not order a purple milk shake."

"I'll stick with vanilla."

For the main course, Kim recommended lasagna, and Jason obliged. A few minutes later she brought the vanilla shake, and Jason knew immediately that he had found the right spot. The shake was otherworldly good, a throwback to the days of real ice cream and real milk, thick enough that you couldn't coax it through a straw. Kim served it in two glasses—the tall aluminum glass it was mixed in and a tall thin glass to drink from. *This* was the way shakes were supposed to be served.

A thought hit Jason just before the food arrived. It was crazy, and way outside his comfort zone, but his competitive instincts edged out his shyness. Kelly Starling would probably be spouting off on television tonight on one channel, while Melissa Davids would be making her case on another. But Jason had an opportunity to find out how real Virginia Beach jurors might think. He got Kim's attention, and she came smiling to the table.

"Do you have any regulars in here?" Jason asked. "I need to bounce something off some folks who live in Virginia Beach. Get their opinion on something."

Kim scrunched her forehead, looking confused.

"I'm a lawyer," Jason said, lowering his voice. "I'm from out of town, and I've got a case I need to try in a few months. I wanted to get a quick opinion from the types of people who might sit on my jury. . . . I'll even pay for their dinner."

Kim asked a few questions about the case, and Jason kept it general. Still, she heard enough to pique her curiosity. "Could I listen too?" she asked.

"As long as you don't get in trouble with your boss."

"That won't be a problem," Kim said. She nodded toward a corner booth. "The guy facing us is a youth pastor named Wayne from a local church. He comes in here about once a week. That couple with him—I can't remember their names—but they're in the church too."

"Think they'll do this?" Jason asked.

"A free meal? Wayne? Uh . . . yeah."

After an awkward introduction, Jason began explaining the facts of the Crawford case. He spoke with as much detachment as he could muster; he didn't even let on whether he represented the plaintiff or the defendant. About three minutes into his presentation, he was forced to start over again when the couple who owned the restaurant joined the discussion, asking lots of probing questions.

He took mental notes as the little group argued about the right verdict. The men tended to sympathize with MD Firearms, but the woman who was part owner of the restaurant proved to be very persuasive. "I'll never forget seeing that shooting on television," she said. "I just think this manufacturer has a duty not to use dealers who are making illegal sales."

Her husband shook his head. "I don't see that. The manufacturer didn't shoot that woman."

"But let's say we hire an employee who we know has violent tendencies. And then he gets mad one day and gets in a fight with a customer. You don't think we'd be responsible?"

The question brought a reflective pause. "I see your point," her husband said.

And so did the others. Once the pendulum started swinging, it didn't stop until it had arrived at $2.5 million.

It wasn't a scientific poll or even a representative focus group. But it served as an effective wake-up call.

"Who do you represent?" Kim asked.

"The company you just nailed for $2.5 million."

When he returned to his booth, Kim asked Jason if he wanted his lasagna reheated.

"Why don't you put it in a box," he said. "I think I lost my appetite."

34

JASON SPENT THE WEEKEND looking for a temporary office and a place to live for the next few months. He was hoping for something affordable near the beach.

The weather took a nasty turn on Saturday, with steady rain and biting winds from the northeast making for a deserted boardwalk. Still, Jason could imagine this place in the summer—teeming with tourists, surfers, and beach cruisers. He learned that the oceanfront economy relied on summer labor from nearly six thousand international college students who were in the country on temporary four-month visas. He also learned that most of them were women.

Moving to the beach permanently was not out of the question.

Each day, he approached his hunt for an apartment and office with the same level of discipline he would bring to bear on a major case. He scoured newspapers and the Internet for possible locations, mapped them out over morning coffee, and drove by later in the day. That way, he could eliminate prospects from his list without talking to somebody on the phone or, worse yet, being subject to an interminable sales pitch. He would go inside only if the place had real promise.

Each night for dinner, he returned to the Purple Cow, where his waiter or waitress would put him in touch with another table of locals looking for a free meal. On Monday night, the locals delivered the first defense verdict, and the owner of the restaurant was so excited for Jason that she comped the family's meal on the spot.

"It's all part of the dining experience," the owner said. "Good burgers, purple shakes, a crazy defense lawyer. What could be more American?"

On Tuesday morning, Jason closed two deals. A one-year office lease on Laskin Road and a month-to-month residential lease for a "cottage"—the

Virginia Beach term for a small detached residence located on the same property as the main house. This particular cottage was a small apartment located over a boathouse on a waterfront estate in the Bay Colony area. The house and cottage shared a backyard that looked out over a body of water called Linkhorn Bay and were located less than a mile from the ocean.

A spry widow named Evelyn Walker lived alone in the main house, except in the summers, when she rented rooms to a number of international students. She was looking for someone to help keep an eye on things, especially during the off-season when the college students weren't around.

The cottage was the perfect size for a young single guy. It had one room on the main floor that served as a combined kitchen and living room. A bathroom and bedroom were upstairs, hanging out over the water in the boathouse. The decor was vintage 1980s. Fluorescent colors dominated—an orange carpet and lime green walls in the living room and a hodgepodge of paintings, beach trinkets, and abstract art for decorations. It wasn't exactly a plush penthouse condo overlooking the ocean, but the price was right.

On the drive back to Richmond, Jason finally garnered the nerve to return a phone call he had received on Monday. Actually, two phone calls on Monday and one on Tuesday morning, all relegated to voice mail when Jason saw the caller ID.

"Thanks for calling," said Andrew Lassiter. Jason thought he could still detect a tinge of panic in Andrew's voice. "I need to get together with you for a few minutes. It's urgent."

It was exactly what Jason *didn't* need. He had already made it clear to Lassiter that he didn't want to get involved in his dispute with Robert Sherwood.

"I don't think that's a good idea."

Lassiter responded quickly. Tersely. "It's not what you think. It doesn't have anything to do with Sherwood. He's screwed me over; I'll deal with that. This is about something else."

"Can we talk about it over the phone?"

Lassiter's sigh signaled his exasperation. "How far are you from your office?"

"Thirty minutes."

"Call me back from your office phone," Lassiter said. "I don't want to talk on this line."

Jason called precisely thirty minutes later, and Lassiter answered on the first ring, sounding every bit as tense as he had earlier. He was trying to put the Justice Inc. controversy behind him, Lassiter said. He needed to launch out in a new direction. Perhaps Jason could help.

Jason would need a jury consultant on the Crawford case, and nobody knew more about picking juries than Andrew Lassiter. He would consult with Jason for free, just to get the marketing push that would come from such a high-profile case. From there, Lassiter could develop his own consulting business.

Jason was intrigued, but red flags shot up everywhere. "Aren't those micromarketing formulas the property of Justice Inc.?"

"They're *my* formulas," Lassiter snapped. "But that's another matter. I'm talking about developing new formulas, better formulas, just for this case."

"Didn't you sign a non-compete?"

"I'm *not* competing, Jason. I know for a fact that Justice Inc. is going to invest based on the outcome of this case. If they're playing games with the gun companies' stocks, they couldn't possibly serve as a jury consultant—it'd be a conflict of interest."

What he said made sense, but Jason still had reservations. He felt like a referee stepping between two angry heavyweight boxers. "I don't know, Andrew. It just doesn't feel right. I wouldn't even be in this case if it wasn't for Mr. Sherwood."

Lassiter didn't respond for several uncomfortable seconds. When he did, his voice seemed calmer, more resigned than the fevered pitch of just a few seconds before. "I'm going to tell you something in absolute confidence," he said. "I need your promise that this goes nowhere."

"Okay," Jason said, though he wasn't really sure he wanted to hear it. The less he knew about the dispute between Sherwood and Lassiter, the better.

"Kelly Starling worked at Justice Inc. several years before you did," Lassiter said. "You won't be able to tell it from her résumé, because it only lists the New York firm that contracted her out to Justice Inc. for an override on her time. Same setup as you had, just a different firm. She's an alum, Jason. I'd rather work your side, but if you're not willing to do this, she'd hire me in a second."

The revelation stunned Jason. His adversary had received the same cutting-edge training that he had? It was like learning your soccer coach was secretly training the other team.

Lassiter would have no reason to lie about this. He had been there. He would have known Kelly Starling.

"Interesting coincidence," Jason said, after taking a few seconds to process it.

"Hardly," Lassiter countered. "Justice Inc. got her involved in the case just like it did you."

"I was being sarcastic," Jason said. "But why do they want alumni on both sides?"

"It makes our models—*their* models—more accurate. It takes some of the unpredictability away if you know the lawyers and their tendencies. It's something Sherwood started doing after a couple cases went south due to poor lawyering."

Jason supposed this information should have been flattering. He was in the case because Justice Inc. trusted him to aggressively represent MD Firearms. But it was a little disconcerting to realize that Sherwood felt the same way about his opponent. It made him feel like a puppet, his strings being pulled by the executives in New York.

"Plus," Lassiter added without prompting, "they know that both you and Kelly are not afraid to try a case. They don't make money if the case settles."

This information changed the trajectory of Jason's thinking. Robert Sherwood wasn't just helping Jason's career; he was orchestrating the next big case. And if somebody like Andrew Lassiter ended up working for the other side, the results could be disastrous.

Still, Jason had that uneasy feeling of a mortal stepping onto the battlefield of the gods. He didn't want either Lassiter or Sherwood angry with him.

"Let me call Robert Sherwood and let him know we're thinking about this," Jason suggested. "That way, he won't find out from somebody else and get all fired up."

"We don't owe Sherwood *anything*," Lassiter insisted. "They used us, Jason. Especially Sherwood. They're still using you."

Jason kept his voice steady, but he was unmovable. He wanted Andrew involved, but he didn't want to take on Justice Inc. He assured his friend that he would present his involvement to Sherwood as a done deal rather than asking for permission. "I don't want him to find out from someone else and assume I'm out here doing stuff behind his back," Jason said.

"You don't owe him anything," Lassiter repeated. "But suit yourself."

When they hung up, Jason sighed deeply. He could feel himself getting pulled into a nasty fight between two men he highly respected. One or the other of them was going to be disappointed in him.

He worried about calling Robert Sherwood and rehearsed the conversation several times in his head. With each passing minute, he thought up another reason to delay the call.

When he finally pulled out his cell phone to call Sherwood, he received an incoming call with an Atlanta area code before he could dial out. He decided to take it. Any call would be preferable to talking with Sherwood.

35

"JASON, IT'S MATT COREY."

Detective Corey didn't make casual calls. A lump formed in Jason's throat.

"What's up?"

"It's about your dad, Jason. Things are getting worse. It's really started to affect his work."

Jason stared at the wall in his office. He knew his father's drinking had worsened. But he always assumed that his father could handle it, would draw a hard line between booze and the job he loved.

"It was pretty bad at Christmas," Jason admitted. "But I thought he kept it off-hours."

"I don't want to go into the details on the phone. He's in some trouble at the station, and there's some stuff that nobody knows about. Point is—he needs help."

"Okay. But he won't listen to me."

"I've already talked to Julie. She's willing to come home next week if you can make it too. The department has this formal intervention program, but I know your dad. He would react badly to it. My thinking is that the three of us—you, me, and Julie—could find a counselor who knows his stuff and work an intervention at your dad's house. Keep it away from the department. We could have a detox facility on standby, and I could work ahead of time to get his cases reassigned. Take away his excuses for not going."

Jason took a deep breath. The thought of confronting his father like this made him physically ill. "He's stubborn, Detective Corey. I don't know if it'll work."

"I'd slap you in the head if I could reach you," Detective Corey said. "How many times have I told you to call me Matt?"

Jason didn't answer. This topic had annihilated his sense of humor.

"Jason, I know this is hard. And I know you and your dad never had a great relationship. . . ."

The words, spoken kindly and matter-of-factly, still cut like a razor. They were heartbreaking and undeniable at the same time.

"But we can't do this without you. They say an intervention doesn't stand a chance if there's somebody important in the person's life who's missing."

Jason could feel his heart beat faster just thinking about it. A headache would soon follow.

"He respects you, Matt. He adores Jules."

And he can't stand me, Jason wanted to add. But he didn't; vulnerability was not his thing. "He and I have some serious issues."

"I can't force you, Jason. And I know he's hurt you in the past. But right now . . . he needs you."

There was a long pause as Jason processed this. He didn't see an intervention ending well, but how could he say no? The man was his father.

"All right," Jason said. "I'll try."

◁▷

The next morning, Jason ignored a call from Andrew Lassiter. There was no sense talking with Andrew again until Jason first talked with Robert Sherwood. Jason had left a message yesterday afternoon and was waiting for a return call.

The call came that afternoon. After Jason gave an update on the case (Sherwood was pleased about Jason's plans to move to Virginia Beach), Jason summoned the nerve to talk about Andrew Lassiter.

Andrew had called and volunteered his services as a jury consultant, Jason explained. But Jason knew that Andrew had left Justice Inc. on contentious terms, and Jason wanted to make sure that Andrew wouldn't be violating a non-compete if Jason hired him.

"There is a non-compete," Sherwood said. "And it's very broad. It would certainly include jury consulting, since that would inevitably require the use of our software or some derivative program."

"Okay," Jason said tentatively. He wanted to tread lightly here; the last thing he wanted was a big argument with Sherwood. But he didn't want Andrew working for the other side.

"Can you make an exception for this case?" Jason asked. "It would help me a lot." He chose his next words carefully—just a hint that Jason might know something about Kelly Starling, just enough to make Sherwood wonder. "I've got a hunch you're betting my side on this one, though both sides are *well represented*," Jason said. "With Lassiter's help, I might be able to cover your bet."

"I see," Sherwood responded, mulling it over. "Did Andrew tell you we've had some experience with your opponent as well?"

Jason felt like an animal who had just heard the trap clang shut, its pain about to register. The question was cleverly worded so as to admit nothing. And Jason's answer would either be a lie or a violation of his promise to Andrew.

Stymied, Jason said nothing.

"Don't play games with me, Jason. I'm sure Andrew talked to you about Kelly Starling."

"Yes, sir. He did."

"We try to get our own people hired on these cases, Jason. That way we know the lawyers will try a good case. We're not attempting to influence the outcome—you won't hear a word from me about *how* to try it. We're just trying to take out some of the guesswork that comes with incompetent lawyers."

Sherwood paused, as if weighing whether he should say anything more. "Kelly was a decent lawyer, Jason. But she wasn't so good that we asked her to leave the program early.

"And I'm a gun enthusiast," Sherwood continued. "That's why I tried to get you hired to defend MD Firearms. And, by the way, we didn't use any undue influence; we just helped MD Firearms see the need for a different kind of lawyer."

"I know that," Jason said.

"Here's what I'm going to do," Sherwood said, his voice authoritative. The man always seemed to be a step or two ahead. "If you can get Lassiter to sign something that would guarantee this is a one-shot thing, so he's not just using it for a springboard to build a business like ours, I'll let him do it."

"I'll try," Jason said. "But I think you're probably right. He wants to build a business out of this."

"Then he can't do it," Sherwood said emphatically. "Tell him he either signs something promising to abide by the non-compete and acknowledging that this is one-time exception, or he can't do it."

"I'll talk to him," Jason promised.

Jason hung up and talked himself out of immediately dialing Lassiter's number. He had three other phone calls he needed to return first. Lassiter could wait his turn.

Ten minutes later, Sherwood's number appeared again on Jason's screen. He took the call.

"Have you called Lassiter yet?" Sherwood asked.

"No, sir."

"Good. Forget what I said earlier. Tell him he can help you win this case."

"Okay. But if you don't mind me asking—what changed?"

"My thinking. That little jerk is going to sue us; there's no doubt about that. Our lawyers say it wouldn't hurt to have him involved in a clear violation of the non-compete. Plus, it will make this case even easier to analyze, because we'll know precisely the type of jury you guys are going to pick."

Not exactly the most noble reasons, thought Jason. But he didn't really care. Anything to get out of this mess.

"I'll tell him," said Jason. "Not about the reasoning of course. Just about what a gracious guy you are."

"You've got good instincts, kid."

"I appreciate that. But honestly, I would love to see you and Andrew patch things up. You're both way too talented and smart to get involved in a war of attrition like this."

Sherwood was silent for a moment; he probably wasn't used to someone being so blunt. "Jason, I would have loved nothing more than to part with Andrew on good terms. Did you know we paid him $2.5 million and let him keep his 15 percent share in the company?"

Jason didn't respond. Maybe Sherwood was fishing to see if Lassiter had been talking about details of the deal. Maybe there was a confidentiality agreement.

"That's what I figured," Sherwood said. "He didn't tell you that. Go ahead and work with him, Jason, but be careful. He internalizes everything, and then suddenly, like a coiled snake, he lashes out."

Jason almost chuckled at the description of Lassiter as a snake. The man would have trouble stepping on a cockroach.

"I'll keep that in mind," Jason said.

36

JASON PICKED UP his prototype MD-45 from Richmond Sporting Goods on Wednesday morning. At the store, he paid careful attention to the paperwork. He was required to fill out ATF Form 4473. He also had to produce a government-issued photo ID and a bill showing his address, then wait for the National Instant Criminal Background Check to clear his name.

The bulk of Form 4473 consisted of a "Certification of Transferee," containing a number of questions that Jason had to answer and a space for him to sign. The very first question was the most important: *Are you the actual buyer of the firearm(s) listed on this form?* The question was followed by a boldfaced warning: *You are not the actual buyer if you are acquiring the firearm(s) on behalf of another person. If you are not the actual buyer, the dealer cannot transfer the firearm(s) to you. (See Important Notice 1 for actual buyer definition and examples.)*

Jason read through all of the examples as the clerk watched him. After a few seconds, the impatient clerk decided to provide a little help. "Most people just answer 'yes' to question 12a and 'no' to questions 12b through 12k. If you answer 'yes' to anything on 12b through 12k, I can't sell you this gun."

"Thanks," Jason said without lifting his head.

Despite the clerk's prompting, he took the time to read each question.

Are you under indictment or information in any court for a felony?

Have you been convicted in any court of a felony?

Are you an unlawful user of, or addicted to, marijuana, or any depressant, stimulant, or narcotic drug, or any other controlled substance?

Have you ever been adjudicated mentally defective?

Have you been convicted in any court of a misdemeanor crime of domestic violence?

Are you an alien illegally in the United States?

At the end of the long list of questions was a paragraph full of boldfaced warnings, informing the purchaser that he or she could face felony prosecutions for falsifying any information.

"They take this stuff seriously," Jason said, signing the form.

"Yeah," the clerk groused. "Unless you buy your guns on the street or at a gun show. The ATF just likes hassling legal purchasers."

Jason had read about the gun show debate. Thousands of gun show sellers skirted Form 4473 because they weren't federally licensed firearms dealers. He decided not to take that bait. The gun used to kill Rachel Crawford had been purchased at a gun store. The straw purchaser, Jarrod Beeson, had certified that he was the actual purchaser and signed his name to this form. The gun store clerk allegedly knew that the gun was really intended for Larry Jamison but sold it anyway, despite the bold-print warning.

Beeson was serving time. The gun store owner and clerk had been indicted and were rumored to be considering a plea bargain.

Jason purchased a few rounds of ammunition, thanked the clerk, and decided to head straight to the firing range.

◁ ▷

Just as he remembered, the gun had a nice heft to it and a sleek feel. It responded cleanly when he pulled the trigger and was easy to sight in. He liked knowing that the gun could only be fired by him. His fingerprints unlocked all this power. *His* gun.

On the way home, it felt a little strange to have the gun in the car. On the one hand, he felt more secure. After all, his MD-45 *was* the great equalizer. But on the other hand, the gun seemed to bring a new aura of danger—as if the world had suddenly become too risky to navigate without firepower.

He called Melissa Davids and told her that he was the proud new owner of an MD-45.

"Have you applied for a concealed carry?" she asked.

He hadn't thought about that. His main concern right now was working on the case, not playing Dirty Harry. "Not yet."

"It might help you get one if you had some actual death threats," Davids said matter-of-factly. "If you need a few, just let me know. I've got extras."

Jason thanked her but said he could probably generate all the death threats he needed on his own.

"I'd like to get together before your deposition next week," he said, changing subjects. "I'm coming to town Friday for some family business. Can we meet then?"

"Why?"

"To prepare for your deposition."

"I've been deposed before," Davids said, her tone dismissive. "I'm a big girl."

The response made Jason bristle. "You haven't been deposed on this case before. You hired me to be your lawyer. We really ought to meet beforehand."

"I hired you to be my *trial* lawyer. This is a deposition. I can take care of myself."

"There aren't many objections I can legitimately make at a deposition," Jason countered, trying hard to remain patient. "It's tough to defend a witness who isn't prepared."

"Jason, I don't care if you go to the shooting range during my deposition. I've done this before. I can handle Kelly Starling."

For a few seconds, Jason let the silence register his objection. "You're the client," he said grudgingly.

"That I am."

37

BLAKE CRAWFORD showed up right on time for his deposition preparation. Kelly started with the general advice. Listen carefully to the questions. Don't guess. Look at the camera. Think before you answer. Those types of things.

Next she spent a few hours playing the role of Case McAllister or Jason Noble, grilling Blake with questions, trying to throw him off or make him lose his cool. Occasionally, she would stop the questioning and give him some pointers.

Overall, the man did amazingly well. He was soft-spoken and sincere. Even during the practice questions, he choked up when he talked about Rachel and the baby. At one point, Kelly stopped and asked him if he needed a break.

"Let's just get through it," he said.

He was at his best when talking about Rachel's hopes and dreams. Blake was a high school math teacher and tennis coach. He and Rachel had moved to Virginia Beach from Florida less than a year earlier when Rachel had been offered a job as an investigative reporter. It was a bigger market and a better assignment than the small station Rachel had been working for in the Florida panhandle. For Blake, it meant moving in the middle of the school year and looking for work as a substitute teacher in Virginia.

"That's quite a sacrifice," Kelly said.

Blake shrugged. "Not really. Teaching jobs are a dime a dozen. But Rachel loved broadcast journalism. And she had a gift. Everywhere I went, I was pretty much known as Rachel Crawford's husband."

After Kelly had asked her last question, she pronounced him ready. "You're going to do great. Just be yourself. We've got nothing to hide."

Blake swallowed hard and stared past Kelly for a moment. "Can I ask you a question now?"

"Sure."

"Your dad's a pastor, right?"

The question caught Kelly a little off guard. "Um, yeah."

"Do you think it's *right* for me to pursue this?" He squirmed a little and toyed with a pen as he spoke. "I don't mean from a legal perspective. I mean as a Christian. Do you think it's the Christian thing to do?"

Kelly didn't hesitate. "Yes. Definitely. Why do you ask?"

Blake put the pen down. Concern furrowed his forehead. "A lot of my friends at church think I'm on the wrong side of this. You know . . . they don't say it that bluntly. But I pick it up from little things. Some of them have a hard time with this suit because they really believe in the Second Amendment. I don't know, maybe they feel like this is a big step toward the government taking away our right to defend ourselves. They're not big fans of the government to begin with."

Kelly wanted to interrupt and maybe suggest a change of churches, but she knew enough to hear him out.

"Others probably feel like I'm just doing this for the money. Especially since we didn't even sue the people who are really responsible. And then there's the whole thing about whether Christians should sue at all."

Kelly's mind raced as her client shared these rambling thoughts. Her own understanding of God as a God of justice was so deeply ingrained that she considered cases like this almost a special calling. How could somebody who apparently worshiped the same God see things so differently?

"God cares about justice," she said. "It's all throughout the Old Testament." She tried to think of some specific examples but she really wasn't much of a Bible scholar. "Even in the New Testament, the apostle Paul appealed his own case all the way to Caesar. And the only reason Christ refused to defend Himself was because there were bigger issues at stake. In His case, justice demanded sacrifice."

Blake looked skeptical. Even to Kelly's ears, her argument sounded muddled. Then she had a thought. "You want me to see if I can get my dad on the phone?"

Blake thought it was a good idea, and Kelly slipped into the hallway so she could talk to her dad on the cell phone and privately explain the situation. A few minutes later, she put him on the speakerphone in the conference room and introduced Blake. "The question, Dad, is whether it's right for Blake to be pursuing this case as a Christian."

She looked at Blake. "Is that it?"

"Basically. Yeah. I mean, I hate to sound so conflicted. But some days, it just feels like I'm on the wrong side of this issue and alienating a lot of people I care about, and most of them are just too kind to say anything right now. I don't know."

"It's a great question," Kelly's dad said. One thing Kelly had always appreciated about her dad was that he wasn't afraid of tough questions. "And it's pretty natural to feel conflicted about something like this." His voice was calm and reassuring—Kelly called it his "pastor's voice," as in, "Don't use that pastor's voice on me." Today, however, it sounded great.

"Like a lot of matters in life, the first thing you probably need to do is search your heart. Only you know why you're really pursuing this lawsuit. Is it for the money? Is it revenge? An attempt to fill a hole in your heart left by Rachel's death?"

Her dad waited, and Blake seemed to be considering these things.

"Or is it a desire to keep others from going through the same pain you suffered? Justice is a noble concept, Blake. But the line between justice and revenge is thinner than most people realize. Vengeance belongs to the Lord, not us."

Blake nodded. "I ask myself those questions all the time. Sometimes, it's hard to tell what's really driving me."

"Fair enough," said Kelly's dad. "And that's a question only you can answer. As for the theological questions—it is true that in the New Testament Christians are told not to file lawsuits against fellow believers, but that wouldn't prevent a lawsuit against MD Firearms. And it may help you to know that our entire tort system is actually derived from the Mosaic law of the Old Testament. When Kelly decided to make a living suing and defending people, I did a little research on this."

Interesting, Kelly thought. *He's never shared this with me.*

"Let me read you a passage from Exodus that might apply here. You've heard the expression 'It all depends on whose ox is being gored'?"

"Yeah," Blake said.

"It comes from Exodus 21. Keep in mind that in those days, they talked about dangerous bulls, not dangerous guns, but you'll see the parallels. 'If a bull gores a man or a woman to death, the bull must be stoned to death, and its meat must not be eaten. But the owner of the bull will not be held responsible. If, however, the bull has had the habit of goring and the owner has been warned but has not kept it penned up and it kills a man or a woman, the bull must be stoned and the owner also must be put to death. However, if payment is demanded of him, he may redeem his life by paying whatever is demanded.'"

"Wow," Kelly said, excited to discover that her lawsuit might actually have a biblical foundation. "It's the exact same principle. We're saying that MD Firearms knew about the dangerous habits of this dealer and did nothing. Didn't keep him penned up, so to speak. Consequently, it's not just the dealer who should pay but MD Firearms as well."

She looked at Blake. He didn't seem to have quite the same spark as Kelly, but the sag in his shoulders had lifted a little. "Does that make sense?" she asked.

"Actually, that helps a lot."

The three of them kicked it around for a few more minutes, and Kelly's dad warned Blake that life seldom served up black-and-white choices. "The apostle Paul understood this when he said he was 'perplexed, but not in despair; persecuted, but not abandoned; struck down, but not destroyed.' Sometimes we have to move forward one step at a time, just waiting for the fog to lift."

When they hung up, Kelly could tell the conversation had helped Blake. But she also knew her dad well enough to realize that Blake may not have been his only, or even his primary, audience.

After her client left, Kelly called her dad again.

"Thanks, Dad. That was exactly what he needed."

"He's asking the right questions, Kelly. He's going to be fine."

They talked for a few minutes, and her dad put her through the usual interrogation. Was she getting enough sleep? Did she need anything? Was she getting any downtime? Her dad told Kelly a few stories about the excitement of his parishioners when they saw Kelly on TV.

"We're praying for you, Kelly. And we're proud of you."

She knew it was true. She had always made the folks back home proud.

Which only made her feel more like a hypocrite. If they knew what she had done, her family would probably still love her. But pride would turn to sympathy and grave concern, swinging on the hinge of a sin that revealed much about her confused and broken heart.

38

JASON DIDN'T SLEEP more than a few hours Thursday night. He took an early flight to Atlanta Friday morning and met his sister and Detective Corey at the airport. He shook hands with Corey and hugged Julie. She was part mother and part sister to Jason. They saw the world differently—she was into recycling and organic foods and thought Al Gore should be anointed King of the Universe—but they shared the same dysfunctional childhood, a bond more important than politics. She taught a sociology course at some California community college whose name Jason could never remember.

Julie had always been the peacemaker in the Noble family, quick with a soft word or a diversion tactic or a compromise for the various skirmishes that erupted between Jason and his dad. She was plain and practical and usually put others first. "Just like her mother," Jason's dad would say.

For this trip, she had brought a small gym bag and a backpack. Like Jason, she apparently didn't plan on staying long.

The three of them huddled in the airport over coffee, plotting strategy for the intervention. Detective Corey briefed Jason and Julie on how things had deteriorated at the precinct. To Jason's surprise, his dad was being investigated by internal affairs for some missing cocaine on one of his cases. His absenteeism was up and case closure rate down. According to Detective Corey, even if Jason's dad was cleared in the internal investigation, there was a risk he would be placed on probation.

"I can't believe he's using cocaine," Jason said incredulously. His dad hated the drug. He had seen how much heartache and havoc it caused.

"He's not," Matt said decisively. "But that doesn't stop the rumors."

The plan was to meet Dr. Paul Prescott, a trained substance-abuse counselor, at Jason's dad's house. Prescott would facilitate the meeting.

Dr. Prescott had urged Jason, Julie, and Matt to write letters to Jason's father that they would read during the intervention. "It's very important to use only 'I' statements in the letter," he had told Jason during a phone call. "When your dad starts saying that we can't tell him what to do, my response will be, 'That's not what's happening. Your family and former partner are telling you what *they're* going to do.'"

Before leaving the airport, Matt, Jason, and Julie each read their letters aloud for the others to hear. Jason had fretted for hours over what he should say and finally just decided to put it all out there. His letter contained things he had never said to his dad out loud. He loved him. He was sorry that he had disappointed him. He respected his dad for working hard all these years, literally putting his life on the line so that Jason and Julie could have a better life than he had. He knew his dad had done his best to raise Jason and Julie after their mom died, and he thanked him for that. Jason ended the letter by saying how much easier it would be just to let his dad continue down the path he was going, but Jason cared too much to sit this one out. He hoped his dad would forgive him if this letter sounded sanctimonious; he just wanted his dad to get help.

When he finished reading the letter, doing his best to keep his own emotions at bay, he saw the tears spilling down Julie's cheeks.

"Dr. Phil couldn't have said it better," Detective Corey joked, trying to lighten the mood.

Julie reached over and gave Jason a hug.

Writing the letter had been one of the hardest things Jason had ever done.

◁ ▷

Paul Prescott was a bear of a man. He had a flushed complexion, curly brown hair, big brown eyes that never seemed to blink, and round cheeks that sprouted dimples when he smiled. He met the others at a Starbucks about a half mile from the house.

"I was an addict too," Dr. Prescott said. "Booze. Drugs. Name the chemical. I know what your dad's going through. Regardless of how he reacts today, this is the right thing to do."

They rehearsed the plan one more time, and Jason felt sick to his stomach. He knew that somehow this would all get blamed on him. His feelings were hopelessly complicated, and he didn't even try to sort them out. He hated being around his dad but suddenly felt sorry for him. The man's own family and his best friend were now scheming against him. In some ways, Jason felt like a traitor.

Jason had serious second thoughts about the whole process. It seemed so heavy-handed, so dramatic. His dad was a private man. He didn't like people pushing him around. If it had been up to Jason, he would have called the whole thing off.

But it wasn't up to Jason. Events had progressed too far for him to back out now. He nodded solemnly as the others talked; he tried to picture his dad after a successful course of treatment, reconciling with Jason and mending years of hurt feelings. For some reason, he couldn't quite crystallize that picture in his mind.

They took two cars to the house. The goal was to have Jason's dad ride with Dr. Prescott to the treatment center. Detective Corey had already taken care of getting work reassigned. Jason and Julie had agreed to split the cost of treatment, so money was not an issue. The idea was to take away every excuse and demand immediate action.

By the time they pulled up to the house, it was nearly noon. His dad's car was in the driveway. The four conspirators walked up to the door, and Jason swallowed his fears and knocked. He would never forget the look on his dad's face when he slowly opened the door.

39

FRIDAY WAS THE THIRD CONSECUTIVE DAY that Kelly ate lunch at her desk. That morning, she had also skipped breakfast after her swim at the LA Fitness club. She'd munched on a package of crackers mid-morning and now polished off some fruit, a sandwich, and a handful of carrot sticks while she reviewed corporate e-mails.

So far this week, she had probably reviewed five thousand pages of documents that one of her corporate clients would be disclosing in response to a discovery request in a big products liability case. Kelly was one of several associates on the case, and it was her job to grind through the boxes of documents lining the floor of her office and decide which documents should be withheld under the attorney-client privilege. It was mind-numbing work, the legal equivalent of operating a toll booth—take a dollar; give fifty cents change; "Thank you very much."

It was ironic how the media talked about the advantages of Blake Crawford having a big D.C. firm and all its resources representing him. The truth was that Kelly felt she had to squeeze the Crawford case in after hours and on weekends, all the while keeping up her billable-hour quotas on other cases where she was low woman in the pecking order.

She read quickly through three more e-mails and placed them in the non-privileged pile. The glamorous life of a big-firm lawyer.

Her tedium was interrupted by occasional pings from her computer—the sign of new e-mail hitting. It used to be a welcome sign, but now she opened each e-mail with a little more trepidation. Since her victory at the Motion to Dismiss hearing, her e-mails had occasionally been sprinkled with hate mail from various gun nuts out there.

She had printed out each of the offending e-mails and kept them in a little file for motivation. "First thing we do, let's kill all the plaintiffs' lawyers," said one. "You can't have my gun but you can have a few bullets," said another. Others were more blunt and full of profanity. Reading them the first time gave Kelly the chills. Reading them the fourth or fifth time made her angry.

The firm had taken the appropriate steps—reporting the e-mails to police, offering Kelly private security (which she refused), and taking her e-mail address off the firm Web site, though any moron could still figure it out. John Lloyd, the senior partner on the case review committee, had actually suggested changing lawyers on the case—which Kelly scoffed at—or that Kelly might want to consider buying a gun for protection. It was the first time in her career that she had asked a senior partner at her firm if he was crazy.

The e-mail Kelly had just received had the name of the Crawford case in the subject line. It looked like it had been sent from another temporary address that would be impossible to trace. She steeled herself for the contents, feeling that familiar mixture of bravado and fear.

As she began reading, she sensed immediately that this e-mail was different. By the third sentence, every ounce of Kelly's bravado had disappeared. She felt like somebody had knocked the wind out of her, like her heart had literally stopped. The blood drained from her face, and for a moment she couldn't move.

> Congratulations on landing the case of a lifetime. Warning: DO NOT SETTLE THIS CASE! Judge Shaver does not need the publicity. As long as you follow my instructions, your secret is safe with me. Otherwise, you'll be able to read all about you and the judge on the Kryptonite blog. Repeat: this case must go to a jury verdict. The day you settle is the day Kryptonite breaks the story.

She read the e-mail a second time, then a third. The Kryptonite blog was a gossip site that broke embarrassing stories about actors, politicians, and rock stars. It was the blog equivalent of *National Enquirer*, more reckless in its accusations than most blogs, but every once in a while it would actually get something right.

Judge Shaver was the district court judge for whom Kelly had clerked nearly seven years ago. He had recently been nominated for a seat on the Fourth Circuit Court of Appeals. He would have his grilling with the Senate judiciary committee if and when the senators found a way to break up the logjam of appointees in the pipeline. In the meantime, he was in limbo.

The timing of the e-mail couldn't have been worse.

What floored Kelly was the fact that somebody else knew about her relationship with the judge. She had never discussed it with anyone. Not a single living soul. Not her father. Not her best friend. Not a psychiatrist or counselor. *Nobody* knew.

Except this person named Luthor.

Luthor. That was the name the writer used to sign off the e-mail. An allusion, Kelly knew, to Superman's greatest nemesis.

She printed the e-mail, folded it in thirds, placed it in a sealed envelope, and put it in the bottom of her briefcase. She deleted the original e-mail from her computer and emptied her computer trash. She realized that the original was still lurking on the firm's server someplace, but she couldn't help that.

It would be hours before she could focus on the corporate e-mails again. The task suddenly seemed incredibly insignificant. Her world had just been turned upside down. A ghost from seven years ago had returned with a vengeance.

She ran down the worst-case scenario in her mind. As a former clerk, she had been interviewed during the FBI's background check on Judge Shaver. She vividly recalled the visit by the agents, the cordial conversation and probing questions they had asked. She had protected the judge and, in the process, placed her own head on the guillotine.

"Is there anything that might make you question his judgment?" they had asked.

"No."

"Are you aware of anything a person could use to blackmail or threaten Judge Shaver?"

"No."

"Are you aware of any intimate relationships between Judge Shaver and anyone other than his wife?"

Though she thought it was none of their business, Kelly had not hesitated. "No."

Now she could be looking at a national scandal, a Shakespearean tragedy, with Kelly in a leading role. The thought of it made her stomach churn with anxiety.

So far, Luthor had demanded something that Kelly fully intended to do anyway—try the case to a verdict. But what would he want next?

She called Judge Shaver, something she had not done since she took the job at B&W. His legal assistant answered the phone and perked up once Kelly said her name.

"It's great to hear from you! How long has it been?"

"Seven years," Kelly said.

They chatted for a while, though Kelly hardly heard a word the lady said.

"Is Judge Shaver in?" Kelly eventually asked.

"No." His assistant drew the word out, hating to disappoint Kelly. "He's at a judicial conference in Phoenix until next Wednesday. But I'm sure he would love to hear from you. Do you want his cell phone?"

"Sure."

As soon as Kelly hung up, before she lost her nerve, she dialed Judge Shaver's cell. Again, there was an exchange of pleasantries.

"I need to see you about something," Kelly explained. "It's fairly urgent."

Shaver asked if they could talk about it over the phone, but Kelly insisted on meeting in person. When he asked if it could wait until next Wednesday, she heard the tension in his voice.

"I think so," Kelly said.

The judge didn't respond immediately. "Should I catch the first flight home?"

Kelly wanted to say yes. She needed to talk this over with him as soon as possible, needed to prepare him for the worst, develop a plan. But having the judge abruptly leave the conference would create its own set of problems. What if Luthor was following him? Maybe Luthor knew about the judicial conference. Maybe he wanted Kelly and Judge Shaver to drop everything and get together for an emergency meeting so he could capture it all on video.

"It'll keep until next Wednesday," Kelly said.

"Okay," Shaver responded, sounding uncertain. "You're sure?"

"Yes."

The judge checked his calendar and said he had a heavy morning docket next Wednesday but could meet at 11:30.

Eleven thirty. The middle of the day, a time when others would be milling around the office. The judge was being careful. He didn't want the two of them to be together alone.

She wished they had both been this circumspect seven years ago.

40

AT FIRST, JIM NOBLE'S FACE LIT UP at the sight of his kids and Matt Corey standing on his doorstep. He looked like a child who had stepped into a surprise birthday party. His expression only made Jason feel worse.

"Jules!" he exclaimed. Julie stepped forward and gave him a hug.

"Hey, Dad."

He smiled at Jason. "Hey, buddy."

"Hey."

Dr. Prescott stepped forward and extended his hand. "I'm Dr. Paul Prescott. I work with the force on a number of matters."

The introduction froze Jason's dad, his impromptu joy quickly turning to realization that something nefarious was going on. He ignored Prescott's hand, looking from Jason to Matt. "What's this about?" he asked. The momentary silence made his eyes narrow and his complexion darken—suspicion giving way to the first vestiges of anger.

"Somebody want to fill me in?"

"We want to talk with you for a few minutes about some personal matters," Prescott said. "Can we step inside?"

"Personal matters?"

"Let's do it inside."

Jason's dad stood there for a few seconds, blocking the way of the much larger Prescott. Jim Noble might be down four inches and seventy-five pounds to the doctor, but there was no doubt where Jason's money would lie if a fight broke out. His dad was one tough dude.

"Please don't make this any harder than it already is," Prescott said, his voice calm.

It took Julie to break the stalemate. When she asked her dad to cooperate, he stepped aside and let them in. "What's going on, Jules?" he asked.

"Can I tell you when we get inside?"

He nodded and followed his daughter into the living room.

The place looked even worse than it had at Christmas. In addition to empty glasses, unopened mail, and dirty clothes, the living room had various case files scattered around the floor. There was an old bowl of Doritos, an empty coffee mug, a few books, and a couple of magazines on the coffee table. Jason counted at least a dozen empty beer bottles strewn around the room. The four visitors each had a seat, Jason bringing in a chair from the kitchen table. They left the reclining chair empty.

Prescott invited Jason's dad to sit, but he refused. "What's going on here?" he asked, looking from one person to the next.

"It would really help if you had a seat," Prescott insisted, his voice firmer this time. Jason knew it was the wrong approach. He studied his dad's reaction. He had lived with the man for eighteen years and had learned to recognize the signs of an impending explosion—veins bulging in the neck and forehead, nose flaring, intense scowl.

"Your kids and Matt care a lot about you," Prescott said. "They've seen some things that concern them enough to come all the way here—in Julie's case from California—and talk to you about them. They're just asking that you hear them out."

Jason's dad snorted, his temper taking control. "Don't give me this psychobabble crap," he said. He turned to Jason. "My son comes once a year at Christmas and then gets out of town as soon as he can. Even Julie thinks of every reason to stay away—"

Matt was on his feet, taking a step toward his former partner. "Don't," he said calmly. "Don't take this out on them."

"If you care so much, couldn't you just pick up the phone and call me?" The old man's eyes were filled with resentment, swinging from one person to the next. "You've got to gang up on me? get some psychologist in here to certify me as crazy?"

"C'mon," Matt said, holding up his hand to get his friend to stop. "We've been through a lot together. Don't say stuff you'll regret."

Jason jumped in as well. He forced himself to ignore his dad's comments and speak past the pain. "You need help, Dad. We've come to help."

His father laughed him off. "*You've* come to help." He turned to Matt Corey. "Isn't that the same thing we tell our targets just before we nail them during interrogation? 'We just want to help.'"

"Why don't you sit down?" Matt said.

Jason's father stared at him, but Matt didn't blink.

"You know I love you, man," Matt said. "But I don't know what happened to the Jim Noble I used to respect. That man would have never acted this way. That man wouldn't have hurt the people he cared about most."

The comment seemed to penetrate Jason's dad's defenses like a tranquilizer dart. He said nothing but sat on the edge of his recliner, his eyes fixed on Prescott.

Matt took a seat as well. "Thanks," he said softly.

Prescott took control of the meeting and explained how Jason, Julie, and Detective Corey had each become independently concerned about their father and friend. "Your drinking is affecting everything," Prescott said. "Your work. Your relationship with your kids, and in Julie's case, her willingness to let you have a relationship with your grandkids. These three folks all care about you very much and decided to do one of the toughest things in their lives—participate in this intervention."

For once, Jason couldn't read the expression on his dad's face. He listened intensely to Prescott, never once looking at Jason or Julie or Matt until Prescott came to the end of his spiel.

Prescott explained that he had asked each of the participants to write a letter and thought perhaps Matt should go first.

Matt Corey read his letter slowly and emphatically, with frequent glances at Jason's dad to assess its impact. He spoke about his great respect for his former partner, of all that the older cop had taught him, about how he had wanted to model his own career after his partner's. "In some ways, you're closer to me than my own father," he said.

The letter pulled no punches in detailing the current state of James Noble's job performance. His hours had become sporadic. A few partners had requested transfers because they couldn't take his mercurial personality swings. His case closure rate was down, and now there were rumors about missing cocaine. "I know it's not you," Matt read. "But let's be honest, you've got an addiction. It's just that yours comes in a bottle."

Jason watched his dad's face redden, but the man made no attempt to respond. Matt finished with a plea for Jim to get help and pledged his own support. In the silence that followed, the attention shifted to Jason.

"I guess I'm next."

Jason's heart pounded as he unfolded his letter. It took every ounce of willpower to look his dad in the eye as he prepared to read. He would have only one chance to do this, and he wanted to get it right. He had to keep reminding himself that the man sitting in this room was not really his father. The booze had stolen James Noble's soul and left a demon in its wake. This might be Jason's only hope for changing all that.

Jason's letter began by recounting some bright memories from his childhood, events that had been lost in the turmoil of the last few years. He glanced at his father as he read, apologizing for disappointing his dad in so many ways. Even during this part of the letter, words he had wept over as he wrote them, his father's expression never changed. Julie's cheeks, on the other hand, were wet with quiet tears.

Jason detailed the changes he had noticed in his dad and how they had affected their relationship. He admitted that his own response had been avoidance and asked forgiveness for staying away. If his dad got help, Jason promised to be there and to work through this with him. But honestly, if his dad didn't change, Jason just couldn't bear to stick around and watch him self-destruct.

"You always taught me that being a man meant you faced your problems and never quit," Jason said. "Don't give up on your family, Dad. We want you back. We love you too much to watch this happen and not do anything. I'm begging you, Dad—get some help."

Jason finished, his eyes stinging with tears, and looked up. His father stared back, still emotionless, looking as if he couldn't believe his own son had turned against him.

"I'm sorry, Dad," Jason said. "But this is the only way we knew to help."

His father nodded grimly and turned to Julie. "I'm sure the old man's let you down, too," he said, the words dripping with sarcasm. "But I really can't take much more of this right now. The stuff about my job performance is all bull." He looked at Matt Corey with eyes flaring again. "You know what that place is like. And you know darn well that this crap against me is just political."

He turned back to Jason. "As for you—I'm sorry I've been such a complete and total failure as a father."

"That's not what I'm saying—"

"That is *exactly* what you're saying," the older man fired back. If the others hadn't been there, Jason had no doubt that his dad would have physically attacked him. "And it's easier to blame it on the booze than it is to talk about the real issues."

"Let's talk about the real issues," Prescott interjected, his voice still calm.

Jim Noble leaned forward, forearms on his knees, hands clasped. He studied the floor for a moment and then looked up at Prescott. "Get out," he said. "You've played your little game, and I get the picture. My drinking days are over. I needed a wake-up call, and I got it. Thank you very much. Now get out."

"You need help, Dad," Julie said.

"You can all leave," Jason's dad insisted. "And you can all leave *now*."

Prescott nodded, and the others followed his cue. They had talked about this. Jason's dad had to know they would follow through. He had to know they would walk out of his life if he didn't change.

They left him sitting there, hunched over and staring at the floor. Julie put a hand on his shoulder as she walked by. Jason left without a touch.

"Give him a day or two to think it over," Dr. Prescott said as the four of them huddled in the driveway. "My guess is that he'll talk to Matt about getting treatment."

Jason had his doubts. He knew in his heart they had done the right thing. But he had little hope that his father would actually change.

He folded up his letter and put it in his pocket. At the airport, he pulled it out and thought about all the emotional energy involved in writing it. He threw it in one of those modern trash cans with an electric compressor. Right on cue, the receptacle vibrated and crunched the letter together with discarded newspapers and candy bar wrappers and Burger King french fries.

It was time, Jason decided, to put that part of his life behind him.

41

KELLY SPENT MOST OF HER TIME on Saturday morning staring out her office window, thinking about Judge Shaver. Perhaps this person named Luthor had intended merely to distract her from preparing for the deposition of Melissa Davids. If so, it was working.

In a naive way, she thought she had put the Shaver chapter of her life firmly behind her. There were scars, to be sure. There was also a type of relentless shame that never seemed to take a minute off, always lingering just below the thin film of the surface. But she had always assumed that these matters were private ones, requiring penance and atonement before God, affecting no one but her.

The e-mail yesterday had shattered that assumption. Somebody else knew. And worse, that person was intent on using this knowledge to manipulate Kelly on the Crawford case.

She was not going to let that happen. Blake Crawford had entrusted her with the most important matter in his life. She would represent him well, even if it meant public exposure and humiliation. She couldn't waver on that, couldn't even allow herself to entertain alternatives. Life might be hell for the next few months. But at least she would be able to look herself in the mirror when it was over.

In some ways, she worried more about Judge Shaver than herself.

She could honestly say she was not bitter or vengeful toward the man. It had been her fault as much as his. If the press found out, they would undoubtedly condemn him as the predator—a powerful federal judge holding sway over a smitten law clerk. Not that Kelly would be unscathed. Though Shaver would bear the brunt of the media scorn, she would be portrayed as an opportunistic manipulator, willing to trade her body for power, mindless of the toll it would take on an innocent wife and children. Her name would be mentioned in the same breath as Monica Lewinsky.

In truth, it was nothing like that.

It began as an emotional attachment. Sure, the man was good-looking, but Kelly had first been attracted to his heart. He championed the causes of the poor and helpless, risking reversal on appeal to rule in favor of justice. He had listened to Kelly's dreams and sympathized with her disenchantment with the political process. In retrospect, she realized that the dynamics had changed when the judge started sharing his own struggles—the pressures of the job, a marriage gone cold, a teenage daughter who no longer wanted to spend time with him.

His vulnerability had only elevated him in Kelly's eyes. He was authentic and transparent, confident enough to break with judicial conventions, secure enough to share his struggles with a law clerk. Kelly had worked harder for Judge Shaver than she had for anyone or anything in her entire life. He inspired her. He helped her regain a respect for the law as a vehicle for changing people's lives, something she had lost in the cynical atmosphere of law school.

Late working nights led to shared dinners and the judge providing Kelly with rides back to her apartment. He didn't want her riding the Metro, D.C.'s subway system, alone late at night.

Sometimes they sat in his car while it idled at the curb for nearly an hour before she finally said good night. Confidences were shared. The judge's struggle to make his marriage work, the way his wife had turned the kids against him. Kelly had met Lynda Shaver, a hard-charging partner at a large D.C. law firm, at a social event. Kelly had no idea why the judge had ever been attracted to the woman in the first place.

Judge Shaver still loved his wife and believed the marriage could work. But as Kelly listened to the judge share, it became clear that Lynda Shaver had divorced him emotionally years before.

The turning point came on a cold night in January. Earlier that day, Judge Shaver, who had been on a short list for the Fourth Circuit Court of Appeals, had been told it was not yet his turn. He had done his job that day with his normal enthusiasm, never saying a word to Kelly about the disappointment. She only found out through his assistant.

Late that evening, in his car outside Kelly's apartment, tears welled up in the judge's eyes. Not because he had been passed over—he still hadn't breathed a word about his professional disappointment—but because his wife, in a fit of anger the night before, had admitted to an affair with another partner in her firm. The affair had been going on for nearly a year.

"We've haven't had a real marriage for a long time," Lynda Shaver had told the judge. "If we want to stay together for the kids and your career, that's one thing. But let's at least be honest about it."

That night, Kelly reached over and touched his hand.

42

KELLY SKIPPED HER MORNING SWIM on Monday. She put on a black skirt with a gray suit jacket and understated earrings. She wore the same sports watch with a small blue Velcro strap that she wore during her swimming workouts.

It took her three and a half hours to reach the Hilton hotel on the Virginia Beach boardwalk at 30th Street. She would have preferred taking depositions in the plush B&W conference rooms, but Melissa Davids wouldn't come to D.C. Rather than get in a big fight and have to postpone the deposition, which was no doubt exactly what Davids wanted, Kelly had agreed to drive to Virginia Beach.

To add insult to injury, Jason Noble had told Kelly that his office wasn't yet furnished, so they would have to use a hotel conference room. After a heated exchange about who should pay, they agreed to split the costs.

Kelly arrived half an hour early to stage the room. The videographer and court reporter both wanted to know where the witness would be sitting. "At that end of the table," Kelly said, pointing toward the end with the view. She wanted Davids looking out at the ocean—maybe it would distract her. Kelly would tell Jason that the lighting for the video would work better this way.

The witness and her lawyers didn't bother showing up until ten minutes after the scheduled start time. They hadn't called Kelly to let her know they would be late and gave no excuses once they finally arrived. There were terse introductions and handshakes. Jason Noble's hand was cold and clammy.

Melissa Davids looked smaller and older than she had when Kelly met her on the set of Fox News. She wore jeans and a sweater, and her hair was pulled back from her face. Case McAllister had on a classic gray suit, monogrammed cuffs on his shirtsleeves, his trademark bow tie, and a pair of scuffed cowboy boots. Jason Noble must have gotten the *dress casual so it looks like we're not worried* memo from Davids. He wore jeans and a blue pin-striped shirt rolled up at the sleeves. He tried to project a casual everyman image, right down to the lack of socks.

A beach thing, no doubt.

◁▷

As Kelly Starling worked her way through the preliminary questions, Jason leaned back in his chair and sized her up. Even in her cross-examination mode, she had that fresh, all-American thing going—smooth skin, intriguing brown eyes, and perfect white teeth. Some intensity came from the angular jawline and the eyes that narrowed as she fired questions at Davids, using the clipped tone of a prosecutor. She was five or six years older than Jason, experienced enough to know what she was doing but young enough to hold the attention of the young men on the jury.

Today, she was all business.

Melissa Davids got off to a good start. She never took her eyes off Starling, paused before each answer, and volunteered no extraneous information. Jason began to relax just a little. Maybe she didn't need his coaching after all.

In law school evidence class, Jason and his classmates had studied the antitrust lawsuit against Microsoft and discussed how arrogant and evasive Bill Gates looked during his deposition. The lesson, according to Jason's professor, was that even smart CEOs needed a prep session.

That professor had apparently never met the stubborn and self-confident Melissa Davids.

◁▷

"Let me turn your attention to the MD-9," Kelly said. At trial, she planned to bring in a replica gun and parade it all over the courtroom. But depositions weren't quite so conducive to grandstanding.

"I wondered when you might get around to that," Davids said.

"A recent study by the *Tidewater Times* found that this gun ranks fourth among assault guns traced by the ATF to violent crimes. Are you aware of that?"

"I don't read the *Tidewater Times*," Davids sneered.

"Your company has had some trouble with the ATF, haven't you?"

"We've never been convicted of a single violation."

"That wasn't my question. Your company has had some trouble with the ATF, haven't you?"

"Objection," Jason said, "asked and answered."

"That's the problem," Kelly said. "It wasn't answered."

Davids stared at Kelly for a few seconds. "I think it was."

"Okay. Then let's walk through it. A few years before the assault weapons ban, the MD-9 was redesigned when the ATF went to court to pull your firearms manufacturing license, isn't that right?"

"The ATF went to court to revoke our license. We settled the case when we got tired of spending money on lawyers. So yes, we slightly redesigned the MD-9 to address their concerns. But the settlement agreement specifically denied any liability."

"The ATF was upset because people buying the MD-9 could easily convert it into an illegal fully automatic machine gun in a matter of minutes using only a file, isn't that right?"

Davids scoffed. "You can convert fertilizer into a bomb, too. That doesn't make fertilizer manufacturers criminals." She turned and looked at the camera. "We sold it as a semi-automatic. What people did when they got it home was their business."

Kelly leaned forward. The witness was getting under her skin. "How many converted MD-9s were traced to crimes?"

"I have no idea."

"More than ten?"

"Who knows?"

"More than a hundred?"

"Could be."

"More than a thousand?"

"She said she doesn't know," Jason interjected, still leaning back in his chair. He didn't have a single piece of paper on the table in front of him, as if this proceeding was too inconsequential to even take notes.

"Maybe this will refresh your memory," Kelly said. She slid a document to Melissa Davids and provided Jason with a copy. She asked the court reporter to mark the document as an exhibit.

"Can you tell me what that document is?" Kelly asked.

"A brief filed by the ATF in the case we've been discussing."

"Please look at page three, the second paragraph. How many MD-9s had been converted into fully automatic weapons and traced to crimes?"

"Eight hundred thirty-three," Davids said.

"And that didn't concern you?"

Davids scoffed. "We redesigned the gun so this couldn't happen. Is that so hard to understand?"

Kelly felt her face redden, the anger rising to the surface. "Just answer the question. Did this fact concern you?"

"Criminals sometimes modify our guns. Criminals sometimes use them to kill innocent people. Every time somebody dies, that concerns me. However, my hope is that sometime before this deposition is over, you might actually want to talk about whether it's fair to try and hold *us* accountable for everything these criminals do."

43

FOR THREE HOURS, Kelly Starling hammered away at the witness while Jason looked on, occasionally lodging an objection. At 1:30 he insisted they break for lunch. Forty-five minutes later, they were back at it, with Kelly focusing on MD Firearms's manufacture of silencers.

"Did Larry Jamison use a silencer?" Jason asked. "I must have missed that."

Kelly shot him a look. "You'll have your chance to ask questions when I'm done," she said.

"Maybe mine will be relevant," Jason responded, though they both knew Jason would have no questions. You ask questions of your own witness at trial, not at depositions. Why give the other side a roadmap of where you're going?

If nothing else, Jason's comment made Melissa Davids smile.

Kelly, on the other hand, did not seem amused. She ratcheted up her intensity, and the questions flew faster.

Davids refused to use the term *silencer,* calling it a Hollywood misnomer, but admitted that MD Firearms sold the outer tubes for "sound suppressors" while other Georgia manufacturers sold the matching internal parts. That way, each company avoided the federal regulations requiring registration by purchasers of complete suppressors. The companies advertised together and sometimes exhibited at the same gun shows with the result that thousands of unregistered sound suppressors were on the street.

The ATF took the companies to court over the suppressor issue, Davids conceded. This time the judge ruled against the ATF. Kelly pulled out a copy of a letter that one of the CEOs had written to the editor of an Atlanta paper the day after an incendiary article about the court's ruling. The letter compared the strong-arm tactics of the ATF to the tactics of Hitler and Stalin.

When Davids said she agreed with those sentiments, Kelly marked the letter as an exhibit.

It was nearly 3 p.m. when Kelly finally started asking questions about Peninsula Arms.

"Do you know what an illegal straw sale is?" Kelly asked.

"Of course."

"Explain it to me."

Davids looked at Jason. "Is it my job to explain the law to her?"

"Not really," Jason said. He was still working hard at acting disinterested. "But maybe if you do, we can get out of here faster."

Davids sighed. "A straw purchase transaction is when an eligible purchaser of a firearm buys a gun on behalf of another person who is an ineligible purchaser of a firearm. Let's say, for example, that you've been involuntarily committed to a mental institution. Jason here couldn't buy a firearm and fill out the paperwork on your behalf and give that firearm to you."

"And if a store knowingly participates in such a sale, they've violated federal law, is that right?"

"Of course."

"Do you monitor your dealers to make sure they don't engage in illegal straw sales?"

It was a loaded question. For the first time, Davids seemed to hesitate before answering. "That's not our job."

"Do you train your dealers on how to avoid straw sales?"

"That's not our job either."

"If it came to your attention that one of your dealers was engaging in hundreds of illegal straw sales and that the guns were ending up in the hands of street criminals, would you cut that dealer off from your products?"

They were on thin ice now. "That's a hypothetical," Jason said. "I'm instructing the witness not to answer."

Kelly's brown eyes flashed. "Do I need to call the judge and get a ruling?"

Jason motioned to the phone. "Help yourself."

He knew she wouldn't do it. Judges hated refereeing deposition disputes. They would always chide both lawyers for acting like a couple of kids fighting on the playground. Plus, Jason was pretty sure he would win this objection—the question called for speculation, not facts.

Kelly turned back to the witness. "You're aware that the cities of New York, Washington, Baltimore, and Philadelphia have filed lawsuits against rogue gun dealers based on guns they sold that were later traced to crimes on the streets of those cities?"

"Yeah, I'm aware. You want my opinion on those suits?"

"That won't be necessary."

"Didn't think so."

"You're also aware that undercover agents from those cities conducted a number of obvious straw purchases in several stores, including Peninsula Arms, and even captured some of those transactions on video—right?"

Davids snorted. "In my opinion, the ATF should have prosecuted those undercover agents for illegally buying guns and the stores for illegally selling them."

"Were you aware that Peninsula Arms received at least three separate citations from the ATF for illegal straw sales?"

"I might have been aware of that."

Jason tensed, fighting the instinct to object in order to keep his client out of trouble. Objections only drew attention to the answer and signaled to the other lawyer that they were on to something.

But Jason knew that Davids's last answer—that she "might" have been aware of the ATF citations—was skating dangerously close to perjury. While reviewing his client's business records to determine which ones to produce, he had looked through MD Firearms's e-mails, electronic documents, and files. Most of the files contained bland records about the design of the MD-9 or sales documents or contracts with various gun distributors and dealers. Jason had barely been able to stay awake as he reviewed the stuff. But one three-page memo from Case McAllister to Melissa Davids had caught his attention. It was entitled "Sales to Dealers Sued by Northeast Cities."

The document was the proverbial "smoking gun," written nearly a year before the Crawford shooting and addressing the issue of whether MD Firearms should stop supplying the rogue dealers who had been sued by the city governments.

In the memo, Case had analyzed precisely how many MD Firearms guns had been traced to crimes in the cities involved in the lawsuits and what dealers had sold the guns. His analysis showed that four dealers, including Peninsula Arms, were responsible for nearly half the guns used in those crimes. Case had analyzed the profits made from sales to those particular dealers and the estimated costs of defending a lawsuit by the dealers if MD

Firearms tried to discontinue sales to them. He also cautioned that taking steps to discontinue sales to some dealers would serve as an admission by MD Firearms that they had a duty to monitor all dealers and could therefore lead to lawsuits whenever their guns were used in crimes.

His conclusion: *"A careful cost-benefit analysis suggests we should continue selling guns to all licensed and qualified dealers."*

Melissa Davids had hand-scratched her response across the top of the memo: *"No kidding. Whatever happened to free enterprise?"*

It was the kind of memo that Kelly Starling would love to wave around during her closing argument, arguing that MD Firearms cared only about profits, not the lives of innocent victims like Rachel Crawford. Jason intended to make sure that she never got that opportunity.

As part of pretrial discovery, Kelly had made an official request for all relevant documents possessed by MD Firearms. But Jason had withheld Case's memo.

In doing so, he knew he was on shaky legal ground. On its face, the memo contained legal advice and was therefore covered by the attorney-client privilege. But when Jason talked to Case McAllister about the memo, he learned that Davids had actually forwarded the document by e-mail to the CEO of another gun manufacturer who was facing the same decision.

"Twice a year, some of the executives of the biggest gun companies get together and talk about issues of mutual concern," Case had explained. "One of the ongoing issues, of course, was the litigation filed by the cities. Another CEO was seriously considering shutting off sales to renegade dealers. Melissa was determined to talk him out of it and sent him the memo without checking with me first."

By providing the memo to a person outside the company, Davids had arguably waived the attorney-client privilege. But that wasn't the end of the analysis. Jason's research had turned up a possible justification for still withholding it from Kelly Starling—something called "joint defense doctrine." If two companies were both targets of a lawsuit and conducting a "joint defense," they could arguably share documents without waiving the attorney-client privilege. It was a stretch, but the doctrine at least gave Jason a good faith reason to keep the memo from seeing the light of day.

Still, it made him uncomfortable when Davids pretended to know so little about the sales patterns of these dealers.

Kelly Starling slid a nineteen-page spreadsheet in front of the witness and provided Jason with a copy. Even though Jason hadn't produced the Case McAllister memo, Kelly had apparently done her own homework.

"This is a spreadsheet containing information about guns traced to crimes in the cities that filed lawsuits and the stores that sold the guns," Kelly said. "In 2006 alone, 251 guns bought from Peninsula Arms were linked to murders or aggravated woundings in these four cities. None of those guns was used by its original owner. Only one other dealer had a greater number of guns involved. Did it ever occur to you that maybe you should discontinue selling guns to Peninsula Arms and this other dealer, Brachman's Gun Shop, based on their obvious involvement with gun traffickers?"

"I told you—it's not our job to monitor gun dealers."

Kelly snorted at the blow-off answer. "That's not my question. Did you ever consider whether you should stop selling guns to Peninsula Arms?"

"No," Davids said. "If anybody had suggested such a thing to me, I would have told them I still believed in the Second Amendment and the free enterprise system."

Because he knew about the McAllister memo, this answer really made Jason squirm. Davids had phrased her answer in hypothetical terms, so she technically wasn't lying. But the answer was not the whole truth, either.

Kelly made a few notes on her legal pad, as if she knew she was getting warm but couldn't quite figure out what she was missing. "Even though you knew Peninsula Arms had been cited for straw purchases three separate times by the ATF, had engaged in straw sales with undercover agents from New York City, and was linked to over 200 guns in one year used in crimes by unregistered owners, you didn't think you had any responsibility to cut them off?"

Davids didn't blink. "Let me put it to you this way," she said. "If you came into a car dealership with three DUIs, do you think that car dealership is going to sell you the car?" She didn't pause long enough for Kelly to answer. "Of course they are. And when you kill somebody on your fourth DUI, you know whose fault that is? The government's, that's who. They're the ones that should have put your sorry butt in jail the third time. It's not the car dealer's fault. It's not *their* job to regulate *your* conduct."

Kelly Starling made a face, as if kicking herself for asking one too many questions. But she was committed to this line of questioning now. "Let's try a different analogy, Ms. Davids. If you're a bartender and your patron has already had one too many drinks and he's searching his pockets for his car keys, you think you can just sell him another beer and not worry about it?"

For the first time all day, Melissa Davids smiled at Kelly. "Perfect example. Maybe the accident victim could sue the drunk driver. And maybe the accident victim could sue the tavern that gave him another drink. But you don't get to sue Anheuser-Busch."

◁ ▷

After the deposition, Jason drove Case McAllister and Melissa Davids to the airport. They had just enough time to check their guns through baggage and make the flight.

"Good job today," Jason said.

"Don't give her a big head," Case warned.

Davids smirked. "It must have been all the practice."

44

JASON SHOWED UP at his new office on Tuesday in jeans and an old sweatshirt. He left his winter jacket on for the first hour while the space heated up. He had leased the second floor of a nondescript brick building on Laskin Road about a mile from the beach. The first floor housed an insurance agent and a mortgage broker. There was adequate parking, the building was fairly new, and the marquee out front now displayed *Jason Noble, Attorney at Law* in the third slot from the top.

The office furniture arrived just before noon—two hours late—and Jason directed its placement while simultaneously meeting with representatives from the phone company and broadband provider. By 2 p.m., he had moved most of his legal files from his truck to the floor of his office, just in time to start the five back-to-back interviews he had scheduled.

The week before, Jason had placed want ads for a legal assistant in the bar association newsletter and local paper. Of the first three candidates, only one had any legal experience, and that was twelve years of real estate closings. One of the three candidates tried way too hard, giggling incessantly, the second had the personality of a tree stump, and the third, the one with real estate experience, spent too much time asking about disability, sick leave, and personal days. "I can't work weekends or evenings," she said, as if the job were already hers.

You won't have to worry about that, Jason thought.

The fourth candidate, Tami Pershing, walked off the cover of *Runway* magazine and into Jason's small conference room, rendering him speechless. She wore a short skirt and tight-fitting sweater and looked Jason right in the eye when they shook hands. Even factoring in the heels, she must have been nearly six feet tall.

Tami had an associate's degree and had just moved to Virginia Beach, she explained. She had no legal experience but Jason immediately began downplaying that factor. "Join the club," he joked. "We can learn together."

The practice of law, Jason knew, was grueling. Having someone like Tami in the office would give him some incentive to get there early. Plus, male clients wouldn't mind waiting a few extra minutes in the reception area.

He got Tami's basic information—experience as an assistant, typing speed, computer skills, etc. She didn't have any of the fatal personality flaws of the earlier applicants—and even if she did, Jason was now grading on a curve, so to speak.

"What brings you to Virginia Beach?" Jason asked.

"My boyfriend's a fighter pilot," Tami responded. "He just got stationed at Oceana."

It wasn't exactly the response Jason would have scripted, but as a lawyer, he was used to looking for loopholes. *Boyfriend,* she had said. Not *fiancé* or *husband*. She wasn't wearing an engagement ring. And she hadn't automatically dismissed working nights and weekends. He wouldn't *try* to break up a solid relationship, but sometimes things just happened.

Tami's forty-five minutes seemed to go much faster than the previous applicants, confirming that she was the best choice so far. They were talking about how much they both liked the beach and how they couldn't wait for the weather to warm up when they were interrupted by the next applicant.

A short lady, heavyset with thinning blonde hair and hound-dog eyes, peeked around the corner of the conference room door that Jason had left open. "I'm Bella Harper," she said in an Brooklyn accent that sounded like something from *My Cousin Vinny*. "I was supposed to meet with Jason Noble."

"That's me," Jason said. "Have a seat in the reception area; we'll be done in just a minute."

Five minutes later, Jason and Tami wrapped it up. Jason escorted her out to the reception area, introduced Tami to Bella, and was struck by the contrast. Tami handled herself with the elegance of a model—straight posture, easy smile, a "nice to meet you" greeting. She towered over Bella, who was slump-shouldered and stiff in her movements, her reading glasses hanging from a lanyard around her neck.

"Good thing these aren't volleyball tryouts," Bella joked.

Tami gave her a quizzical expression and a curious smile. Then Jason saw a glint of mischief in Tami's eyes. "Oh," she said, her face reflecting surprise. "You thought I was interviewing to be Jason's assistant."

Jason watched Bella, who seemed to have lost a little of her color.

"He's my boyfriend," Tami said.

Before Jason knew what was happening, Tami reached over and squeezed Jason's arm. "See you later, honey," she said, and gave Jason a quick peck on the cheek.

"Okay, thanks," Jason said, reddening. "See you tonight."

He turned to Bella Harper, who was looking at him with a curious expression. "Let's talk in my conference room," Jason said.

His BlackBerry buzzed, and the number on the screen belonged to Andrew Lassiter. "Give me just a minute," Jason said to Bella. He answered the phone and wandered down the hall to his new office, closing the door behind him.

He wanted to get Lassiter involved in the Crawford case as early as possible. They had already negotiated a consulting agreement. "Can you come to Virginia Beach and watch the video of Melissa Davids's deposition?" Jason asked. "She's a little difficult to coach. It might help get her attention for trial prep if we could show her the reactions of a few Virginia Beach focus groups."

◁▷

Jason had intended to make it a quick interview, but Bella wasn't cooperating. She had nearly thirty years' experience as a legal assistant, knew about all the courts and procedures in the Hampton Roads area, possessed superior typing and filing skills, and even knew how to keep the financial records required for trust accounts and operating expenses. "Mr. Carson didn't need to hire a bookkeeper for the first five years," she said proudly.

It would be nice, Jason thought, to hire Tami as a receptionist and let Bella to do the grunt work. But he couldn't afford two staff members just yet.

He studied Bella's résumé. She had jumped around when she first entered the workforce, but the last twenty years had all been at one firm. "Why did you leave Carson and Associates?" Jason asked.

"Brad Carson is probably the best lawyer in this area," Bella said defensively, as if Jason had just insulted the man's character. Her face changed expressions, and Jason thought he noticed her get a little misty-eyed. "I was with him when he started. But lately, well . . . um, to be honest, he brought in a hotshot young lawyer who thinks she's God's gift to the legal profession, and, well, we just fought constantly, and I finally decided it was time for one of us to move on."

"Does he know you're interviewing?" Jason inquired.

"No. He'd probably try to talk me into coming back. He's very persuasive, and I love him like a son, but I . . . well, you know."

Jason didn't know, but figured he probably shouldn't probe any deeper. Bella had about thirty years on Tami in the experience department. But Bella was brusque and seemed to be a little emotional. And Tami had already proven herself to be pretty quick-witted.

"Thanks for coming in and meeting with me today," Jason said. "I'm going to take a couple of days to think about this and then get back in touch with everyone."

Bella didn't move.

"Should be no later than Thursday or Friday," Jason said, standing. "Should I use this e-mail that's on your résumé?"

"Can I be frank?" Bella asked.

Jason gave her a twist of the head, a nonverbal cue that the answer was no. But what came out of his mouth was, "Sure."

"You do a lousy interview, Mr. Noble. But then again, there are lots of questions you probably can't ask without getting sued."

Jason stiffened. At least she was making his choice easy. The last thing he needed to deal with every day was a brash New Yorker.

"I'm single," Bella said. "I work weekends and nights. I might complain about it, because that's what I do, but I really don't even mind getting your dry cleaning.

"You seem like a nice young man and probably need somebody in the office to play the bad cop. That just happens to be my specialty. That, and collecting fees. With all due modesty, if it wasn't for yours truly, Brad Carson would have been bankrupt about three times over by now."

Jason stared for a moment and, sensing she wasn't done with her sales pitch, sat back down.

"You just moved here from Richmond, right?" Bella asked.

"Right."

"Ever spent much time in Florida?"

Though he wasn't used to the interviewees asking the questions, Jason decided to play along. "Not really."

"Didn't think so." Bella leaned forward. "Your . . . *girlfriend*—" Bella made quote marks with her fingers—"drove away in a car with Florida plates. I watched out the window while you were back in your office on the phone because I had my suspicions. Now, she's obviously pretty clever, and she's got other . . . *assets* that I don't have, but what does she know about client trust accounts and generally accepted accounting principles and drafting pretrial orders for Virginia Beach Circuit Court?"

Now it was Jason's turn to be a little embarrassed. He gave Bella a tight-lipped and sheepish smile. *Busted.*

"Plus," Bella said, "you've got to wonder whether a girl who dresses like that knows anything about guns and the Second Amendment." She glanced around and lowered her voice. "I'm packing," she said conspiratorially. "It's not one of MD Firearms's guns, but I've got a concealed carry."

Jason wasn't really sure how that struck him. Something about the idea of the firm secretary carting around a gun in her handbag was a little unsettling.

Bella bent over and reached into her massive handbag. "Don't worry," she said. "I'm not going for the gun."

She pulled out two manila folder files and placed them on the table. The first one was labeled "research" and the other "deposition summary."

"I took the liberty of pulling a few Virginia cases on issues like superseding cause and the definition of 'aiding and abetting,' since that's the language of the exception to the Protection of Lawful Commerce in Arms Act," Bella explained. "This second folder is a deposition summary with page citations for Melissa Davids's deposition yesterday. I know the court reporter. She sent me a digital file."

Jason knew it was important to have depositions accurately summarized so that the lawyers could have easy access to a witness's prior testimony. Summarizing a six-hour deposition could easily take three hours or more.

He leafed through the folders. "Impressive," he said.

"Now," Bella said, "can we talk health plans?"

A fleeting image of Tami Pershing made one last dramatic run through Jason's mind. It was tempting, but he had a duty to his clients. With Bella in the office, there would be no distractions, no office romance, no drama. The thought of it made him a little melancholy.

"When can you start?" Jason asked.

45

KELLY SLEPT VERY LITTLE on Tuesday night. On Wednesday morning, she spent a little extra time on makeup, lipstick, accessories, and what she should wear, but still she was unable to remove all evidence of the dark circles that had formed under her eyes. After three outfit changes, appraising herself in the mirror each time, she settled on a modest gray suit and matching silver earrings. She chastised herself for caring at all about how she looked. When was the last time she had stressed out this much over which outfit to wear?

It seemed fitting that the day was one of the coldest and windiest of the entire D.C. winter. Banks of clouds blocked a sun that seemed to have lost all its heat in those rare moments when it did break free.

Kelly's car was parked nearly a block from her apartment—the price of getting home late from the office the night before. She buttoned the top button on her overcoat and pulled up the collar, but her face still stung from the biting wind by the time she reached the shelter of her Toyota.

She arrived at the federal courthouse about fifteen minutes early, carrying a thin briefcase as if she had an important motion to argue. She slid into the last row of benches in Judge Shaver's courtroom and watched him preside over a discovery dispute between two experienced litigators. His eyes caught hers momentarily, a greeting so subtle it would have been lost on anyone else, and then he turned his attention back to the proceedings.

His face was still square and handsome with the perpetual five-o'clock shadow that Kelly had always found alluring. He had a touch of gray around the temples and wore half-moon reading glasses that were a new addition since the days of Kelly's clerkship. The glasses alone added ten years to his face.

She could remember watching him seven years ago presiding over cases, the aphrodisiac of power weaving its spell. She could still recall, with no small amount of shame, how she had marveled at the thought of being a confidant to a man this powerful. Lawyers would jump through hoops to curry favor with him, yet the judge would ask Kelly, in the solitude of his car in front of her apartment, how she thought the most important cases on his docket should come out. They normally saw things the same way, so much so that Kelly had convinced herself they might have been soul mates under different circumstances. A different time. A different place. A younger and unmarried Judge Shaver.

Her standards had been raised just by being around him.

She tried to remember when her guilt about the two of them spending so much time together had left her. That was the problem with this type of thing—it was all so gradual. There was no single defining moment, although the night she learned about his wife's affair was surely a turning point. From then on, Kelly no longer felt she was breaking up a marriage. The ugly truth was that the marriage had been over long before Kelly arrived on the scene.

How long had it been after that night? A week? Two weeks? Events blurred together between the night of their first touch and the night he asked to come in. Somehow, she had known he was going to ask that night. She had promised herself that she would say no, but she had cleaned the apartment anyway. At the time, it all just seemed so natural, one emotion leading to the next, the excited beat of her own heart, the judge's sensitivity. They talked for a half hour, and Kelly knew he wasn't going to leave.

She didn't want him to leave. They both knew how it was going to end.

When he leaned over to kiss her, she closed her eyes and didn't resist. Later that evening, she took his hand and led him to the bedroom.

When he left at midnight, guilt arrived in waves.

He must have been able to read her face the next morning. He called her into his office, shut the door, and told her that the night before had been the most incredible night of his life.

"It was wrong," Kelly said in response. "We both know it. We can never let it happen again."

He looked devastated. "Are you sure about this, Kelly?" He was thinking about a future together. Somehow, he would make it work.

It had taken every ounce of moral fiber she had left, but Kelly did not let him dissuade her. She could still picture it clearly in her mind—the look on his face, his quiet pleading, his apologies, and ultimately his pledge to accept her decision.

To his credit, the judge never raised the issue again during her clerkship.

She began taking the Metro. They never spent another unguarded moment alone together. Judge Shaver treated her with professional courtesy and worked hard at rehabilitating his own marriage.

Two years later, he had called. "They're talking about a spot on the Fourth Circuit again," he told Kelly.

"You deserve it," she had said. And she meant it.

"If I'm nominated, they'll do a careful vetting. They'll talk to all my former clerks, try to find out whether I've done anything that could be used to blackmail me. There's a chance they might ask about affairs."

The thought of it stunned Kelly. FBI agents asking questions about Judge Shaver's private life. The wrong answers could destroy his chances. "I can't lie, Judge."

"I know," he said softly. "I wouldn't ask you to lie."

"Then why did you call?"

The judge inhaled deeply on the other end of the phone. "Kelly, you know how sorry I am about what happened. Lynda and I are still together and trying hard to make it work. I'm just saying, anything you can do short of lying, I would really appreciate."

"Maybe you should pull your name," Kelly suggested. "Family reasons. Not wanting the spotlight. You like being a trial judge. There could be a million reasons."

Shaver didn't respond right away. "I know I could," he eventually said. "But Kelly, the things you and I believe in are the right things. The right causes. We need judges on our highest courts who are willing to stand up for the most vulnerable in our society. I can't sell them out just to save myself some potential embarrassment."

No longer blinded by her infatuation, the words sounded hollow. The president could find a hundred other judges who shared Shaver's judicial philosophy. This was about his ego, his opportunity to go as far as he could go.

"I'll do what I can," Kelly had said.

"That's all I can ask."

46

WHEN THE HEARING ENDED, Judge Shaver invited Kelly back to his chambers. He introduced her to his current clerks and waited while Kelly exchanged a few pleasantries with the judge's secretary. Kelly then followed the judge into his spacious chambers, where he took off his judicial robe and hung it on a coatrack.

"Can I take your coat?" he asked.

"I'm fine," Kelly said, though it was a little warm.

Shaver's chambers showed even less wear and tear than the judge himself. Paperwork was neatly stacked. The same pictures and diplomas adorned the walls. Even the kids' pictures on his desk looked like the same ones Kelly remembered from seven years ago. He had left his office door open, but his desk was on the other side of the massive office from the doorway. If they talked quietly, they wouldn't have to worry about being overheard.

The judge made the kind of conversation you might expect when a former clerk stops by. "How's the law practice? . . . I read that article about you in the *Post*. . . . Interesting case you're handling against that gun company. . . ." Etc., etc.

Kelly responded politely, asking her own softball questions. Judge Shaver expected the confirmation hearings to start in a few weeks or maybe months. It was hard to predict. "This is the third time my name's been floated but the first time I've made it this far," he said. "I'm hoping the third time's the charm."

"Me, too."

The judge leaned forward and softened his voice. "Thanks for what you did with the FBI."

It was a tone that used to give Kelly goose bumps. Today, she just left the comment hanging. She reached into her briefcase and retrieved the e-mail from Luthor.

"We've got a problem, Judge. This showed up in my inbox last week."

She watched Judge Shaver put on his reading glasses, his face darkening as he read the e-mail. He placed the letter on his desk and stared at it.

"Who knows about us?" he asked.

"If by that you mean, 'Whom did I tell?' the answer is no one."

"I wasn't accusing you, Kelly. I'm just trying to think this through."

Kelly looked down at the desk. There was something she had never shared with the judge, preferring to shoulder the pain on her own. She had dealt with it, condemned herself for what she had done, and then willed herself to forget about it and move on.

"I was pregnant," Kelly said. She swallowed, her voice suddenly thick. "I took the RU-486 pill five weeks later."

She glanced up at the judge and saw nothing but sympathy on his face. She tried to continue, stopped, pulled herself together, and started again. "I went to a clinic and got a prescription. They guided me through the process and had me return to the clinic the day the abortion occurred for some counseling and observation." She blew out a deep breath. "I expelled the fetus at home. But half a dozen people at the clinic probably know."

Saying it out loud brought back a rush of emotions and images. At the time, Kelly had worked hard not to think about the implications, knowing she would probably talk herself out of what she felt she had to do. She took the initial dose of RU-486 at the clinic and suffered through a few hours of nausea, headache, and fatigue. For the next forty-eight hours, she walked around like a zombie, trying not to focus on what she had done.

She took the Cytotec pill at home and a few hours later began to dilate. According to the information she had read, the fetus would be tiny at this stage, about half an inch or so. She made it a point not to look before she flushed the toilet.

She was businesslike when she returned to the clinic for observation. But she fell apart when she returned to her apartment, sobbing deep into the night. Just before dawn, emotionally exhausted and weak with grief, she had finally collapsed into a fitful sleep.

Weeks later, she couldn't keep herself from researching fetal development. She'd even looked at a few pictures on the Internet. At five weeks old, tiny arm and leg buds would have been formed. The baby's tiny heart would have been beating. The image of the fetus was burned into her mind.

"I'm so sorry," Judge Shaver said. "I had no idea."

He got up from his chair and walked over to close his office door. Then he sat down again and handed Kelly some Kleenex.

"I just wanted to deal with it on my own," Kelly said. "I wanted to get my life back on track."

She pressed her lips together and held back the tears, watching the recognition dawn on the judge's face. This wasn't just his and Kelly's word against the world. Somewhere there was proof that Kelly had been pregnant.

Kelly had spent the last few days wondering how he would react. Would he question whether the baby was his? be angry at her for not telling him? go immediately into damage-control mode?

She saw none of those calculations in his eyes. Just an overwhelming sadness and an almost palpable sense of sympathy.

"I can't believe you had to go through that alone," Judge Shaver said. He paused, searching for words. "I can't change the past, Kelly. I wish I could . . . but I can't do anything about that. The thing I *can* do is keep you from suffering any more. It's not too late to withdraw my name."

She appreciated the offer, but he wasn't thinking this through. "That won't really change anything, Judge. If the press gets hold of this, they'll still run the story to explain why you withdrew. The coverage might not be as intense, but it would be out there just the same. My statements to the FBI have already been made. Everyone we care about would be hurt. Your family. My family."

Judge Shaver nodded solemnly. She was right, and he knew it.

For a second, Kelly was struck with the irony of it—this man who had so mesmerized her with his Solomonic wisdom a few years ago now seemed so overwhelmed. It was amazing how love—or was it just passion?—had destroyed her objectivity and neutered her common sense.

For Kelly's part, she had steeled herself for whatever lay ahead. A part of her just wanted this whole thing out in the open—the secrets that haunted her finally revealed. Maybe on the other side of humiliation she would find liberation. But the thought of disappointing everyone who mattered most held her back.

"I need to play this out a little," Kelly said, trying to sound more confident than she really was. "Dance with this guy for a while. See if he makes a mistake. Maybe I can represent my client zealously and still figure out who Luthor is before the case goes to trial."

Shaver looked skeptical. "There's a lot at risk here," he said.

"Tell me about it."

47

BEFORE SHE LEFT her condo Friday morning, Kelly checked the Kryptonite blog one last time. Though her blackmailer's threat had been very specific—exposure of her affair *only if* she settled the case—she still couldn't keep from obsessively monitoring the site.

The blog seemed to consolidate everything evil about the Internet in one URL. For starters, it was a vicious rumor site, populated by sordid stories attributed to unnamed sources. The comments were smarmy and full of vulgarity. It was basically a place to verbally tar and feather defenseless public figures based on either pure speculation or the flimsiest evidence imaginable.

Kelly breathed a sigh of relief every time she checked the latest post and saw that it wasn't about her. Her fears were compounded by what she had learned in the past few months about the public-relations aspects of gun control. The mainstream media would be her ally. The "intellectual elites," as the right-wingers called them, generally believed that the country's fascination with guns was unhealthy, that its frontier mentality was a bad thing. Civilized countries, like those model democracies in Europe, solved their disputes with clever editorials and dueling political philosophies, not guns at high noon.

But the "flyover zones" were filled with rabid gun enthusiasts. Many of the ordinary folks in battleground states lost all sense of objectivity when the government made noises about controlling firearms. Kelly had already seen a little of that fury in the e-mails she had received and the letters to the editor that mentioned her name. If word about her affair ever hit the press, she would be red meat for a pack of Second Amendment wolves.

The fickle media would probably abandon her as well. She would be like a pup-tent camper in the middle of a hurricane, exposed to its destructive fury with nowhere to turn.

Today's Kryptonite story, thankfully, was about the latest political sex scandal. In the few days she had been checking the blog, Kelly had noticed a definite pattern. Political stories focused on sex and corruption. For movie stars, the stories were about sex and drugs. For rock stars, who were expected to be stoned and promiscuous, Kryptonite trotted out the really bizarre accusations, accompanied by unflattering photos of the stars looking either bulimic or severely overweight.

And then the "fans" would crucify them.

The common denominator to all the stories was sex. It wasn't lost on Kelly that her escapade with Judge Shaver certainly fit the profile.

Kelly read a few comments, said a prayer of thanks that it wasn't her turn yet, and started to get ready for work. The gossip rag sheets could wait. Today would be the crucial deposition of Jarrod Beeson.

◁▷

Beeson's deposition started at 1 p.m. in a dingy conference room in the Patrick Henry Correctional Unit near Martinsville, Virginia. The site was a minimum security facility that housed about 150 inmates. It was classified in the Virginia system as Level 1 High Security, not a country-club prison but also a far cry from the types of places where violent felons served long stretches.

Because of the difficulties associated with having Beeson transported to Virginia Beach for the trial, Kelly and Jason had agreed that this would be a *de bene esse* deposition, meaning it could be used at trial in lieu of Beeson himself appearing.

Kelly knew that Beeson would be dressed in an orange jumpsuit and look like a felon, so she had ordered only a court reporter and not a videographer. That way, the deposition would be read to the jury, but they wouldn't be watching a static head shot of a guilty-looking Beeson on videotape. Unfortunately, Jason Noble had anticipated this move and paid for his own videographer, determined to show Jarrod to the Virginia Beach jury.

Beeson had an unnerving stare as he answered Kelly's questions. He was a small man with thick black eyebrows that nearly touched in the middle and short, wiry facial hair covering his chin and jaw. His leg was in constant jittery motion, and he leaned forward as he talked, eyes glued on Kelly, as if he couldn't get enough of her. She wanted to tell him to look at the camera, but she knew Jason would object and accuse her of coaching the witness, thereby drawing more attention to Beeson's creepy demeanor.

Kelly got through her preliminary questions without incident. Beeson had purchased a total of twenty-three guns from Peninsula Arms. When the ATF agents carried out a search warrant at his apartment, they had found only three of those guns remaining, along with a fourth gun that had its serial number filed off.

Under questioning by the ATF agents, Beeson had cracked, admitting that he was acting as a straw purchaser for felons and others who couldn't buy guns on their own. Two of the guns he had purchased had been traced to violent crimes. One of them was the MD-9 used by Larry Jamison to kill Rachel Crawford.

That part of his testimony was undisputed. The key would be showing that the clerks at Peninsula Arms knew Beeson was a straw purchaser who would resell the guns to unqualified buyers.

"How did you get your customers?" Kelly asked. "How did you learn about men who needed guns but couldn't purchase them on their own?"

"Objection, calls for hearsay," Jason said.

Jason had been sitting back during most of the deposition, watching more like a bemused spectator than an attorney. He had shown up in jeans and a long-sleeved pullover, knowing that he wouldn't be on camera. It was also, Kelly realized, a subtle form of psychological warfare. *This witness isn't worth dressing up for.*

"It's a deposition," Kelly responded. "Hearsay is allowed."

"I'm just preserving my objection for trial, where hearsay is most definitely *not* allowed."

"You can answer," Kelly told the witness. "Mr. Noble is just objecting for the record."

"How did I get my customers?" Beeson snorted. "The gun store sent 'em to me. I didn't go looking for 'em."

"Move that the remarks be struck from the record," Jason said, his voice monotone, as if it was hardly worth the bother. "There's no foundation for that other than hearsay."

"Let's talk about *this* sale," Kelly suggested. "The MD-9 used to gun down Rachel Crawford. When did you first learn that Larry Jamison needed a gun?"

"Objection. Hearsay."

Kelly blew out a breath and looked at Jason. "Why don't you just make an objection to this whole line of questioning and quit interrupting every single question?"

Jason gave her a tight smile. "Thanks for the suggestion. But I think I'll try my own case."

"That dude Jamison called me," Beeson said, not waiting for a prompt. "He said he tried to buy a gun at Peninsula Arms but didn't pass the background check. Said the clerk at the gun store gave him my number."

"Move to strike," Jason said. "Hearsay."

Kelly shot him a look.

"Did he say which clerk sent him to you?" Kelly asked.

"Objection. Hearsay again."

Give it a rest!

"Nah," Beeson said. "It didn't matter."

"Had this happened before? Ineligible gun buyers calling you and saying they were referred by the store?"

This time Jason snorted at the question. "Let's see," he said. "Hearsay—actually double hearsay—leading the witness, relevance . . . Am I missing anything?"

"You mean other than that class in law school where they teach you to reserve your objections until trial?" Kelly asked.

"Tell you what," Jason said, his tone friendly. "You stop asking objectionable questions, and I'll stop objecting."

Kelly shook her head. In the past five years, she had learned her deposition lessons the hard way—don't let the men push you around. Always get the last word. "It's a shame," she said, "that the rookie has to learn how to practice law on my case."

Beeson chuckled. "Man, I wouldn't mess with her," he said to Jason.

The squabbling continued for several more questions until Kelly got back on solid ground. The phone conversation was only one way of showing that the clerks at Peninsula Arms knew this was a straw purchase. The other was the transaction itself.

According to Beeson, he and Larry Jamison had entered the store together. Jamison had talked with the clerk and inspected the firearms while Beeson looked on. Once Jamison selected the gun, Beeson and Jamison went outside the store, and the money changed hands—the cost of the gun and a 50 percent "handling fee." Beeson went back inside on his own and purchased the gun, gave it to Jamison in the parking lot, and never saw the man again.

It was, Kelly thought, as good a place as any to end the testimony. Beeson wasn't the best witness, but Kelly didn't get to pick them. She already knew how she would explain it in her closing argument.

"Boy Scouts don't participate in the gunrunning business. The other people who know how this transaction occurred are either dead or taking the Fifth. We don't pick the witnesses, ladies and gentlemen, we just put them on the stand.

"But is he telling the truth? Consider this—Beeson's confession earned him a twelve-month prison sentence. What human being lies so that he can spend a year of his life behind bars?"

48

JASON WAS IN FULL ACTING MODE NOW. He was so nervous he could feel his heart pounding against his chest. Nevertheless, he pushed his nerves aside and adopted a condescending air, an acerbic tone.

Jarrod Beeson was scum. It was important that every part of Jason's cross-examination deliver that message.

"You seem to be mighty friendly with Ms. Starling," Jason said. "Have you rehearsed your testimony?"

"Objection," Kelly snapped. "That question completely mischaracterizes the witness's demeanor."

"I thought we were saving our objections for trial," Jason said.

"Just ask your questions."

"Well," Jason said thoughtfully, "let's probe it a little bit. Have you been sued by Ms. Starling?"

"Maybe. I dunno."

Jason smiled. When witnesses tried to play it coy, it only hurt their credibility. "Okay, let me help you. Have you been served with any official-looking legal documents while you've been sitting in jail—documents that demand you pay Rachel Crawford's husband a lot of money?"

"No."

"Then let's assume you haven't been sued."

"I'll save you the trouble," Kelly said, her voice curt. "I didn't sue him because he's penniless. It would be a waste of time."

Jason pondered this for a minute. He could tell he was getting under Kelly's skin. She was a good lawyer, but she took everything personally. Maybe he could exploit that. "Will you also stipulate that you didn't sue the gun store because they're in bankruptcy?"

"That's got nothing to do with this deposition," Kelly said.

"Or how about the fact that you sued my client because they seem to be the only ones that do have money?"

Kelly turned to the court reporter. "Strike that from the record," she said. Then back to Jason. "Are you going to ask this witness questions, or do you just want to pick a fight?"

"All right." Jason turned back to Beeson. "Do you know Melissa Davids?"

"No."

"Have you ever talked to *anybody* who works at my client's company, MD Firearms?"

"You mean other than the gun store clerks?"

"Nice try. But they don't work for us. I mean anybody actually employed by MD Firearms?"

"Don't think so."

"And when you illegally buy these guns for criminals, you don't always buy guns manufactured by MD Firearms, do you?"

Even Beeson knew he couldn't deny this one. The records were clear. "No. Though most felons seem to like that MD-9."

Nice touch. Jason gave Beeson a quick smile and reminded himself not to get sloppy. "In fact, some of your straw purchases were at stores other than Peninsula Arms, correct?"

"If you say so."

"Do you need to see the receipts?"

"Nah. I believe you."

Jason paused. He knew that periods of silence could sometimes help refocus the attention of the jury. "Then let me ask you this question: If for some reason MD Firearms had decided to no longer sell guns to Peninsula Arms, you could have bought a different gun for Jamison, or you could have gone to a different store and bought the MD-9 there—right?"

Kelly let out a frustrated sigh. "That calls for speculation."

"And so does your lawsuit," countered Jason. He honed in on Beeson. "You need to answer the question. The judge will rule later as to whether the jury will hear it."

"Can you repeat it again?" Beeson asked. It seemed to Jason like he was trying to buy time.

Jason had the court reporter read back the question and Beeson's face went from concern to triumph—a dull math student finally understanding the formula.

"Maybe," Beeson said. "But I would have never known that Jamison existed if Peninsula Arms hadn't sent him to me."

"Which is all hearsay," Jason said. "The only person who told you that Peninsula Arms was involved in referring Jamison to you was Jamison himself; isn't that right?"

"Objection. Asked and answered."

"Do I answer again anyway?" Beeson asked, looking at Kelly.

She nodded.

"That's right," Beeson said. "Jamison told me. And it might be a little hard to cross-examine him."

◁▷

As Kelly was leaving the prison, Jason held the door for her. After two hours of fighting tooth and nail, she wanted to tell him he could dispense with the Southern gentleman charade. Instead, she found herself saying thanks. But when he tried to civilly discuss scheduling dates for other depositions and discovery matters, she blew him off. "Call me at the office," she said. "It's been a long day."

"Can I buy you a cup of coffee?"

Kelly stopped and looked at him. *The audacity.* "No, thanks." She knew she should probably let it go at that. Jason was young. He was good at depositions, but he obviously had a few things to learn about life. "This isn't Ralph Wolf and Sam Sheepdog," Kelly said. "Try to kill each other all day, punch a clock, wish each other a pleasant evening."

Jason looked a little stunned, but Kelly was just getting started. "Your client pumps useless semi-automatic assault weapons into the black market and turns its back while people die. My client has to live the rest of his life without a soul mate. I know you're just doing your job, but it doesn't mean I have to like it."

Jason stood there for a second, taking it all in. "Okay," he said. "All right, I get that. But did I mention the coffee's on me?"

Kelly sighed. It was hard to stay mad when he wouldn't fight back. "Call me at the office," she said. She turned and headed toward her car, hiding the faintest hint of a smile.

"Drive safe," Jason called out.

Was he playing mind games with her, or was he really that clueless?

49

BELLA HARPER, it turned out, had an opinion on everything. Between smoking breaks, lecturing Jason on how to run a law office, and organizing everything in sight, she also tried to get Jason's spiritual life squared away. She talked about her own dramatic conversion to Christianity just a few short years ago and how much it had changed her. "Maybe not in the smoking department," she admitted. "But everything else."

Jason must have given her a sideways look, because she immediately read his mind. "You think I'm bossy now? You should have seen me before."

Jason had a hard time imagining how it could have been any worse. Bella was overbearing, but he would tolerate it because she got the job done.

The last week or so, they had been in an unspoken who-can-get-to-work-first race. Jason came in at 8:30 on Monday. Instead of welcoming him to the office, Bella said she had been worried that maybe he was taking the day off and forgot to tell her. On Tuesday, he arrived at 8:00 to find Bella at her desk with the coffee made. Wednesday, it was 7:45. When he arrived at 6:30 on Friday only to find Bella on her first smoke break, Jason threw in the towel.

"Are you sleeping here?" he asked. "Let's talk about setting some reasonable office hours."

They were out on the front stoop. It was dark, cold, and windy.

Bella took a puff on her cigarette and blew the smoke away from Jason. "You're the one sending out e-mails at one in the morning. Pot, meet kettle."

Jason smiled. "Maybe we're not exactly good for each other's workaholism," he admitted. "Maybe we should both take a day off once in a while."

"Yeah, like maybe Sunday. Go to church together."

"Nice try," Jason said. The invitation had become a running gag. Jason was careful not to disrespect Bella's faith but made it clear that he really wasn't interested. Bella had nevertheless declared her intention to drag him to church with her someday, kicking and screaming if necessary. She had already tried every angle, including telling Jason about all the single young women who attended.

"Okay, I might need a little assistance in the religion department," Jason had said. "But I definitely don't need your help in the dating department."

"Right," Bella said. "I forgot about that steady stream of bachelorettes beating down your door. Hard to know how you keep them all straight."

Jason gave her his best I'm-the-boss-and-I'm-not-happy look.

She threw up her palms. "I get it. I mean, not really, but I hear ya."

"Okay, thanks."

Jason thought the conversation was over and started walking away. But something about Bella's facial expression stopped him. She looked sheepish, a look he hadn't seen from her before.

"What is it?" he asked.

Bella grimaced. It was obvious she was holding out on him.

"Bella?"

"If you get a call from *Beach Weekly* about their ten most eligible bachelors edition . . ." She stopped and braced for the reaction. "I sent that in before we had this conversation. So don't get all huffy on me."

◁▷

The call came when Kelly was waiting in line for lunch at the small deli on the ground floor of her building. Judge Shaver's cell phone.

"Hey, Judge," Kelly said. She tried to sound natural, but her heart was in her throat. Shaver wouldn't call unless it was very important. "Can I call you right back?"

"How long?" Shaver asked.

"A minute. Literally."

"Okay."

Kelly paid for her lunch, carried her tray to a table, and left it there. She looked for a private spot in the lobby. There were people milling around, and the granite floors created an echo. She decided to step outside, even without her winter coat, in the middle of February. She figured the call wouldn't take long.

Shaver answered on the first ring. "Just wanted to follow up on our meeting the other day," he said blithely. "Thanks for stopping by."

His tone, Kelly knew, was intended to send its own message: Be careful what you say; someone might be listening.

"Thanks for asking about the confirmation hearings," he continued. "And for asking my advice about settlement."

Kelly had not, of course, sought any such advice. The man was sending her some kind of signal, being careful so that his choice of words wouldn't haunt him later.

"The politicians are working on a compromise for judicial nominations. They say my hearings could start as early as next month, or it could be as long as three or four months."

"That's a pretty big window," Kelly responded, running the timetables in her head. Either way, it would probably happen before the start of her trial.

"Yeah. Quite a system," Shaver said. "I'm so frustrated with the whole process, I'm thinking about just withdrawing my name."

Kelly had been walking down the sidewalk, trying to keep warm. She was drawing a fair number of looks. The tension and the frigid air made her voice tremble a little. "Hang in there, Judge. You've come this far; don't back out now."

Kelly had thought this through from every angle. If Shaver withdrew his name, it wouldn't solve many of her problems. Luthor would still have his blackmail threats, though the story about the affair wouldn't have quite the same national appeal. Still, Kelly's friends and family would all find out about it.

"Yes, well, for the time being I'm content to see where it heads. But I like being a trial judge. I do wonder sometimes whether this whole process is worth it."

There was a momentary silence, as if Shaver was waiting for some type of coded message in response. It would have been easier just to meet with the man, but Kelly could understand why he didn't want to take that risk.

"Changing subjects," Shaver said, "I've been thinking about that gun case you mentioned and the advice I gave you about settlement. One thing I've been asking myself is who would benefit if you went to trial. It seems to me that two very different groups benefit. The Handgun Violence Coalition, the group that referred you the case, would benefit because this case will generate a lot of donations.

"The second group that would benefit is the NRA and its allies. Think about it. What they need is a villain to help them raise cash, a boogeyman that threatens to disarm all of America. Trial lawyers in general—and you in particular—fit that role very nicely. So these advocacy groups benefit handsomely if the case goes to trial. But Kelly . . ."

"Yes, Your Honor."

"Your role is to ignore them. Your only role is to do what's best for your client."

"Yes, sir," Kelly said.

There were no settlement discussions on the table, so from that perspective, the judge's comments were all nonsense. But it didn't take a rocket scientist to decode the message. Shaver thought Kelly was being blackmailed by the Handgun Violence Coalition or one of the NRA's allies. Both groups certainly had financial incentives to see this case tried, but how would either of them have learned about the affair?

"In any event, how's the case going?" Judge Shaver asked.

Kelly kept it short and sweet; after all, it was freezing outside. She headed back toward the warmth of the building lobby, explaining her frustrations with the deposition of Jarrod Beeson and other aspects of the case. Shaver listened politely but was careful not to give her any legal advice.

After they hung up, Kelly hustled back inside the lobby of her building. She took a deep breath, rubbed her freezing arms, and ran through the conversation in her mind.

The whole phone call felt strangely off-kilter. She'd heard paranoia in Shaver's voice. He'd even made a second offer to pull his name from nomination in hopes that all this might somehow go away.

But it wouldn't.

His references to settlement made Kelly even more leery. Shaver had made it clear that Kelly should do what was best for her client. Yes, he had been sending signals about who he thought might be the blackmailers, but this phone call, if it had been recorded, would be Shaver's Exhibit A to show that he had urged Kelly not to give in to the blackmailer. *If it's in the best interest of your client you should settle*—or words to that effect.

He didn't *need* to say that. Kelly had already told him she was not going to let Luthor dictate what she should do on this case. But now Judge Shaver had made a special phone call to go on record distancing himself from Kelly's decision.

It felt vaguely like a setup, as if Shaver was trying to keep her mollified yet at the same time separate himself from her decisions. If Kelly tried to say that the judge had urged her not to settle in order to keep their affair a secret, he would just trot out this phone call as evidence to the contrary.

It was clever and subtle, but she saw right through it. Judge Shaver didn't trust her. He was trying to erect a wall of separation between her decisions on the case and their adulterous relationship.

In the world of D.C. politics, it was, as usual, every man for himself.

50

FOR JASON NOBLE AND ANDREW LASSITER, it was almost like old times.

But not quite.

The air between them was noticeably chillier now—not quite see-your-breath chilly but not exactly warm bayou nights either—as they sat together in Jason's conference room and watched the videotaped depositions of Melissa Davids and Jarrod Beeson. There was an unspoken acknowledgment that Jason had not stepped up for Andrew when Justice Inc. had done Andrew wrong. That pall hung over their meeting, though both men were too reserved or stubborn to talk about it.

While he watched the depositions, Andrew toyed with a number of spreadsheets on his computer, tweaking the characteristics they wanted for their model jurors. He would need to do some focus groups to test his thinking, he told Jason, but he had researched the gun-control issue in the past.

They needed to avoid African American women and upper-class white women, according to Lassiter. No Democrats. Baptists and Pentecostals were fine; mainline Protestants were trouble. Catholics could go either way. Intellectual elites were disastrous—especially readers of *Atlantic Monthly* or the *New York Times.* Same for environmentalists unless they were avid hunters. Jason wanted folks who shopped at Kroger and Target, not Fresh Market and Nordstrom.

And Lassiter pointed out one other surprising correlation. Law enforcement personnel would side with the gun manufacturers 90 percent of the time.

"Why is that?" Jason asked.

"Most cops are firearms and hunting enthusiasts," Lassiter responded, blinking rapidly. "They believe that disarming honest citizens does nothing to reduce crime and might deprive those citizens of the means of self-defense."

During one of the breaks, while Lassiter was using the men's room, Jason wandered out to the reception area.

"That guy's *weird*," whispered Bella, loud enough to be heard down the hall.

"But very talented," Jason said in a much softer whisper, hoping that Bella would take the hint.

"He's got this blinking thing going on," she complained, her volume unaffected. "And he won't look you in the eye. When he was sitting over there waiting for you, he had the jitters like crazy."

"He's not trying the case, Bella. He's just helping pick the jury."

She shook her head, unconvinced. "Something's not right about him," she said, making a face.

Three hours later, Bella peeked into the conference room where Jason and Lassiter were still watching the videotaped depositions. "It's six o'clock," she said. "You need anything before I leave?"

"No, we're fine," Jason replied, his attention still on the monitor. But before Bella could turn to go, a thought hit him. He pressed pause.

"Bella, come here a minute." He handed her the transcript from Melissa Davids's deposition. "Pick out a question on any page," Jason said. "Andrew, let's see if you can guess the answer."

"There's no point in this," Andrew said.

"Just humor me. Bella, go ahead and pick out a question."

Bella and Andrew looked at Jason with matching frowns, but he wouldn't let it go. A frustrated Bella exhaled forcefully enough to move a small sailboat and turned to the middle of the deposition. "'Do you know what an illegal straw sale is?'" she asked, her tone registering her protest.

"'Of course,'" Andrew said.

Bella shot Jason a look, like she'd just seen an impressive card trick. "'Explain it to me,'" she read.

This time, Andrew stared at the wall for a moment and fluttered his eyelids. "'Is it my job to explain the law to her?'"

Jason smiled. He remembered the line from the deposition—and his own response. "You don't have to explain it," Jason said, "but it might help us get out of here."

"Actually," Andrew said, "your precise line was, 'Not really. But maybe if you do, we can get out of here faster.' Then Ms. Davids says, 'A straw purchase transaction is when an eligible purchaser of a firearm buys a gun on behalf of another person who is an ineligible purchaser of a firearm. Let's say, for example—'"

"All right," Bella said. "I get it. You can stop now. But let me just check something. . . ." Like a true skeptical New Yorker, she flipped through a few pages in the deposition and started reading again.

"'You're aware that the cities of New York, Washington, Baltimore, and Philadelphia have filed lawsuits against rogue gun dealers based on guns they sold that were later traced to crimes on the streets of those cities?'"

"'Yeah, I'm aware,'" said Andrew, playing the part of Melissa Davids. "'You want my opinion on those suits?'"

"'That won't be necessary.'"

"'Didn't think so.'"

"Wow." Bella shook her head, a converted skeptic. "How do you do that?"

Lassiter twitched and looked back to his computer program—game over. "I don't know. I've just always been able to remember things."

"Un-flippin'-believable," Bella said. "You oughta go on *Jeopardy!*"

"Thanks, I'll keep that in mind."

51

HIRING RAFAEL JOHANSEN was not Jason's idea. It had been suggested—no, it had been insisted on—by Andrew Lassiter. "What good is a micro-marketing program for selecting jurors if we don't know enough about their lifestyles to match them up?"

According to Lassiter, nobody could do a better job of providing detailed background information for prospective jurors than Rafael Johansen and his investigative team.

"I thought Rafael was employed by Justice Inc.," Jason said.

"Are you kidding? Robert Sherwood is not about to put Justice Inc. on the hook for Johansen's actions. Rafael works as an independent contractor. Sherwood gets all the dirt on the real jurors without ever having to know how it came into Johansen's greasy hands. Plausible deniability. Richard Nixon style."

Jason eventually agreed to bring Johansen on board but insisted on calling Robert Sherwood first. This caused a heated argument between Jason and Andrew Lassiter, but Jason was not about to back down. "If Sherwood has a problem with it, I'll find another investigator," Jason said.

"It's none of Sherwood's business," Andrew replied.

Jason called anyway and learned, much to his surprise, that Sherwood thought it was a superb idea. Jason got the impression that Sherwood was going to put a lot of money on Jason's side of the case and wanted to see Jason get all the help he needed. "Just be prepared," Sherwood warned. "He doesn't come cheap."

Jason's next call was to Case McAllister to obtain the client's approval. Everything was a go until they found out how much Johansen's services cost. After two days of phone negotiations, they finally talked Johansen into a billing rate of "only" $325 for himself and $200 for his associates. To Jason's chagrin, his jury investigator was now making more per hour than he was. To secure payment, Johansen required a $50,000 retainer.

Not surprisingly, Bella gave Johansen a cold reception when he showed up at the office a half hour late for his first meeting. He came decked out in black pants and a tight, black, long-sleeved pullover that showed off bulging pecs. His hard eyes and icy stare made everyone around him uncomfortable.

In his office, Jason explained the kind of information he would need for each potential juror and the types of reports he preferred. When he finished his spiel, he handed Johansen a two-page retainer agreement with the terms of the undertaking spelled out in detail.

Johansen looked at the agreement, snorted, and put it back on Jason's desk. "I don't do agreements," he said.

"Then we don't have a deal."

"Fine." Johansen stood and headed for the door.

"Wait," Jason said. The big man turned around, his face as emotionless as before. "We'll do it without a written contract," Jason offered.

Johansen nodded and returned to his seat. "I'm here because Robert Sherwood asked me to help. To me, you're just another punk lawyer getting paid a lot of money before you've proven anything in the courtroom." Johansen hardened his stare. "I'll do my job and get you the information you need. But I do it my way and that means we don't put anything in writing."

The venom caught Jason by surprise. He didn't expect to be Johansen's buddy, but he didn't appreciate being called a punk by a guy he had just hired at $325 an hour.

"Fair enough," Jason said brusquely. "Then let's put a few more things on the table. You work for me on this case. You don't call the client unless I give you permission. You don't do any investigative work unless I authorize it, and I want weekly reports on all your activities. Your primary responsibility will be compiling information for each potential juror. You'll be working directly with Andrew Lassiter." Jason sat back and let his demands hang in the tense air for a few seconds. Working with Johansen was going to be tiring. "Any questions?"

Johansen shrugged. "No."

"Then here's what I need done. . . ." For the next several minutes, Jason detailed the information he wanted on each jury member. He ignored Johansen's stare and pretended not to be bothered by the fact that Johansen didn't take a single note.

"I expect a trial date in June or July," Jason said, wrapping up. "We'll have a list of prospective jurors—there will probably be nearly a hundred of 'em—about a month prior."

"Is that it?" Johansen asked condescendingly.

"For now."

"You don't need me to investigate anybody else?"

"No, just the jurors."

"I see," Johansen said, nodding. "Then what do you want me to do with the information I've already got on the plaintiff, the plaintiff's attorney, and Judge Garrison?"

"What information?"

Johansen sneered. "Does that mean you want to hear it?"

"How about we quit playing games," Jason said. "If you've got information I need to know, let's have it."

Johansen crossed his legs and gave Jason a little smirk. "I thought maybe your curiosity would get the better of you. Let's start with the plaintiff."

Instinctively, Jason picked up a pen and jotted a heading on top of his legal pad. He was grinding his teeth, trying to prevent himself from saying something he might regret.

"What are you doing?" snapped Johansen.

"What do you mean?"

"No notes," demanded Johansen. "You don't take notes on this stuff."

Jason shook his head and put down his pen.

As far as Blake Crawford was concerned, it turned out to be much ado about nothing. A guy named Tony Morris, one of Johansen's top men, had followed Crawford around, managed to hack into a private e-mail account, discreetly asked questions of friends—"and used a few other techniques as well." The result? Crawford was squeaky clean. No affairs before his wife died; no female companions since. No Internet porn, no drugs, no financial shenanigans. According to Johansen, he was the male version of Mother Theresa. "Good luck ripping into him," Johansen said sarcastically.

But the judge . . . there were definitely rumors about the judge. There was talk about an affair with an assistant at his law firm nine or ten years ago. Some questionable rulings in favor of local developers with ties to his father. A young female defense attorney who never seemed to lose a motion in Garrison's courtroom.

Johansen certainly had Jason's attention now. The last thing Jason needed was a judge on the take. "Have you checked his finances since this case was filed?" Jason asked. "Any strange spikes in his standard of living?"

"Is that authorized?" Johansen said derisively "I thought I had strict orders to do only what I'm told."

"Just answer the question."

"The judge's standard of living and his known bank accounts have not changed in any dramatic way."

"Will you continue to monitor him?"

"Of course."

Jason contemplated this for a moment. Garrison had seemed to play it straight at the Motion to Dismiss hearing. Still, it couldn't hurt to keep an eye on him. Jason had no idea where Johansen got his information—didn't really want to know—but it was handy data nonetheless.

"What do you know about Kelly Starling?" Jason asked.

"I'm sure you're aware of her time at Justice Inc.," Johansen replied. "She was a good trial lawyer—tenacious, uncompromising, a true believer. She's done a lot of work with human trafficking victims in D.C. We did a thorough background check before she worked for us at Justice Inc. and found no skeletons in her closet. Nothing out of the ordinary during her last five years at B&W. Seems to be quite the workaholic with no time for romance. Typical Justice Inc. alum."

Jason asked a few more questions, but Johansen had little additional information. After Johansen left, Bella came in and wiped down his chair with disinfectant. It was an obvious ploy so that Jason would ask her opinion on the matter; therefore, Jason tried to ignore her altogether.

"The man's got issues," Bella said when it became obvious that Jason wasn't going to ask. "I know an investigator named O'Malley who could run circles around him."

"Thanks for your advice," Jason said.

"I'm just sayin'. . . . You wrestle with a pig, and you both get dirty. But only one of you likes it."

"Thanks for the cliché."

"I've got instincts," Bella said, throwing the paper towels she had used into Jason's trash can. "And that guy gives me the heebie-jeebies."

"Noted," Jason said. "Now, if you don't mind, I've got work to do on this brief."

52

THIS WAS THE LAST PLACE Kelly Starling wanted to be.

The Hillside Clinic was a nondescript medical facility with red brick, lots of glass, trim shrubs, and a small professional sign. It seemed so harmless and sterile. But as Kelly pulled into the parking lot, the memories came back with a debilitating vengeance, like someone had just ripped a fresh hole in her heart.

Kelly backed into a spot in the far corner of the lot and left the car running as she stared at the building.

She had read a few online journals written by other women who had taken the RU-486 pill and later spilled their emotions for the entire world to read. The women featured on the pro-life sites said they thought about their babies every day. How old were they now? What would have been their first words? their favorite toy?

Some wrote about the deception they had experienced at the clinics they used. The women had been promised that the abortion would be like any other period. But some had seen an embryo larger than expected. Some talked about their desire to have a burial.

Kelly's experience had not been like that. A nurse at Hillside had made it clear that the RU-486 pill was not convenient and painless. She had carefully explained the differences between chemical abortion and surgical abortion with patience and sensitivity. Kelly's impression, which proved to be right, was that the RU-486 pill would be like a miscarriage with bleeding and cramping and a sense of loneliness.

And plenty of guilt, something the nurse had *not* talked about.

Most women said they chose the pill rather than surgery because it seemed more natural and allowed them to have a semblance of control. These were definitely factors in Kelly's thinking. She could start the process at home, on her schedule. And it felt like something she did to herself, rather than something somebody else did to her.

But in hindsight, Kelly realized that she had also picked RU-486 precisely *because* it was not easy and quick and painless. In a convoluted way that Kelly couldn't quite express, it felt right to suffer, as if the process itself should be the beginning of her penance.

Six years old. Her baby would have started first grade this year.

She blinked back tears and forced herself to focus on the job at hand. She had turned this over and over in her mind, always reaching the same conclusion. The leak must have come from someone at the clinic. She would walk in and demand a meeting with her doctor, refusing to leave until he gave her a few minutes of his time. She would tell him that somebody had threatened to disclose the fact that she had been pregnant. She would explain that she had talked to no one outside the clinic about it. She would demand that he investigate.

But even as she rehearsed the conversation in her mind, she recognized the problems with this approach. There was a good chance her doctor would become defensive. Even if he initiated an investigation, it would probably be clumsy and ineffective, serving no purpose other than to make the blackmailer more circumspect. If the doctor brought in outside authorities, it would only increase the number of people who knew about Kelly's abortion.

Kelly knew she might temporarily feel better if she gave the doctor a piece of her mind, but it would solve nothing. Everyone at the clinic had treated her with kindness and respect. In her heart, it was hard to believe that somebody in there was working with the blackmailer.

She stared at the clinic and tried to honestly assess her own motives. Was she hesitating because she was scared? Or was this genuinely a bad idea?

Either way, she couldn't make herself go in there.

She put her car in drive and pulled out of the parking spot. She would find out who was behind the blackmail; her resolve hadn't been weakened one bit.

But this was not the way.

53

JASON HAD HEARD that the ability of opposing lawyers to get along decreased exponentially as trial approached. Now he knew it was true. Throw in a high-profile case, a frosty relationship at the outset, and two young lawyers both trying to make a name for themselves, and the result was a constant parade to the courthouse so the judge could resolve petty disagreements.

The first two Fridays in March found Kelly and Jason arguing over various discovery disputes. They took turns accusing each other of improperly withholding information, operating in bad faith, filing burdensome and harassing discovery requests, and other forms of underhanded lawyering and general thuggery. Judge Garrison ruled for Kelly on some points and for Jason on others, frustrating everybody.

On the third Friday, the lawyers found themselves in Garrison's courtroom again, this time arguing over Kelly's desire to take a follow-up deposition of Melissa Davids. "I won't need more than two hours," she claimed. "There are some things I know now that I didn't know when I first deposed her."

"Like what?" Jason asked.

"I'm not required to divulge my deposition strategy," Kelly responded.

After twenty minutes of heated argument, Judge Garrison banged his gavel and told the lawyers he'd heard enough. He started with a lecture aimed at Kelly—he wasn't going to keep letting her have a second and third shot at the defendant every time she thought of something new. But then he talked about the purpose of discovery and how both sides should have more than adequate opportunity to question the other party on all matters relevant to the case.

Jason could see where the ruling was headed and wanted to scream. He understood the rules of full and open discovery, but Melissa Davids had already answered questions for nearly six hours. His client was going to have a fit.

"You're only getting two more hours with the witness," Garrison told Kelly. "Not a minute more."

"Thank you, Your Honor."

"And you'll have to fly to Atlanta at your expense. I'm not making Ms. Davids come back here for two hours."

"Yes, Your Honor."

"Anything else?" Judge Garrison asked.

"No, Your Honor," Kelly said cheerfully.

Jason shook his head, refusing to give Judge Garrison the satisfaction of a verbal reply. At first, Jason had thought Garrison was a good draw for the case. The judge had risen through the ranks of the Republican party and was certifiably conservative. But now the information provided by Rafael Johansen was never far from Jason's mind. The judge had issues. . . . Maybe somebody on the other side was pulling his strings. Jason didn't think Kelly was capable of such a thing, but there were a lot of strident gun-control groups with an active interest in the case.

Or maybe it was something less nefarious. Maybe Garrison just subconsciously favored nice-looking female attorneys.

Either way, there wasn't much Jason could do about it right now. After the hearing, he would call Case McAllister and tell him to get Melissa Davids ready for another two hours of deposition. What new angle did Kelly Starling want to pursue?

◁▷

Ten days later, Jason stopped by his office early in the morning on his way to the airport. Not surprisingly, Bella was there. She had his trip folder organized and ready to go, including directions from the airport to MD Firearms, the prior deposition of Davids indexed and summarized, and every other possible item Jason might need on his trip, including the phone number for Judge Garrison's chambers if the court needed to rule on something during the deposition.

Jason thought about the day he had interviewed Bella, how he had almost hired that other woman—what was her name? Going with grit, girth, and experience over beauty and seduction had been one of the smartest decisions of his young legal career.

But on this particular morning, Bella's one major weakness was also in full bloom. She wasn't satisfied just running her own life; she had to mother Jason, too.

She did it from a familiar vantage point—blocking the door to Jason's office, her arms folded across her chest, clutching manila folder files and legal documents.

"Brad Carson used to always say a trial is a marathon," Bella pontificated. "You can't keep up this pace for a marathon."

"What pace?" Jason asked without looking up. He didn't have time for this.

"Let's see . . . at 11:30 last night, you e-mailed me the first draft of a Motion to Compel in the MD Firearms case; two hours later, a draft of our expert's opinions on the McAfee case—so now we're looking at nearly two in the morning. Four hours later, I'm getting more e-mails about the need to set up appointments with fact witnesses for each of these hair cases."

Jason shrugged. "I'm nocturnal."

"Mmm-hmm," Bella said, as if Jason's answer had somehow confirmed her point. "When's the last time you went to the beach?"

Jason looked up. "Like every other normal human being, I don't spend much time at the beach in January and February."

"I'm not talking about layin' out or swimmin' or something. I'm just talking about strolling on the boardwalk when the tourists are gone or eating at one of those restaurants that overlook the ocean. When's the last time you did *anything* that wasn't work related?"

Jason put down his pen. She had a point. A small one, but a point nonetheless. When he moved to Virginia Beach, he had been drawn by the ocean, the sand, the water, the laid-back culture. He was going to learn to surf or maybe master the paddleboard. He would run on the boardwalk and join a gym and be part of the young lawyers' association.

He had done none of those things. Instead, he'd done what he always did: thrown himself into the intellectual challenges. Sure, he had played soccer in high school and starred in the school play, but mostly he studied. In college he avoided the fraternities and extracurricular activities so he could focus on the books. Because of what he'd been through, he didn't drink and felt out of place at parties. He went to an SEC school but never attended a football game. It wasn't until law school, where it was finally okay to be a nerd, that he had begun to thrive. Law review, moot court, and high class rank made him the envy of classmates rather than an outsider.

But even in law school, he ate lunch alone every day at an out-of-the-way restaurant or in the kitchen of his one-person apartment. Jason was an unrepentant introvert. He had always considered himself a paradox—a loner who liked to perform. Since law school, he had learned that a lot of other public speakers and actors were introverts as well. He couldn't change who he was, so why not accept it?

"When's the last time *you* went to the beach?" Jason asked, turning the tables on Bella. Deflect and distract, always a good defense.

But Bella had worked for a lawyer for thirty years. "This isn't about *me*," she said. "Besides, you want to be like me someday? Fifty years old and all I have is my job?"

The honesty of her assessment surprised Jason. And it may have surprised Bella a little as well, because she quickly added, "And my faith and friends at church. But . . . I mean, I wish I had done more stuff when I was your age."

In that moment of transparency, Jason felt a wave of sympathy for his assistant. He hadn't really given much thought to what it would be like in Bella's shoes. For Jason, the law was an intriguing mistress, a challenging intellectual exercise, and a way to make money while serving the clients. For Bella, it must have been a grind—all menial and administrative tasks. And worse, after spending most of her career with one lawyer, she had to start all over again with somebody new.

But Jason wasn't a counselor. Quite the contrary, he hated talking about personal issues. He decided to resort to another time-tested advocacy weapon—procrastination.

"Let's just get through the Crawford case first," Jason said. "And then we'll both turn into Virginia Beach socialites."

"Speak for yourself," Bella said. "You can't teach an old dog new tricks."

54

THE LOOK ON MELISSA DAVIDS'S FACE had been smug and impatient in her first deposition, but today it was pure contempt. Jason worried that his client might say something she would regret later, something that Jason might not be able to overcome no matter how skillfully he picked and cajoled the jury.

Even as Kelly asked her preliminary questions, Jason's palms were practically dripping with anxiety. He caught his leg bouncing nervously under the table and stopped before he bumped Case McCallister, sitting next to him. *What did Kelly Starling have that was so important it required a follow-up deposition?*

"In your last deposition, I asked if you were aware of the fact that Peninsula Arms had received three citations from the ATF even before Rachel Crawford's death. You said you might have been aware of that. Do you remember that testimony?"

"Yeah."

"Do you want to amend that answer?"

"Of course not."

"Were you aware of those citations?"

"Objection," Jason said. "How many times does she have to answer the same question?"

Kelly ignored him. "Ms. Davids, are you saying today, under oath, that you don't recall whether you were aware of those three ATF citations?"

"I said it before and I'll say it again: I *might* have been."

Kelly snorted at the answer. Jason tensed even more, leg bouncing, heart pounding. He didn't like where this was headed.

"I also asked you whether you ever considered shutting down Peninsula Arms as a dealer." Kelly consulted her bound copy of the prior deposition's transcript. "And your response was, 'No. If anybody had suggested such a thing to me, I would have told them I still believed in the Second Amendment and the free enterprise system.' Do you remember that testimony?"

"Not particularly. But if that's what the transcript says, I don't deny it."

"Isn't it a fact, Ms. Davids, that you *definitely* considered whether MD Firearms should cut off rogue dealers and *definitely* decided against doing it because you wanted to protect the company's bottom line?"

Jason opened his mouth to object but it was too late.

"Of course not," Davids shot back. She looked like she wanted to jump across the table and attack Kelly. "That's just your fantasy."

Jason knew what was coming next. Part of it was the smirk on Kelly's face. Part of it was the way she let the answer hang out there as she deliberately pulled out a set of documents, slowly removed the paper clip and separated three copies.

She kept one copy, handed one to the court reporter, and slid the third across the table to Jason. "Since your last deposition had twenty-six exhibits, I'm going to ask the court reporter to mark this next document as Plaintiff's Exhibit 27," she said calmly. "Then I'll ask if you've ever seen this document before."

Jason glanced through the document quickly. Just as he feared, Kelly had somehow obtained a copy of the memo from Case McAllister.

"I object," Jason interjected, even before the court reporter handed the document to Davids. "This document is protected by the attorney-client privilege. I'm instructing the witness not to answer any questions about it."

Without saying a word, Kelly Starling pulled out another set of documents, removed a paper clip, and separated three single sheets of paper. When Jason got his copy, his throat constricted.

It was a copy of Davids's e-mail to Gerald Franks, CEO of Walker Gun Co., urging him not to blacklist renegade dealers from the Walker distribution chain. The e-mail was cryptic and to the point—vintage Melissa Davids.

> Gerry:
>
> If just one manufacturer caves in on this, it will require that all the rest of us also monitor every dealer and shut off dealers with troubled legal histories. For a lot of reasons, this is a bad idea. Attached is a memo Case put together on the subject. For your eyes only.
>
> Don't open the floodgate for lawsuits.
>
> Melissa

While Jason stared at the memo, Kelly had it marked as Plaintiff's Exhibit 28. "Do you recognize this?" she asked Davids.

"Hold on," Jason said. He turned to Kelly. "Where did you get this?"

She shrugged. "I don't have to answer that."

"This e-mail and the attached memo are protected by the attorney-client privilege. I'm instructing the witness not to answer."

"You're kidding," Kelly said.

Jason felt his face flush, but he was committed now. "I'm basing my objection on the joint defense privilege. Both companies faced the prospect of being named as defendants in a lawsuit. Under those circumstances, it's not a waiver of the attorney-client privilege to share a privileged document with an executive from another company."

Kelly laughed cynically. "That's creative. But it's also total garbage. Do you have any cases where the joint defense privilege has been applied to two companies that aren't even defendants in the same case together?"

Jason sat up straighter. "You're not going to talk me into this. If you want to call the judge, be my guest."

Kelly gave one final harrumph and suspended her questions so they could get Judge Garrison on the phone. Halfway through Kelly's explanation of the issue, the judge cut her off.

"Is this true?" he asked Jason. "Did Ms. Davids send this memo to another company's CEO?"

"Yes, Your Honor. But both companies were potential targets in the lawsuits filed by the northeastern cities. MD Firearms had already been named as a defendant. In fact, that's the very reason the memo was drafted in the first place."

"Save your breath," Garrison said. "Your objection is overruled. Tell Ms. Davids to answer Ms. Starling's questions or I'll hold her in contempt."

Melissa Davids was still in the conference room and stared at the phone, her nose flaring. "I'm right here," she said. "May I say something?"

"No," Case McAllister said quickly, surprising even Jason.

Davids glared at her general counsel for a second and then apparently decided that twenty years of building trust ought to be worth something. "Okay," she said to the speakerphone. "On the advice of my lawyer, I'll just keep my mouth shut and answer the questions."

"Good call," Judge Garrison said.

55

FOLLOWING THE PHONE CALL, Melissa Davids increased her level of belligerence—jaw jutting out, scowling for the camera. Jason could see the deposition being played back in court—a large monitor in front of the jury box, Davids's fury visible for all the jurors to see.

Kelly had the witness read Case McAllister's conclusion: "A careful cost-benefit analysis suggests we should continue to sell guns to all licensed and qualified dealers."

"Did you agree with Mr. McAllister's cost-benefit analysis?"

"No."

The response seemed to surprise Kelly, causing a double take. "What's wrong with it?"

"There should be no cost-benefit analysis in the first place."

"Why not?"

"Two little things called the Second Amendment and free enterprise. It's a game of dominos played by gun-control zealots like you. Shut down the worst dealer, and the next in line is then by definition the world's worst dealer. So you shut him down, and then people start pointing at the next one. Where does it stop?"

"Let me ask you a few specific questions about Mr. McAllister's data. Do you see in the memo where he indicates that four dealers in particular account for more than half the guns traced to crimes in these northeast cities?"

Davids took her time reading the document, generating a long silence.

"Page two, second paragraph," Kelly prompted.

"What was the question again?" Davids asked.

Kelly read the question a second time.

"Yes, Case says that."

"And Peninsula Arms was one of those dealers, right?"

Again, Davids took her time reading the document. Kelly waited her out.

"That's correct," Davids said. "You want me to just read the whole memo into the record?"

"That won't be necessary," Kelly said sharply. "Now, Mr. McAllister says that cutting off dealers might result in litigation by those dealers and would also play into the cities' hands by acknowledging that MD Firearms has a responsibility to monitor dealers. Isn't that right?"

"The document speaks for itself," Jason said. "Do you have a question for this witness?"

Kelly sighed and put the document down, staring at Melissa Davids. "Is there one single sentence, anywhere in Mr. McAllister's memo, stating that one of the factors you ought to consider is the life-threatening danger that occurs when felons and other illegal purchasers obtain firearms?"

"No," Davids said decisively. "And if he had put something like that in there, I probably would have fired him."

Kelly chuckled aloud at the perceived absurdity of the answer.

"You find this funny?" Davids challenged.

"Yes. As a matter of fact, I find most of your answers hilarious."

"Objection," Jason said, using the most condescending and disdainful tone he could muster. "Counsel's remarks are childish and disrespectful and should be struck from the record."

"You're calling me childish?" Kelly asked with a small ironic snicker. She shook her head and turned her attention to the witness. "Why would you have fired Mr. McAllister if he had suggested that you ought to consider the risk to people's lives?"

"Because anybody who believes that stopping the sale of guns to Peninsula Arms will keep criminals from getting guns doesn't have enough sense to work at MD Firearms."

"Maybe they could be a plaintiff's lawyer," Kelly said sarcastically.

"Your words, Counselor. Not mine."

◁▷

When the deposition was over and everyone had cleared out, the MD Firearms brain trust huddled in the conference room.

"I want to know where that leak came from," Melissa Davids demanded, looking at Case. "I want somebody looking through every one of our e-mail servers and employee accounts. I want you to interrogate every area manager. We can't afford to have traitors working at our company, Case."

Davids was on her feet, pacing next to the conference table, her face tight with anger. In contrast, Case remained seated, a soothing presence as his volcanic CEO spilled her lava.

"Do you have any idea who did this?" she demanded.

"There's no guarantee that it's somebody at our company," Case said. "It might have been somebody at Walker Gun Co., or somebody could have hacked into our network."

The two of them speculated for a while about who might be behind the leak. Case promised he would leave no stone unturned in his investigation.

After Melissa left, Case blew out a deep breath.

"What do you think?" Jason asked.

"She handled the questions well. Unfortunately, her previous deposition answers painted her into a corner." Case tugged on his bow tie. "Bottom line, she's going to look like she was lying when Starling plays her previous testimony denying that anybody ever suggested she look at the possibility of shutting down Peninsula Arms."

The two men sat there for a moment. Jason let his silence indicate his assent.

"She's been getting mixed results from our focus groups," Jason said. "They either love her or hate her."

"No surprise there."

Case arranged his legal pads and deposition transcript into a neat little pile. He stacked copies of the day's exhibits on top.

"You've got good judgment, Jason. And I've watched the tapes from Justice Inc." Case stopped fiddling with the stack of papers in front of him and looked at Jason. "You're one heckuva trial lawyer."

To Jason, it felt like a strange turn for the conversation. "Thanks," he said.

"I may need you to try this case alone," Case said.

"What are you talking about?"

"I might need to take the stand."

Jason furrowed his brow at the suggestion. "Why?"

"We need somebody who can really explain that memo," Case suggested. "Some of the jurors might think that Melissa is a little over the top, but maybe they would relate better to me. The question is whether I add more value to the case as a lawyer or as a witness. Right now, I'm thinking witness."

Jason felt pressure building in his chest; his head throbbed from these rapid developments. Kelly Starling had a possible mole inside MD Firearms and a smoking-gun memo for her arsenal, and now Jason might have to try the case alone.

"Let's sleep on this for a few days before we do anything rash," Jason suggested.

"Of course," Case said. "You know me. I never make rash decisions."

56

FLYING BACK TO NORFOLK, alone in the window seat, Jason had time to take inventory. He made a list of things he needed to get done prior to trial—two solid pages on his legal pad, and there were probably plenty of things he hadn't remembered to include. Maybe he was just tired, but the deposition had somehow caused him to turn an emotional corner in the case.

Given the choice, he probably would have picked the plaintiff's side. He loved representing the underdog. He wasn't a natural fan of the Second Amendment, though he was getting more comfortable with the thought of having his MD-45 in his house or car. In some undefined way, it gave him a sense of security and empowerment.

For a while, he had talked himself into liking this case. It was by far the biggest case of his legal career, and he had grown to genuinely respect Melissa Davids. Plus, there was this whole individual responsibility thing. Wasn't MD Firearms really just an innocent scapegoat? Weren't the real culprits Jamison and Beeson and Peninsula Arms, none of whom had been sued?

But now that Case's memo had come to light, Jason's enthusiasm for the case was about nil. Melissa Davids had shown her worst side today. And though he had given Kelly a hard time in front of his clients, Jason found himself respecting her crusader mentality. Kelly carried herself like somebody who had justice on her side—somebody willing to bleed for her client. Jason realized, in a moment of unguarded candor, that he didn't feel the same way.

But he *was* Jason Noble. Law student prodigy. Ace trial lawyer. The greatest actor who would never be considered for an Oscar.

Jason had once heard a Hollywood veteran say that sincerity was the key to all good acting. *"Once you can fake sincerity, you've got it made."* It was, Jason thought, true in the courtroom as well.

By the time the plane started its approach, Jason had talked himself into once again being the Great Defender of the Second Amendment. The memo might have cost him a co-counsel, but if so, Jason had gained a great witness in the process. Melissa Davids had her rough edges, but Case McAllister was a pro. He would sit there on the witness stand, adjust his bow tie, and systematically dismantle Kelly Starling's case.

Jason's BlackBerry vibrated before the plane hit the ground. As usual, he had refused to turn it off during flight, secretly switching the mode from normal to vibrate. The habit was probably indicative of some deep personality flaw born out of his rebellious and contrary nature, but his reasoning was simple: if cell phones actually messed up the navigational equipment, would they really let passengers even bring them on planes?

He did, however, have the good sense not to check his messages until the plane touched down. As the flight attendant started her welcome-to-Norfolk spiel, Jason pulled the BlackBerry from its clip and started scrolling through his messages.

Seven e-mails. Not bad for a ninety-minute flight. He could get through these before they hit the gate.

But when he opened the third one, his hand froze around the device. The words sucked the wind from his lungs, causing an audible gasp. He read it twice and bowed his head, leaning against the seat in front of him, staring at the screen of his BlackBerry.

> Jason:
>
> The retired chief of police for the city of Atlanta would make an excellent expert witness in your case. His name is Ed Poole. Hire him.
>
> And Jason, you'll want to do what I say. Otherwise, the entire world will be reading on the Kryptonite blog all about that little accident you had in high school.
>
> I know who was driving and I've got the proof.
>
> Don't make me use it. I want to help. The Second Amendment is the only thing that staves off tyranny. *Sic semper tyrannis!*
>
> Luthor
>
> PS: Don't let anybody talk you into settling this case. It's very winnable.

Jason took a deep breath and tried to calm his racing heart. His hands literally trembled, as if he had just watched an old friend rise out of the grave, point a finger at Jason's chest, and accuse him of murder.

He closed his eyes and, like a recurring nightmare, it all came rushing back.

57

Ten years earlier

THE IRONY WAS THAT JASON and his friends avoided the big party that night—the one with all the football players and cheerleaders and rich kids—because Jason and his buddies discussed it, and they thought there might be trouble.

For the most part, Jason avoided parties altogether, feeling lonelier in big groups than he did staying home. But on this night, he had made plans with four of his soccer teammates and a small group of girls to hang out in a parking lot next to the tennis courts of a northern Atlanta subdivision. A senior with a fake ID brought the beer. Another kid grew his own weed.

Jason rode to the party with a buddy named LeRon, a fast left wing on the soccer team, a player so full of bravado and bluster his teammates affectionately nicknamed him the Mouth.

In some ways, they made a strange pair—the quiet son of a cop and the outspoken son of an AME preacher—but sports brought them together. The Mouth could hold his own intellectually, quoting King and Plato and T. D. Jakes, and he brought a nice balance to Jason's biting sarcasm. The Mouth was an eternal and irrepressible optimist, even on a soccer team that hadn't logged a winning season in five years.

The Mouth also harbored big dreams. One day, he was going to be the next Johnnie Cochran. The next day, the world's greatest sports agent. Once Jason tried to goad him toward politics, but the Mouth scoffed at the idea. "There's no money in *that*."

On this night, like many others, the Mouth had a few too many beers and smoked a little too much weed. After a few hours hanging out, including the last thirty minutes inside the cars while a light rain fell, they all decided to go to a nearby Steak n Shake for something to eat. LeRon, to the surprise of everyone, begged off and handed his car keys to Jason. "Your daddy's the cop," he said. "They won't bust you for DUI. You can take me home and crash at my house."

Jason agreed to drive, but not because he thought his dad would cut him any slack. He wasn't as wasted as LeRon. He'd only had a few beers during the past two hours, four or five at the most. If he wanted to get home in one piece without calling his father and triggering the old man's wrath, his own hand on the wheel provided the best hope of getting there safely.

Trouble hit on the Highway 400 exit ramp. Jason lived off a different exit and nearly passed LeRon's out of habit. At the last second, he swerved to make the ramp. It might have been this abrupt maneuver, or the sharp curve of the ramp, or the slick road, or the nearly bald tires, or the wipers that smudged rather than cleared the windshield. It might have been the speed. It might have been the booze.

The car started fishtailing, and Jason overcorrected, fighting back a surge of panic. LeRon reached out an arm to brace against the dashboard, shouting expletives. The car skidded, hit the shoulder, and flipped—once, twice, who knew how many times?

The world spun and tumbled, turning violent and chaotic as if some giant had picked up the car, shaken it around, and thrown it against a tree.

The tree. Jason saw it coming for a split second—nothing but a flash in his peripheral vision during one of the flips—and then felt it. The car slammed against it, metal crashing, shearing, practically exploding, Jason's head bouncing violently against a doorframe, followed immediately by a jolt and the smell of smoke.

Air bags?

Within a split second, almost instantly, everything was quiet. Jason moaned—his head spinning, his subconscious screaming danger. Was he even alive? There was pain that said he was. A shoulder. His right leg. He could taste blood in his mouth.

His chest. It felt like somebody had crushed his rib cage.

He struggled for breath. He fought back darkness.

He was hanging nearly upside down, his weight on one shoulder and his neck, the whole front seat of the car crushed. The driver's-side window was pinned against the ground. There was no way out.

"LeRon?" he said. It came out as a whimper. "LeRon?"

He tried to twist around, pain shooting through his body. He had to see his friend. A surge of adrenaline-fueled panic blew away some of the cobwebs. The smoke—was the car going to explode?

He twisted enough so he could see LeRon. His friend was not moving. His neck was wrenched around at a horrible angle, as if some superhuman force had twisted it like a bottle top. LeRon's eyes were open, staring . . . lifeless.

"No!" Jason tried to reach out to him, but the darkness was winning, overwhelming Jason, clouding his thoughts.

He needed to get out, must get away from the car and get LeRon help . . . but he was trapped. He couldn't focus. He started sinking deeper, faster, into a black hole of unconsciousness.

Somehow, he reached into his pocket and pulled out his cell. He flipped it open and speed-dialed his dad. Jason was fading fast, gasping for breath. He spoke in chopped sentences. His dad said something—get away from the car? don't move your friend?—the instructions were lost in the whirlpool of thoughts Jason could no longer control. He mumbled something about the off-ramp, exit 6, a tree. The phone dropped from his hand.

The pain receded and the panic died, replaced by an oozing darkness and a sense of overwhelming loss.

◁▷

Jason awoke in the hospital, his mind woozy from pain medication and trauma, his father sitting next to his bed. Jason stared at him for a moment, allowing the world to come into focus again. His father's face was drawn, his eyes bloodshot.

"LeRon?" Jason asked.

His father shook his head.

The pain medication blunted the grief, keeping Jason from lashing out or shouting. Instead, he closed his eyes, sadness seeping through every fiber of his being. He felt his life had changed forever.

Immediately the questions started flowing.

Why did LeRon die?

Why did I survive?

Who wants to live like this?

When he opened his eyes again, his father had not moved. Jason felt tears rolling down his cheek, soaking into his pillow. His father leaned forward, glancing toward the door.

"You weren't driving," he whispered.

Huh? Jason furrowed his brow, trying to comprehend.

"I called the accident in to Officer Corey, who was patrolling that area. Then I called 911." His dad edged a little closer to Jason's bed. "Matt Corey is a friend. He managed to get you both out of the vehicle before the paramedics arrived."

Jason shook his head. At least he tried to shake it. Small shakes. Adamant.

He wasn't going along with this.

"Listen to me," his father said sharply. "We've already lost one life. I'm not going to lose another."

Jason stared back. Even in his drug-induced state, he knew he had to fight this. He had already done enough damage to LeRon's family.

"Matt Corey put his career on the line for *us*," Jason's dad said emphatically. "If you don't handle this right, you're not just tossing away your life. You're ending the career of a great and selfless cop."

◁▷

The hardest day of Jason's life was the day of LeRon's funeral. Jason showed up with his broken right leg in a cast and his left arm in a sling—nursing a broken collarbone, a compound fracture of his tibia, two cracked ribs, and a serious concussion. He used a crutch under his good arm to walk.

He was showered with kindness and love by LeRon's family.

The physical pain was nothing compared to Jason's broken spirit. During the investigation, he had nodded along as Officer Corey described the scene, even when Corey talked about prying Jason out of the passenger seat. Jason gave vague details about the events of that night—claiming that the last thing he remembered was being at the tennis court parking lots. He had downplayed the amount of drinking he had done. There was no mention of drugs.

At the funeral, Jason watched in horror as LeRon's mother sobbed uncontrollably in front of the casket. He cried quietly as LeRon's dad eulogized his son, bringing the large crowd to laughter and tears and eventually to their feet as they applauded a life well lived.

◁▷

For the next few months, suicide was never far from Jason's mind. Nor was confession. On at least three separate occasions, he drove to the parking lot of LeRon's church but couldn't muster the courage to go inside and talk to LeRon's dad about what had really happened.

The accident changed him. He vowed never to touch a drop of alcohol again. He became more cynical, less social, at times despondent.

It also served as the tipping point in an already strained relationship between father and son. Jason's dad thought Jason should be grateful for a second chance at life. Instead, Jason felt resentment toward an officer of the law who would abuse the system and pressure his own son to lie about a matter of life and death. And he felt ashamed for his own part in the deceptive scheme.

As time wore on, it became harder for Jason to think about setting the record straight. It would destroy both Officer Corey and Jason's own dad, and what would it help? Would LeRon's parents really find any relief in knowing that their son wasn't driving? It wouldn't bring him back. Jason would probably go to jail, which in some ways might be an improvement—the guilt he already carried seemed more suffocating than any jail cell.

For months, remorse and shame stalked Jason, hanging over every waking moment, lurking in his nightmares, and reasserting their stranglehold the moment he woke up to face another tortured day. He rationalized his way through life, convincing himself each day that it was too late to turn back now.

He went to LeRon's grave and asked for his friend's forgiveness. He left with the same weight on his shoulders he had brought there.

◁▷

Two years later, during his sophomore year in college, Jason decided to pursue a career as a lawyer. Maybe it was a sense of guilt that he had survived the accident and LeRon had not. LeRon had wanted to be a trial lawyer, the next Johnnie Cochran. Maybe he would have been.

Jason couldn't bring his friend back. But he could at least honor his friend in some small way. Perhaps this accounted for Jason's willingness to take on criminal defendants as clients. That's certainly the type of law LeRon would have practiced.

LeRon's style would have been very different from Jason's. LeRon argued out of passion; for Jason it was mostly theater. But maybe someday Jason would find himself sitting at his counsel table, defending someone who faced the full wrath of the state, and realizing that this is exactly what LeRon would have done.

Jason would be switching seats again.

But this time, he would make his good friend proud.

58

JASON STAYED AWAKE the entire night after receiving the e-mail from Luthor. He paced around his small apartment over the boathouse. Eventually he went outside and sat on the bulkhead, staring at the bay.

Mostly, he asked questions.

What "proof" could there be about the accident? It was ten years ago. Maybe some investigator at the time could have reconstructed the accident based on the damage to the interior of the automobile, the blood in the car, the injuries sustained by Jason and LeRon—that type of thing. But the car had been hauled to the junkyard and the case file closed. There could be no evidence left.

Unless Matt Corey had preserved something. But why would he do that?

The prospect of a lie-detector test popped into Jason's mind and caused his pulse to pick up speed. As a lawyer, he knew he couldn't be required to take a polygraph. But what if somebody raised a question about who was driving and suggested a lie detector to put the issue to rest? What reason could Jason give for refusing?

Did Luthor really want Jason to win the Crawford case? If so, why had he threatened blackmail? If you want somebody to win, you call them in the full light of day using your real name.

Jason had looked up the résumé of former Atlanta chief of police Edward Poole. The man's credentials were impressive. And Jason could use an expert witness to testify about the black market for guns, someone to explain that criminals like Jamison can obtain guns regardless of whether stores engage in illegal straw sales. But did Jason dare use someone suggested by Luthor?

What was Luthor's real agenda?

As the darkness of the cool spring night gave way to the first hint of sunrise, Jason began focusing on the most important question of all.

Whom could he trust?

Certainly not Rafael Johansen. In fact, it occurred to Jason that both the Case McAllister memo leak and the e-mail from Luthor had occurred not long after Rafael joined the team.

The more he thought about Rafael and the amount of dirt Rafael always managed to dig up on the jurors for the Justice Inc. trials, the more Jason became suspicious of his own investigator. He decided to limit Rafael's access to the files. The man could conduct his juror investigations at arm's length—Jason didn't need him around the office. He thought about firing him the next day but knew he needed Rafael's skills to properly select the jury in the Crawford case.

Besides, Jason believed in the principle of keeping your friends close and your enemies closer. He wouldn't fire Rafael until a week or two before trial, until Rafael had completed his investigative profiles on each of the jurors.

What about the others? Could Jason confide in Matt Corey? Andrew Lassiter? What about Case McAllister? Or Bella? What did he really know about *her* background? For that matter, could Jason even trust his own father?

Maybe he was just dog tired. Maybe it was the gut-wrenching prospect of his past finally catching up with him. Maybe he was just being paranoid.

But right now, Jason Noble didn't know *anybody* he could trust. He would play it the way he had always played it—alone. He would buy some time by meeting with Poole and listing him as an expert. Jason could always withdraw that designation later if something came up.

But he had a sickening feeling he had not heard the last from Luthor. Figuring out a strategy to win this case could well become the least of his worries.

Before heading to the bathroom for a shower, Jason he checked the Kryptonite blog. He had a feeling he would be doing this the first thing every morning and the last thing before going to bed at night for a while. Just like he would open every e-mail addressed to him with a nagging sense of dread and uncertainty.

◁ ▷

Kelly Starling spent the three months prior to trial in what she called "the zone"—an adrenaline-laced focus that allowed her to work fourteen-hour days for weeks on end. She was billing nearly thirty-five hours a week for her paying clients and spending another forty hours on the Crawford case. She reduced her morning swims to four times a week, ate meals at her desk or in her car, and could barely find time to go to the dry cleaner. E-mails piled up in her inbox, and phone messages from her dwindling list of friends went unanswered.

Kelly's life had been pretty much reduced to keeping the plates spinning for her other cases while focusing on the single most important case of her legal career.

Judge Shaver's confirmation hearings remained stalled. He checked in with Kelly occasionally, ostensibly calling for an update on her high-profile case, encouraging her like a proud dad. But the phone calls always contained a nebulous question or two—"Any new developments? Have you heard anything from our mutual friend? Any settlement negotiations, or are you still planning to go to trial?"

Each time, Kelly assured him there were no new developments. She was beginning to think she might never hear from Luthor again—that he (or she) just wanted to ensure that the case would go to trial.

Luthor certainly wasn't much of a pen pal. And without more frequent contacts, Kelly had given up trying to figure out who it was. How could she draw out information if the mysterious Luthor never bothered to contact her?

For three months, she focused on getting ready for trial. Blake Crawford was counting on her. She couldn't let speculation about Luthor distract her from the task at hand.

Even Luthor seemed to understand this. For three months, Luthor was silent.

PART V
THE TRIAL

59

June 29

THE PACKAGE ARRIVED on Monday morning, one week before trial. The printed message inside was short and cryptic:

> Glad you haven't settled. Thought you might need some help with Ed Poole. Maybe you could turn these over to his wife's divorce attorney when you're done.
>
> Luthor

Among other things, the package contained bank statements for the last few months from what looked like an offshore account in Poole's name. The account balance showed nearly $300,000 at the beginning of June. There were sporadic deposits into the account and a $10,000 wire payment each month from the account to a bank in the United States. The recipient account was listed on the statement.

There was also a bill for a cell phone registered to Poole. Luthor had highlighted several phone calls and text messages to a number that Poole had called at least once a day, sometimes talking for twenty or thirty minutes. The phone bill was from the previous fall.

Kelly had deposed Poole a few weeks after Jason named him as an expert. Poole came across as folksy and patronizing, a former chief of police trying to educate a naive young D.C. attorney on the harsh realities of law enforcement. Criminals could get guns anytime and anywhere they wanted, according to Poole. Dealers like Peninsula Arms didn't help, but if Kelly thought that closing down one dealership would have prevented Jamison from getting a firearm, then she was living in a dream world. Poole had seen underhanded dealers come and go in the Atlanta market for years. It didn't make one bit of difference in the gun trade.

Poole even cited a few facts to back up his opinions. He was particularly fond of a Justice Department study based on interviews with nearly 18,000 state and federal inmates. More than 80 percent had obtained their guns through friends or family members or had bought them on the street. Only 9 percent of the guns used by criminals had been purchased at retail outlets illegally, either through straw purchases or otherwise. In addition, a relatively small number of guns used in crimes were what the media referred to as "semi-automatic assault weapons." That number was about 8 percent.

And so it went, the personable former chief of police spewing out statistics and homespun Southern advice while Jason Noble could hardly suppress a smile.

Kelly knew she would have her hands full with Poole at trial. For that reason, the documents from Luthor intrigued her. But she was also skeptical. Evidence from Poole's divorce case probably wouldn't be admissible to impeach him as a witness.

Still, it was at least worth a few phone calls.

Kelly's first call was to the number highlighted on the phone bill. A female voice answered, and Kelly asked for Angela, Poole's estranged wife. The woman on the other line hesitated before she told Kelly it was the wrong number. "Who is this?" Kelly asked. "A wrong number," the woman repeated.

Kelly's second call was to Angela Poole's divorce lawyer. Kelly told her about the documents, and the lawyer asked Kelly to scan them and send them as a PDF file.

Within the hour, the lawyer called back. "We thought he was hiding assets," she said. "These documents give us everything we need to prove it. Poole didn't include this account in his list of assets. The phone number is Poole's mistress. We already had that information. I've got my investigator on it, but I'll bet the wire transfers go to her account."

Just like that, Kelly had some serious ammunition for cross. Poole had lied to the divorce court about his assets. Plus, who knew the source of the money getting deposited into that offshore account? She wondered if Poole had reported that income to the IRS.

But now Kelly also had a dilemma. Technically, Jason Noble had filed discovery requests demanding all documents that Kelly intended to use at trial. But with these particular documents, it would be a lot more effective if she could hold them back and surprise Poole on cross-examination. Sure, it would be a little sleazy, and the judge might chew her out, but only *after* she had embarrassed Poole on the stand. Some courts would even overlook her duty to disclose documents that were well known to the witness and used only for cross-examination.

She had no doubt what Jason would do if the shoe were on the other foot. He would withhold the documents, ambush the witness at trial, and then feign shock when the judge lectured him about it.

Which, of course, didn't make it right. Kelly ran her hands through her short blonde hair, reminded herself to get a haircut before trial, and tried to balance her ethical responsibility with her duty to zealously represent her client.

After a few minutes, she gave her client a call. Blake Crawford was the one with the most at stake. Why not let him weigh in on the decision?

60

THE FOURTH OF JULY fell on a Saturday, meaning that businesses and courts would be closed the following Monday. Accordingly, the Crawford trial was scheduled to start first thing Tuesday morning.

For Jason, the Fourth of July would be a twelve-hour workday like virtually every other day for the past three months. He rose early and checked the Kryptonite blog, though he hadn't heard a thing from Luthor in twelve weeks. He took a quick shower, decided he could skip shaving today since no clients were coming to the office, and threw on a pair of shorts, the same T-shirt he wore yesterday, and a pair of worn-out Crocs. It was already 6:30, so Bella would probably be there. Andrew Lassiter would show up at about nine and work until midnight.

The day promised plenty of sunshine, heat, and mugginess. The beach would be hopping. With tourism in full swing, the allure of the surf drew tens of thousands. There would be fireworks at night and concerts at three different venues.

Jason would ignore it all. He would spend the day and evening hard at work. At most, he and Bella might drive a mile down the road to the empty parking lot of the vacant Surf and Sand movie theater and see if they could watch the fireworks from there.

Until then, he would spend the day preparing for the fireworks that started Tuesday morning.

To Jason's surprise, he was the first one in the office. He went into the kitchen and put on a pot of coffee. He watched it brew, thinking about a thousand things he still needed to do before the trial started.

Jury selection would begin first thing Tuesday morning. The entire case was being telecast on truTV, the channel that had replaced Court TV. Big portions were also scheduled to air on CNN, Fox News, CNBC, and some local public-access stations.

Once the actual jury was in place, Bella and Andrew would recruit a shadow jury, composed of Beach-area residents with the same micromarketing profiles as the real jury. The shadow jury would view the actual court proceedings and provide real-time feedback on how various witnesses and exhibits affected them. Jason would adjust his trial strategy accordingly.

It was an ambitious plan for an outfit as small as Jason Noble, Attorney at Law. Robert Sherwood would be proud.

But trying to pull it off was taking its toll.

Bella came dragging in at 7:45, looking pale, eyes bloodshot, wearing no makeup. She had on a baggy white T-shirt and black capris that must have taken ten minutes to squeeze into. She was huffing from the climb up the steps and smelled like she'd already been through a pack of Camels.

"Good morning," Jason said.

"Hardly. It's July Fourth, and here we are, grinding away at the office, no plans for tonight, no social life, no barbecues with the family. Instead, we get to sit around all day and figure out how to keep a good Christian widower from getting any money to compensate for the loss of his wife."

"You need some coffee," Jason suggested.

By 9:00, Bella was in full swing, putting together trial notebooks, organizing documents, making arrangements for witnesses. She gave Andrew Lassiter a hard time for arriving late; as usual, he ignored her, heading back to the conference room he had commandeered for his jury research.

At 10:00, Jason ventured out to the reception area, where Bella was hard at work.

"I'm going to make your day," Jason said.

Bella looked up at him and grunted, as if it was already too late to salvage this one.

"We've got all the juror information we're going to get from Rafael Johansen," Jason said. "Andrew is inputting the micromarketing data and should have his recommendations for jury selection ready by Tuesday morning. I think we can finally fire Johansen. Want to do the honors?"

"Are you kidding?" asked Bella, rubbing her hands in obvious delight. She had clashed with the arrogant investigator every step of the way. "I think I might be able to squeeze that in."

Jason smiled. "Go easy on him. He's given us some good stuff."

◁▷

At 8 that evening, Jason decided it was time to show a little leadership. He walked down the hall to the conference room where Andrew Lassiter sat hunched over his laptop. The man had his nose practically on the screen; his black-rimmed distance glasses sat on the table.

He looked up at Jason, his brown bangs hanging in his eyes.

"Let's go see the fireworks," Jason suggested. "Take a few hours off."

"Can't."

"Yes, you can. C'mon."

Andrew put his glasses on, tossed his hair back, and looked at Jason. "I've got way too much to do."

"It can wait."

Andrew blew out a breath. "I've still got holes in this jury information." He scrolled through his spreadsheets. "Basic stuff. Do they attend church? Magazine subscriptions? Political parties? Private schooling? Rafael only gave us complete information on about two-thirds of these people."

Jason knew the data wasn't perfect. There were sixty jurors on the panel, and even Rafael's clandestine operations had their limits. But Jason knew that Andrew Lassiter would improvise, using the available data to help select the best possible jury.

Jury selection was the least of Jason's worries.

"I'll let you sit next to Bella," Jason promised.

This brought a smirk from Lassiter. He took off his glasses and rubbed his eyes. "I'll pass," he said.

Jason had better luck with his assistant. At first, she tried to play the martyr too. But when Jason went into begging mode, Bella gave in.

They hopped in his truck, fought the traffic for a mile and a half, turned left on Atlantic Avenue, and eventually found a parking spot on 53rd Street a few blocks from the beach. They headed first to a souvenir store on the strip, and Jason bought two aluminum beach chairs. He and Bella walked barefoot across the sand and set up their chairs a few feet from the high-tide line. It was just before sunset and the sky was gorgeous. They leaned back to enjoy the festivities.

The beach wasn't crowded, but there were plenty of others who'd had similar ideas. Families on blankets, couples huddled together, small bands of tourists throwing Frisbees or footballs, locals with their dogs. A few father-

and-son combinations were already lighting sparklers and setting off their own firecrackers.

Bella and Jason faced the southern end of the beach. "I think they set them off from a barge in the ocean, down that way," Bella said.

They watched the other beachcombers while the light faded, Bella making snarky remarks that had Jason smiling to himself. She started talking about the case once or twice, but Jason shut her down—"No shop talk tonight." With work off-limits, it didn't take long for them to run out of things to say. They waited for the fireworks in relative silence.

As Bella predicted, the fireworks were launched from a barge anchored several hundred yards offshore, lighting up both the night sky and the spectators on the beach, turning the ocean waves luminescent purple, red, blue, and green. Each new burst brought a smattering of ooohs and aaahs, and an occasional after-burst or particularly bright explosion seemed to suck the collective breath out of the crowd.

Jason hadn't been to a fireworks display in years and found himself, strangely, thinking back to the times his dad had taken him to Stone Mountain on July Fourth when Jason was little. They always left a little early, catching the grand finale over their shoulders on the way to the car as they tried to beat the traffic out of the parking lot.

It was one of the few pleasant memories Jason had of time spent with his dad.

"Did you see that?" Bella asked, suddenly transformed into a kid. "I love those ones that spiderweb out like that."

As Jason left the beach that night, the sand squeezing between his toes while he walked toward the boardwalk, Bella huffing and puffing beside him, gushing about what a great idea this had been, Jason found himself feeling melancholy. He wondered about his dad. The last word from Matt Corey had been that his father was still struggling at work. He had been cleared in the internal investigation but, in Detective Corey's opinion, that had only prolonged the inevitable.

His dad was going to crash. And nobody would be there to help pick up the pieces.

"Don't you agree?" asked Bella, between breaths.

"Sure," Jason said.

"Good, I'll pick you up at nine."

"For what?"

"Church," Bella said. "You just agreed that you needed to get away from the office more. Maybe go to church or something."

"I wasn't listening," Jason said. "This is my last break until the trial's over."

In truth, he was anxious to get back to work. The pressures of an impending trial had an amazing way of keeping him from thinking about anything else for very long.

That was a blessing.

61

THE FIRST DAY of any big trial starts with a scintillating media buildup followed by the drudgery of picking a jury. To most observers, it is the legal equivalent of going to a big football stadium with bands and cheerleaders and hot dog vendors just to watch the grass grow. But to Jason Noble and Andrew Lassiter, jury selection was the most critical and intriguing aspect of the case.

Judge Garrison, preening for the cameras he had allowed in the courtroom, took some of the fun out of it by planting himself firmly center stage. Jason knew there were basically two models in the jury selection world—the judge could have the starring role or the lawyers could. Garrison made it very plain from the outset that in this process the lawyers would stay backstage.

Before he started court, Garrison ushered Kelly Starling and Jason Noble into his chambers. Sitting behind his desk in his seersucker suit, the pudgy judge took off his wire rims and laid down the law. Court would start each day on time or maybe even a few minutes early. Lawyer hotdogging would not be tolerated—was that clear? He would ask most of the questions to the jurors himself; the lawyers could weigh in only when granted permission by his honor.

Throughout the five-minute conference, Kelly and Jason did a lot of nodding and muttered, "Yes, Your Honor" often.

"I've got a number of standard questions I'll run through with the jury," he informed them. "I'll follow up one-on-one with any jurors that we might have to dismiss for cause. When I'm done, we'll take a break, and you can submit any supplemental questions you want me to ask and make your Motions to Dismiss. Any questions?"

"No, sir," Jason and Kelly said in unison.

Jason still found the judge hard to read. Rafael's team had continued to monitor Garrison's financial accounts and extracurricular activities prior to trial but had seen nothing to indicate the judge was on the take. "He's got his eye on the Virginia Supreme Court," Rafael told Jason. "And the other Beach judges would be happy to see him go. He's obnoxious and narcissistic—but as far as we can tell, he's clean."

Judge Garrison started the first day of the trial with a thirty-minute lecture for the media and court observers. There would be no displays of emotion. No whispering or talking during court. Court would start on time, and he didn't want spectators coming in late and disrupting the proceedings. Fifteen-minute breaks would actually be limited to fifteen minutes—no more, no less. All cell phones, beepers, and computers must be checked at the metal detectors. "The first time somebody's cell phone goes off, I own it," Garrison declared. This was a very important legal proceeding, the judge said gravely, not entertainment. If anyone wanted to be entertained, go watch Judge Judy.

"Now," asked Garrison, "are there any questions?"

There were none. The judge looked like Elmer Fudd, but he spoke with the authority of General Patton. His bailiff scoured the spectators to see if anybody dared violate even one of the judge's recently pronounced rules.

Jason Noble, already sweating like a steel worker, began to perspire even more. Case McAllister, sitting next to him at counsel table as the representative of MD Firearms, looked like he was stifling a yawn.

Finally, after asserting his unchallenged authority, Judge Garrison directed the bailiff to bring in the jury panel. Four rows of wooden benches that served as spectator seating in the courtroom had been cleared for the first panel of sixty prospective jurors. Each attorney was handed a numbered list of the jurors with some minimal background information. The first fourteen jurors on the list were seated in the jury box; the next twelve sat in the first row of seats behind the plaintiff's table, the next twelve in the next row, and so on.

After the jury panel was sworn in, Judge Garrison delivered a civics lecture on how important their job was and how lucky all of them were as Americans to have a jury system.

Jason stole glances at the jurors, giving them a pleasant but closed-lipped smile. When he turned around, he saw Andrew Lassiter, seated immediately behind Jason, staring at the jurors like a serial killer. He would check his laptop, zero in on a particular juror, type in a few lines, and then stare at the next victim. Most ignored him. Or at least tried to.

Jason reminded Andrew not to study them as if they were animals in a zoo. Andrew nodded and kept staring.

Virginia law required seven jurors for a civil case. In a complex matter like this one, it was customary for the judge to impanel at least two alternates. Jurors who demonstrated bias would be dismissed for cause. After that, each side would have three preemptory challenges for the main jury and one for the alternates. The lawyers could use those preemptories on whomever they wanted.

Jason moved his chair back so he was sitting next to Andrew Lassiter and turned sideways so he could face the jurors. Garrison started in with the standard questions: Do you know either of the parties in this case? How about the attorneys? Have you heard about this case? Would what you've heard affect your ability to be fair and impartial?

On and on he went. Sometimes he had the jurors raise their hands as the group answered his questions; other questions he asked them individually. Jason took notes of any juror responses that bothered him.

Not surprisingly, many of the jurors had strong opinions about gun control. Others were probably just looking for a way to avoid jury duty and thought that if they demonstrated bias they might get dismissed by lunch. By the end of the morning, Garrison's questions had claimed thirty casualties.

Garrison adjourned for lunch with a long diatribe about how the jury panel should avoid talking to anybody about the case, including "your therapist, your spouse, or your lover." He ended with a veiled warning about sequestering the jury if they didn't behave themselves and then told the jurors to enjoy their lunch.

As soon as Garrison left the bench, Andrew Lassiter began to complain. "He's destroying this jury panel," Andrew whispered frantically, eyes blinking like crazy. He shook his head at the computer screen, as if by staring hard enough he could will the data to change. "These gun lovers have got to learn to keep their mouths shut."

It was true that Garrison had dismissed more gun-rights advocates than gun-control advocates, but Jason had expected that. In some respects he was pleased that the jurors were so passionate about his side of the case. So far, the gun-rights advocates seemed to outnumber their counterparts by a margin of about two to one, confirming Jason's decision to leave this case in Virginia Beach state court.

"Let's see how it plays out," Jason said. He was nervous enough without being sucked into Andrew's paranoia. "The jury's still out."

Andrew didn't even smile at the remark. "I'm just saying—" he turned his palms up in frustration, his face showing concern—"I don't like where this is headed."

◁ ▷

Jason and Case ate lunch at a nearby deli.

During his trials at Justice Inc., Jason had often found himself wound so tight that he skipped lunch on the first day. As the trial progressed, he eventually went for something light—a salad or some kind of wrap. At night, when the pressure of the day was over, he ate pizza or burgers or some other greasy meal while reviewing documents in preparation for the next day's proceedings.

But Jason was in character mode now—the calm, cool, collected trial wizard—and Case wanted company for lunch. Jason went along and ordered soup and a sandwich.

Andrew Lassiter begged off, choosing instead to pore over his computer program and fret over the waning and anemic-looking jury pool.

Eating lunch with Case was the next best thing to therapy. Case only wanted to talk about the trial for a few minutes before he launched into stories about other trials or hunting trips or political figures with whom he had crossed swords. He spilled a little mustard on his white shirt and cursed, then dipped his napkin into his water glass and tried to rub it out.

This brought to mind the story about the time he had spilled his drink into his lap during lunch just before an opening statement. "I get a little nervous sometimes," he had told the jury.

By the time they returned to the courthouse, Jason felt better. He enjoyed watching Case banter with the reporters who followed them across the parking lot toward the courthouse.

"What do you think of Judge Garrison?" someone asked.

"The wisdom of Solomon," Case shot back.

"Are you worried about all the publicity this case is generating about MD Firearms?"

"Not if they spell our name right."

"Does MD Firearms have any regrets about supplying guns to Peninsula Arms?"

"I don't know," Case said. He stopped walking for a second. "What about you?"

The reporter looked at Case, confusion on her face. "What do you mean?"

"Have you stopped beating your kids yet?"

She rolled her eyes, and Case resumed leading his little parade toward the courthouse.

They arrived upstairs at the courtroom fifteen minutes early, and Jason decided to head to the men's room. A call arrived from Bella at precisely the wrong time, and Jason just let it ring. A few minutes later, she called back.

This time he answered. "What's up?" He was back in the hallway heading to the courtroom.

"I just got a strange call," Bella said. She sounded shaken. "One of those digitally altered voice deals."

Jason's heart stuck in his throat. He waited for the punch line.

"It was a man's voice. He said to make sure you check your e-mail," Bella said. "There's supposed to be some information about potential jurors that you won't want to miss."

"That's it?"

"He said to make sure you check it over your lunch break. Then he hung up."

"I don't suppose his number showed up on your screen."

"He had it blocked."

They talked for a few more minutes as Jason answered Bella's questions about the morning's events. He kept it short; he needed to get off the line and check his e-mail.

"Sounds like we're off to a good start," Bella said. "I'm praying for you."

The comment caught Jason off guard. He found it a little strange to invoke the help of the Almighty against a grieving widower.

He thanked Bella, ended the phone call, and checked his e-mail. There were no new messages since lunch. *Strange.*

Three minutes later, while he was sitting at counsel table, his BlackBerry vibrated.

> Jason:
>
> Do not strike Juror 3 or Juror 7. It would be a bad time for publicity to surface about your DUI.
>
> Trust me, I'm only trying to help. These jurors will be your champions.
>
> Luthor

62

HEART RACING, Jason turned to Andrew Lassiter. "Can I see where we are?"

Andrew brought up his summary screen, showing the first thirteen jurors left on the panel if Judge Garrison didn't throw anyone else off for cause. As it stood now, Andrew was recommending that Jason use a preemptory challenge on Juror 3. Juror 7 had a low score in Andrew's system but was safe at the moment—but only because three jurors with even worse scores were still on the panel.

What did Luthor know about these two jurors that Jason and Andrew didn't?

It would be hard to justify keeping Juror 3. His name was Rodney Peterson, an African American professor of history at Virginia Wesleyan. He had several strikes against him from a micromarketing perspective. Wrong political party. Wrong religious affiliation. He lived in Virginia Beach, but he did a lot of work with the Boys and Girls Club in inner-city Norfolk, seeing firsthand the lethal combination of guns and gangs. He had a doctoral degree, another strike. Jason preferred blue collar. The only thing in his favor was his gender. The focus groups showed that women had far more sympathy for Blake Crawford than men.

Juror 7, a middle-aged white woman named Marcia Franks, had some pluses and minuses. Another Democrat, strike one. No religious affiliation, strike two. She had other issues as well, maybe not complete strikes but at least foul balls. She read the wrong magazines, enrolled her kids in a private, nonreligious school, and shopped at organic grocery stores. She had an Obama bumper sticker on her car.

On the plus side, her spouse was retired military and now worked in a private security firm. There were guns in the house. Occasionally, her husband went hunting on the eastern shore.

Jason pointed to a few other jurors with low scores, though not as bad as

Marcia Franks. "I've got bad vibes on these two," he said. He didn't know yet whether he would strike Jurors 3 and 7, but he wanted to start laying some groundwork just in case he decided to keep them. The best way would be to put the focus on other potentially bad jurors and build a case against them.

But Lassiter wasn't buying it. "Trust the formulas," he said. "Unless the jurors say something in *voir dire* that totally changes our information, we've got to stick with the formulas."

Even before Jason had received the e-mail from Luthor, he and Andrew had gone back and forth on this issue. Jason saw the formulas as a guide. Andrew saw them as a mandate, the tablets from the Mount—thou shalt strike the bottom three jurors according to the formula.

Jason tapped his chest. "This is part of the formula, too."

Andrew pointed to the screen. "This thing is based on objective information, not emotions." He turned to Jason, intensity lining his face. The pressures of the case affected everyone, but Andrew showed it most—he was a volcano ready to erupt. "Don't throw out months of hard work just because you have a gut feeling. Feelings change." He blinked, and his neck twitched a little. "And even if they didn't—"

"All rise!" the bailiff called out, rescuing Jason from the rest of Andrew's lecture.

"Jason, you know this stuff works," Andrew whispered.

Over the next few hours, as the questioning of the jury panel droned on, Jason focused on his dilemma. If he used a strike against either Juror 3 or 7, his past would be revealed, right in the middle of this high-profile case, distracting him from the task at hand and besmirching his client by association. What if Luthor really *was* trying to help? Luthor had suggested Ed Poole as an expert witness, and Poole had done great in his deposition.

But if Luthor knew things about these jurors that would make them favorable to Jason's case, why hadn't he provided details? Face it, the whole thing was dirty. Had to be. Luthor was blackmailing Jason. Chances were good that he was blackmailing these jurors as well. Even if he was blackmailing them for Jason's benefit, wasn't Jason now a party to Luthor's fraud by not reporting Luthor's e-mails?

And what if Luthor was blackmailing the jurors to get a decision for the plaintiff? If Jason allowed the jurors to stay on, the web of lies he had started ten years ago would ensnare another victim—Jason's client.

On the other hand, he couldn't even bear to think about the consequences of the truth being exposed after all these years. What would he say to Bella? What about LeRon's family—Jason had compounded their grief by making them think their own son had been driving. Why open those old wounds again? And then there were the legal ramifications. Even for a decade-old cover-up, he could be disbarred—maybe even do jail time.

Virginia required unanimous jury verdicts. Even if Jason allowed Jurors 3 and 7 to stay on the case, they couldn't decide it on their own. Two jurors couldn't sway the panel if Jason had the others firmly in his camp.

He couldn't tell anything from their faces. Both jurors just sat there impassively, answering the judge's questions, avoiding eye contact with Jason and everyone else seated at counsel's table. A few other jurors were dismissed for cause, and Jason was pretty sure that both Juror 3 and Juror 7 would now be on Andrew's list of recommended strikes.

In a few hours, it would be time to choose.

◁▷

At 4:30, Judge Garrison ran out of questions and relinquished his starring role to the lawyers. About half the jury panel had already been eliminated for cause. Jurors 3 and 7 had made the initial cut and would be on the final panel of thirteen. The only thing that would keep them from serving on the jury would be if Kelly or Jason used one of their three preemptory challenges to excuse them or asked questions that revealed a bias.

Kelly went first and did her best to goad the gun lovers on the jury into saying something inflammatory so she could get them kicked off for cause. She also pitched some softball questions to her favorite jurors so they could again reiterate how fair and impartial they intended to be.

When it was Jason's turn, he took the occasion to argue his case in the form of questions. If he could show that his client had done nothing illegal, would they be able to put aside their sympathies and render a defense verdict? Did they understand that just because guns can be dangerous, it doesn't mean that you hold the manufacturer responsible for everything that happens with that gun? Even if you don't agree with the Second Amendment, are you willing to follow it as the law of our land?

Neither lawyer was able to reveal any serious prejudice that would disqualify other jurors. When they had finished asking their questions, Judge Garrison gave them an opportunity to huddle with their respective clients to see if they had missed anything.

"Any more questions?" Garrison asked after a few minutes.

"No, sir," Kelly said.

Jason stood. "Just one."

Garrison sighed and told Jason to proceed.

Jason walked to the front of the jury box and gave them another smile. "Judge Garrison and the lawyers have asked you a lot of questions today, and Judge Garrison has explained, in general terms, what this case is about. I was just wondering, before we get started, what questions you might have for us."

"What?" asked Kelly, immediately on her feet. "I object."

Jason turned toward a red-faced Judge Garrison. "Get up here," the judge barked.

When they reached his bench, the judge leaned toward Jason. "What was that stunt? *We* ask the questions during *voir dire*, not the jury. How many cases have you tried?"

Jason spread his palms. "I thought the whole point of *voir dire* was to find out about the jurors. What better way than to see what questions they have? I wasn't going to answer them—but Ms. Starling and I would be fools not to govern our case accordingly."

Kelly was flabbergasted. "Judge," she stammered, as if the absurdity of it was so plain that she couldn't find words to describe it. "I mean . . . that's ridiculous."

"I agree," Judge Garrison said. "Return to your counsel tables."

Jason and Kelly did as they were told and Garrison turned to the jury. "Mr. Noble is not allowed to solicit questions from you at this stage," Garrison said. "Hopefully, all your questions will be answered during the presentation of evidence."

From the looks on their faces, Jason could tell that the jury was at least grateful he had asked. One thing he had learned from interviewing jurors at Justice Inc. was their frustration at never getting to ask their own questions. If they were such a critical part of the trial process, why didn't anybody care what they thought?

At least now, they knew that Jason cared.

When Jason sat down, Case McAllister leaned over and whispered one word.

"Brilliant."

63

THE BAILIFF APPROACHED Kelly Starling and handed her the list of thirteen remaining jurors. She checked some notes, whispered to Blake, and crossed a name from the list.

The bailiff brought the list to Jason. He huddled with Andrew Lassiter on one side and Case McAllister on the other. Not surprisingly, Kelly had struck the highest-rated juror, putting the symbol for "plaintiff" next to her mark. "That one was a no-brainer," Andrew whispered. He pointed to Juror 2 and shrugged. "Here's our no-brainer."

Juror 2 was an African American principal who had demonstrated a distaste for big corporations that made money from a culture of violence and death. Jason had tried to get him dismissed for cause but the man swore he would keep an open mind.

Jason looked at Case, who nodded his assent. The principal was sent packing.

Kelly and her client took considerably longer with their next strike. When the bailiff returned with the sheet and Jason saw the line through Juror 9, he was somewhat surprised. Lassiter's system had at least four jurors ranked higher.

"That's great!" Andrew exclaimed. His voice was a whisper but loud enough that Kelly probably overheard.

"Shhh," Jason cautioned.

"They don't get this stuff," Andrew whispered excitedly. "They should never have struck number nine."

Andrew pointed to the next obvious strike for Jason—Juror 3. To Jason's chagrin, he saw that Juror 3 and Juror 7 now had the two lowest remaining scores.

"I can't strike him yet," Jason whispered. "I'd get a Batson challenge."

Case law prohibited lawyers from basing their strikes on a juror's race. If a lawyer's opponent raised a Batson challenge, the lawyer making the strike would have to articulate a legitimate reason for making the strike that was not race-related.

"You've got race-neutral reasons," Andrew insisted. "He's got to go."

"Do him third," Case suggested. "Get rid of Juror 7 next."

Jason squirmed for a second and considered his options. He looked at Jurors 3 and 7—no overt hostility showed on either face. Maybe he was just looking for a reason to keep these two jurors on the panel, but he was starting to think it was worth a gamble.

Justice Inc. had orchestrated Jason's hiring in the first place. Then an anonymous source named Luthor had helped Jason find a valuable expert. Now this same Luthor was suggesting that Jason keep these two jurors on the panel.

The MO had all the markings of Justice Inc. Inside information about the jurors and about Jason himself. The company certainly had a huge financial incentive for influencing this case. The only thing that didn't fit was the threat of blackmail. Justice Inc. liked to skirt around the edge of the law, but Jason never thought they would stoop to something so blatantly illegal.

Jason looked at the sheet again. The juror with the lowest score, other than Jurors 3 and 7, was Juror 12. Jason pointed to her name. "I've got a really bad feeling about her."

"What?" Andrew whispered. "We've been through this. Put your *feelings* aside."

"I'm not a robot," Jason protested. "I've got to have jurors I can connect with."

Andrew responded with a string of statistics from the focus groups, the importance of this factor versus that factor. "She's a bona fide bumper-sticker liberal," he pleaded, pointing to Juror 7. "Get rid of her with this strike and Juror 3 with your next one."

The bailiff was hovering over the table, his arms crossed. The entire courtroom waiting with bated breath.

"Give me that sheet," Case said. "We look like the Three Stooges."

He turned to Jason. "You sure about this?"

Jason looked at the table. *No.* "Yes," he said softly.

Case struck a line through Juror 12, putting the defense symbol next to it. "I hired *you* to defend my company," he said. "Not some computer program."

When the bailiff brought the sheet back for the third strike, Andrew Lassiter didn't say a word. "I'm sorry, Andrew," Jason said, striking out the name of Juror 11.

When Jason handed the sheet back to the bailiff, Andrew closed his laptop. For a moment, Jason thought his friend would walk out of the courtroom right in the middle of the jury-selection process.

If he had, Jason wouldn't really blame him. Jason had just flushed weeks of work and thousands of dollars down the drain. The truth was, he did have a bad feeling about the last two jurors he had struck.

But the deeper truth, the one that made him sick to his own stomach, was that Jurors 3 and 7 would have been gone if not for Luthor's e-mail. Perhaps he had stacked the odds against himself, perhaps not. Hopefully he could still pull it out. Or, in a worst-case scenario, at least get a hung jury.

Because Case had gone to bat for him, Jason was more determined than ever to try his hardest. Maybe in the process, Jason could expose Luthor and whoever was behind this attempt to manipulate the justice system.

Or perhaps these were just the rationalizations of a traitor. MD Firearms had hired Jason to defend them. On the first day of trial, he had been too busy defending himself.

64

JUDGE GARRISON gave the jury another stiff lecture about not discussing the case with anyone, then dismissed the panel and invited the lawyers back to his chambers. When they arrived, Garrison took off his black robe and motioned toward two unoccupied chairs.

"We're off to a good start. But, Mr. Noble?"

"Sir?"

"We could have done without your asking the jury that question."

"Yes, sir."

"You don't have any stunts cooked up for tomorrow, do you?"

"Not yet."

Garrison had been glancing through some papers on his desk but the comment stopped him cold. "Say what?"

"Just a little humor, sir."

"Yes, well . . . let's try to keep this thing on track and keep the showmanship to a minimum."

Jason wanted to ask if that applied to judges as well, but he let it go. For the next few minutes, they discussed scheduling matters and how long the case might take.

"Have the parties discussed settlement?" Judge Garrison asked.

Kelly responded first. "My client's not willing to settle. It's a matter of principle."

"Yes, yes, I've heard that a few times." He turned to Jason. "Why don't you put some money on the table so we can find out how much those principles cost?"

"I'm sorry, Judge. For my client, it's a matter of money—and she's not willing to pay any."

Garrison sighed. "Well then, be ready to start opening statements at nine."

After he warned the lawyers not to make any inflammatory comments to the press, he sent them on their way.

Kelly stopped Jason in the hallway and handed him a manila folder.

"These are some documents responsive to your discovery requests," she said. The look on Jason's face must have telegraphed his suspicion at not receiving them earlier. "Before you blow a gasket, you should know I just received them myself," Kelly continued. "Most lawyers wouldn't even produce them to you—they would just surprise you with them on cross-examination."

"Cross-examination of whom?" asked Jason.

"The documents speak for themselves," Kelly said.

Jason ignored reporters on his way out of the courthouse and walked straight to his truck. When he opened the truck door, it felt like a blast furnace inside. He threw his suit coat over the passenger seat and loosened his tie.

He started the air-conditioning, braced himself for the worst, and opened the manila folder. He perused the bank documents—an offshore account under Ed Poole's name—and the pages of cell phone records.

Jason didn't recognize any of the phone numbers and didn't understand the full significance of the offshore account, but he did know one thing—if Kelly Starling intended to use the documents on cross-examination, they must be bad.

Which in turn led to another sickening conclusion—Luthor had set Jason up. Jason's main expert witness had a serious Achilles' heel. Luthor had undoubtedly known about it all along. And now, like an idiot, Jason had dug an even deeper hole by keeping Luthor's suggested jurors on the panel.

He cursed and pounded a fist on the dash. Why hadn't he seen this coming?

Perhaps because he didn't want to see it. He was so intent on keeping his past a secret that he had closed his eyes to the obvious and stepped right into the middle of Luthor's trap.

A tap on the window shook Jason out of the fog. He looked at Case McAllister and rolled down his window.

"You okay?" asked Case. "You look a little peaked."

"I'm fine. It's just been a long day."

◁▷

Kelly Starling didn't check her phone messages until she was on her way to the Hilton Oceanfront hotel, her temporary headquarters for the next two weeks. Sometimes being part of a big firm had its privileges.

The fourth caller had called from an unidentified private number during lunch. Kelly had returned to the courtroom early and shut off her phone. She must have just missed him.

The voice sounded like a male's, but it was hard to tell because it had been digitally altered. The connection wasn't the greatest, and Kelly had to listen twice in order to make out exactly what the person said. What she heard made her heart stop cold.

"Kelly. This is Luthor. Keep Juror 3 and Juror 7 on your jury. If you do, your secret's safe with me."

After listening the second time, she hung up the phone without checking her other messages. She had kept both jurors on the panel—why wouldn't she have?—but that's not what bothered her. Luthor was interfering with the case. Giving her direct orders. If he had been watching jury selection, he would think that he had her, that she had acquiesced to his requests.

In truth, she had resolved to do just the opposite. She was going to represent Blake Crawford to the best of her ability no matter the cost.

From the looks of things, the price could be high. She had gone along with this demand, albeit unintentionally. How long before Luthor made another demand that she couldn't comply with?

She called Judge Shaver to let him know she had heard from Luthor again. He didn't answer his phone, so she left a cryptic message.

"This is Kelly Starling. I just heard from a mutual friend named Luthor. He's fine right now, but I'm afraid it might just be a matter of time. Thought you'd want to know." She left her cell number and hung up.

She wondered what she had missed about Jurors 3 and 7. She had frankly been a little surprised that Jason had not struck Juror 3, Rodney Peterson. Now she wondered: *Were they plants for the other side?*

It seemed unlikely. Luthor appeared to be on her side. He had already provided the damaging cross-examination material for Ed Poole and the copy of Case McAllister's cost-benefit analysis. But how could she know for sure? Maybe Luthor was just trying to gain her trust in order to betray her in the end.

She still didn't have the foggiest idea who Luthor was. The only thing she could do was focus on the case. Maybe in the meantime Luthor would slip up and Kelly would learn his, or her, identity.

Either way, if Luthor thought he could control Kelly Starling, he had another think coming. If her affair with the judge ever became public, it would get ugly, but Kelly would survive. After that, Luthor would wish he had never met her.

That was all for later. Right now, she needed to focus on her opening statement.

65

JASON DROVE BACK to the office slowly. He didn't want to face Andrew Lassiter. In fact, he wasn't even sure that Lassiter would be there. Andrew believed so strongly in his jury vetting system that he would likely take Jason's actions today as a personal slight.

Jason also dreaded seeing Bella Harper and Case McAllister. They believed in him. They had worked so hard on the case. Now, to save his own skin, Jason had sold them all out.

He rolled up his sleeves on the way home, stopping at a 7-Eleven to fill up with gas and grab a soda. He was in a funk. He felt as if he were walking around with his soul separated from his body, suspended in some weird state of purgatory after being purchased by Luthor and his e-mails. Yet even in the emotional darkness, Jason recognized a single ray of light. It might not be a way out . . . but it *was* a place to start.

Ironically, the documents sitting on the passenger seat provided the one advantage Jason had in his battle with Luthor. Jason assumed that Luthor had provided these documents to Kelly. If Jason hadn't been so shocked when he first received the documents, he would have asked Kelly about Luthor right there in the hallway and watched closely to see if she flinched. He still planned to ask her at some opportune time during the trial.

Luthor's only mistake thus far was that he hadn't factored in Kelly Starling's ethical standards. He had counted on her to keep the documents to herself and spring them on Poole during cross-examination, the way most lawyers would. That way, Jason wouldn't have known until later in the case that Luthor was definitely working against him. Instead, Kelly had provided the documents to Jason early, and now he knew, right from the beginning of the case, that Luthor was trying to sabotage him, not help him.

It was a slim and temporary advantage, but it was something. In order to leverage this knowledge, Jason needed an investigator he could trust.

He pulled his truck into the parking lot of his office and let it idle for a few minutes. He pulled out his BlackBerry, took a deep breath, and called his father.

Listening to the phone ring, Jason almost hung up. He put his mind in neutral, forcing himself to say on the line.

"Yeah."

"Dad, it's Jason."

A pause. "I know," his dad said. "Caller ID." He waited another few seconds. "It's been months."

There's no law that says that you couldn't have called me. "I'm sorry, Dad. I've been busy."

They talked for a few minutes, a clipped and awkward conversation about the case. His father's bias against MD Firearms was still evident. The man spoke with a thick tongue, and Jason could picture him sitting in his living room, wearing jeans and a white undershirt, empty bottles scattered around the room.

Jason stared out the windshield, wondering if this was the right move after all. "I could really use some help on this case, Dad. I need somebody I can trust to investigate a couple of the jurors." He hesitated, his dad's silence unnerving him. "I was thinking, I dunno, like maybe you could take a few days off to come and help."

The silence on the line seemed interminable. Jason's heart pounded in his ears. A second passed . . . two. Jason wished he had never asked.

"Seems like you'd want an investigator who didn't need to be in rehab," his dad said bitterly.

Jason didn't know how to respond. "Dad, I did what I thought I needed to do. Julie and Matt too. If that hurt you, I'm sorry."

"You're not sorry, Jason. You need something. It's what you've done your whole life. You come crawling home to fleece the old man; then I don't hear from you for months."

Jason wasn't in the mood for this. It had already been a long day. He didn't need his dad piling on. "You know what, Dad? Just forget it. I shouldn't have called."

His dad snorted. "What do you need?"

But it was too late. Every time he tried to reach out to his dad, this was the reward. Rejection. Humiliation. Criticism. Jason just wanted to punch something.

"I don't need anything from you," Jason said.

And with that, he hung up.

A few minutes later, after calming down, he walked into the office. Bella was at her station.

"Turkey and cheese on your desk," she said.

"I'm not hungry."

"Eat it anyway. Trials are like a marathon. You've got to stop at the juice stations."

Actually, trials are more like waterboarding, Jason thought.

He made his way back to the conference room, which looked worse than ever. He had to step over a box and a pile of documents to get through the door.

"Didn't expect to see you here," Jason said.

Andrew Lassiter thumbed through some papers. "We've got to get our shadow jurors in place," he replied, not looking at Jason.

It was Andrew's way of saying he was going to stick around despite what Jason had done in court. They talked for a few minutes about the shadow jury, neither saying a word about Jason's selection of the actual jurors. Andrew thought that he could have a shadow jury in place by Thursday.

"Do the best you can," Jason said. "And Andrew—" his friend looked up—"I appreciate you hanging in there with me."

"Don't worry about it," Andrew said, the eyes blinking. "You're going to make me rich."

Jason furrowed his brow. "How?"

Andrew put on his glasses, brushed his hair out of his eyes, and stared at Jason for a few seconds. "When we impanel this shadow jury, I'm going to bring in two extra jurors who will be just like the last two that you kicked off the panel. When the case is over, we'll compare the opinions of the two you picked with the two I recommended that you leave on. It'll make for great marketing materials: man versus machine—look what happens when you rely on your instincts."

"Clever," Jason said.

"Yeah. And if you lose with the panel you selected, particularly if my jurors would have gone the other way, it will be great for business."

"No offense," Jason said, "but I hope your marketing plan goes down in flames."

66

"MS. STARLING, does the plaintiff have an opening statement?"

"We do, Your Honor."

Kelly stood and walked toward the jurors, holding nothing but a remote control. After months of pretrial discovery, deposition disputes, and a bevy of motions, she couldn't believe that the moment had finally arrived.

"'By our readiness to allow arms to be purchased at will and fired at whim, we have created an atmosphere in which violence and hatred have become popular pastimes.'"

She looked at Juror 3, Rodney Peterson, the only African American left on the jury. A history professor. A Democrat. A man active in the inner city. "Those are not my words," Kelly said. "They are the words of Dr. Martin Luther King Jr."

She stopped a few feet in front of the jury box and surveyed all the jurors. "What Dr. King said is true. And nobody has been more ready to allow guns to be purchased at will and fired at whim than the defendant—MD Firearms."

Kelly had placed a large screen hooked up to an LCD projector in front of the witness box. She pushed a button on her remote, and the first fact flashed on the screen.

"According to the Bureau of Alcohol, Tobacco, and Firearms, the federal agency tasked with oversight of our gun laws, one percent of gun stores sell the weapons traced to 57 percent of gun crimes. 'How can that be?' you might ask. That doesn't seem statistically possible. And you're right—it's not.

"Unless . . . those gun stores help things along a little bit. Unless a few stores, a few renegade dealers, find ways to supply the black market for guns and make money from it. Maybe they sell a bunch of guns to legal purchasers, knowing that those purchasers are supplying the guns to criminals. Maybe they fudge the paperwork. Maybe they lose the paperwork. However they do it, these dealers are merchants of death, making money by supplying the street gangs and thugs and drug dealers with lethal firearms.

"The evidence in this case will show that Peninsula Arms was one such dealer."

For the next few minutes, Kelly took the jurors through a series of PowerPoint slides that demonstrated her point. She started with a map of the United States, highlighting those cities that had filed lawsuits against renegade dealers. Using a blowup of the federal firearms transaction record, she explained how a straw sale occurred—having an eligible purchaser fill out the paperwork knowing that the gun was in reality going to somebody else who couldn't have purchased it on his own.

She showed them slides full of statistics gleaned from the various lawsuits. Two dealers had sold 30 percent of the guns traced to street crimes. One was Peninsula Arms. In 2006 alone, 251 guns previously sold by Peninsula Arms were linked to murders or aggravated woundings in Philadelphia, Washington, Baltimore, and New York City. As part of their investigation, undercover agents from New York City had enticed Peninsula Arms clerks into an illegal straw sale. It wasn't hard.

"MD Firearms knew about these lawsuits and these statistics. And what did they do with this knowledge about one of their biggest dealers?" Kelly asked. She walked over to the table where Jason Noble and Case McAllister were sitting. "Did they stop selling to Peninsula Arms until the dealer straightened up?"

Kelly looked down at Case, who returned her gaze with an unrepentant stare. At that moment, she was pretty sure Case wanted to shoot out her kneecaps. *Perfect.*

"Did they help the ATF set up a sting so that Peninsula Arms could be prosecuted? Did they even send their dealer a lousy warning telling them to curtail the straw sales or MD Firearms might have to stop supplying them?"

Kelly gave a small derisive laugh and headed back toward the jury. "No. I'll tell you what they did—they kept on selling guns to Peninsula Arms. And you know why?"

Kelly hit the button and showed the profit margins on an MD-9. "Here's why—two hundred dollars per gun. Nearly a million dollars last year from Peninsula Arms alone."

She paused, letting that number sink in. "Now, in case you think I'm just making this up—that MD Firearms isn't really motivated just by money, they did us the favor of putting it all in writing. How fitting that in a case about distribution of firearms, Mr. McAllister over there should be so kind as to create a memo that can only be referred to as a 'smoking gun.'"

Page by page, Kelly took the jury through the McAllister memo. The man had analyzed the profits made through four troublesome dealers, including Peninsula Arms. He had argued that shutting off these four dealers (which, Kelly pointed out, together accounted for over 50 percent of the guns traced to crimes in the northeast cities) would generate lawsuits by the dealers and serve as a tacit admission that MD Firearms had a duty to monitor its dealers.

"According to Mr. McAllister, a cost-benefit analysis suggested that MD Firearms should continue selling guns to all licensed dealers—even if they were acting illegally in the sales of those guns."

Kelly got mad just thinking about it. She didn't have to manufacture emotion—her anger was real. If McAllister and Davids had acted responsibly, Rachel Crawford might still be alive.

"Do you know what's missing from Mr. McAllister's cost-benefit analysis?" Kelly demanded. "Do you know what just happened to slip his mind, just fall through the cracks?"

She stopped, jaw clenched, lips pursed. "The cost of innocent human life—that's what. The devastation to a young couple like Rachel and Blake Crawford. The death of a tiny baby twenty-two weeks into gestation, little Rebecca Crawford, tucked safely inside her mother's womb."

Kelly paused, pulling the images from the 3-D ultrasound up on the screen. "Unfortunately for MD Firearms, Mr. McAllister is not the only one who gets to do a cost-benefit analysis on whether they should have stopped selling guns to Peninsula Arms.

"You, ladies and gentlemen, get to do your own cost-benefit analysis. Was MD Firearms acting responsibly by knowingly selling to dirty dealers? Or did their failure to exercise reasonable care cost Rachel Crawford her life?"

Kelly let the question hang there for a moment as she prepared to change gears. She wanted to tell the jury about Ed Poole. She needed to make sure Jason Noble either put him on the stand or paid the price for pulling him as an expert.

"The defendant has retained an expert witness named Ed Poole," Kelly explained. "A former chief of police for the city of Atlanta. He's going to tell you that the man who shot Rachel Crawford could have obtained his gun from the black market. That it wouldn't have made any difference if MD Firearms had cut off dealers like Peninsula Arms.

"But then I'll get a chance to ask him a few questions on cross-examination. And without giving away what I'm going to say, I'll promise you this: By the time he leaves the stand, you won't be willing to believe a word the man says."

Kelly lowered her voice. She went to her counsel table and picked up the MD-9 used to kill Rachel Crawford. "This case is really the story of a gun," she said. "This gun."

It took her ten more minutes to tell the story. The illegal purchase by Larry Jamison. His vendetta against Rachel Crawford because of the investigative report Rachel had prepared. His plan to take Rachel hostage and execute her on live television.

"Unfortunately," Kelly said, her voice nearly a whisper, "his plan worked to perfection. What you're about to see is graphic, but it's the reason the stakes are so high when a company like MD Firearms does a cost-benefit analysis about the way it distributes its products. What you're about to see, what many of you have already seen, are the last few minutes of Rachel Crawford's life. . . ."

67

JASON NOBLE LEANED BACK in his chair, frowned a little, shook his head occasionally, and jotted a note or two. He stifled a yawn for the jury. On the outside, the epitome of boredom. On the inside, butterflies in full riot mode, heart pumping, perspiration factory working overtime.

He noticed that Kelly Starling had no trouble keeping the rapt attention of the men on the jury. She had recently cut her short blonde hair, making her appear even more businesslike. She wore a white blouse, gray suit, heels, understated earrings, a silver necklace, and a touch of lipstick—very classy, but nothing to purposely draw attention to herself.

She didn't have to. She walked around the courtroom with elegant grace, her eyes blazing with intensity, yet still she managed a beguiling smile here and there. The four men on the jury followed her every move. The three women kept glancing over at her client. She was, thought Jason, a formidable opponent.

She stood now at the edge of the jury box, out of the way, and for the first time nobody paid any attention to her. She played the video of the shooting. It started with Rachel live on the air, and then somebody yelled something about a gun. The screen went dark for what seemed like an eternity.

When it came back on, Jamison was on camera along with Lisa Roberts, the news anchor, and Rachel. Jamison forced the women to introduce themselves and told the television audience they had just heard a bunch of lies. He paced behind Lisa and Rachel, then pointed the gun at Rachel's face.

While Jamison ranted about the investigative report, Jason watched the looks on the faces of the jurors. Most of them grimaced, bracing themselves for what they knew was coming. They seemed to be holding their collective breath.

Jamison questioned Rachel about her sources, threatening her as he did so. He forced Rachel to apologize and beg for mercy. He questioned Lisa: "Do you agree that it's her fault?" Lisa shuddered and sobbed, "She made a mistake."

Though the jury knew it was coming, the gunshots still managed to startle them. Some jolted back as they watched Rachel dive for the floor, Jamison pumping bullets into his victim even as his own body was torn apart by the SWAT team bullets. There was shouting and chaos. Both Rachel and Jamison lay dead on the set, blood splattering their bodies.

The screen went blank.

Kelly moved to the front of the jury box and stood there. She didn't say a word. Her back was to Jason, so he couldn't tell if she was crying or just trying to hold it together. The tension in the courtroom was off the charts.

"Ms. Starling," Judge Garrison finally prompted. He said it softly, as if trying to nudge her from a trance.

"Silence," Kelly said. "Since the time those gunshots were fired, for my client . . . there's been nothing but silence. Where once there was the laughter of a spouse, a greeting when he came home from work, soft breathing on the pillow next to him at night, all those sounds that brought joy and contentment in life . . . now, there's just silence."

Kelly hit the remote again, and the screen displayed the ultrasound images. "Where once there was a heartbeat, there is silence.

"What would my client give to spend one more day with his wife? I'll tell you what he'd give—anything in the world. You can't put a price on a soul mate."

Kelly stopped and turned toward Jason's counsel table, her eyes locking on Case McAllister.

She turned back to the jury and lowered her voice. "Not even Mr. McAllister could do a cost-benefit analysis on that."

◁ ▷

Watching on the large flat-screen television in his office, Robert Sherwood gave Kelly's opening an approving grunt. He took a long pull on his cigar and wafted the smoke toward the ceiling. Kelly Starling had risen to the occasion.

At Justice Inc. she had been a good lawyer—a pleasant face, an ultra-competitive personality, and a hard worker. But she had never shown the flashes of brilliance that Sherwood had seen from Jason Noble. Five years of trial experience had changed her. Sherwood had expected a solid opening. But this one bordered on greatness.

At heart, Robert Sherwood was still a trial lawyer. He loved watching the cases unfold. He had spent the months since Andrew Lassiter's departure rebuilding trust with investors. For once, the stars were truly aligning on a case. If things stayed on course, it could be Justice Inc.'s biggest payoff yet. There were dozens of publicly traded gun companies that would be affected by this trial's outcome.

He took another puff on the cigar and watched Jason Noble rise to face the jury. This would be good. Kelly Starling had thrown down the gauntlet. *Let's see how the whiz kid responds.*

68

JASON NOBLE STOOD, took a quick look around the courtroom, and froze. Leaning against the back wall, arms folded across his chest, was Jason's father. The bailiffs had closed off the courtroom earlier that morning when the seats were full, but his dad had must have used his law enforcement credentials to talk his way through.

Jason wasn't used to having his father in the audience. Even in high school, the man always had an excuse during Jason's soccer games. It got to the point where Jason didn't even tell him the game schedule. But now he was standing there against the back wall, and he gave Jason a little nod, adding an extra jolt to the adrenaline already surging through his body.

Jason knew his first job was to take the emotion out of the courtroom. The jurors needed to use their heads, not their hearts.

"Some of you may have seen the movie *A Beautiful Mind*, the true story of a mathematical genius named John Forbes Nash. He won the Nobel Prize for economics. He may be the most impressive mathematical genius the world has ever seen."

"Objection, Your Honor." Kelly Starling was on her feet, a small smile on her lips. "Perhaps I'm in the wrong case. But if not, this can't be relevant."

Jason had not objected during Kelly's entire opening, though he'd had plenty of opportunities. He thought objecting during opening statements made lawyers look petty and simply called more attention to what the other side was saying.

He spread his palms. "I'm getting to the point, Judge. If opposing counsel could give me sixty seconds or so before making her first objection, she'd see how it's relevant."

"Make your point quickly," Garrison said, as if Jason had been stalling for hours. "Objection overruled."

"Where was I?" Jason mused for a second. "Right. This brilliant man, John Forbes Nash, also believed that extraterrestrials spoke to him. As a result, he was confined to a mental institution. When a Harvard professor visited him and asked how a mathematician like him could possibly believe that extraterrestrials were sending him messages, Nash told him this: 'Because the ideas I had about supernatural beings came to me the same way that my mathematical ideas did. So I took them seriously.'"

Jason paused and let the jury think about this. He had no notes and spoke matter-of-factly, like a lecturer in a college classroom. "Judge Garrison will give you the jury instructions at the end of this case. He will tell you that your job is to decide the case based on the facts and the law, using your own common sense. But you cannot let your emotions influence your decision.

"The left side of your brain uses logic, math, and science. It is detail-oriented, where common sense rules. But the right side of your brain uses feelings and emotions and is impetuous. What the judge will be saying is that anybody with half a brain can get this case right—I know, bad pun. But maybe not somebody with a full brain.

"To do justice, especially on an emotionally charged case like this, you need to use the left side of your brain. Because if you engage that right side, your emotions will overwhelm justice. And that's what makes it so hard to render unbiased justice—because your thoughts and ideas, whether they are primarily based on logic or emotion, all seem to come to you the same way. They all seem to come from the same source.

"It will be your job to constantly ask yourself: Logic or emotion? Facts or feelings? In this case, you must work hard to separate your common sense from your emotions."

A few of the more favorable jurors seemed to have relaxed their tight facial expressions, but most still looked skeptical. The visual image of Rachel Crawford had been burned into their brains—right side or left, it didn't seem to matter.

"I will help you do that as much as I can. I want you to know that I have sympathy for Mr. Crawford too. Nobody should have to bear the silence that Ms. Starling talked about. The question here is not whether life has been fair to Mr. Crawford. The question is who should be blamed."

Jason hesitated. This next promise was a bit of a risk, but it was a manageable risk. The conventional wisdom was that a good defense attorney wouldn't cross-examine an innocent victim like Blake Crawford who had no factual knowledge about the event itself. Plus, Jason already had the man's video deposition. He could play the video if he needed it.

"I don't want Mr. Crawford to be sitting there wondering if I'm going to put him through the meat grinder on cross-examination." Jason turned slightly and caught a glimpse of Crawford. "So I'll tell you and him right now. When Mr. Crawford takes the stand, I'll have no questions for cross-examination. The man has already suffered enough."

A few of the jurors gave Jason a curious look. They hadn't been expecting that.

Jason picked up the MD-9 firearm that Kelly had left on the exhibit table and took it back to his own counsel table. He placed it in the middle of the table, a foot or so from Case McAllister's legal pad. He had warned Case to keep the table clear of everything else.

"I want you to keep your eye on that gun," Jason said. "The murder weapon. The one used by Larry Jamison. Sold by Peninsula Arms. Purchased by a man named Jarrod Beeson. And manufactured by my client, MD Firearms.

"I want you to watch it closely during my entire opening statement."

69

JASON MOVED BACK in front of the jury box. "Larry Jamison is not here today. He caused all of this heartbreak and chaos and loss. But he is not here. Why? Because the SWAT team took him out before he could kill other innocent victims in his vile rage. They used a standard issue Colt CAR-15 to do it. And you won't see that gun being introduced into evidence in a lawsuit against its maker. It's a military assault weapon, every bit as deadly as the MD-9—no doubt about that. But it was used to *protect* innocent life, not take it."

Jason walked over to his counsel table and stood behind the chair he had been sitting in. "There's an empty chair at the defense counsel table. Until now, I've been sitting here. But I've decided I'm not going to sit here anymore. Why? Because this is the number one chair at the defense counsel table, and the person sitting in this chair ought to be a lawyer for Larry Jamison. He's the one who pulled the trigger."

Next, Jason leaned over and asked Case McAllister to move down a seat, freeing up the second chair at the defense table. "This chair," Jason said, "ought to belong to Jarrod Beeson. Right now, he's a little busy, spending twelve months behind bars for participating in a gunrunning operation. He bought the gun for Larry Jamison, knowing that Jamison couldn't purchase it on his own. In fact, Beeson bought more than twenty guns from Peninsula Arms and turned right around and sold many of them to criminals."

Jason stood there for a moment, his hands on the chair in front of him. "This is Beeson's seat."

There was only one chair left at the counsel table, the seat now occupied by Case McAllister. Behind the table were several other leather chairs for legal assistants and others helping the lawyers. Jason took two of those chairs and moved them parallel to the counsel table but several feet away, on the opposite side of the table from the jury. He asked Case McAllister to move into one of those seats.

For the rest of trial, Jason and Case would be sitting there, with no table to put their notes on. It would be awkward but it would be a lasting visual reminder of his opening statement.

But Kelly Starling was on her feet. "Judge, I object to this . . . whatever it is. It's certainly not an opening statement; it's more like musical chairs."

"It's unusual," Jason said, "I admit. But I'm not aware of any rule that says we've got to sit *at* the table instead of *next to* the table."

"Let's get on with it," Garrison said. "Objection overruled."

"This last chair," Jason continued, "the last one actually *at* the table, is for Peninsula Arms. They engaged in numerous straw sales. They have actually been cited three times by the ATF. And they sold this gun to Jarrod Beeson knowing that he would in turn sell it to somebody else who wasn't a legal purchaser. Yet you won't hear from the store's owner or the clerks; they're all taking the Fifth Amendment."

Jason surveyed the table and walked back to the jury. "There are only two reasons the plaintiffs are trying to put my client at that table. The first is because my client has money—"

"Objection!"

"Sustained. Watch yourself, Mr. Noble."

"The second is because my client sold guns to Peninsula Arms even though they allegedly knew the gun dealer had sold some guns illegally. But let me ask you a question. When you buy a car, do you expect the car dealer or car manufacturer to check your driving record and refuse to sell you a car if you've got a few speeding tickets? No. You expect the government to suspend your license if you've got too many tickets to be driving. But if the government allows you to drive, and you've got a valid license, you expect the car dealer to sell you a vehicle. Ford's job is to sell cars, not police the roads.

"In the same way, it is the responsibility of the Bureau of Alcohol, Tobacco, and Firearms—we commonly refer to them as the ATF—it is the ATF's job to police the gun stores. It is MD Firearms's job to manufacture guns—good guns, guns that work as advertised—and then sell those guns to any licensed firearm dealer."

Jason pointed to the defense table. "I asked you to watch that gun," he said. "Did you notice that the gun hasn't moved? It's not an animate object with a conscience and a sense of good and evil. That gun is simply an object.

It can be used for good, like the SWAT team used their guns, or evil, the way Jamison used this particular gun.

"Jamison pulled the trigger. Beeson supplied the black market. Peninsula Arms sold guns illegally. And MD Firearms? All they did was manufacture a lawful product that worked as advertised and then sell it to a licensed firearm dealer operating with the blessing of the federal government.

"Use the left side of your brain, and ask yourself this simple question: Other than the fact that my client has money, why is MD Firearms even sitting in this courtroom?"

70

AFTER LUNCH, Kelly put Blake Crawford on the stand to tell his story. His lips forced a smile or two as he talked about Rachel, but his eyes never joined in. The dark circles under them reflected a lifetime of sadness at the age of thirty-two.

Kelly walked Blake through several old videos and still photos to illustrate the life and times of Rachel Crawford. Blake was careful not to turn his wife into a saint. Rachel had an ornery side, he said—that was part of the reason he loved her. But she also had this sense of justice. If the good Lord intended for Rachel to die young, then at least she died while fighting for something she believed in—the rights of young international students who fell victim to Larry Jamison's human-trafficking schemes.

Kelly had provided Blake with a general outline of the questions she would be asking, but she hadn't gone over them word for word. She wanted the testimony to be spontaneous, and she was hearing many of the answers herself for the very first time. As she listened, she realized that she had been so focused on Blake as a client that she had really not spent much time thinking about Rachel.

"You quoted Martin Luther King Jr. in your opening statement," Blake said. "One of the things that motivated Rachel was another quote from Dr. King: 'Injustice anywhere is a threat to justice everywhere.' It's why she did investigative reports on people like Larry Jamison."

At that moment, Kelly realized how much she and Rachel were alike. Their mutual desire to help the poor and oppressed. Their crusader mentality. Even the focus on this particular issue: human trafficking.

A few minutes later, as Blake struggled to explain what it was like not having Rachel in the house, he choked up, fighting back emotion. Kelly felt tears stinging her own eyes, both in sympathy for Blake and in the stark recognition that Blake and Rachel had enjoyed something together that Kelly had never experienced.

"Do you need to take a break?" she asked.

He shook his head, as she knew he would. "I'm sorry," he said. Kelly could tell every jury member wanted to tell him there was no need to apologize. "I just miss her so much."

Kelly let that statement linger and then started a series of questions about the plans Blake and Rachel had for a family. It was the part of Blake's testimony that Kelly had been dreading most, but she found it easier to get through than she had anticipated.

At the end of nearly three hours of testimony, interrupted by only one fifteen-minute break, Kelly circled back to Rachel's quest for justice.

"Did that sense of who Rachel was—the way she fought for fairness and justice—did that impact your decision to file this suit?"

Kelly half expected an objection from Jason, but her opponent hadn't objected once during the entire testimony. He sat there in his chair next to his client, legal pad on his lap, looking both pitiful and silly as he tried to make do without a table to write on.

"I'm not one for conflict and confrontation," Blake said. "I believe in forgiveness. But if we can save one other family from going through this kind of pain, it will be worth it. I know it's what Rachel would have wanted me to do."

"No further questions," Kelly said, returning to her seat.

Jason stood up at his chair and didn't even move toward the witness. "I'm sorry for your loss, Mr. Crawford."

"Thank you."

"Your Honor, I have no questions for this witness."

◁▷

During the remaining hour of court on Wednesday, Kelly called Bob Thomas, the WDXR news director, to the stand. She wanted to end the first day strong and emblazon that video footage on the jury's mind.

Thomas had been in the studio when Jamison entered, and it was Thomas who had called 911 for help. After the initial round of shooting, he had been hiding from Jamison behind some equipment. While plotting a strategy to thwart Jamison, Thomas had been pointed out by Lisa Roberts. After that, he had gone into the control booth to make sure the WDXR feed was live on the air as Jamison had demanded.

He described in vivid detail how he had watched Jamison threaten both Lisa and Rachel with his gun, spewing his vitriol for the live television audience. Thomas described how helpless he felt and how it seemed like forever before the SWAT team arrived. At the end of his testimony, Kelly asked him to identify the tape and then introduced it into evidence. At a few minutes before five, she asked the judge if she could show the tape to the jury again.

Jason stood. "They've already seen it once, Judge. How many times are we going to make them watch it?"

"I'm entitled to show it once during opening and again during the case," Kelly said.

"I don't think it's changed any," Jason countered. "And the jury's got a pretty good memory. But if you insist, I'll withdraw my objection."

You jerk, Kelly thought. Jason's well-timed objection had just blunted the effectiveness of her second showing. Now it looked like Kelly was just trying to play to the jury's emotions.

Which, of course, she was.

Still, she had no choice but to roll the tape a second time. She noticed that the jury's reaction was more muted this time. Halfway through, she wished she had saved it for closing.

The tape concluded at a few minutes after five. "No more questions," Kelly said.

Judge Garrison looked at Jason. "Shall we save cross-examination for tomorrow?"

Jason stood and shrugged. "Actually, I only have a few quick questions. No sense making the witness come back a second day."

Garrison frowned. "Make it quick."

Jason positioned himself in the middle of the courtroom. "So if I understand this correctly, for a while you were hiding from Jamison."

"That's correct."

"How far away—ten feet, twenty?"

"I don't know; probably more like thirty or forty."

"Okay. Did Jamison ever have his back turned toward you?"

"Yeah. Once or twice."

"Do you own a gun, Mr. Thomas?"

"No."

"On that particular day, do you wish you'd had a gun?"

The witness hesitated, shifting in his seat. "I wish I could have done something to stop that madman. So, yes, I guess I would have liked to have had a gun."

"No further questions," Jason said, returning to his seat.

Before he sat down, Kelly was on her feet. "Redirect, Your Honor. Just one question."

Garrison nodded.

"On that day, Mr. Thomas, do you wish Larry Jamison had *not* had a gun?"

"Oh, most definitely."

71

WHEN COURT ADJOURNED, the adrenaline that had been coursing through Kelly's body all day suddenly disappeared. It felt like somebody had just squeezed every ounce of emotion out of her, leaving her drained and lifeless. The wear and tear of a day in court was worse than her most demanding swim meets had ever been.

She left court side by side with Blake Crawford, stopping on the steps of the courthouse to field questions from the press. It seemed like years ago that she had entered the courthouse jacked up to give her opening statement. She had hours of work still ahead of her tonight, and then she would be back first thing tomorrow to do battle all over again.

The pressure was unbelievable. The high points of a trial were so exhilarating, the low points so devastating. And the crazy thing was, she loved every minute of it.

She answered a dozen or so questions, keeping her responses bland and professional, then headed to her car. She had spent the early evening hours of the previous day preparing Blake for his testimony. Afterward, she worked on her opening until 1 a.m. She hadn't had time to get a minute of exercise in nearly four days. As she climbed into her car, she felt sluggish, hungry, and physically exhausted.

As she started the car, her BlackBerry buzzed—Darcie Rollins, her firm's PR director. "Are you on your way to the hotel?" Darcie asked.

"Yeah. What's up?"

"I need you to go to the WDXR studios. They're letting you use the satellite uplink for some interviews tonight. First one starts at 7:00."

"What interviews?" Kelly said.

"You haven't checked your messages?"

"*What* interviews?"

Kelly waited. When Darcie finally answered, her voice sounded less enthusiastic. "We set up three interviews with cable shows—CNN, CNBC and Fox. You can get them all done by 8:30."

Kelly almost lit into the poor woman. She didn't have time to play TV celebrity. She'd be lucky to get in bed by midnight even if she went straight to work. Somehow, miraculously, she kept her temper in check. "I can't do these interviews," she said. "I'm in the middle of a trial."

But Darcie wouldn't take no for an answer. The senior partners at the firm sensed an unparalleled marketing opportunity. Darcie was just following orders. She had already committed Kelly; they couldn't back out now.

This time, Kelly let her anger play itself out. She vented for nearly three minutes, blasting the firm and her senior partners and even Darcie for being so insensitive. She ultimately agreed to do two of the shows but made Darcie cancel the Fox interview. "And Darcie . . ."

"Yes?"

"Don't you dare schedule one more interview without checking with me first."

"O-kay," Darcie sounded hesitant. "No more after tomorrow morning."

"What?"

"You were such a hit on the *Today* show last time around. They really wanted you back. They're sending a crew to your hotel."

◁▷

By the time Jason arrived at the office, his father and Case McAllister had already met. They were comparing guns and swapping firearms stories like old friends. You would have never known that Jason's dad harbored a deep resentment toward MD Firearms.

Andrew Lassiter, meanwhile, was hunched over a computer in the conference room, oblivious to everyone else. Bella was playing hostess and providing a running commentary on the status of various tasks.

Jason gathered his team in the cramped conference room, nudging aside Andrew Lassiter's stacks of documents and spreadsheets so they could all have a place to sit. Bella brought in dinner in Styrofoam containers—lasagna and salads from the Purple Cow.

Jason hardly touched his food as he focused on the list of tasks to be completed. "Our first priority is to get this shadow jury in place," he said. "I feel like I'm running blind until we start getting that feedback."

Andrew launched into a five-minute explanation of why the process was taking so long. Bella rolled her eyes.

"Can we have them in place by tomorrow night?" Jason asked.

Before Andrew opened his mouth, Case chimed in. "A simple yes or no will do," he said.

"It's not that easy," Andrew murmured, though he wouldn't look at Case. "Bella and I have interviewed close to two hundred prospects on the phone. If we want exact matches, it takes time." He shook his head a little, a nervous twitch that Jason hadn't seen before. "This isn't what I'm good at—talking to potential shadow jurors. At Justice Inc. I had other people doing that."

"Can you help him, Dad?" Jason asked.

Jason's father shrugged. He was probably thinking that he hadn't flown in from Atlanta to do secretarial work, but he didn't say no.

"I'll take that as a yes," Jason said.

They spent another half hour bickering about the mountain of tasks that needed to be addressed: witnesses to prepare, deposition designations to complete, preparation of cross-examination questions, legal research, factual research . . . Jason got depressed just talking about it. Every item they surfaced generated five additional unfinished items. Bella kept grousing about how it would be impossible to get it all done.

Finally, Case had heard enough. He took charge of the meeting and assigned responsibilities and deadlines for each task. He insisted that Jason be freed up to focus on developing his cross-examinations of the witnesses.

"I'll make another pot of coffee," Bella said. "It's going to be a long night."

Two hours later, Jason took a break and wandered down the hall to a makeshift office his dad was using as he called potential mock jurors. His father occupied the only chair in the room, so Jason leaned against the wall, waiting for his dad to finish his call.

"Thanks for coming," Jason said.

"You're still my son," his father said, locking onto Jason with bloodshot eyes. "From what I was hearing, it sounded like you could use a little help."

Jason wasn't sure what that meant, so he let it pass. He closed the door and placed a sheet of paper on the desk in front of his dad. "I didn't bring you up here just to help manage the shadow jury," Jason said.

"That's a relief."

"I really need you to investigate a couple of jurors." Jason nodded toward the sheet. "Three and Seven. Nobody else can even know you're doing this."

"What for?" Jason's dad narrowed his eyes and his thick eyebrows drew together. Jury tampering was a felony.

"Nothing illegal, Dad. I've just got a feeling that they're holding something back, that for some reason they're out to nail me."

"A *feeling*," his dad said sarcastically.

"It's complicated," Jason replied. "I can't tell you anything else right now."

Jason's dad stood. "I'm your father, Jason. If you're in trouble, I need to know."

For a moment, Jason seriously considered telling him. It would feel so much better to have someone else share this burden. But he knew what would happen. As soon as his dad was brought into the know, Jason would no longer control the response. His options would disappear; his dad would try to dictate what to do. Another cover-up would be in full swing.

"Will you do it?" Jason asked.

"You're not going to tell me why?"

"Not yet. I can't."

Jason's dad blew out a big sigh, one of those where-did-I-go-wrong exhalations that Jason knew all too well. "When do you need it by?"

"Anything you can have by tomorrow night would be great."

"You need any other miracles with that?" his dad asked. "A Red Sea parting maybe? Water into wine?"

"Nope. I'm good," Jason said. Despite the pressure of the case, something about this conversation seemed right. It was the first time they had talked without fighting since Christmas day.

"By the way, whenever you're done and ready to go, just come and get me," Jason said. "I can always finish my work at the cottage."

"Thanks," his dad said. "But I already checked into a hotel."

◁ ▷

Jason arrived at his cottage well past midnight, so tired he could barely move. He took off his shoes, threw his suit coat, shirt, and tie on a chair, and sat down on the couch in front of the TV. He flipped from one channel to the next, anything to distract his mind from the case. Before long he had curled up on the couch and fallen asleep with the remote in his hand, the channel stuck on a late-night talk show.

A few hours later, his neck stiff from being propped against a pillow on the armrest, Jason woke up. Instinctively, before he staggered up to bed, he checked his BlackBerry. The e-mail jolted him awake:

> Slow the trial down. Don't put Poole on the stand until Monday. Keep up the good work. Your secrets are safe with me.
>
> Luthor

72

ROBERT SHERWOOD arrived at work early on Thursday, content in the knowledge that the three mock juries hearing the Crawford case would start their day, as they had the day before, precisely at 7:00 a.m. The case was proceeding beautifully on all fronts except for the timing. Trials moved fast in the Virginia Beach Circuit Court. Maybe a little too fast.

If they worked from 7 a.m. until about 10 at night, Sherwood figured his trial team should be able to complete the truncated version of the Crawford case that evening. All three mock juries would return a verdict by midnight.

On Friday, Justice Inc. would make its move in the stock market. That would leave the weekend to meet with the various hedge fund managers who would in turn make their market moves on Monday. The actual verdict in the Crawford case would not come back until late Monday afternoon at the earliest. Most probably it would be Tuesday or Wednesday.

The timing could work, but it was tight. There was no margin for error.

◁ ▷

The pro-gun demonstrators had shown up in droves outside the courtroom on the first day of trial, but their numbers had dwindled by day two. They would probably be back tenfold for closing arguments, but unlike the colorful parade of characters who protested G8 summits, these folks had real jobs. Protesting was just a hobby. Plus, the forecasters were saying the temperature could reach a hundred degrees by early afternoon.

The jury wasn't ushered into the box until nearly 10 a.m., a full hour later than Judge Garrison had wanted to start. He apologized to the jury, told them that he and the lawyers had been working on a few housekeeping matters (Jason and Kelly had argued for an hour over Jason's objections to certain portions of the Beeson deposition), and thanked the jurors for their patience.

The jury began the day watching the videotaped deposition testimony of Jarrod Beeson. The felonious gunrunner came across every bit as disreputable on the screen as he had in person. His dark eyes darted back and forth from the camera to Kelly, and his facial expressions alternated between a smirk and a sneer. He had about three days' worth of facial hair and wore an orange jumpsuit.

Despite the man's obvious status as a prison inmate, the jury watched carefully, and several members took notes.

Beeson admitted that he had purchased a total of twenty-three guns from Peninsula Arms. Most of the guns he resold at a profit to convicted felons who weren't eligible to buy the guns outright. Sometimes he filed off the serial number first; sometimes he didn't. Two of the guns he purchased had been traced to crimes.

Judge Garrison had sustained Jason's hearsay objections to the portions of the deposition describing the alleged phone call between Larry Jamison and Beeson. But that didn't prohibit Beeson from talking about the way he purchased the gun.

On the video, Beeson explained that he and Jamison had arranged to meet at Peninsula Arms. It was Larry Jamison who talked to the sales clerk and checked out various guns while Beeson watched. Once Jamison had settled on the MD-9, the two men went outside the store, and money changed hands. Beeson returned to the store, filled out the paperwork, and gave the clerk the money. He then carried the gun out to the parking lot and handed it to Jamison. He never saw Jamison again.

Jason's videotaped cross-examination followed. He had focused on Beeson's lack of connection with MD Firearms. Beeson had bought and resold all kinds of guns, from several different gun stores, and it just so happened that this particular gun was manufactured by MD Firearms. Plus, Beeson was an admitted liar—he had lied at least twenty-three separate times, on twenty-three separate forms, all signed under oath and under penalty of jail time for dishonesty.

But as Jason watched the jury, it seemed that they believed every word Beeson said. His confession had earned him twelve months in a federal pen. Why would he make it up?

Kelly followed Beeson's testimony by calling Lisa Roberts, WDXR's photogenic news anchor, to the stand. In Jason's opinion, the witness tried way too hard, milking her time on national TV for everything it was worth. She broke down crying at least twice and used all kinds of animated facial expressions and hand gestures in talking to the jury. Jason could read the frustration on Kelly's face as she tried to rein in the witness.

Lisa had not exactly played the role of hero on the day Larry Jamison had walked into the studio, so she worked hard to recast events in a more favorable light. But a few things were undeniable. She had ratted out the show's director, Bob Thomas, when he was hiding. Later, she had refused to stick up for Rachel Crawford's innocence. Granted, she had the business end of the MD-9 pointed at her face, but the jury still seemed to dislike her, folding their arms in stone-faced disapproval as she tried her best to charm them.

The irony of a jury trial, thought Jason. *They believe the felon. But they don't like the innocent news anchor.*

After Lisa Roberts's direct examination, Jason announced he had no questions for cross and thought he noticed some disappointed looks from the jury box. "Oh, wait," he said, "I do have one question."

Lisa had already climbed halfway out of the witness box, and Jason waited for her to sit back down.

"Are you going to sue MD Firearms too?"

"Objection," said Kelly Starling. "That's not relevant here."

"Goes to bias, Your Honor," Jason said calmly.

"Overruled."

The witness stared at Jason for a moment. He knew that MD Firearms had already received a letter from her lawyer.

"Depends on how this case turns out," Lisa said.

"I see," Jason said. And he hoped the jury did as well. The slippery slope—*Where would it all stop?* "So you're thinking about suing even though you weren't actually shot by Jamison, am I right?"

"Objection!"

Jason held up his hands. "She's right, Your Honor. That was two questions. I promised the jury just one. I'll withdraw it."

73

THE PARADE OF WITNESSES continued throughout the morning and into the early afternoon. The WDXR station manager testified about how much potential Rachel had demonstrated as a reporter. The medical examiner certified the cause of death. Kelly even trotted two Peninsula Arms clerks and the store owner to the stand and forced them to plead the Fifth Amendment in front of the jury.

Then Kelly called Case McAllister and asked him just enough questions to lay a foundation for the memo he had written to Melissa Davids. Just to preserve the record, Jason objected to the memo on the basis of the attorney-client privilege. Judge Garrison overruled the objection again, stating that Melissa Davids had waived that privilege when she shared the document with others.

Jason had no questions for Case at this time. He planned to call Case to the stand when it was his turn to put on witnesses, unless Melissa Davids did so well that Case was not necessary. In either event, Jason would save his questions until later in the trial.

After lunch, Kelly cued up portions of the videotaped depositions of Melissa Davids. The MD Firearms CEO looked angry as Kelly grilled her about the redesign of the MD-9 after 833 of those guns had been converted by criminals into full automatics and later traced to crimes. She responded testily as Kelly quizzed her about the silencer parts MD Firearms sold and the company's run-in with the ATF, including Davids' agreement with the letter to the editor that compared the ATF to the regimes of Hitler and Stalin.

Jason watched despondently as Kelly asked in the first deposition whether Melissa Davids had ever considered whether she should stop selling guns to Peninsula Arms based on their three ATF violations and the number of their guns that had been traced to crimes.

"No," Davids said. "If anybody had suggested such a thing to me, I would have told them I still believed in the Second Amendment and the free enterprise system."

Kelly followed that response with excerpts from the second deposition, where she showed Case McAllister's memo to Davids. This time, the witness became outright hostile. It was not hard for Jason to read the jurors' body language; every one of them demonstrated a thinly veiled contempt for his client.

The last witness of the day, an ATF agent named Bill Treadwell, took the stand with an air of unmistakable confidence. He wore a buttoned blue blazer, a white shirt with a red tie, and khakis. He had short red hair and a freckled complexion—a young man's face that invited trust.

When he settled into the stand, he removed a pair of reading glasses from his pocket and placed them on the rail in front of him. Kelly Starling led him through a series of artfully phrased questions—the choreographed waltz of direct examination.

Treadwell had been one of the agents who obtained the confession from Jarrod Beeson, and he described his investigation into the straw purchase. He also taught the jury about the paperwork and process required to purchase a firearm—the background check, the ATF Form 4473, and other aspects of the sale. He testified about the three other times Peninsula Arms had been cited for straw sales.

Treadwell spoke softly, listened carefully, and confined his answers to the precise questions before him. Through his testimony, Kelly managed to put a boy-next-door face on the ATF, making Davids's statements about the ATF seem even more outrageous.

Kelly finished her direct examination of Treadwell at about 4 p.m., ending with the introduction of the gun into evidence.

Jason rose quickly to begin his cross. He was so caught up in the competition of the moment that he was hardly even nervous.

"Are you aware of any gun manufacturers in the entire country who refuse to sell guns to licensed firearm dealers because they don't trust those dealers?"

Treadwell thought for a moment. "No. Not that I'm aware of."

"As a point of fact, it's the ATF's job to police firearm dealers, is it not?

"We regulate dealers, yes."

"The ATF can revoke licenses of gun dealers, true?"

"That's correct."

"And you have personally been involved in that process, isn't that right?"

"Yes."

"Are you aware that fifteen years ago there were about 250,000 licensed dealers in America, and today there are less than half that number—about 108,381?"

Treadwell shrugged. "I'm not aware of the precise numbers. But that sounds about right."

"Do you recognize the name Red's Trading Post of Twin Falls, Idaho?"

Treadwell's face dropped a little. He had been transferred east a few years earlier. "Yes."

"That store's been in business for seventy-one years, correct?"

"I don't know. Sounds about right."

"You tried to revoke their license, right?"

"Objection," Kelly said. "What's this got to do with the Crawford case?"

"I'll link it up," Jason promised.

"Make it quick," Garrison said.

Jason turned back to the witness. "You tried to revoke their license, right?"

"We *did* revoke their license. In 2006. For multiple violations over a series of years."

"But the gun store appealed that case to federal court, didn't they?"

"Yes."

"And let me ask you if this is a statement that the federal judge made in that case: 'The ATF speaks of violations found during the inspections of 2000 and 2005, but fails to reveal that additional investigations in 2001 and 2007 revealed no violations or problems.'"

"I don't have the opinion memorized, but it was something like that."

"So the court overturned the revocation, didn't it?"

This brought Kelly to her feet again, palms out. "Judge, I still don't see how this can possibly be relevant to this case."

"I agree," Garrison said. "Objection sustained."

"Isn't it true," Jason said, checking his notes again, "that the number of gun dealers dropped by at least 50 percent in the ten years leading up to 2005 and that revocations of licenses increased nearly sixfold between 2001 and 2006?"

"I wouldn't know if those statistics are accurate or not."

"But you would agree that the ATF has stepped up its enforcement activities, aggressively going after gun stores that violate the law?"

"We've always done that, Mr. Noble."

"Then what actions did you take to revoke the license of Peninsula Arms after its third straw purchase citation?"

"We issued a license revocation notice on September 18 of last year."

"That's after Mr. Jamison shot Rachel Crawford. I'm asking what you did before that—given the fact that Peninsula Arms had already been cited for three prior straw purchase transactions."

Treadwell adjusted himself in the chair and tried to make eye contact with Kelly. Jason took a half step to the side, placing himself directly in the witness's sight path.

"We didn't deem those other citations—which were spread out over nearly ten years—sufficient to take revocation action," Treadwell said.

"But you were also aware, were you not, that a number of guns from Peninsula Arms had been traced to crimes in cities in the northeast—cities like Philadelphia, Baltimore, New York, and Washington?"

"Yes. But without information that the sales of those guns somehow violated the law, we couldn't take legal action against the dealer."

"My point exactly," Jason said.

"Objection!" Kelly said. "Move to strike."

Judge Garrison cast Jason a castigating glance and then turned to the jury. "Please ignore that last statement by Mr. Noble," the judge said. "I will strike it from the record. And Mr. Noble—please keep your editorial comments to yourself."

"Yes, Your Honor." Jason checked through his notes. "I do have one other question," he said. "To your knowledge, has Ms. Starling filed any lawsuits against the ATF for its failure to take action against Peninsula Arms?"

"No, she has not."

"No further questions."

Before he sat down, Jason casually moved one more empty chair up to the defense counsel table. When he sat in his own seat, next to Case McAllister, all eyes were on him.

Case leaned over. "After this case, you need to raise your hourly rate."

74

AT THE END of Agent Treadwell's testimony, Kelly stood up and announced that she rested her case.

Inside, she was already second-guessing her strategy. She had started strong with the videotape of the shootings and the testimony of Blake Crawford. But she had wanted to finish strong too. She had toyed with the idea of ending on the videotaped testimony of Melissa Davids—a guaranteed high point for her side. Instead, she decided to end her case with Treadwell's testimony, hoping to demonstrate in the flesh that ATF agents were the furthest thing from Hitler and Stalin.

Unfortunately, Treadwell had been a disaster.

Now Jason Noble was on his feet again. "I have a motion to make," he said.

The lawyers and Judge Garrison all knew what was coming—a Motion to Strike. Defense lawyers routinely made such motions at the end of a plaintiff's case, asking the judge to throw out the case because the evidence was legally insufficient.

"Okay," Judge Garrison said, checking his watch. "I'm going to let the ladies and gentlemen of the jury go home for the night, and then we can discuss the motion."

Kelly nodded her head. This was normal and no cause for alarm.

But then Judge Garrison added something that twisted her stomach in knots. "I'm also going to ask the jury not to arrive tomorrow until 1 p.m. It's going to take us a while to work through this motion, and I'd like to give the jurors the morning off."

Almost every member of the jury smiled. Judge Garrison had just become a very popular man.

And Kelly was sick with worry.

◁▷

Jason stayed off the phone during the twenty-minute drive back to his office. His success in court had only made him feel like a bigger hypocrite. Only he knew that even if he tore apart witnesses like Agent Treadwell on cross-examination, his case would ultimately implode when Chief Poole took the stand.

It was bad enough that Jason was forced to call Poole as a witness, bad enough that he had been manipulated into keeping two jurors on the case whom he really didn't want, but now he was being forced to use Poole as his last witness. By waiting until Monday to call Poole, Jason would end his case the same way Kelly had ended hers—with a whimper.

Maybe he was just being paranoid. Maybe this guy Luthor really thought Poole would be a good witness. Maybe Luthor wasn't the one who had provided the damaging documents to Kelly; maybe Luthor had no idea that Poole would get destroyed on cross-examination. Jason couldn't communicate with the man, so it was impossible to know what he was really thinking. Maybe Jurors 3 and 7 would be strong advocates for Jason's cause.

And maybe Santa Claus would show up tomorrow and grant Jason's Motion to Strike.

If nothing else, Jason's life had taught him to be a realist. Mothers die. Fathers disappoint. Friends get killed in car accidents. You get fired for doing a good job. Life is not fair. You move on the best you can.

What made it harder was that Jason had developed such great respect for Case McAllister. The man had done nothing but encourage and coach Jason since the day they met. Case was entrusting his entire company and career to a rookie lawyer. And Jason was rewarding that trust by selling Case out to an anonymous blackmailer.

But what else could Jason do? Betray his father and Matt Corey? If he did that, the case would be declared a mistrial, and MD Firearms would have to start over. He could quite possibly lose his law license, and serious jail time was not out of the question.

But maybe then he could at least live with himself.

He stopped at a red light, his knuckles white on the steering wheel. He was actually trembling from all the pressure, his mind racing wildly from one thought to the next.

The light turned green, and Jason took a few deep breaths. He forced himself to think logically. *Left brain, Jason; filter out the emotions. Slow down.* He needed to play this out one step at a time. If he won the Motion to Strike tomorrow, the case would be over. Even if he lost, he could call Melissa Davids as his first witness. That would buy him the weekend.

He would run out of time on Monday morning—either rest his case or call Chief Poole to the stand. Honor or reputation? Should he sacrifice his own father or MD Firearms?

His hands started shaking again as he drove slowly through the intersection.

◁ ▷

When Jason got to the office, it was deserted except for Case McAllister. The veteran lawyer was in the firm's small kitchen, finishing dinner from the Purple Cow disposable containers.

"I'm going to pick up Melissa at the airport," Case said. "I'll take care of getting her ready to testify."

"Thanks."

"You look like death," Case said. "You need to get something to eat and take an hour or two off."

He shoved a couple of the Styrofoam containers at Jason. Chicken wrap, turkey club, or Caesar salad. Jason didn't care.

"I've got to work on my argument for the Motion to Strike," Jason said. He tried to sound upbeat but felt like he was on autopilot. "I'll rest this weekend."

"You might want to call Bella. She's been trying to get in touch with you."

Jason smiled. "I know. Four messages on my BlackBerry."

After Case left, Jason dialed Bella's number. She was at the Courtyard Marriott hotel at the oceanfront with the shadow jury. She and Andrew Lassiter had shown them the opening statements and the first few witnesses. Each individual juror had filled out a brief questionnaire.

"Andrew says we can't give them any hint who we're working for," Bella reported. "He says it might sway their opinions."

"Yeah, that's standard procedure," Jason replied. "Don't want them to know which side is paying them."

Bella scoffed at the notion. "That wouldn't influence me any. If I don't like somethin', I tell people. Makes no difference who's paying me."

"I've noticed."

"Anyway, they like you a lot. But they like Ms. Starling too."

This didn't surprise Jason. He would talk with Andrew later and get a full report on any subtle strategy changes he needed to make based on the shadow jury's feedback.

"Andrew says to tell you that the two jurors he would have selected are more favorable than the two you left on the jury," Bella said. "But I still say you've got to trust your instincts."

The mention of Jurors 3 and 7 made Jason's gut clench. "Is my father down there?" he asked, changing the subject.

Bella hesitated. "Your dad's not exactly the easiest guy to work with." Jason could just picture the friction between Bella and his dad—the bellicose secretary and the no-nonsense detective. "He basically left halfway through the day, said he had some investigative work to do. Wouldn't tell me what it was."

Jason thanked Bella and walked from the kitchen into his office. There was a manila envelope on his chair with his father's handwriting on the outside. *Jason Noble, private and confidential. Not to be opened by anyone else.*

Jason tore open the envelope and pulled out a memo from his father with a number of backup documents attached. The memo was written with the clinical detachment of a criminal detective documenting interviews. The information confirmed Jason's worst fears.

Among other things, his dad had interviewed students who had taken a course from Rodney Peterson, Juror 3. They had all praised Professor Peterson's teaching but labeled him as "progressive" or "liberal." On the issue of gun control, most remembered how passionate Peterson became when talking about the assassination of Martin Luther King Jr. and JFK. He bemoaned the culture's fascination with guns and violence. Most students acted surprised that Peterson had been allowed to stay on the jury.

But during jury selection, Jason recalled, Peterson had claimed to have an open mind. He had answered every question truthfully, and this additional information gave Jason no legal basis to have him disqualified now.

At the end of his memo, Jason's dad couldn't resist the urge to temporarily depart from his detached writing style and editorialize a little. *Why is a guy like Peterson even on this jury? Didn't your other investigator pick this up? I looked in the file on Peterson and there were NO interviews with former students.*

Why indeed? Jason thought.

The memo on Marcia Franks, Juror 7, was even more troubling. Nothing in Rafael's investigation was wrong: Marcia was a registered Democrat with no religious affiliation, had her kids in a private academy, and proudly displayed her Obama sticker.

But what Rafael Johansen's original report did not contain caused Jason to go weak in the knees. He had been set up. There was no longer any doubt about that.

He glumly read through the details. Marcia Franks had been through a nasty divorce more than ten years ago. She had accused her husband of hiding assets but could never quite prove it. There had been an extended custody battle, and it looked like Marcia had been the loser, receiving joint custody until their son turned sixteen, at which time he had decided to live with his father. Marcia Franks would hate Chief Poole, a man who would undoubtedly remind her of her own ex-husband.

Jason slumped in his chair, the stark reality of his dilemma hitting home. Luthor was playing it smart. Neither of these jurors had a thing in their background that would disqualify them from serving. But the toxic mixture of Chief Poole, Marcia Franks, and Rodney Peterson would guarantee only one result.

Jason could see the endgame now. If Judge Garrison didn't grant the Motion to Strike, money would flow into short sales of gun-company stocks and put options—options that would become incredibly valuable if the stocks went down.

The justice game was in full swing. And the house held all the cards.

75

THAT EVENING, Luthor ran the figures one last time. Luthor had already established a number of offshore companies to hide the millions of dollars that would be flowing in when the gun companies—MD Firearms in particular—began to collapse. After Ed Poole took the stand on Monday, Jason Noble's case would tank and the stocks would nose-dive. With any luck, Luthor's investments would more than double.

Luthor had also considered a worst-case scenario. Plan B was premised on the unlikely scenario that Jason Noble might try to play the hero and report the blackmail scheme to the authorities. By manipulating the paperwork and forging signatures, Luthor had ensured that ownership of the offshore companies would lead to none other than Jason Noble and Kelly Starling.

Luthor knew the authorities were naturally suspicious of blackmail claims. Many times, the "victim" was, in fact, the mastermind behind the crime, setting up an elaborate scheme to bilk innocent third parties out of their cash, much like guilty mothers who tried to blame a kidnapper for the "disappearance" of a child. The feds had learned to put the person reporting the claim on the short list of suspects.

Luthor would help that predisposition along by planting some subtle references to the offshore companies in Jason's and Kelly's e-mail histories. There would be just enough of a trail that the feds could piece it together. Luthor would walk away with the money, but the feds would think Jason and Kelly had fled the country and were now spending their millions under new identities in exotic locations. Everyone would marvel at the audacity of the young lawyers' plan. They would become the Bonnie and Clyde of the twenty-first century.

Rumors would surface about the two lawyers reappearing in this country or that country, but the rumors would be false.

The sad truth was that under Plan B, neither Jason Noble nor Kelly Starling would ever be heard from again.

◁ ▷

Jason tried to focus on preparing for the Motion to Strike hearing, but his heart wasn't in it. He kept checking the Kryptonite blog, though he knew his name wouldn't be there. At least not yet. His mind wandered to LeRon's family—their shock if they ever learned that their son had not been the one driving the car on the night he died. Facing LeRon's parents was a prospect worse than facing jail time.

"How could you let us live with this for ten years?" they would ask.

The other picture that wouldn't leave Jason's mind was of Chief Poole taking the witness stand. Kelly Starling's cross-examination would be devastating. Anger would smolder just beneath the surface for Marcia Franks, Juror 7. Worst of all would be the look on Case McAllister's face as the trial went up in flames.

Plus, the more time Jason spent researching the issue, the more he realized that Judge Garrison wasn't going to grant the Motion to Strike. Jason still couldn't get around the precedent of *Farley v. Guns Unlimited*. Garrison had ruled against Jason on this same legal issue at the Motion to Dismiss hearing earlier in the case. Unless Case's friends in the Virginia legislature had convinced Garrison to change his mind, the case was going to the jury.

Jason's spirits were buoyed a little when Andrew Lassiter and Bella returned with the feedback from the shadow jury. They were split four to three in Jason's favor after the opening statement. One juror had then switched to the plaintiff's side after Blake Crawford's testimony, but one had left the plaintiff's side after the testimony of Agent Treadwell and was now undecided. The net result was a virtual deadlock after the plaintiff's evidence—not a bad place to be for a defense lawyer.

Lassiter had a three-page list of suggestions that they discussed until about 11:30. Jason tried to focus on the details, but in reality, the minutiae of the case no longer interested him.

When Jason decided to pack it in for the night, Bella went into mom mode.

"Are you eating anything?" she asked. "You look awful."

"Yeah. I had a club sandwich."

"A trial is a long campaign," Bella lectured. "Not a single skirmish. You've got to rest, and you've got to eat."

"Good night," Jason said.

◁ ▷

Instead of going straight home, Jason decided to stop by his father's hotel. He couldn't explain why he felt this need to sit down and talk with his dad—*really* talk with him—but right now Jason was operating on emotion, not logic. The right brain had taken over.

He had decided to put it all out on the table—from Luthor's first e-mail to the impact of the investigation his dad had just concluded. Jason was ready to suggest that they do the right thing, though he feared his dad would resist it.

In a way, Jason didn't really care anymore. He was so tired of carrying this weight alone, so desperate to talk with someone about it, so sick of waking up and wondering if perhaps it had all been a bad dream, of wishing the nightmare that controlled his life would finally go away.

The desk clerk at the Holiday Inn Express dialed his dad's room, but there was no answer. Jason tried his dad's cell phone—still no answer. Jason pleaded for his dad's room number so he could go and knock on the door, but the clerk refused, citing hotel policy. With no other options, Jason settled in at a table in the hotel lobby and waited. His guess was that his dad was out on the town.

It was 1:30 before his dad staggered in through the lobby door. Jason had seen his dad like this before, the unsteady gait and the faraway look in his eyes.

Jason was out of his dad's line of sight and thought about just watching his dad stagger to the elevator so he could leave without saying anything.

But that was the whole problem. Avoidance. Procrastination. Running from the truth.

"Dad," Jason said.

His father stopped, startled. He looked at Jason, as if seeing a ghost. "Did you get the stuff I left in your office?" his dad asked, leaning back.

"Yeah. Can I talk to you for a minute?"

His dad sneered and chuckled a little. "A little late for talk, isn't it, Son?" He was speaking louder than normal, and Jason knew immediately that this was not the time.

But when would be the time?

"Have a seat," Jason said.

"Why? You got your buddy Prescott waitin' under the table? You want to embarrass the old man again?" Jason's dad spread his arms. "I'm right here. Anything you've got to say to me—say it right here."

"It's not about that, Dad. I need your help."

His dad reached into his pocket and pulled out a wad of bills. "Here. You want my help. This is all I got left." He walked over to Jason and slapped the money on the table. "You already took everything else," his dad said, his words slurred. "It wasn't enough for you to hate me, you had to get Jules on your side too—make her hate me."

Jason shook his head. He stood and tried to hand the money back to his father. "All right. Let's not talk about this now."

"Yeah. That's right," said his dad, rejecting the money. "Walk away from it, Son. That's what you always do." His father stepped closer, and the stench of his breath just about knocked Jason over. "All I ever wanted was a son with a little bit of backbone." He paused, his mind evidently working hard to stay on track. "And all I ever got was a son who just turns tail and runs."

Jason told himself his father didn't mean it. The alcohol was talking, not his dad. But the tears welled up anyway, though Jason fought them back and kept them from spilling over.

"That's right," his dad said. "Let's just have a good cry. That's what real men do." He patted the outside of Jason's arm, shook his head in disgust and turned to walk away.

"Wait," Jason said. He reached out and grabbed his father's arm, almost knocking him off his feet. "I love you, Dad." The words had slipped out before Jason knew what he was saying. "I don't care if you hate my guts. You're my father, and you're all I've got."

His father stood there for a moment, as if trying to make the slightest bit of sense out of what he had just heard. To Jason he looked pitiful—confused and at a total loss for words. If Jason had thrown a punch, his dad could have handled it. Somehow, drunk or not, he would have instinctively fought back.

But for this the man had no response.

He lowered his gaze and brushed Jason's hands from his arm. "I'm going to sleep." He staggered toward the elevator.

Jason watched until his father disappeared from sight.

"Good night, Dad," he said.

76

IN THE PACKED COURTROOM Friday morning, Jason had an unsettling sense of déjà vu. He had made these same arguments before, and this same judge had rejected them.

Kelly Starling quoted liberally from *Farley v. Guns Unlimited* for the proposition that proximate cause is a jury issue in these types of cases. This time, she reinforced her arguments with quotes from Judge Garrison's own ruling on the earlier Motion to Dismiss.

As before, Jason tried to argue that this case was prohibited by the Protection of Lawful Commerce in Arms Act. But Garrison quickly brushed that argument aside. "We're dealing with an exception to the Act, Counselor. The issue is whether your client's conduct aided or abetted the illegal activities of Peninsula Arms."

Garrison's questions were so one-sided that when Kelly Starling was arguing, Jason leaned over and whispered to Case, "I thought your boys in the state legislature were going to straighten him out."

Case just shrugged.

Garrison let the lawyers argue their positions for nearly two hours as the squat little judge enjoyed his turn in the spotlight. At eleven o'clock he took a short recess and fifteen minutes later returned to announce his ruling. He admonished the spectators that he would not tolerate any emotional outbursts, as if he believed his decision would be so controversial that the courtroom would erupt.

He read his opinion from the bench, alternately looking down at his notes and glancing up so the television cameras could enjoy a view of something more than the top of his bald head. He said he was duty-bound to follow the law. He didn't write the laws, and in fact many times he didn't even approve of the laws, but his job was to interpret them as written. A judge who attempts to rewrite laws is working for the wrong branch of government, Garrison said. He paused after that line, appearing confident that every evening news broadcast would use it as their lead.

"It is clear," he concluded, "that the plaintiff has presented a viable case under the law as it now stands. Accordingly, I am overruling the defendant's Motion to Strike."

◁ ▷

Kelly Starling's relief at surviving the Motion to Strike was short-lived. After lunch, Jason called his first witness to the stand. He didn't waste any time on supporting actors.

"The defense calls Melissa Davids," he announced.

The CEO of MD Firearms apparently had decided to take the Joe Six-pack approach. She wore jeans, boots, and a white blouse. She held her hand up, head erect, and proudly took the oath.

"Do you swear to tell the truth, the whole truth, and nothing but the truth, so help you God?"

"Absolutely."

The jury eyed her suspiciously. The pretrial publicity and her deposition had already made the diminutive woman infamous in their minds.

Kelly was no expert in body language, but if Osama bin Laden had climbed into the witness seat, she doubted the expressions on the jurors' faces would have been much different.

Jason stood and smiled at the witness. "Good afternoon, Ms. Davids."

"You can call me Melissa," she said. "As much as my company's paid you, we should be on a first-name basis by now."

Kelly rolled her eyes, hoping a few jurors were watching.

The next two hours made Kelly feel like throwing up. Jason did a good job of personalizing Davids and, by association, her company. Over Kelly's objections, Davids was allowed to talk about getting raped at age sixteen and trying to protect herself by learning jujitsu. She talked about another sexual assault that occurred two years later and how that second life-shattering experience had driven her to purchase her first gun.

She also talked about her struggles as a small-business owner. There were protestors to deal with and harassment by the ATF and all the normal personnel issues. When Jason mentioned that she must make a lot of money as the CEO of a large gun manufacturer, Davids laughed. She talked about mortgaging her house and borrowing from her 401(k). Sometimes she had to borrow from her husband's family and friends so she could make payroll. She regularly received death threats and hate mail, and once someone had tried to set her factory on fire.

And worst of all, of course, there were plaintiffs' attorneys. She had been sued a dozen times or so; frankly, she had lost track. But MD Firearms had never lost a case.

"You must have good lawyers," Jason said.

"Not really. We like to hire kids fresh out of law school. Give 'em a chance to learn." She smiled, and to Kelly's chagrin some of the jurors smiled with her. "We win because we're right."

At least twice, she corrected Jason in his terminology about guns. She turned to the jury when she talked about why they sold guns to anybody with a federal firearms license.

"My job is to make the best guns possible," she said. "And to pay my taxes so the government can monitor gun dealers for safety violations. Think about it in the context of air safety. Boeing makes the planes, but the federal government licenses the pilots. If a plane goes down due to pilot error, you don't sue Boeing.

"Gun dealers are the same way. The ATF decides who gets to sell guns and who doesn't. Our job is to supply them with the best-made guns possible."

After two hours, Jason checked his notes and looked at the witness. "Did I forget anything?" he asked.

"No," Davids said. "I think I'm ready for the part where Ms. Starling and I get into a catfight."

77

KELLY'S ORIGINAL STRATEGY had been to ask Melissa Davids as few questions as possible on cross-examination. She had already grilled the witness on all the good stuff during the depositions that the jury had watched. Before the CEO took the stand, Kelly had even thought about saying, in a self-satisfied way, that she had already asked her questions in the deposition and would stand on that testimony.

But the longer Davids testified, the more angry Kelly became. By the time Jason sat down, the entire Green Bay Packers football team couldn't have stopped Kelly from going after this witness.

"Cute answer," Kelly said sarcastically. "You think this is a joke?"

Jason stood to object but Davids waved him off.

"Getting sued is never a joke," Davids said. "I take it very seriously when somebody accuses me of causing another human being's death."

"Good. Because I have some serious questions." Kelly prowled the well of the courtroom, a panther stalking her prey. "Let's start with the types of weapons you sold in your nice little family business."

"Objection, Judge," Jason said. "Argumentative."

"Sustained. Ms. Starling, we can do without the sarcasm."

"Let's start with the original design of the MD-9, a design that made it easy for customers to convert the gun into an illegal fully automatic assault weapon."

"The MD-9 was a perfectly legal semi-automatic pistol," Davids responded. And before Kelly could ask her next question, Davids tried to preempt her. "I know . . . next you're going to ask whether I was aware that a large number of customers converted it into a fully automatic pistol and whether the ATF got involved and all that—am I right?"

The arrogance of the woman's answer infuriated Kelly. "Your Honor," she said, "please tell the witness to just answer the question."

Garrison complied, delivering a stern little lecture to Melissa Davids.

"I was just trying to save us some time," Davids said.

"You also had a run-in with the ATF over your sales of silencers; is that right?"

Davids nodded. "The ATF ranks right up there with trial lawyers."

Kelly ignored the answer, firing off a series of questions about the way MD Firearms had circumvented the laws regulating the registration of silencers.

"You sold the outer tubes for the silencer, and other companies sold the internal parts, right?"

"If you're talking about sound suppressors, that's correct."

"More than six thousand tubes sold by MD Firearms, and only four buyers registered their *suppressors*. Does that sound right?"

"Approximately."

"What did you think folks were doing with all those suppressors?" Kelly asked. "Sneaking up on deer if they missed with the first shot?"

Davids smirked. "Do you think this is a joke?" she asked mockingly. "I thought we were going to ask serious questions here."

"You seem to have a knack for providing criminals with the weapons they need," Kelly stated.

"Objection!" Jason said. "That's not a question."

"I'll withdraw it," Kelly said.

"I'll answer it," Davids said testily. "We already had one court rule in our favor when the ATF sued us on the issue of the suppressors. Unless I'm missing something, you don't get to appeal that decision here."

The women dueled for a half hour, keeping each juror on the edge of his or her seat. For Kelly, it was like beating her head against a brick wall. She decided to end on a sure bet.

"The jury watched your first deposition, where you denied under oath ever thinking about whether you should stop selling guns to Peninsula Arms." She handed Davids a copy of the memo from Case McAllister.

"Is that your handwriting at the top of this memo, which has been marked as Plaintiff's Exhibit 27?" Kelly asked.

"Yes."

"And this is a memo where the company's attorney, that man right there,

Case McAllister, was analyzing the pros and cons of whether you should discontinue sales to certain problematic dealers, including Peninsula Arms, right?"

"Objection. The memo speaks for itself."

"Sustained."

Kelly nodded, taking a step closer to Davids. "Why don't you read Case McAllister's conclusion and what you wrote right next to it?"

Davids studied the memo for a moment. "Case wrote, 'A careful cost-benefit analysis suggests we should continue selling guns to all licensed and qualified dealers.' And I wrote, 'No kidding. Whatever happened to free enterprise?'"

"If Mr. McAllister had included in his memo the fact that keeping these gun dealers in business would cost many innocent people their lives, would you have come to the same conclusion?" Kelly asked.

"Objection," Jason said. "Calls for speculation."

Davids turned to Judge Garrison. "I'd like to answer the question if I could," she said.

"I'll allow it," Garrison ruled.

"I would have told him that a lot of innocent people have already lost their lives on the field of battle to protect our rights as Americans," Davids said, "including the right to bear arms as memorialized in the Second Amendment. I would have told Mr. McAllister that he should remember those lives the next time he starts weighing which side of the debate the innocent deaths stack up on."

Kelly waited a few seconds before asking the next question. Now they were getting somewhere. "Does the Second Amendment say you have to supply shady dealers? Is the Second Amendment a license to kill?"

"The Second Amendment," Davids said emphatically, "is a license to prevent tyranny, arm the innocent, and thwart criminals."

"I have one last question, Ms. Davids. And I would appreciate a yes or no answer." Kelly took another step toward the witness. She waited two or three seconds, absorbing the total quiet of the courtroom. "Was the Second Amendment in place on the date that Rachel Crawford was gunned down by Larry Jamison?"

"Of course."

"Then maybe the Second Amendment is not enough. Maybe we need to use a little common sense and discretion too."

"Objection," Jason said.

"Withdrawn," Kelly said, returning to her seat.

78

JASON ENDED THE AFTERNOON by calling Case McAllister to the stand. Case provided fewer fireworks than Melissa Davids and provoked a far less inspiring cross-examination. Maybe everybody was just tired. But by the time Case stepped down at 5:15, it felt like somebody had long ago let all the air out of the room.

Garrison issued his standard set of warnings to the jury and dismissed them for the weekend. "How many more witnesses does the defense intend to call?" he asked Jason.

"We should be done Monday morning."

"That's good to know," Garrison said. He informed the lawyers that they would start closing arguments right after lunch on Monday. That way, the jury could begin deliberations Monday afternoon.

As they were packing their stuff to leave, Case gave Jason a note. "This is from Melissa," Case said. "She had to run and catch some television interviews."

Jason unfolded the note and read his client's hurried handwriting. *You're doing a great job. Thanks for hanging tough.*

More encouragement from a grateful client. Given the circumstances, it only made Jason feel worse.

◁ ▷

Jason was supposed to meet Bella and Andrew Lassiter at the office Friday evening to go over feedback from the shadow jury, but he no longer cared what they thought. Everything would change on Monday if Chief Poole took the stand. Jason called Bella and told her he wanted to postpone their meeting until Saturday morning.

"What's up?" she asked.

"Kelly Starling called," Jason lied. "She wants to discuss settlement."

"What? Does Mr. McAllister know?"

"Not yet," Jason said. "And I'd appreciate it if you didn't say anything."

"He's not coming back in tonight. It's just me and Andrew."

Bella hesitated, probably considering whether she should push the point.

"What is it?" Jason asked.

"Well, with all due respect, I think some cases are basically a matter of principle. I like Mr. Crawford and all, but I really don't think MD Firearms wants to pay him a dime."

"I understand that," Jason said. "But it never hurts to listen."

After he hung up with Bella, Jason tried reaching Kelly Starling on her cell but had to leave a message. He drove to his cottage, changed into shorts and a T-shirt, and sat down in front of the TV.

He flipped from one channel to the next and then turned it off. If things didn't change, on Monday morning he would put Chief Poole on the stand, and the trial would implode. Juror 7 would lead the charge for the plaintiff. Jason would have betrayed his client in order to protect himself, his father, and Matt Corey.

Jason wasn't very religious and hated clichés. Nonetheless, this felt like the proverbial deal with the devil. Once Poole took the stand, Jason's decision would be irrevocable. How could he live with himself if that happened?

Even if he wanted to do the honorable thing and not call Poole, there was no way to salvage the trial now. If Poole didn't take the stand, Marcia Franks probably wouldn't turn against him. But he would still be stuck with Juror 3, Rodney Peterson, meaning that the best Jason could hope for would be a hung jury.

And Luthor would still reveal to the world what had happened ten years ago. Jason would face potential disbarment, national shame, and the scorn of LeRon's family, along with possible jail time. The Crawford case would be tried all over again by somebody else.

And that was the *best* case.

Jason's only hope was to figure out Luthor's identity. That was the real reason he needed to meet with Kelly. He was going to confront her about how she had obtained the incriminating information on Poole. He would mention Luthor's name. He would watch the look on her face.

By the time Kelly returned his call, it was nearly nine. She had been doing some television interviews, and they had made her turn off her phone. "I like to try my cases in court, not on TV," Jason said.

"Good then; I'll see you there Monday."

"Actually . . . I was hoping to get a few minutes of your time tonight."

"For what?"

"Can I tell you when we meet? It's not something I want to talk about on a cell phone."

79

THEY AGREED TO MEET AT CATCH 31, a bar and restaurant located on the ground floor of the Hilton. At a few minutes after nine, Jason found a spot in the 31st Street parking garage just across the street. He left his gun under the passenger seat and started walking toward the corner of the garage where the stairs and elevator were located.

His mind was on his meeting with Kelly. How would she respond when he mentioned Luthor? How much should he reveal?

The garage was dark and about half full on the fourth level where he had parked. He could hear people on the street below, a band playing at Neptune Park, Atlantic Avenue buzzing with tourists.

He was preoccupied with thoughts of the upcoming meeting and didn't even notice that a few cars on this level were actually running. Without warning, two vehicles on the far side of the garage turned their lights on—high beams—putting Jason directly in their spotlight. He turned toward them, shielding his eyes with his hands.

The blow came from behind, something solid against the back of his skull. Jason tried to pivot, but his knees went weak. Before he realized what was happening, someone had grabbed him and yanked a hood over his head.

Almost simultaneously, someone drove a fist into Jason's side, and he felt the wind leave his lungs, his ribs screaming with pain.

"Yell out, and you're dead," said a thick voice in his ear. The man pulled the hood tighter, cinching it around Jason's neck.

A second person pulled Jason's hands behind his back and snapped some plastic handcuffs on his wrists.

"Get in the car!" the first man hissed. He pushed Jason's head down and shoved him into the backseat of some vehicle. Every breath Jason took sent pain shooting through his side. It felt like his ribs were broken, and he could only breathe in short, painful bursts.

"We told you not to settle." The voice was hoarse and raspy. Jason didn't recognize it. He was sandwiched between two men in the backseat.

One of them leaned over so his mouth was just a few inches from Jason's ear. "With the heel of my hand, I once hit a guy so hard that I drove the bone from his nose all the way up into his brain. You have any idea what that feels like?"

Jason shook his head emphatically.

"Why are you getting ready to meet with Kelly Starling?"

Jason tried to catch his breath. "We had some things to go over for Monday. Just . . . logistical stuff—"

"Umph!" Another blow to the ribs sent the wind out of Jason's chest. He doubled over in the seat and moaned in pain.

"Sit up!" One of the men jerked him back in his seat, causing a fresh wave of agony. The man pulled up the bottom part of the fabric covering Jason's face and jammed the hard steel of a gun barrel into his mouth. Jason gagged. Cold sweat broke out on his back and forehead.

"Cross me again and you die," one of the men hissed. "Understood?"

Jason nodded his head.

He froze when he heard the hammer cock back. "You still want to settle?"

Jason shook his head, trembling uncontrollably.

"Good boy," whispered his captor. "'Cause I'm going to tell you a little secret."

He waited, torturing Jason with the silence. "This gun is a revolver with three bullets in the chamber. Kind of like that *Dirty Harry* movie. You feel lucky?"

Jason shook his head again. Vigorously. But the more he squirmed, the harder the man shoved the barrel down his throat.

"Tough," said his captor. "We're going to see if you are anyway."

He pulled the trigger.

Jason flinched . . . but nothing happened.

"This must be your lucky day," the man said. He pulled the barrel out of Jason's mouth and pressed it against Jason's neck.

"C'mon." the man said. He yanked Jason out of the car. The man was larger than Jason, strong as an ox. "When I release you, walk straight to your car. Don't look back or I'll fill you with bullet holes."

With that, his captor cut the plastic handcuffs and pulled the hood off. He pushed Jason forward, in front of the headlights. Jason stumbled and scrambled to his feet, barely able to breathe. Doubled over, he hobbled toward his truck. Just as he was opening the front door, he heard the squeal of tires and looked behind him.

The black sedan was out of its parking spot and gunning around the corner of the garage. A second car followed.

Jason climbed gingerly into his truck and picked up his gun. He tried to get his bearings. He was dizzy with pain, trying to recover from the shock of being attacked. This was the kind of stuff that happened in movies, not in real life to a civil litigation lawyer.

He realized he should probably file a report with the police, but he didn't want to involve them. They would ask questions that would force Jason to choose between lying and telling the truth about how Luthor was blackmailing him. The truth about the accident ten years ago.

Instead, Jason dialed his father's number. When his dad didn't answer, Jason left an urgent message on voice mail.

In that moment of pain, every shallow breath more difficult than the last, a thought hit Jason. Something he should have realized a long time ago. Something that suddenly seemed so obvious he wondered how he could have missed it.

His BlackBerry had been provided by Justice Inc. as part of his severance package, his yearly subscription paid in advance. Possibly—no, almost certainly—somebody was monitoring it. The call to Bella had been intercepted. That's how they knew he was coming here.

This theory confirmed a lot of things. Justice Inc. wanted to control the outcome of the litigation. They might have a hundred million or more riding on the case. And up until now, they had been able to track Jason's every step.

Jason turned the BlackBerry off and stared at it as if it were a coiled snake. He thought about his time at the company. In every case, the company put millions of dollars of its own money on the line. How could they be sure that the lawyers trying the mock cases weren't providing information to hedge fund operators on the side? Those lawyers, like Jason, knew the outcome of every shadow jury trial.

Maybe Justice Inc. had monitored every phone call he had ever made during his time at the company. That might explain how they found out about the DUI accident in the first place—his conversations with his father would allude to it. Jason had probably also mentioned Matt Corey from time to time. It wouldn't be hard to figure out.

He felt betrayed by the device he had carried with him everywhere, every minute of the day, on his hip, like a Trojan horse. Maybe even now, with the device turned off, Justice Inc. still had some kind of GPS system embedded into the phone that could track his every move. He was dealing with a huge and powerful organization with untold amounts of money at stake.

And he still had the same intractable dilemma that he had thirty minutes ago. Play the game and betray his client, or refuse to play and betray his father. Refuse to play and hurt LeRon's family. Refuse to play and go to jail.

He powered the phone on and dialed Kelly's number.

"I can't make it tonight," he said. "Something's come up."

"Do you need to push it back?"

"No. I just need to call it off. Events have more or less preempted it."

"Fine," Kelly said. "I'll see you in court Monday."

"Yeah. See you Monday."

After the call, he waited several more minutes, trying to catch a few breaths without the sharp pain that had been accompanying each inhalation.

Strangely, the attack had increased his resolve. Waiting for the other shoe to drop for the last few weeks had been like torture. Thinking about the fall-out from having his treachery exposed had been paralyzing.

But a few minutes ago, he'd thought he was going to die. And at that moment, all he wanted was another chance at life.

Coming that close to death could do something to a man.

He needed to go to the hospital and get his ribs checked out. But first, he had to take care of some other business. He drove out of the parking garage and cruised down Atlantic Avenue a few blocks. He found a metered spot on a side street, strapped on his shoulder holster with his MD-45, and threw a Windbreaker over top even though the temperature was still in the mideighties.

From now on, Jason and his gun would be inseparable; his BlackBerry would stay in the truck. He wouldn't throw it away entirely, though, or Justice Inc. would realize that he knew how they were monitoring him.

He ducked in and out of the pedestrian traffic for a few minutes, checking behind him, the rapid pace causing more pain in his chest. Eventually, he worked his way to the lobby of the Hilton, where he called Kelly from a hotel phone.

"I'm in the lobby," he said. "I know this sounds a little schizophrenic, but we really need to meet."

80

IT WAS LATE IN THE EVENING. Kelly's meeting with Jason Noble had been over for more than an hour, and there was no way in the world that she was going to sleep. She walked out onto the balcony of her room, overlooking the boardwalk, and breathed in the night air.

She loved this view, had retreated to this spot numerous times in the last few days with the pressure of the trial bearing down on her. It was here, listening to the rhythmic beat of the ocean, that she had fine-tuned her opening statement. Last night, pacing back and forth on the small balcony, staring out at the ocean, she had imagined every minute of the cross-examination of Melissa Davids.

The night air was muggy, but a nice breeze blew in from the ocean, and the air carried a curious blend of salt water and the aromas from the Catch 31 restaurant twelve stories below. She could hear the country band playing next door, at the outdoor Neptune Park. She could see tourists strolling the boardwalk, others walking in the sand, kids playing on the blue playset just below the statue of King Neptune.

But tonight, none of this could begin to calm her nerves. This case had enough pressure of its own. But after her meeting with Jason, the intrigue and mind games had increased tenfold.

Could she trust Jason Noble? Nothing in the history of this case suggested that he had much integrity.

Kelly was confused and restless. She was on the verge of emotional exhaustion, yet at the same time she felt almost jittery with nervous energy. In some ways, this was expected at the end of a long week of trial. She hadn't exercised all week. The adrenaline just bounced around in her body with no productive outlet, draining her reserves.

She needed some kind of release. She needed to think. Maybe she could hit the hotel pool and do a few laps. The exercise might clear her mind.

She changed into a one-piece swimsuit that she used for training, threw on flip-flops and a pair of shorts, put her goggles around her neck, and grabbed a hotel towel.

The Hilton's outdoor pool was on the roof of the hotel, twenty stories above the boardwalk, surrounded by a waist-high brick railing topped with a wire fence.

Kelly rode the elevator with businessmen and businesswomen dressed for a night on the town. The Hilton's rooftop also featured a plush bar, and it was apparently a hot spot for the upscale locals.

When she stepped off the elevators and headed toward the pool, she knew immediately that this was a dumb idea. There were couples lounging in the lawn chairs. A few women in bikinis stood in the water with boyfriends or husbands, some draped all over each other, some holding drinks. Kelly chuckled at the absurd thought of trying to swim laps in this pool. The patrons cast a few suspicious glances her way, as if she had just shown up with a six-pack at an AA meeting.

Turning around, she headed back to the elevator.

Instead of hitting twelve, she pushed the button for the ground floor. She exited the lobby and stepped into the muggy Virginia Beach night. She crossed the boardwalk, headed toward the ocean, and took off her flip-flops.

The sand was smooth and cool on her feet. The expansive beach was unguarded and open to tourists at night, many of whom took advantage of it. Couples were sitting in the sand talking or holding hands as they walked in ankle-deep water at the edge of the ocean. A few guys were throwing a Frisbee by moonlight. A family walked their dog nearby.

The moon was three-quarters full, and there wasn't a cloud in sight. The lights from the boardwalk and night sky cast a pale glow over the water of the Atlantic, an alluring invitation to do some real swimming.

Kelly picked a spot for her towel, flip-flops, and shorts. When nobody was looking, she buried her hotel room key in the sand, a few inches below her left flip flop. She put on her goggles and waded into the water until it was about knee deep, splashing some cold water on her shoulders and back.

A couple walking on the beach checked her out—*What's with the crazy woman?* There were probably others staring as well. She took a deep breath and waded forward, the cold waves crashing against her and sucking her breath away. *Here goes!* She picked a large swell and dove under.

She came up instantly refreshed, raked back her hair, checked her goggles, waded a little deeper, and dove under another wave. This time she came up swimming. First she angled away from the shore, swimming under a few more large swells as they broke. Within seconds, she was out past the breaking waves, parallel to the shore, swimming freestyle, her body rolling with the rhythm of the ocean.

For the first few minutes, Kelly concentrated on getting in sync with the waves, timing her breaths to avoid swallowing salt water. Before long, she was in the zone. It felt great to be in her element, channeling her pent-up tension into each stroke. It seemed like the longer she swam the stronger she became. She kicked harder and lengthened her stroke, practically sprinting down the back side of the swells.

She knew she should be careful about holding some energy in reserve—a riptide could carry her out a half mile or more in no time at all. But tonight, she didn't really care.

Fatigue came more quickly than she anticipated, but still she swam. After twenty minutes, she stopped long enough to glance at her watch. A good workout in the pool would be thirty minutes. But here, fighting the ocean swells, she had already been swimming twenty minutes and hadn't even turned around.

She had drifted a little farther from shore than she had intended. She put her head down and plowed farther ahead, muscles beginning to burn. The pain was exactly what she needed. The risk was exactly what she wanted.

At twenty-five minutes, she turned and headed back toward the Hilton. Going in this direction, she rotated her head toward shore as she breathed, catching a glimpse of the lights from the oceanfront homes with every other stroke.

Ten minutes later, she started struggling a little. It was harder to breathe, and her arms and legs felt like lead weights. She was still dangerously far from shore, but tonight she had this inexplicable desire to flirt with danger. She knew how dangerous this was. Bordering on insane. She had a promising career. A family who loved her. She was on the verge of being a national figure—a hero in the fight against gun violence.

But none of that seemed to matter now. Because the one thing Kelly cared about most—her reputation, her integrity—was about to be shattered. Luthor would be forced to reveal what he knew. The Monica Lewinsky taint would follow Kelly forever. How often had her father said that if you lose your integrity you lose everything?

She swam harder. Longer. Pushing herself for one more minute . . . one more breath . . . one more stroke.

Finally she reached the point of exhaustion and started angling toward shore. As soon as she got there she would rest on the sand for a few minutes and then walk the rest of the way to the hotel.

But as she turned toward shore, at nearly the height of her fatigue, she felt the subtle pull of the current and realized she had miscalculated. The tide was taking her farther out—not a full-blown riptide but something close.

She stopped to tread water for a second and get her bearings but quickly started swimming again as she watched the shore grow more distant. A surge of adrenaline kicked in, and she nearly panicked as she realized that she was still losing ground. She knew the drill—don't fight the riptide. Swim parallel to shore, out the side of the current, not against it.

But that required energy and stamina. She tried to get a deep breath and relax, but she was so tired. She gamely fought back the panic, put her head down, and started swimming parallel to the shore. Two minutes. Three minutes. Five.

She swallowed some water and coughed it up. The swells seemed larger now, though she knew it must be just an illusion. The shore was still fading away.

Thoughts about the trial had succumbed to a single-minded focus on survival. A prayer and another rush of adrenaline sustained her for a few more minutes, but at this rate it would be over soon. Her arms and legs burned with fatigue as lactic acid took its toll. She resisted the urge to shout out. It would be a waste of breath; nobody could hear her this far from shore.

There was only one thing to do—keep swimming.

She put her head down and continued pushing—past the fatigue, past the pain, one stroke at a time, each one more difficult than the last. In her competitive days, she was legendary for her will to win. Tonight, it would take every ounce of that will just to survive. She thought about everything worth living for—her faith, her family, her friends, the clients who needed her.

Nothing helped. She was going to lose this battle.

But just when she was ready to concede defeat, she felt a small shift in the current, very subtle—the gradual release of the riptide's fingers. It was as if the fist of death had been pried opened by the hand of God.

She swam a few more aching strokes until she had completely cleared the current. She caught her breath by floating on the surface for a few minutes before starting the grind toward shore. She picked the right angle, rode the waves, relaxed between swells, and eventually felt sand under her exhausted legs.

She walked toward the beach and collapsed on her knees in the ankle-deep water. She stayed there for a minute, trying to catch her breath. How close had she been to dying? How many more minutes could she have fought the tide?

She knew God had snatched her out of danger. In a private moment that no one else would share or comprehend, He had rescued her. But only after she had quit fighting against the riptide. Only when she had been ready to give up and let the powerful ocean claim its victim. That's when she had felt Him move.

Kneeling in the sand, she thought about some verses her dad had often quoted. The words of Jesus, though Kelly couldn't remember when or where. *If you try to hang on to your life, you will lose it. But if you give up your life for my sake, you will save it. And what do you benefit if you gain the whole world but lose your own soul?*

The whole world—a law career, a reputation, national fame.

What do you benefit if you gain the whole world and lose your soul?

To her horror, Kelly realized how much she had been toying with that bargain. Her pride and her shame had driven her away from God. She had been swimming against the need for repentance and reconciliation, trying to curry His favor with her crusades when what she really needed was mercy and acceptance.

Kneeling there in the sand, she asked God to forgive her.

81

FIRST THING SATURDAY MORNING, Kelly called her dad. "Can we talk?" she asked.

"Sure, Kell. What's up?"

They had talked a few times during the trial, but Kelly was usually so busy that mostly her dad left voice mail messages telling Kelly how proud he was of the way she was handling the case.

Last night, she had decided to call him today and tell him everything she had been hiding for the past seven years. But now that he was actually on the phone, it felt awkward.

"I know you've got church tomorrow, but is there any way we could get together for a few minutes? I just really need to see you."

Kelly knew that Saturday was her dad's day to fine-tune his sermon. Rule number one in the Starling house: don't mess with Dad on Saturday. And the drive from Charlottesville to Virginia Beach one way would take nearly four hours.

But her dad must have heard the catch in Kelly's voice. He said he could be there by two that afternoon. He would get someone else to preach the next day. He had wanted to watch her closing argument anyway.

She backtracked a little and put up some token resistance but it was a done deal.

Early that afternoon, her dad called from the hotel lobby. He came up to Kelly's room, and she told him everything.

They sat on the edge of the bed, and her dad gently assured her of God's forgiveness. She cried in his arms for what seemed like an hour.

◁ ▷

Jason didn't arrive at the office on Saturday morning until nearly 9 a.m. After his meeting with Kelly on Friday night, he had gone to the Virginia Beach

General Hospital ER. The emergency-room staff had made him wait for an hour before they X-rayed his ribs and did a CT scan of his head. Though he hadn't lost consciousness, they wanted to be cautious.

The good news was that there was no discernible brain damage, and the ribs were just bruised, not broken. After a few pain pills, Jason managed to get about five hours of sleep.

The pain was back in full force on Saturday morning, but he needed to think clearly, so he stayed away from the pain medication.

"Sleeping Beauty's in the house!" Bella announced when Jason came in the door. He smiled and grimaced all at once.

"What's wrong with you?" she asked.

"I got mugged last night in the parking lot," Jason said. He figured a half-truth would be easier to remember than an outright lie. This elicited lots of sympathy and required about a ten-minute explanation filled with enough small fibs that Jason was sure he'd never be able to tell it the same way again.

Lassiter came out to the reception area about halfway through Jason's explanation, requiring that Jason repeat it from the beginning. Bella cross-examined Jason for a few minutes and gave unsolicited advice on how to treat his injuries. Eventually, Jason managed to change the subject back to the day's agenda. Both Lassiter and Bella were anxious to go over feedback from the shadow jury. Proposed jury instructions had to be drafted. And Jason needed to prepare his closing argument.

"How good is Brad Carson?" Jason asked.

The question about her former boss seemed to surprise Bella. "You mean in court?"

"Yeah. Do you think he could come over for a few hours and help me with my closing? I need an outside perspective."

Bella lit up at the idea. "He'll come," she said confidently, "if I have to drag him here myself."

Before they got down to the day's business, Bella handed Jason an envelope. "Somebody slid this under the door last night."

It had Jason's name on it and it was marked *personal and confidential.* Jason recognized his dad's handwriting. "I'll meet you guys in the conference room in a minute," Jason said.

He went into his office, closed the door, and ripped the envelope open. His hands shook a little as he read the one-page note.

When we get together, it usually doesn't turn out the way I planned, so I thought I would leave this note instead. I'm sorry about Thursday night. I don't remember everything I said, but I remember enough to apologize for it.

I think I've helped about as much as I can. I wish you trusted me enough to tell me what's really going on. Watching you do your thing this week and getting to know Case has been good.

I want you to know that I'm proud of you.

I'm going back to Atlanta and I'm going to get help. Thursday night was the last straw. I thought about staying for the verdict but I realized that I'm a distraction. The best thing I can do for you is get better.

Maybe after a few weeks in rehab, you'll get your old man back. Maybe we could get together then.

Good luck.

Dad

Jason stared at the note for a long time. He wasn't really sure how he should react. He knew how it made him feel—thankful, proud, confused. He tried dialing his dad's number but ended up in voice mail. Later in the day he would call both his sister and Matt Corey. But for now, he just stared at the letter and read a single line over and over and over.

I want you to know that I'm proud of you.

His dad needed help, and today he had finally admitted it. Maybe in a few weeks, they really could get together. Maybe there was hope.

So long as Jason didn't blow it all up by forcing Luthor's hand.

Jason thought about how hard it had been to write the intervention letter to his dad a few months ago. For the Noble family men, swallowing your pride and being vulnerable did not come easy. It must have been even harder for his dad to write this letter. But admitting that he had an addiction was the first step toward recovery.

What kind of son would turn on his dad at a time like this?

PART VI
THE VERDICT

82

ON MONDAY MORNING, Jason swallowed hard and called Chief Ed Poole as a witness for the defense. Poole was a large and powerfully built man with the sloped shoulders of a football lineman. He moved slowly and methodically to the stand, glancing at the jurors as he did so.

Poole was mostly bald with undersized facial features, gray hair on the sides of his head, and wrinkles that radiated from his eyes and creased his forehead. He was dressed in a gray blazer and white shirt, his tie so tight around his neck that the skin bulged at the top of his collar.

He seemed comfortable and self-assured. He was a former police chief of a large city. He had seen a few things.

Jason began by taking the witness through his impressive list of credentials. Like any good expert, Poole seemed reluctant to mention everything he had done and managed to come off as both highly qualified and charmingly humble. When Jason moved to have Poole qualified as an expert on the issue of gun trafficking, there was no objection.

As Poole testified, he turned periodically to face the jury, throwing in a few wisecracks to keep them amused. He told them that 80 percent of guns used in crimes were purchased by criminals on the street or from their friends and family members. Those sales, of course, were entirely unregulated. Only 11 percent were bought legally at gun stores, and 9 percent of guns used in crimes were purchased illegally at retail stores like Peninsula Arms.

"What about the designs of the guns?" Jason asked. "The jury's heard a lot about semi-automatic assault weapons like the MD-9. In what percentage of crimes are these types of guns used?"

"Actually, not very often," explained Poole. He proceeded with a lecture about gun nomenclature and how he didn't even like the phrase "semi-automatic assault weapon" because it was so misleading. At the end of his lecture, he looked back at Jason. "What was the question again?"

"In how many crimes are these types of guns used as compared to other types of guns?"

"Oh yeah," said Poole, smiling. "Less than one in ten."

Jason ended with his payoff question. "Do you have an opinion, to a reasonable degree of certainty, as to whether Larry Jamison could have obtained a gun from the black market even if every gun store in America had refused to sell him one?"

Poole laughed. "Surveys show that nearly 60 percent of high school boys say they can obtain access to a gun if they need to. That's high school, Mr. Noble. For an adult like Jamison, give him a few hundred bucks and a few hours on the streets of downtown Norfolk, and you can take your pick."

Jason didn't return the witness's self-satisfied smile. "Thank you, Chief Poole. Please answer any questions that Ms. Starling might have."

Kelly stood quickly, anxious to attack. She was wearing a blue pin-striped matching jacket and skirt, navy blue heels, and a white blouse. She looked even leaner than normal, professional and sophisticated. Unlike Jason, she looked well rested.

How did she sleep at all last night? Jason wondered. In the mirror that morning, his own bloodshot eyes had reflected another sleepless night. He had thrown on a suit that he had worn three times in two weeks without taking it to the dry cleaner and barely made it to the courthouse on time.

"Are your answers, given under oath and under penalty of perjury, all truthful and correct?" Kelly asked.

Poole leaned back a little and grunted, as if Kelly didn't know whom she was accusing. "Of course."

"Have you ever lied under oath?"

"Absolutely not."

"Are you presently in the midst of divorce proceedings?"

Jason stood and objected. But it was merely a formality; he knew Garrison would overrule him.

"I'll link it up," Kelly promised. "It goes directly to his credibility."

"You're on a short leash, but go ahead," Garrison said.

Poole sighed heavily and shot daggers at Kelly. "Yes. Though I consider it none of your business, my wife and I are getting divorced."

"Did you have to file an accounting in your divorce case, under oath, that detailed all your assets?"

Poole started to turn a little red around the ears. "Yes . . . and I did."

"*All* of your assets?"

"Of course."

"You didn't hide any secret accounts that you had used, let's say . . . to pay a mistress?"

The courtroom buzzed, and Poole's brow furrowed—indignation giving way to concern.

"Objection!" Jason said.

"Overruled."

"I'm not sure what you're talking about," Poole said. "Or what it has to do with this case."

Kelly smiled. She walked over to Jason's chair and handed him a copy of the bank documents he had seen the week before. She asked the court reporter to mark for identification a copy of a bank statement as Plaintiff's Exhibit 33 and a cell phone bill as Plaintiff's Exhibit 34. "May I approach the witness?" she asked Judge Garrison.

"Yes."

She handed the documents to a stricken Poole. "Can you identify what's been marked as Plaintiff's Exhibit 33 and Plaintiff's Exhibit 34?"

Poole took his time looking at both documents. Kelly stood in front of him, unmoving, like an avenging angel. "Well?" Kelly asked.

Poole looked at the judge and then back at Kelly. "I'm invoking my Fifth Amendment privilege against self-incrimination," he said. "I refuse to answer the question."

There was an audible gasp in the courtroom, followed by murmuring and the banging of Judge Garrison's gavel. "Order! Let's have it quiet in here." Juror 7 had her arms crossed and her lips pursed in disgust. Jason could feel the stares of the courtroom audience. It was painful watching your case go down in flames.

"Plaintiff's Exhibit 33," Kelly said. "Isn't that a statement from a bank account you own that was not declared in your divorce case?"

"I'm invoking the Fifth."

"Where did the deposits come from? Isn't this more money than you were making from your consulting work?"

"I'm invoking the Fifth."

"And what about Plaintiff's 34? Does that show cell phone calls to the same woman who was receiving payouts from this account?"

Poole's face was crimson now, as if he might explode at any moment. His lips barely moved when he talked. "I'm invoking the Fifth, Counselor."

"Let me ask you one more time," Kelly said, "because you forgot to invoke the Fifth Amendment for this one earlier. Have you ever lied under oath?"

"I plead the Fifth Amendment," Poole said.

83

ED POOLE was off the stand by 10:30. He left the courtroom with his tail between his legs. He would fly back to Atlanta and probably face perjury charges or at least an irate divorce-court judge.

Though Kelly had gone after him hard, she actually felt a little sorry for the man. With everything going on in her personal life, Kelly found no pleasure in watching somebody else's past catch up with him.

Jason stood and announced that the defense rested. Kelly told the judge that she had no rebuttal witnesses. Everybody could sense that the jury was anxious to begin their deliberations.

Judge Garrison announced that his jury instructions and closing arguments would begin after a fifteen-minute break. The tension in the courtroom increased exponentially.

◁ ▷

Fifteen minutes later, after Judge Garrison read the jury instructions, Kelly walked to the front of the jury box and surveyed the panel. She caught the steely-eyed gaze of Marcia Franks, Juror 7, and the attentive look of Rodney Peterson, Juror 3. All of the jurors had benign looks of encouragement, as far as Kelly could tell. She sensed that the case was hers to lose.

"We're not here to raise Rachel Crawford from the dead. I wish somehow we could, but her warm and cheerful light has been extinguished forever—at least this side of heaven.

"We *are* here to correct a grave injustice. As my client so eloquently reminded us, quoting the words of Dr. King: 'An injustice anywhere is a threat to justice everywhere.'

"Mr. Noble doesn't want to talk about justice. He wants us to focus on the left brain. Remember what he said during opening statements? Use logic, not emotions. So let's humor Mr. Noble for a minute. Let's talk left brain.

"What could be more left brain than statistics?" Kelly hit a button on her remote, and numbers flashed up on the screen. "One percent of gun stores sell 57 percent of the weapons ultimately traced to crimes. I know, Chief Poole testified that most guns used in crimes came from street sales. But if you trace them back far enough, how did they get on the streets in the first place? Through a few renegade gun dealers who specialize in illegal sales.

"According to MD Firearms's own study, four renegade dealers accounted for approximately 50 percent of the MD Firearms guns linked to crimes. One of those dealers was Peninsula Arms. That gun store accounted for 251 guns linked to murders or aggravated woundings in Washington, Philadelphia, Baltimore, and New York during 2006 alone."

She took a few steps, and the screen flashed one more time, displaying another number: $2,763,960.00. "This is the reason why MD Firearms keeps selling guns to dealers like Peninsula Arms. Two million, seven hundred sixty-three thousand, nine hundred sixty dollars. That's the amount of revenue that MD Firearms made from Peninsula Arms in the last three years."

She turned to squarely face the jury again. "You want left brain? Let's talk legal definitions. A few minutes ago, Judge Garrison read a set of jury instructions to you. He told you that negligence is a careless act or omission by the defendant.

"An act *or omission.*

"In other words, it's no defense for MD Firearms to do nothing if a reasonable manufacturer would have acted.

"Oh, they're good at pointing fingers." Kelly turned and stared at her three adversaries—Jason Noble, Case McAllister, and Melissa Davids, who had obviously decided to be present for closing arguments—all sitting in that ridiculous position off to the side of the defense counsel table. She walked over to the table. "Mr. Noble is great at putting everybody else on trial." She pointed to the empty chairs. "Larry Jamison. Peninsula Arms. Jarrod Beeson. He even added a seat for the ATF."

She turned back to the jury. "Larry Jamison already got his verdict—at the hands of the SWAT team. Beeson's in jail. Peninsula Arms is bankrupt. The ATF has qualified immunity. But for these individuals representing MD Firearms, *this* is their judgment day."

Her voice grew tighter, angrier, more intense. "And it's no defense for them to sit back smugly and say, 'We did nothing. We hid behind the Second Amendment. We knew people were dying, we knew this dealer was supplying the black market, but we also knew we made nearly three million dollars from them the past three years, so we did *nothing*.'"

Kelly stopped. Took a breath. Lowered her voice. She thought about her dad leading Communion, about the words of the liturgy that applied to her own life. *We have sinned against You by what we have done, and by what we have left undone.*

"MD Firearms didn't pull the trigger. They didn't make the illegal sale. Those were the wrong things that were done. But MD Firearms is guilty by what they have left undone. They knew about this renegade dealer but didn't act. They knew people were losing their lives because Peninsula Arms was supplying the black market, and they turned their heads. They came into court and brought out the proverbial bowl of water and washed their hands of the matter, blaming everyone else."

The jury was anxious to start their work; Kelly could see that. And most jurors had probably made up their minds already. She needed to keep this short. But she also needed to end with a little emotion.

"And so if you do what Mr. Noble suggests and use only your left brain, I respectfully submit that you will find in favor of the plaintiff. But I must say, ladies and gentlemen, that there's a reason the left brain and right brain are connected. Because, you see, justice is not just a matter of the head; it's a matter of the heart."

Kelly stepped in front of the jury and turned to a dry erase board. She pulled the top off a red marker and wrote the name of Larry Jamison. "Follow the trail of blood," she said, drawing an arrow. "From Jamison to Jarrod Beeson." She wrote names and drew arrows as she spoke. "From Beeson to Peninsula Arms. And from Peninsula Arms to MD Firearms.

"No amount of fancy lawyering can remove the blood from their hands."

She put down the marker, the red ink staining her fingers.

"Follow the trail of blood, ladies and gentlemen. It will take you straight to the door of Melissa Davids and MD Firearms."

84

JASON STOOD and took only a few steps from his chair, trying to look calm and relaxed. His insides churned from the tension.

"In the ancient Jewish tradition, the priest would lay his hands on the head of a goat during the Day of Atonement and confess the sins of the people. The goat would then be cast out into the wilderness to make atonement for the people's sins.

"The ancient Greeks had a similar custom when a natural disaster, like a plague or famine, would occur. They would pick a beggar or someone crippled from inside the city, place the blame on that person's head, stone and beat him, and then cast him out of the community."

Jason stepped into the middle of the courtroom, keeping his eyes on the jury. He would do his closing without notes. For the most part, he would keep his voice even and measured—the very picture of reasonableness.

"Scapegoating. It's been around for thousands of years. But American plaintiffs' lawyers have perfected it."

"Objection!" Kelly said, and Jason wanted to thank her. "That's improper argument, Judge."

Judge Garrison looked a little perplexed. He told Jason to tread lightly and reminded the jury that this was just argument from the lawyers, not evidence in the case.

"A tragedy occurred on August 25, when Larry Jamison broke into the WDXR studios and executed Rachel Crawford in cold blood. A family was destroyed. A career was cut short. A wife was killed. A baby was lost. Somebody has to pay. And so Ms. Starling comes over and lays her hands on the head of my client, the manufacturer of the gun, and declares them responsible for all of this evil."

Jason shook his head in disbelief. "Why? Because they pulled the trigger?

No. Because they committed an illegal act in selling the guns? No. All they did was manufacture a perfectly legal gun and sell it to a perfectly legal dealer in a country that protects the constitutional right of its citizens to do so."

By the skeptical looks on their faces, Jason could tell that some of the jurors weren't buying this. Marcia Franks was not. Rodney Peterson was not. But Jason didn't really care about them any more. He was talking to other jurors now.

"There's been so much smoke and so many mirrors deployed in this case that I need to remind us all what this case is *not* about. It's not about sound suppressors or fully automatic machine guns or whether ATF agents are Nazis. It's not even about whether or not you like my client." Jason turned and looked at Melissa Davids. Not surprisingly, she didn't smile.

"I actually like Ms. Davids," Jason said, as if that might surprise the jurors. "She's a straight shooter, if you'll pardon the pun. She has her convictions, and she's not willing to compromise them. She's a living example of how guns can level the playing field and help women protect themselves.

"But it really doesn't matter whether you like her or you think she's the devil incarnate. She's not running for Miss Personality here. She's at the bar of the court seeking justice. And Lady Justice wears a blindfold for a reason."

Jason knew he had to deal with this next subject, unpleasant as it might be. Poole had been decimated on the witness stand. For the sake of appearance, Jason had to at least talk about the issue.

"This case isn't about Chief Poole's divorce either," Jason said. "And you may think I've lost a lot of credibility by putting him on the stand." Jason looked straight at Marcia Franks. "But if that's the case, there's something you need to know.

"Lawyers have certain obligations in what we call pretrial discovery. One of those is to turn over documents that we intend to use at trial. Before the first witness took the stand, I received the documents from Ms. Starling that she used this morning on cross-examination." The jurors looked a little surprised—exactly the reaction Jason anticipated. "I didn't share them with Chief Poole. I knew he would get crucified on cross-examination, and I put him on the stand anyway. From the looks on your faces, I can tell you're wondering why."

Jason took a few steps, looking down, giving the jury a moment to contemplate the issue.

"First, because I figured if he was trying to cheat on his ex-wife during their divorce proceedings, it probably needed to come out in open court. And second, because I knew that everything he said about guns being available on the streets is independently verifiable. Think about it—what does the fact that he cheated during his divorce proceedings have to do with his testimony concerning the availability of guns on the streets?"

Jason surveyed the entire jury, but he took special note of Marcia. She seemed to at least be considering this. "I put him on because I knew that you were smart enough to distinguish between the character of the man and the quality of his data. Thomas Jefferson wrote the Declaration of Independence yet never released his own slaves. Does that mean we should throw out the Declaration?

"You will recall that even though Ms. Starling made a fool of Chief Poole, she didn't even try to attack the statistics the man presented."

Jason took a deep breath and thought for a moment, drawing the jury in with him. He was no longer nervous. *This* was what he loved. Being on stage. High stakes. The audience hanging on the next line.

"Larry Jamison is not here today to punish. The SWAT team took him out. But there are other killers like Larry Jamison out there watching. And believe it or not, they probably hope that you will give a big verdict to the plaintiff. Why? Because these criminals know that *they* can always get a gun. And their plans will be that much easier if law-abiding citizens cannot.

"Two wrongs do not make a right. Larry Jamison murdered Rachel Crawford. An unjust verdict against the manufacturer of the gun will not bring her back."

◁▷

"Any rebuttal?" Judge Garrison asked.

"Very briefly, Your Honor."

Kelly turned on the monitor in front of the jury and loaded the DVD. Without saying a word, she began running the tape again. Jamison bursting into the WDXR studios. The bullying, the threats, the demands of Lisa Roberts, forcing Rachel to apologize. Resolve lined Rachel's bloodied face as Jamison screamed about the lies and declared the television studio a "court of law."

The jury watched intently as Jamison held the gun to Lisa's head and asked her if Rachel was guilty. They heard the commotion off camera and watched Jamison pivot toward Rachel, hatred and desperation in his eyes.

Kelly Starling paused the video right there. The frame perfectly captured both the hatred and the fear. Jamison spinning in rage toward his prey. Rachel diving toward the floor. The WDXR news studio a split second before the bullets started flying.

When Kelly spoke, her voice was barely a whisper. "Using his MD-9, purchased illegally at a gun store that never should have been allowed to sell that gun, Larry Jamison made a mockery of justice. In the final seconds of her life, Rachel Crawford had to bear the indignity of a kangaroo court, run by a madman, a court that declared her guilty of something she didn't do."

Kelly paused, letting the silence underline everything she was saying. "I believe that in those last few seconds of terror, her soul was crying out for rescue, hoping that real justice would somehow prevail. And I believe, as does my client, that she is watching now, crying out for justice again. *You* are the only ones who can deliver it.

"Don't let Larry Jamison and the merchants of death who supplied him with firepower win again. Don't add insult to injury. Despite what Larry Jamison said, that television studio was no court of law. *This* is where people come to have wrongs made right. *This* is where people come to plead for justice.

"Do the right thing.

"Yes, we want you to use your head. We're not afraid of a clearheaded review of the evidence. But we also ask you to unashamedly follow your heart. That's where justice resides. That's where you'll find the truth."

85

JUDGE GARRISON instructed the jury to select a foreperson before lunch and begin their deliberations as soon as they returned from eating.

Most observers expected the deliberations to last a few days. Some were predicting a hung jury; others thought that the scales had been tipped in favor of the plaintiff by the devastating cross-examination of Chief Poole.

Nobody expected the jury to return with a verdict that same afternoon.

"Just in case," Garrison told the lawyers, "I want you within reach by cell phone. I'll give you thirty minutes notice before we reconvene. Govern yourselves accordingly."

◁ ▷

Jason desperately wanted to call his father during the twenty-minute drive to the Courtyard Marriott at the oceanfront but knew he shouldn't. For starters, he was pretty sure that every call from his BlackBerry was being monitored by the folks at Justice Inc. And even if they hadn't been, Brad Carson had been adamant about this part of the plan.

"We operate from here on out on a strictly need-to-know basis," Brad had said. "Trust no one. Not even your own father."

Two days earlier, on Saturday afternoon when Brad and Jason were alone in a conference room supposedly working on Jason's closing argument, Jason had hired Brad Carson as his lawyer. Under the protection of attorney-client privilege, Jason had confessed everything.

Brad had agreed to take Jason on as a client, but only after laying out some ground rules. And ground rule number one was, "Follow my advice without question and without exception."

But the more Jason pictured his dad trying to get sober, and the more he thought about the letter his dad had left on Saturday morning and the pain his dad would feel at being betrayed, Jason couldn't live with himself if he didn't say *something*.

He gnawed on his fingernails as he drove down the highway. Ten years ago he had gotten himself into this mess by going along with other people's advice—his dad's and Matt Corey's to be specific—instead of doing what he knew was right. This time would be different.

He decided to veer by the office.

He pulled into the parking lot and raced upstairs. He assumed nobody would be there—Bella and Andrew were with the shadow jury—but he called out just to be sure. Quickly, he checked each room and then closed the door to his own office.

He dialed his dad's number from his desk phone. It rang several times and kicked into voice mail. Jason hung up and immediately dialed again. He reached voice mail a second time.

"Dad, it's Jason. Thanks so much for the letter you wrote this weekend." He paused. "Um . . . listen, things have gone pretty crazy here with the case. It's hard to explain, but somebody found out about me driving the car when LeRon was killed. They're trying to blackmail me with it, Dad. The only way I can do my job and represent my client is to let the chips fall. If the truth comes out, it comes out. Um, I don't know. I guess I just wanted to call and let you know this and tell you I'm sorry."

The message seemed so inadequate, but what else could he say?

"Oh yeah. Don't try to call on my cell phone. I think it's bugged. I'll call you back later this afternoon."

Jason hung up the phone and took a deep breath. He stared at it for a moment. "I love you, Dad."

◁ ▷

When James Noble heard his son's message, he played it back twice. His mind was already reeling from his attempts to quit drinking. He had a splitting headache and couldn't seem to string one thought together with the next.

His first call was to Case McAllister. Voice mail kicked in. He hung up and cursed. He just wanted to get a message through to Jason somehow—tell him to do the right thing.

He tried Jason's office number. More voice mail.

His third call was to Matt Corey.

He told Matt what little he knew about Jason's predicament. Matt nearly came unglued. He wanted to talk with Jason. There must be some way out of this. What kind of blackmail? Who? How could he get through to Jason?

James Noble had no answers.

◁▷

Matt Corey hung up the phone in a state of panic. Never in a million years had he thought Jason Noble would defy the blackmailers. That little twerp had shown some spine.

Six months had passed now since the phone call. It sounded like a man's voice, though Corey couldn't be sure; it was digitally altered. The person had called himself Luthor.

He said he had proof that Corey had falsified the accident report for Jason Noble's accident ten years ago. There were apparently recorded conversations between Jason and his father indicating as much. Luthor intended to use this information to his advantage in the Rachel Crawford case.

Luthor had assured Corey he wouldn't go public with the information as long as Jason Noble cooperated. Luthor swore he had no interest in ruining the careers of Detectives Matt Corey and James Noble.

"Why are you telling me this?" Corey had asked.

"My guess is that Jason would call you first if he decided to defy me and go to the authorities. If he does, you should try to talk him out of it. And if you can't, at least give me a heads-up."

Corey had tried to play it coy. Maybe this person named Luthor was just fishing—trying to get Corey to admit something on a recorded call.

"I don't know what you're talking about," Corey had said.

"I'm sure you don't," Luthor responded. "But I have a theory. Once a crooked cop, always a crooked cop. If it appears that your boy Jason is about to divulge your dirty little secret, you might want to let me know so I can have a talk with him before he does anything irrevocable."

"Get out of my life," Corey had said, his suspicions of a setup growing. "If Jason comes to me for advice, I'll tell him to *never* give in to blackmail."

"I'm sure you will." The digital voice was flat, nearly monotone, like a robot. "But if you ever want to talk with me, just leave a comment on the blog at the Kryptonite site. Sign your name. I'll give you a call."

That was the last time Corey had heard from Luthor—nearly six months ago. At first, Corey thought about telling Jason. But then he realized that doing so would just entangle him deeper in this nightmare. For a while, he had tried to stay close to Jason. He at least wanted to know if Jason intended to go to the authorities and ruin Corey's career.

And now, Corey couldn't believe this was happening. He had tried to help a friend ten years ago, and this was his payback? He thought about the embarrassment, the investigation, the legal issues. His family would be put through hell. His name would be a byword for police misconduct. LeRon Tate's family would publicly fillet him.

How could Jason Noble, a kid who owed Corey everything, even think about doing this? And if Jason was going to defy Luthor and risk exposure, why didn't he at least have the decency to call Corey himself? Instead, Corey had to learn secondhand from Jason's father.

Corey went to his computer and found the Kryptonite site. He left a comment about the latest athlete on steroids and signed his name.

Twenty minutes later the phone rang. By the time Corey hung up, he was sick to his stomach.

An hour ago, he thought he had everything going his way. A great family. A career on the upswing. The respect of his coworkers.

Now, his entire life was in limbo. His fate was in the hands of a blackmailer he had never met and a scared kid he had never really liked.

86

JASON CHECKED HIS REARVIEW MIRROR constantly, though the oceanfront area was humming with tourists and so much traffic it was impossible to tell if he was being followed. Just to be safe, he parked a few blocks from the Courtyard Marriott. He strapped on his gun, threw his suit coat on over it, and half-walked, half-jogged toward the hotel. The temperature was in the nineties, and by the time Jason hit the lobby, he had worked up a good sweat. His ribs were still sore and hurt each time he took a deep breath.

He checked behind him one last time and turned left down a hallway to Conference Room C. He entered without knocking and quickly took inventory. Everyone except Melissa Davids had already arrived. Jason shook hands with Case, Kelly Starling, and Blake Crawford. Andrew Lassiter and Bella were standing behind the others.

"I guess everybody has already met," Jason said. They nodded and spent time in awkward small talk until Melissa Davids arrived.

The deal had been finalized by phone the night before, shortly after midnight, just twelve short hours ago. On Sunday, in a meeting with Case McAllister, Jason had explained that he had been blackmailed into leaving Jurors 3 and 7 on the panel and calling Chief Poole as an expert. Brad Carson had been in that meeting as well, acting as Jason's attorney, and would not let Jason share the particulars of the leverage the blackmailer had used. But Jason and Brad had a plan that they proposed to Case.

Case listened carefully and handled the entire situation with a level of grace and understanding that had Jason hoping he could one day be just like the man. "Trust me," Case said, "when you've been in this business as long as I have, you've seen it all."

Case had called Melissa Davids, who was considerably less sanguine about the whole affair. She exploded on the phone, threatening to fire Jason and maybe even Case along with him. "Why don't we just expose the fraud of our own lawyer and demand a mistrial?" Melissa suggested. "This has the Coalition's fingerprints all over it."

But Case wouldn't let it go. He talked Melissa through her initial anger and helped her see the benefits of Jason's plan. MD Firearms would still get an unbiased verdict—up or down. The company would be seen as more than fair to Blake Crawford. The media coverage would be unprecedented.

"So what you're saying is that our little Benedict Arnold has actually done us a favor?" Melissa asked.

"You could look at it that way."

"I don't," snapped Melissa. "But I guess this plan makes the best of a bad situation." There was a pause on the phone line. "But Case, if I agree to this, we'd darn well better win."

After the call, Case had relayed the conversation to Jason and Brad, including Melissa Davids's final warning. "No pressure," Case said. "But if this thing goes south, I hope one of you will need a law partner."

Melissa had flown into Norfolk late Sunday evening in no better spirits. She had barely spoken a word to Jason all day Monday. And even now, as she finally arrived at the conference room, Jason could tell she was in no mood for introductions.

Jason grabbed some paper napkins sitting on the conference table and wiped the sweat from his face. His mouth was dry, and he was so tense he could hardly think straight. He hadn't been half this nervous even during his closing argument.

"Bella and Andrew, I'm sure you're wondering why everyone's here. Thanks for getting the shadow jury settled in."

The night before, Jason had given Bella strict instructions. "Assemble the shadow jury at 11:30. Don't let them watch Chief Poole's testimony or the closing arguments until I say so."

Jason cleared his throat and continued. There was no easy way to say this—he could hardly bear to look at Bella and Andrew. "This weekend, I've been in discussions with opposing counsel about some problems in our trial caused by my own misconduct. Those problems were severe enough that they would have justified a mistrial and perhaps my own disbarment. I told Kelly I was ready to make a motion for a mistrial first thing this morning unless we could find some other way to resolve the matter."

Because everyone in the room except Bella and Andrew had already heard Jason's confession the night before, he forced himself to focus on them now. Bella looked crestfallen and wounded—the look of a mom who had just found out her son was on drugs. Andrew wouldn't even return Jason's eye contact; his face showed the pain of a betrayed friend.

But Kelly nodded her encouragement, and Jason took another deep breath. Melissa Davids pierced him with her intensity as he continued. "The trial has been tainted from day one. Without going into details, let me just say that I have been pressured into putting Chief Poole on the stand and keeping two jurors on the panel who should never have been there in the first place."

Jason stopped and looked at Andrew. "I'm sorry, Andrew." His friend looked at him, pursed his lips, and nodded, though he couldn't hide the disappointment on his face.

"I told Kelly about the shadow jury and about the fact that we've been very careful not to let them know which side of the case impaneled them. I suggested that we dismiss the two members of the shadow jury who were chosen to mimic Jurors 3 and 7 on the real panel. I also suggested that we not let this shadow jury hear the testimony of Chief Poole or any comments the lawyers made in their closing arguments about Chief Poole.

"To cut to the chase—we've all agreed to be bound by the verdict of the untainted shadow jury, not the actual jury. If the shadow jury comes back with its verdict before the actual jury, we'll inform Judge Garrison that the case has been settled. If the shadow jury comes back after the real verdict, we just settle the real case then. Either way, we ignore the real verdict even though we decided to let that case run its course this morning because . . ." Jason paused. "Well, for reasons I can't disclose, it's best that the real case continue."

Kelly piped in, her voice far more upbeat than Jason's. "My only caveat was that I wanted a chance to eyeball these jurors and ask them a few questions, like my own private *voir dire*. Jason can ask questions as well if he wants. I just need to make sure they haven't been influenced by something other than the evidence in the case."

Heads were nodding. Bella was still wide-eyed, trying to take it all in.

"One other thing I didn't mention last night," Kelly said. "I would like to leave someone here to monitor things." She was speaking to Jason. "You've got Bella and Mr. Lassiter. The rest of us may be called back to court. My dad's in from out of town, and he can be trusted to keep this confidential. If we decide to move forward with this, I'd like to have him stay with this jury and your team as part of the monitoring process."

Jason shrugged and looked at Case. He knew better than to seek Melissa's approval on anything right now.

"It's fine with me," Case said. "If you can't trust a minister, we're all in trouble."

Other logistical details were discussed, and a stunned Bella and Andrew Lassiter were dispatched to prepare the jurors for a meeting with the real attorneys and real parties in the case.

A few minutes later, Bella came back and directed traffic. She was already taking to her new role, a kind of shadow judge for the shadow jury. She explained to the litigants that the jurors were in the hotel's largest conference room, right down the hall. They were seated around a conference table, and Bella had put some chairs in front of the table for the lawyers and their clients.

She had Kelly and Blake enter first, followed by Jason, Case, and Melissa. There were astonished looks on the faces of the shadow jurors, as if the actors from a TV show had just walked into their living room. Bella introduced the parties and their lawyers and asked them to take a seat. Then she turned to her jury.

"Folks, the lawyers are going to ask you a few questions to make sure you've not been biased by some outside source in this case. The actual case has had a few—" she searched for the right word—"hiccups. It's now going to be incumbent on you to render a fair and impartial verdict in this case. And the parties have agreed to be bound by whatever you decide."

87

AFTER NEARLY AN HOUR of *voir dire*, Kelly and Jason stepped into the hallway to consult with their clients. They huddled for a few minutes; then Kelly pulled Jason aside, out of earshot of the others.

"We'll go with it," Kelly told him.

Jason took a deep breath, and Kelly's heart went out to him. Though Jason hadn't shared any details about his conversations with his clients, it was obvious that Melissa Davids was not happy.

"Thanks," Jason said.

"Let me go to the feds with you," Kelly said. It was an offer she had already made, and Jason had already refused.

Jason shook his head. "Part of the deal was that I go alone. There's no use destroying more lives than we have to."

He had the same determined look in his eyes that he did on Friday night when they met at the Hilton. Jason had told Kelly about the attack in the parking lot and the way Luthor had blackmailed him in the case. Jason said that he had decided not to call Chief Poole to the stand. He suggested that he and Kelly settle the case. If they couldn't agree on a settlement, Jason would move for a mistrial based on his own misconduct. Either way—settlement or not—he was going to blow the whistle on himself and go to the authorities.

Later on Friday night, after her ocean swim, Kelly had reconciled herself to the fact that her past would be exposed. The one thing Luthor had demanded of her was that she refuse to settle. But her client's best interest now demanded settlement—it was either that or face a mistrial motion from Jason that would undoubtedly be granted. Afterward, they would all be back at square one.

But Jason had no authority to settle unless he could get his client to go along.

Over the weekend, a slightly different plan evolved, fueled by the objective thinking of Brad Carson. Why not submit the case to the shadow jury? That way, both sides could get a fair resolution and they could still nail Justice Inc. for trying to blackmail the litigants in the real case.

As the plan unfolded, Kelly began to trust Jason and decided to tell him in confidence about Luthor's e-mails to her. She had offered to go the authorities with him, but Jason had been adamant that he wouldn't settle the case if she did.

"You didn't do anything wrong," Jason insisted now, as the two lawyers stood alone in the hallway. "I kept two jurors on the panel who I knew would hurt my case. You didn't do anything to hurt yours. Luthor wasn't sabotaging your case; he was helping it. Why ruin your career too?"

"But he was *trying* to manipulate it from both sides. His e-mails to me are still a crime."

"We've been over this, Kelly. Your duty is to your client. The terms of settlement I offered include you *not* going to the authorities unless your testimony is later deemed necessary to convict Robert Sherwood and Justice Inc."

He was right; they had gone over this ad nauseam last night. On this point, Jason would not budge. Kelly didn't understand why he was so adamant about protecting her, but she couldn't really fight it. The agreed-upon resolution was in the best interest of her client.

"Okay," she said with a sigh.

"I'll let everyone know we have a deal," Jason said.

They shook hands, and Kelly thanked him. He nodded grimly.

Even in the best case, his reputation would be shattered. His green eyes had gone from piercing to resolved, the look of a martyr heading into the Coliseum. He seemed so much older to Kelly than when they had started the case. She felt a little ashamed at the way she had initially judged him and belittled him.

"You tried a good case," she said.

"Not half as good as you."

◁▷

Kelly's dad arrived at the hotel a few minutes later, and another round of introductions followed. The plan now was for Blake and Kelly to head back to the Virginia Beach courthouse and chat with reporters while the jury deliberated. They would be joined there by Melissa Davids, who would provide the media with plenty of ammunition from her side. Brad and Jason thought it would seem a little suspicious if every participant in the trial suddenly disappeared for the entire afternoon.

The shadow jury would be monitored by Kelly's dad, Bella, and Case McAllister. It was never explicitly stated, but everyone knew what Jason would be doing. It was time to turn state's evidence and cut a deal.

Kelly decided to stop at her hotel on the way to the courthouse. She wasn't looking forward to another round of fending off reporters, especially when she needed to be careful not to say something inappropriate during jury deliberations. She figured she could spend a few minutes packing her stuff and watching the news coverage. She could grab a sandwich and eat lunch while driving to court.

She parked in the 31st Street garage, on the fourth floor. By now she knew the routine—she would walk down two flights of stairs and cross over the street on the covered concrete bridge that connected the parking garage to the hotel.

She reached the stairwell at about the same time as a man from another spot on the fourth floor. He looked vaguely familiar—maybe one of the other regulars at the Hilton? He was wearing jeans, a Windbreaker, and a baseball cap with a ponytail hanging out the back.

A Windbreaker? It was pushing ninety-five degrees.

Kelly walked down the first flight of steps as quickly as her high heels would allow. The man followed close behind, literally breathing down her neck. If she kicked off her heels, she could surely out-sprint him. The man must have tipped the scales at 250.

As she turned the corner to head down the next flight, he reached out and grabbed her arm. She gasped as he drew her next to him, face-to-face, a gun suddenly in her ribs.

"Not a word," he hissed.

He yanked her toward the door that opened to the third level of the garage as a car came skidding around the corner. The back door flew open.

Kelly screamed at the top of her lungs.

"Shut up!" The gunman threw her in the backseat and climbed in behind her, catching her as she scrambled to get out the other side. The driver took off even before the door closed behind the beast beside her. The man's bulk pinned Kelly against the door on her side, muffling her screams.

He whipped his gun across her face and she felt her cheekbone crack.

"Shut her up!" yelled the driver.

The ponytailed man forced her face up against the side door, wrenching her arms behind her back so he could handcuff them. Once she was cuffed, he bore down on her with his full weight until she stopped squirming. She felt a needle in her neck and the world started spinning.

The driver pulled into a parking spot and popped the trunk. Kelly tried to yell again, but her tongue wouldn't cooperate. Her attackers were fading, spinning, zooming in and out of focus.

Her eyes rolled up in her head, and she quit fighting it, her assailants' words lost in a blur of scrambled noise and jumbled thoughts.

◁ ▷

Rafael Johansen paid the cashier at the exit to the parking garage. He calmly made a left on Atlantic and another left on Laskin Road. Jason and Kelly had surprised him. Jason in particular. The little jerk had mustered the guts to defy Luthor and sacrifice his own reputation.

The stupid kid had no way of knowing it would cost him his life.

Johansen called Robert Sherwood and detected a hint of panic in the great man's voice. Things had not exactly gone according to plan on the Crawford case.

Johansen ended the call, checked his rearview mirror, and took a left into the deserted parking lot of the Surf and Sand movie theater. The yellowed signage on the large marquee still displayed its final message: *Goodbye Surf and Sand. We will miss you. Love, the staff.*

Last week, the locals had told Johansen the place had been sitting vacant for the past eighteen months. The doors had been locked and chained.

Johansen had scoped out the place two days ago. The parking lot was shielded by tall marsh grass and a wildlife area protected by the Chesapeake Bay Preservation Act. The theater was only a mile or so from the Hilton, set back from Laskin Road and bordered by the marsh on every side except the west end of the parking lot, which abutted the Purple Cow parking lot. Earlier today, using a bolt cutter and a crowbar, Johansen had pried open one of the back doors of the theater.

He parked the car behind the building and took a final glance around. The car could only be seen from the marsh.

Johansen opened the trunk, and a partner from his investigative firm, a large weight lifter named Tony Morris, lifted Kelly out and carried her into the abandoned theater building. Except for Johansen's flashlight, the place was pitch black.

They duct-taped Kelly to a seat in the front row directly in front of the big screen, gagged her with a cloth, and left to abduct their second victim.

"How long before she comes out of it?" Johansen asked.

"Fifteen minutes."

"Just in time for the feature show."

88

IT HAD ALREADY BEEN A DISASTROUS DAY before Olivia ushered Special Agent Billingsley of the FBI into Robert Sherwood's office. The agent was short, stocky, and young. He had perfect posture and light blond hair clipped short. If Sherwood had met him on the street, he would have guessed West Point graduate.

"Nice view," Billingsley said, admiring the floor-to-ceiling windows that overlooked the Hudson River. "Do you ever find yourself taking it for granted?"

"Have a seat," Sherwood said, motioning toward the navy blue leather chair. "I'm a busy man, and I understand you've got some questions."

"Right." Before Billingsley sat down, he placed a digital recorder on Sherwood's desk. "Do you mind if I tape this?"

Sherwood sighed. "No."

Billingsley took a seat and ran through a little intro for his recording—time, plaçe, the consent of Robert Sherwood. Then he began his questions.

"Does the name Luthor mean anything to you?"

"No."

"Have you been following the Crawford trial in Virginia Beach?"

"Yes."

"I understand that both Jason Noble and Kelly Starling at one time worked for you. Is that correct?"

"Technically, no. They worked for two law firms in town. Justice Inc. was a client of those firms. But they did spend most of their time working on mock cases for our research department."

"Are you aware of any other clients either one of them had while supposedly working at these New York law firms?"

This brought another big sigh from Sherwood. Why did they always have to play these cat-and-mouse games? "No."

"Are you aware of anything in either Mr. Noble's or Ms. Starling's past that might be used to blackmail or embarrass them?"

Sherwood narrowed his eyes. "What's this about?" he asked.

"Somebody has been blackmailing Mr. Noble in the Crawford case and possibly manipulating jurors," Billingsley said. He seemed to be watching Sherwood for any possible reaction. "We think it might be somebody with a lot of money at stake."

Sherwood scoffed at the implied accusation. "You think I'm blackmailing Jason Noble?"

"I'm just asking questions," Billingsley said.

"I'll tell you one thing," Sherwood replied. "If I'm blackmailing Jason Noble, I'm doing a pitiful job of it."

◁ ▷

Jason was in his office, printing off e-mails and pulling together the documents he would need to present to the U.S. Attorney. He was supposed to be at Brad's office by 2 p.m.

In the conference room down the hall, Andrew Lassiter was doing the same thing. When Jason had told him he was spilling the beans on Justice Inc., Lassiter had wanted to help. "I can testify about all the data they collected on employees," he told Jason. "I know for a fact they were checking your e-mails, tapping your phones, and all that."

At first, Jason hadn't wanted to involve anyone other than himself. But Lassiter insisted, and Jason had to admit that his friend could provide a lot of corroborating evidence. Jason called Brad, who saw no downside in bringing Lassiter along.

As he organized his evidence, Jason was consumed with thoughts about the fallout from his decision. What would happen to his dad? Detective Corey? What would LeRon's father say? How could Jason face him?

"Jason!"

It was Andrew's voice from the conference room, shattering the silence, startling Jason. It was followed by the sounds of a scuffle and another muffled shout.

Jason grabbed his gun and bolted from his office, sprinting toward the conference room. When he turned the corner in the hallway, he stopped in his tracks. A large man with a ball cap and light blond hair had taken Lassiter hostage and was using him as a shield, holding a gun to his temple. The big man's hand was covering Lassiter's mouth.

"One more step and I shoot," he said to Jason.

Before Jason could react, he felt a blow to the back of his head. There was a flash of color, a kaleidoscope of sparks . . . and this time Jason's world went dark.

89

JASON DRIFTED IN AND OUT of the fog. Stray thoughts and nightmares tumbled together through the cobwebs of his mind. He heard voices at the end of a long tunnel and felt the intense pain of a pounding headache radiating from the back of his skull. His head felt like someone had it in a vise and was screwing it tighter and tighter as Jason regained consciousness. His mouth was dry as cotton.

He felt something sting his cheek. Once. Twice. He flinched. Another slap.

"Wake up, Boy Wonder."

He realized he was sitting in a chair. He blinked a few times into the darkness, trying to clear his head. Somebody pointed a bright light into his eyes—some kind of spotlight? He squinted and slit his eyes—a flashlight.

He felt the sting of the next slap on his cheek, a hard shot with an open palm, and he shook his head. He tried to retaliate, but his wrists were handcuffed together in front of him. As he tried to stand up, a strong arm shot out and jammed him back into his seat. He couldn't yell—they had stuffed something in his mouth; he could feel fabric on his tongue. A rag, maybe, held in place with some kind of tape wrapped around the back of his head.

"Welcome back to reality," a deep voice said. "Unfortunately for you, reality sucks."

Jason squinted to get his bearings. He was in an auditorium. A theater? It was dark except for the light shining directly in his eyes. He could make out the shadows of two figures behind the flashlight.

He felt a gun barrel at the back of his skull.

"That's enough," someone said. "He's awake." It was a softer voice. The person who had just spoken took the flashlight from the first man and placed it on the floor. He knelt in front of Jason.

Andrew?

Jason stared at him, and Andrew Lassiter stared back, blinking. "I never meant for it to turn out like this," he said.

◁ ▷

Robert Sherwood parried questions from Agent Billingsley for nearly thirty minutes, a battle of wits between a brilliant CEO and a savvy investigator. The one thing Billingsley had that Sherwood did not was time. And patience.

Sherwood had clients to call. Fires to put out. His entire business plan was imploding.

"Turn that thing off," he said, motioning to the recorder.

Billingsley leaned forward and switched off the device.

"Our corporation is a highly sophisticated research firm that provides advice to a number of clients," Sherwood said in a condescending tone. He would try to keep it simple so Billingsley wouldn't glaze over with the technical details. "We have a state-of-the-art system for analyzing potential jury verdicts in big cases like the Crawford case. It's complicated, but the heart of the system is a mock trial we conduct using three different jury panels, all designed to reflect the characteristics of the jurors on the actual case." Sherwood paused. "Are you following all this?"

"You might want to slow down a little," Billingsley said sarcastically. "FBI agents can be a little thick."

Sherwood frowned at the gamesmanship. "Last Thursday evening we heard from our three jury panels. They all came back with a defense verdict based on what we thought the evidence in the Crawford case would be. Over the weekend, we advised our clients, most of them hedge fund managers, that it was our considered opinion that the stocks of gun manufacturers like MD Firearms would not be damaged by this verdict. In fact, we anticipated that a defense verdict would boost the stocks higher."

Sherwood watched closely as Billingsley processed the information. The agent showed no reaction.

"Today, of course, the final witness for the defense imploded, the case went south, and we look like idiots." Sherwood leaned forward on his desk. "If the plaintiff gets a verdict in this case, and I suspect he will, our firm might never recover." He paused, again giving the FBI agent time to process the information.

"So I would appreciate it, Agent Billingsly, if you would get out of my office and find out who's been blackmailing Jason Noble. I've got a few ideas of my own, and I can promise you this—whoever it is had better pray that you find him first."

90

"YOU WERE SUPPOSED to go along with the program," Andrew Lassiter said, the words clipped with emotion. "This wasn't about *you;* it was about getting back at *them*. Sherwood took everything, Jason. He took my entire life's work."

Jason stared at Lassiter, trying to comprehend the man's betrayal. He tried to ignore the jackhammer that seemed to be pounding away at the back of his head. *There has to be some way out.*

There were three men here, as far as Jason knew. Lassiter, a guy behind Jason holding a gun to his head, and a third man—larger and stronger than Lassiter—the man who had slapped Jason awake.

"Let's get on with it," that man said to Lassiter. It was a familiar voice. A New York accent. Hispanic. "He's not your priest, and we don't need your confession."

Jason's eyes were growing accustomed to the dark, and he could finally make out the big man's features. It was the first time Jason could ever remember seeing him smile.

Rafael Johansen.

"That's right, Boy Wonder," Rafael said. "I guess I'm a mercenary. Although Sherwood never offered me a share of the profits like the mad professor here." He inched a little closer, and Jason leaned back. "You sure screwed things up with your Johnny-Be-Good routine. Now things have gotten a little complicated."

Jason was still processing his surroundings. He seemed to be in the first row of the second section of a movie theater, about ten rows or so away from the screen. They undoubtedly intended to kill him—why else would they be brazen enough to show their faces?

Unless Andrew Lassiter had a sudden change of heart, Jason was a dead man. And for some reason, coming to terms with that indisputable fact took away some of his terror. *Courage comes when you have nothing left to lose.*

He quickly decided things could only get worse. The one advantage he had right now might be the element of surprise.

Jason bolted up and twisted, swinging his handcuffed fists toward the gunman behind him. He whiffed. Rafael was instantly on him, pile-driving him into the cement floor. Rafael's weight landed on Jason's shoulder, and he screamed into the gag. He nearly blacked out a second time as Rafael hauled him to his feet and threw him back into the chair.

"You're trying my patience, boy," Rafael said, catching his breath.

The other man had moved in front of Jason now, a few feet away, pointing the gun at Jason's forehead. He was another bodybuilder, a private security guard who worked with Rafael. Jason recognized the ponytail.

Toward the front of the auditorium, Jason thought he heard a muffled scream. They weren't alone? His mind raced through the possibilities. The most likely scenario was also the one that Jason dreaded the most.

"We'll deal with you in a minute," Rafael yelled over his shoulder.

91

"GO EASY ON HIM," Andrew sputtered.

Rafael laughed and turned toward Andrew, who had stepped a few feet away. "Go easy on him," Rafael repeated, mocking his coconspirator. "We're going to kill him, genius."

"No, we're not," Andrew said. "I've been thinking this through."

Though it was hard for Jason to see Andrew in the shadows, his voice had a desperate edge to it. Maybe he was starting to understand the monster he had unleashed. "We don't need to risk murder charges. I've got a better way."

"There is no other way," insisted Rafael. "Let's get it over with."

He turned the flashlight on Andrew, and for the first time Jason noticed that his friend was wearing plastic gloves. In his right hand, he was holding Jason's MD-45.

"I've already set them up," Andrew said, his voice trembling now, his words coming out in a torrent. "The offshore investment companies I created to short the gun companies' stocks have Jason's and Kelly's fingerprints all over them. I used their BlackBerry accounts to exchange e-mails about their conspiracy. We can drug them both, let them live, dump them outside the country. Everyone will assume they gamed the system and—"

"That's not the plan," Rafael said matter-of-factly. "Too many loose ends."

"They can't come back, because the police will be looking for them. We go to the cops first—"

Rafael shook his head, determined. "That's not the plan."

"If these two ever come back to the country, nobody will believe—"

"Shut up."

The room went silent as Rafael shone the flashlight directly in Lassiter's eyes. Andrew stared back at Rafael for a long moment—his eyes blinking, the neck twitching, every feature on his face reflecting his tortured conscience.

He took a step back, raised the gun, and pointed it at Rafael and his ponytailed partner, back and forth, his arms trembling.

The man with the ponytail kept his gun trained on Jason. Rafael made no move for his own gun, tucked into the waist of his jeans.

Instead, he calmly took a few steps toward Andrew. "Pull the trigger," Rafael taunted. "Let's see if the genius has any guts."

Andrew stiffened his arms, his face contorted. "Stop," he said, but Rafael took another step. Andrew took a half step back. "Stop."

Rafael just kept coming.

Andrew closed his eyes, flinched, and squeezed the trigger.

When nothing happened, Rafael reached for his own gun and smiled. "It always amazes me how dumb you genius types can be. Or maybe I just never told you that Jason's gun has a safety lock that's only released by his fingerprints."

A look of sheer terror filled Andrew's eyes. He dropped the gun and held his hands in front of him, as if to push the larger man away. "No," he said, shaking his head. "I can get us out of this. Nobody has to die!"

"That's where you're wrong." There was a smug grin on Rafael's face, then a flash from the barrel of his gun, and a bullet ripped through Andrew Lassiter's eye socket. He was blown backward, landing lifelessly on the row of seats behind him, his mouth open in midscream, blood trickling from the hole in his head.

Jason gagged and felt vomit rising in his throat. He heard another muffled scream from the front row.

The man with the ponytail stared at Lassiter's lifeless body. "What the—?" He turned on Rafael. "Are you crazy?"

This brought another smile to Rafael's face. "Tony. How long have you known me? Eight years? Nine?" Rafael put his gun back in the waist of his jeans. "I've got a plan, Tony. You know I don't like loose ends."

"But this is nuts," Tony protested. "Out of control."

"Think about it," Rafael said. "Lassiter's plan had a big problem. When you frame somebody, it's got to be airtight. But if these two lawyers were going to fix the case, set up offshore companies to bet on the stocks and then run off with the money, why wouldn't they wait until a few weeks after the verdict when the spotlight on them was gone? Why would they disappear while the jury was still deliberating, guaranteeing there would be a national manhunt for them? It doesn't make sense."

Tony shrugged. "I don't know. But we've still got the same problem."

"Not anymore." Rafael smiled at the brilliance of what he was about to share. "Because now we've got three people missing. We make it look like the lawyers and Lassiter were all in the scam together. Lassiter gets greedy, anxious, whatever . . . jumps the gun, so to speak, and kills both lawyers. The police find the bodies of Jason and Kelly and a gun with Lassiter's fingerprints. The money and Lassiter disappear forever."

Even without seeing Tony's face, Jason could sense the big man relaxing.

"See what I'm saying?" Rafael asked.

"Maybe," said Tony, his voice still a little unsure. "But we shoulda talked about that first."

The next part must have been planned in advance, because the men didn't say a word as they pulled Jason from his seat and dragged him to the front of the theater. They pushed him into a seat a few chairs down from Kelly and cuffed Jason's right wrist to the armrest.

In the shadows, Jason exchanged a glance with Kelly. She had a look of fierce determination.

To Jason's surprise, Rafael reached down and peeled away the duct tape holding Jason's gag. Jason spit the gag out and looked up at Johansen.

"Tony, shine that flashlight on the big screen," Rafael said.

Tony did as he was told, propping the flashlight on the arm of one of the theater seats.

At the same time, Rafael started unwrapping the duct tape that held Kelly to her seat, talking as he did so. "We're going to require your cooperation, Mr. Noble, in order to make this as painless as possible for your coconspirator here. The cops know that anybody can type a message into a BlackBerry. So I need you to leave a voice mail on Ms. Starling's phone. You're going to tell her to meet you and Andrew Lassiter at First Landing State Park. That will be the final resting place for you and your opposing counsel."

This time it was Jason who scoffed. "Whatever you say." He already knew he was going to die—why cooperate with the cover-up? "What's the worst you can do, kill me?"

This made Rafael laugh—long and hard, as if Jason had just delivered the perfect punch line. Johansen took out a switchblade and pulled Kelly from her seat, her hands cuffed behind her back, her legs taped together, the gag still in place. "I'm glad you asked," Rafael said. He pushed Kelly facedown on the floor and knelt on her back.

"Because you're about to see the worst I can do."

92

RAFAEL JOHANSEN flicked open the switchblade and held the edge of the blade next to Kelly's ankle. "They say that slitting the Achilles tendon is the most painful thing that can happen to a human being," Rafael said, business-like. "That tendon is like an incredibly strong piece of elastic, connecting the foot to the calf muscle. When it's snapped, the calf muscles just pull the whole ligament in and curl it up toward the knee. The foot just kind of dangles at the end of the leg, held loosely in place by skin and the bone socket."

Jason saw the look of terror on Kelly's face, sweat covering her forehead, her eyes wide with a combination of fear and rage. She caught Jason's eye and gave a small but defiant shake of the head. Then she squirmed and kicked with all her might.

Rafael jerked her back into place and pinned her shoulders and upper body to the floor. "Try that again, and I'll cut your face instead."

Jason cursed at Rafael and promised to say whatever the man wanted. "If you hurt her, so help me . . ."

Rafael laughed again. "So help you *what*? You going to give me another stirring legal argument? Maybe talk me to death?"

"You win," Jason said. "Give me my phone."

Rafael grinned. "Nope. It doesn't work quite that way. Instead, we'll want you to speak into this little digital recorder that Tony has. Once you get the message right, *we'll* make the phone call and use the recorder to leave the message. Takes away the margin for error, wouldn't you say?"

Jason knew Rafael would somehow make sure the cops found Kelly's cell phone and Jason's BlackBerry. Or maybe he was counting on the fact that Justice Inc. monitored Jason's calls, that the FBI would find recordings of those calls when they executed their search warrant. Either way, Jason would be establishing a perfect cover for these men.

Tony stood in front of Jason and took out the recorder. He pointed his gun at Jason's knee. "It's not quite the same as slitting the Achilles tendon, but having a kneecap blown out hurts a little, too. Let's make sure we get the message right the first time."

"It's very simple," Rafael called out. "Just tell her to meet you and Andrew Lassiter at First Landing State Park. Plans have changed. Come immediately."

Jason stared at the recorder, feeling incredibly helpless. Either way, he was going to die. Did he have enough guts not to go along with the cover-up?

Kelly answered the question for him. Without warning, she kicked again and rolled away from Johansen. She tried to stand but with her ankles taped fell back on her side. Rafael reached out and grabbed her, pulling her back toward him. "Feisty," he said, waving the blade in front of her face. "It's a shame to ruin such a pretty face."

He flicked the knife toward her just as Jason heard the blast of a gun and watched Rafael's arm jerk backward, away from Kelly, the knife flying from his hand. The shot distracted Tony, and Jason lurched into him, head-butting the big man and forcing him backward.

Another series of shots rang out, three of them, so close together they sounded almost like one explosion. The bullets ripped into Rafael, and he collapsed backward in a heap.

From behind Jason, a fraction of a second later, another series of bullets flew, exploding into the head and chest of Tony. He was dead before he hit the floor.

As quickly as it had started, it was over.

Jason hardly dared breathe. "Are there any more?" Melissa Davids shouted from the entrance to Jason's left.

"I think we're done," Case McAllister said, limping up from behind Jason. He grabbed the flashlight and, along with Melissa, did a quick search of the theater, guns drawn as they went from row to row like a couple of trained detectives.

When they finished, Case came down to help Jason, who had buckled to the floor.

"You all right?" Case asked.

"Not really."

Melissa knelt next to Kelly, using Johansen's knife to cut the duct tape from around Kelly's ankles. Next, with the gentleness of a mother, Melissa peeled off the duct tape holding Kelly's gag.

"Thank God," Kelly said, her face a mixture of relief and tears. She leaned into Melissa Davids, her hands still cuffed behind her back. Melissa held her for a moment.

Jason watched the women as Case searched through the pockets of the dead men for the handcuff keys.

"I'm not sure how much we were planning on charging for those GPS options on our guns," Case said over his shoulder. "But whatever it was, we oughta double it."

A few minutes later, after Case had unlocked the handcuffs, the SWAT team burst through the theater doors. "Hands on your heads! Freeze!"

"That's it. Now take two steps back away from your guns."

"Glad you guys could join the party," Melissa Davids said.

93

THE MEDICAL STAFF at Virginia Beach General treated Jason like royalty. Though Jason was still in shock from the pain and trauma, he realized that in the big scheme of things he was miraculously unhurt. He had dislocated his shoulder and suffered a serious concussion from the blow to his head. He now had a big bald spot where they had shaved his head for the stitches, though they had since covered the wound with gauze and a bandage.

His first visitor was Bella Harper.

"Look at you," she said. "I leave you alone for one hour, and you just about get yourself killed. You look terrible."

"Thanks," Jason mumbled. He motioned with his hand for Bella to keep her voice down. "I've got a splitting headache."

Bella shook her head, tears welling up in her eyes. "I'm just so glad you're okay," she said, choking up. The bravado hadn't lasted long. It looked like she wanted to give Jason a hug but didn't dare touch him for fear she might hurt him. Instead, she squeezed his hand.

"From the minute we figured out you were missing, I started praying for you," Bella said.

"Thanks."

Bella gave him the rundown about the search. She had discovered Jason and Kelly were missing when she tried to call the lawyers with news about the shadow jury's verdict. After fifteen minutes of unanswered calls, Melissa Davids had called her company and obtained the information for the GPS unit in Jason's gun.

"When she found out the location, she and Mr. McAllister were on their way before they even called 911," Bella said. "I don't think Ms. Davids trusts the cops."

Jason thanked Bella for everything she had done. He was tired and hurting and just wanted to sleep. Unfortunately, all the nurses were determined to keep him awake for another twelve hours because of the concussion.

"Don't you want to know about the verdict?" asked Bella.

From the tone of Bella's voice, it was hard to tell whether they had won or not. Maybe it was the painkillers, or the trauma he had just seen Kelly endure, or the horror of seeing Andrew Lassiter shot right in front of him. For whatever reason, the verdict didn't seem to matter as much anymore. He would certainly take no great solace in a defense verdict. As hard as it had been to watch Andrew and the others die, he couldn't imagine what Blake Crawford must have gone through watching the tape of Rachel being shot.

"They gave the plaintiff a million dollars," Bella said.

Jason closed his eyes and absorbed the news. Was it justice? In his drug-induced state, it was hard to tell.

"I'm kidding," Bella said, grinning. "It was a unanimous defense verdict."

Jason's first thought was that he wanted to kill his assistant. There were some things you didn't joke about. But the drugs had made a pacifist out of him.

"Very funny, Bella," he said as sharply as possible, though his voice didn't have much edge to it. "How did Blake Crawford take it?"

"That's it?" Bella asked. "I just told you we won the biggest case of your career, and you don't even smile?"

"I don't know," Jason said. He was too drugged to be anything but honest. "It doesn't really feel like anybody won."

"I know what you mean," Bella admitted. The two were silent for a moment, as if they were honoring the memory of Rachel Crawford.

"In answer to your question," Bella said, her tone reflective, "Blake Crawford wasn't there. But Reverend Starling was, and he was incredible. He thanked every one of the jurors and then called Kelly and Blake. Kelly, of course, didn't answer. You want to know what Blake said—according to the reverend?"

Jason shrugged.

"He told the reverend to congratulate you and thank you for setting up a fair process for resolving the case. He said he had to accept the jury verdict as God's will."

Jason thought about that for a moment. "Amazing," he said.

"My thoughts exactly," Bella said.

94

THE FALLOUT from the Crawford case was swift and severe.

Matt Corey and James Noble were dismissed from the Atlanta police force pending the outcome of an internal investigation. Given the fact that ten years had passed since the altered accident report and the difficulties of proving that Jason was actually driving, few expected Jason or his dad to be charged with a crime. Matt Corey, on the other hand, was facing a grand jury indictment for conspiring with Andrew Lassiter by warning him about Jason's intent to go to the authorities.

To Jason's surprise, the FBI found no evidence to suggest that Judge Garrison had been blackmailed or otherwise involved in the plot. On the contrary, his disciplined handling of the case was now receiving widespread acclaim, earning him mention as a possible candidate for an appellate job down the road.

Meanwhile, Judge Shaver apparently had second thoughts about his own appellate aspirations. In a move that only a few insiders knew was related to the Crawford case, the judge withdrew his name from consideration for the Fourth Circuit Court of Appeals.

The major media outlets enthusiastically embraced Kelly Starling as a hero and were even forced to admit that Melissa Davids and Case McAllister had also acted courageously—in a vigilante sort of way. Public opinion about Jason's role was hotly contested. Gun supporters eagerly gave him the benefit of the doubt, while others noted that his web of deceit had nearly cost Kelly Starling her life.

Even before the shootings in the Surf and Sand Theater, Brad Carson had discussed a deal with the FBI to grant Jason immunity in exchange for his cooperation. While Jason was in the hospital, Brad also discussed the matter informally with the head of the state bar's disciplinary committee. According to Brad, Jason could expect to be reprimanded and placed on probation for his conduct in the Crawford case but would not lose his license since he had gone to the authorities before his client was ultimately harmed.

Jason was released from the hospital on Tuesday morning, shaved his hair down to a nub so the bald spot wouldn't look so conspicuous, donned his Georgia Bulldogs hat, and booked a flight to Atlanta. He stayed overnight with his father and, to his great disappointment, discovered that the events of the last few days had knocked his dad off the wagon.

"I don't want to hear any of your sanctimonious crap about my drinking," his father said after half a dozen beers. "What else is a man supposed to do when he loses his job and his reputation just for trying to help his son?"

In the past, Jason might have responded in anger. But on Tuesday night, he just murmured an apology and headed to bed.

On Wednesday morning, Jason faced one of the most difficult ordeals of his life. He tried to get his father to go with him but was refused.

"I can't say anything while this investigation is ongoing," his dad said, hunched over a cup of strong, black coffee. "And even if I could, I'm not going to apologize for protecting my son. I'd do the same thing again."

"Your call," Jason said with a shrug. Change would not come easy for someone as proud as Jim Noble.

But a few minutes later, as Jason was rising from the table resigned to the fact that things with his dad would never change, the man said something that stopped Jason in his tracks.

"I understand why you're doing this," his father said without looking up. "It might not be the way I would handle it, but . . . regardless of what I might've said last night, I understand."

Jason stared at the top of his dad's head for a moment. The man was complicated.

"That's all I can ask," Jason said. He turned and headed for the door.

◁ ▷

When Jason arrived at the church, he sat in his rental car for nearly five minutes, envisioning the upcoming meeting, talking himself out of turning the car around and leaving. There would be no acting in this one. Jason would have to take responsibility, fall on his sword, and ask for forgiveness. He would look them straight in the eye and explain how sorry he was. He would tell them that his lies had haunted him every day of his life.

He would sit there and take all of their anger, all of their vitriol, every one of their accusations and indictments. He deserved every word.

Anything he said would, of course, be a self-incriminating statement. If the Tates decided to press charges based on this meeting, so be it. Anything would be better than continuing to live with this lie.

He was sick to his stomach by the time he meekly introduced himself to Reverend Tate's assistant. He desperately wanted to bolt, but there was no turning back now. The reverend had the door to his office closed and made Jason wait five more minutes. It was the longest five minutes of Jason's life.

Reverend Tate came out looking serious and sad, shook Jason's hand, and ushered Jason into the office. He looked the same way Jason remembered him—beefy and intimidating with intense brown eyes. He was a little heavier now, and his hair was peppered with gray.

Mrs. Tate was also in the office, and she greeted Jason with a hug. She had put on more weight than her husband, and her sad eyes sagged even when she briefly smiled.

Jason sat down on a small couch, as if he were at a counseling session. Reverend and Mrs. Tate sat in front of him in two side chairs, holding hands.

"We appreciate you coming," Reverend Tate said. "Do you mind if I start with a prayer?"

The request shouldn't have taken Jason off guard, but it did. He took off his hat, put his elbows on his knees, and bowed his head. He was so nervous he hardly heard a word the reverend said.

When Reverend Tate finished praying, he asked Jason about his shoulder.

It actually hurt like crazy, but Jason tried to shrug it off. "Just a flesh wound," he said in a lame attempt at humor.

"Look, Jason, I know how hard it must have been coming here and facing this." Reverend Tate stared at Jason—right through him, really—and Jason couldn't look away. "This is all pretty fresh to us and picks the scabs off some raw wounds, but I want you to know—" he paused and looked at Mrs. Tate, who nodded along—"we *need* you to know that we hold nothing against you, son."

Mrs. Tate dabbed at her eyes, and Jason realized that the reverend's voice was cracking a little as well. "You were LeRon's best friend, and he loved you like a brother. You boys were young, and you made a big mistake. God chose to take LeRon home. We've learned to accept that."

The words stunned Jason, rendering him speechless. He hadn't known quite what to expect, but he surely had not envisioned this. His planned *mea culpa* speech seemed so inadequate now. What could he say in response?

Jason was not an emotional guy, but he found himself choking back tears as he offered a meager apology. "He deserved a better friend than me. I've lied to you, disrespected him, used my dead friend as a . . ." Jason struggled for the right word, then reached back to his closing argument. ". . . as a scapegoat."

He had more to say, but Mrs. Tate cut him off, her motherly instincts kicking in. "You were young. You had your whole life in front of you. We don't blame you."

"How can you not?" Jason asked.

"What good would bitterness do?" Reverend Tate asked, his voice strong and confident again. He was in pastor mode now. "Would anger bring our son back? Would punishing you bring him out of the grave?"

Jason shook his head, but that apparently wasn't good enough for the reverend.

"Would it?" he insisted.

"No, sir."

"You know that's right," the reverend said. "All that's left is all that's left. LeRon wouldn't have wanted us puttin' no guilt trip on you."

They talked that way for nearly an hour, with the last half focused on memories of LeRon. As they did, Jason felt a suffocating weight leave his chest. For ten years, he had lived with guilt and deception. Now he felt like he could breathe again.

By the time Jason was ready to leave, Reverend Tate had him convinced that LeRon would actually be proud of the type of trial lawyer Jason had become.

"He's probably watching you right now," the reverend suggested, "talkin' smack. 'Have you seen my boy Jason? Ain't nobody better than him.'"

Reverend Tate locked his eyes on Jason. "Do you mind if I preach at you for a minute, son. Sometimes, I just can't help myself."

"No problem," Jason said.

Mrs. Tate smiled.

"Don't back away from the hard cases, son. The clients nobody else wants to touch—the people everybody else gives up on. You want to honor LeRon's memory?"

"Yes, sir."

"Then seek justice, son. That's what you're good at. But let me leave you with a passage from the Word to think about. You ready for this?"

Jason nodded.

"'So speak and so act as those who are to be judged under the law of liberty. For judgment is without mercy to one who has shown no mercy. Mercy triumphs over judgment.' That's James chapter two, verses twelve and thirteen."

It sounded profound, but to be honest, Jason didn't know exactly what it all meant. He borrowed a piece of paper and a pen. He wrote down the reference.

Later, when he had time, he would look it up. He would think about it with the same intensity he brought to his cases. He would read what the experts said. *The law of liberty. Mercy triumphs over judgment.* The words were familiar, but the way they were strung together created concepts that were foreign. Like a mystery.

Maybe someday he would understand.

EPILOGUE

AFTER A TWO-DAY MEDIA BLITZ, Melissa Davids settled into her nondescript office in the out-of-the-way industrial park that served as the national headquarters for MD Firearms. The factory was running full bore, trying to keep up with the orders flooding in for MD-9s and MD-45s with the new GPS system and fingerprint-activated safety lock. Almost every employee was working overtime.

At 10 a.m., Melissa called Case McAllister to her office for a quick meeting.

Before he arrived, she picked up the memo and moved in front of her desk. As usual, this would be a stand-up meeting. If it took five minutes, it would be too long.

"How's Annie Oakley?" Case asked as he walked in the door.

"Remind me never to do CNBC again," Melissa replied. "Hopeless liberals."

"That's what you said last time," Case reminded her.

"Yeah, well . . . they haven't changed."

"There's a surprise."

Melissa handed Case the memo. "Look this over and let me know what you think."

She watched his eyes glance over the page and then lock on the handwriting at the top. The document was a copy of the memo Case had written two years ago entitled "Sales to Dealers Sued by Northeast Cities."

But Melissa had crossed through her original handwritten instructions and replaced them with new ones. Case, the consummate pro, didn't show the slightest hint of surprise as he read.

> Let's cut off the worst of these renegade dealers. I'll leave it to you to separate the sheep from the goats. All licensed dealers might be entitled to buy guns. But not all dealers are entitled to buy our guns.

"I think I can make this happen," Case said. "After all, the Second Amendment's not a license to kill."

Melissa shot him a look. "Quotes like that—you oughta work for CNBC."

◁ ▷

It took Robert Sherwood two days to get the FBI off his back. Once he provided documented proof that Justice Inc. and its clients would have stood to lose tens of millions of dollars from a plaintiff's verdict, the feds had to concede that Andrew Lassiter, Rafael Johansen, and Tony Morris must have acted outside the purview of Justice Inc. But the feds were not willing to concede total defeat; they made noises about possibly prosecuting Sherwood for illegally tapping into Jason Noble's phone calls and intercepting his e-mails.

"Maybe Rafael Johansen was intercepting those calls and e-mails," Sherwood argued, "but he wasn't passing that information back to us. Think about it. If I had been monitoring Jason Noble's e-mails, I would have known he was being blackmailed. And if I'd known he was being blackmailed, I wouldn't have invested millions in MD Firearms and other gun companies."

The logic was unassailable, and Sherwood knew that his firewall of legal protection would hold. While attorneys like Jason were working for Justice Inc., their company phone calls and e-mails were closely monitored—all perfectly legal. Justice Inc. had tens of millions of dollars riding on each case. The cell phones and e-mail accounts were company property. Permission to monitor them was contained in a bunch of legalese buried in the small print of contracts the lawyers signed when they handled company cases.

Andrew Lassiter's access to those records, along with the repossessed computers of those lawyers, was undoubtedly how he had learned about Kelly's affair and been alerted to something fishy with Jason's car accident.

Once the attorneys left the New York City firms and quit working for Justice Inc., they were on their own. From time to time, Sherwood might use Rafael Johansen to investigate or monitor the lawyers, particularly if they were suspected of harboring proprietary information that belonged to the company. But Sherwood was a master at plausible deniability.

"Just how Johansen did the monitoring was his business," Sherwood explained. "He was an independent contractor, and I didn't ask any questions. I just continued to stress that everything needed to be done on the up-and-up."

By the third day, the FBI had run out of questions, and Robert Sherwood was ready to make some serious money.

The company was flush with cash from the Crawford case, and the clients had never been happier. Sure, Sherwood had received some panicked phone calls on Monday right after the devastating cross-examination of Chief Poole. In the sanctuary of his office, he had paced and cursed and called Jason all kinds of names for not vetting Poole properly. But on the phone with clients, Sherwood had been the epitome of composure, urging them to ride it out, assuring them that Jason would pull a rabbit out of his hat during closing arguments.

Then came the shocking events of Monday afternoon. A mistrial in the real case. A defense verdict by the shadow jury. A shoot-out at the Surf and Sand that had turned Melissa Davids into a folk hero.

MD Firearms stock had skyrocketed, and Justice Inc.'s clients cashed in.

In the following weeks, the only cloud on the horizon for the firearms manufacturers was the newfound popularity of plaintiff's attorney Kelly Starling. There were rumors her firm was already preparing half a dozen new cases on behalf of gun victims. According to Sherwood's sources, she had turned down a gig as a legal commentator for CNN to stay focused on her crusades against gun makers and sex traffickers.

But such matters no longer concerned Robert Sherwood. He had already moved on. There were millions of AIDS victims in Kenya, and Sherwood was never one to rest on his laurels.

"Brett Lawson, line one," Olivia called out.

Sherwood spent the next fifteen minutes talking to the father of Carissa Lawson, the backup singer who had died with high levels of cocaine and oxycodone in her blood. Despite the jury verdict in the criminal case acquitting Kendra Van Wyck, Brett Lawson was convinced she had poisoned his daughter. Months ago, Mr. Lawson had filed a wrongful death suit and promised to bankrupt Kendra Van Wyck and all of her associated companies. He reminded the world that O. J. Simpson had won the criminal case and lost the civil case. The standard of proof was different. He wouldn't rest until justice was served.

But now, the civil case had bogged down due to the ineptitude of the L.A. celebrity lawyer handling the matter. Robert Sherwood had called some of his connections in the entertainment industry, who in turn had talked Brett Lawson into calling the CEO of Justice Inc.

"I've got just the lawyer for you," Sherwood promised. Due to Jason's notoriety from the Crawford case, it didn't take long to convince Mr. Lawson he'd be better off changing attorneys. Jason Noble could win this case in his sleep.

Sixty seconds after Sherwood hung up, Olivia was standing in the doorway, arms crossed. She knew why Brett Lawson had called.

"Well?"

Robert Sherwood looked up and smiled. He pulled a cigar out of his desk drawer and lit it.

"Game on," he said.

ACKNOWLEDGMENTS

This is where I get the chance to thank the real characters who made the fictional ones possible. And because I've used up every ounce of creativity in the book, I will keep it pretty straightforward.

Let's start with the publishing team that is second to none. Thanks to Karen Watson, Jeremy Taylor, Stephanie Broene, Cheryl Kerwin, Ron Beers, and so many others at Tyndale House. You not only believed in this story but made it stronger at every phase. I can honestly say that without the unflagging encouragement and insights of Karen Watson and my agent/friend Lee Hough, there would be no *Justice Game.*

In my efforts to achieve balance and accuracy, I leaned hard on readers and friends. Mary Hartman and Michael Garnier did their stellar job of checking local and legal facts while Jack Spitler and O. E. Burke, two of the most knowledgeable sportsmen and gun enthusiasts I know, provided insight on the technical aspects of the book.

Also, thanks to those of you who watched the preview video and voted for the verdict reflected in this story. A special thanks to the bookstore owners gathered in Hershey, Pennsylvania, who opened the voting and the lawyers and judges of the James Kent American Inn of Court who closed it out. It might interest you to know that the voting was 63 percent in favor of the verdict that I incorporated into the book and 37 percent for the opposite result. A special thanks to Mark Allen for producing the video and Debbie Lykins for getting the word out.

As with most novels, the story is the boss and I've not hesitated to use literary license to help it along. For example, Virginia Beach residents will know that The Purple Cow restaurant has now closed. But The Cow was such an authentic and fun slice of Beach life during its heyday, I kept it open for purposes of my book. Hey, other authors make up entire cities. In the same manner, you should take the arguments made by the lawyers and the facts surrounding the gun case as rough fictional reflections of real life rather than as claims to factual truth.

In addition to those who directly helped on this book, there are many others who made it possible by showing the author grace in other areas of life. Trinity Church had to suffer through a few sub-par sermons. Willcox and Savage had to embrace the idea of having a loose cannon novelist on deck. And the Singer family had to allow these fictional characters to take up residence in our home and infringe on our conversations for the better part of six months.

In short, this book is not the product of a solitary and lonely attempt to produce literary genius. Instead, it's the natural result of my interactions with readers and editors and family and friends. The good in it can be traced to the fabric of rich and colorful relationships God has put in my life. Not even Justice Inc. could put a price tag on that.

"Blessed are they who maintain justice, who constantly do what is right."
Psalm 106:3 (NIV)

ABOUT THE AUTHOR

Randy Singer is a critically acclaimed author and veteran trial attorney. He has penned nine legal thrillers, including his award-winning debut novel *Directed Verdict*. In addition to his law practice and writing, Randy serves as a teaching pastor for Trinity Church in Virginia Beach, Virginia. He calls it his "Jekyll and Hyde thing"—part lawyer, part pastor. He also teaches classes in advocacy and ethics at Regent Law School and serves on the school's Board of Visitors. He and his wife, Rhonda, live in Virginia Beach. They have two grown children. Visit his Web site at www.randysinger.net.

ALSO BY RANDY SINGER

Fiction

Directed Verdict
Irreparable Harm
Dying Declaration
Self Incrimination
The Judge Who Stole Christmas
The Cross Examination of Oliver Finney
False Witness
By Reason of Insanity

Nonfiction

Live Your Passion, Tell Your Story, Change Your World
Made to Count
The Cross Examination of Jesus Christ

www.randysinger.net

CP0232